Books by Lee Charles Kelley

'TWAS THE BITE BEFORE CHRISTMAS
TO COLLAR A KILLER
MURDER UNLEASHED
A NOSE FOR MURDER

LEE CHARLES KELLEY

'TWAS THE BITE BEFORE CHRISTMAS

AVON BOOKS
An Imprint of HarperCollinsPublishers

AVON BOOKS
An Imprint of HarperCollins*Publishers*
10 East 53rd Street
New York, New York 10022-5299

Copyright © 2005 by Lee Charles Kelley
ISBN-13: 978-0-06-073228-8
ISBN-10: 0-06-073228-8
www.avonmystery.com

First Avon Books paperback printing: November 2005

Avon Trademark Reg. U.S. Pat. Off. and in Other Countries, Marca Registrada, Hecho en U.S.A.
HarperCollins® is a registered trademark of HarperCollins Publishers Inc.

Printed in the U.S.A.

10 9 8 7 6 5 4 3 2 1

Dedicated to the memory of Roark—
he was a very good boy.

Acknowledgments

Thanks as always to my editor, Erin "How-Does-She-Put-Up-With-Me" Richnow. Thanks also, as always, to my technical advisor, NYPD Detective (Ret.) Melanie Weiss, for her gift of gab and for letting me steal some of her stories.

Speaking of stories, this one wouldn't have been quite as good as it is if not for the input from a nine-year-old kid named Michael. He and his older sister Emilee were very helpful, even if they didn't know it at the time.

I also have to mention the smart, talented, and sexy (she made me say it) Jen Bausch, the best dogwalker in Brooklyn, who keeps all the canines in The Heights happy.

Thanks, too, to Alex Levi and Howard Jurofsky (Saki), Jane Marino (Cassie), and Kirstin Baars (the late, great Roark).

And a special thanks to all the Jack-and-Jamie fans who send me e-mails asking me to write more books. Don't worry—they're on the way!

Disclaimer

The following is a work of fiction.
Only the dogs are real.

The Meeting of the Dogs

The dogs all met one Christmas.
They came from near and far.
Some dogs came by Greyhound Bus,
while others came by car.

The purpose of their meeting?
To fill the world with glee,
and put a brand new puppy
under every Christmas tree.

But a special hall was rented,
and the landlord did declare
he didn't want them running 'round,
just pooping everywhere.

So before inside that rented hall
the dogs could even look,
they had to take their hineys off
and hang them on a hook.

Then once inside the meeting—
each mother, son, and sire—
some cat dressed in a dog suit
began to holler, "Fire!"

They all rushed out, that pack of dogs.
They had no time to look,
to see which type of hiney
they grabbed off its little hook.

They got their hineys all mixed up.
It really made them sore,
to have to wear a hiney
they'd never worn before.

Then, once the chaos ended,
so did the dog's grand scheme.
And kids who'd dreamed of puppies
were left with just a dream.

It's also why you'll see a dog
give up a juicy bone
to go and sniff a hiney,
to see if it's his own.

Anonymous
(adapted by Lee Charles Kelley)

'TWAS THE BITE BEFORE CHRISTMAS

Prologue

Ebeneezer Scrooge, The Grinch, Old Man Potter—these are my secret Christmas heroes. Don't get me wrong. They're my *secret* heroes, which means I try not to let my anti-yuletide sentiments sour the eggnog. And yes, there are even a few people (Jamie, for one; and my sister Annabelle, for another) with whom I don't mind spending the holidays, and who can even get me halfway into the Christmas spirit, as long as they don't push me too hard, make me shop too long, or try to make me sit still while some overly enthusiastic yet singularly untalented relative reads " 'Twas the Night Before Christmas."

So while you shouldn't expect me to happily join in with the carolers, or to gaily return your festive "Merry Christmas!" as you pass me beneath ye olde, foil-bedecked street lamp, neither will I slam the door in the muffled singers' faces or tell you to go shove it. The sad truth is, I'm not as committed to my Scroogery, or my Grinchitude, or my Potterlike ways as my secret heroes are. That's what I admire about them. They don't grudgingly give in to the holidays the way I do every year. They fight back, tooth and nail. But not me. No, I'll decorate the boughs of fir, and hang the lights from the eaves, and shop, and have dinner with family, and hide presents under the tree—all that crap—and the whole time I'm silently wishing for it to be over with as soon and as painlessly as possible.

There are a *few* things I like. I like the smell of the Christmas trees, and hearing Bing Crosby and Nat King Cole, and "Little Saint Nick," by the Beach Boys. And I like the way Annabelle calls me every year from San Diego, and how the first words out of her mouth are always, "At ease, General," which is her favorite line from *White Christmas.* But do I *like* that movie? Hardly. I prefer *The Apartment,* which is usually on another channel at the same time of year. Greed, betrayal, adultery, broken lives, attempted suicide—that's my picture of what life is *really* like at the holidays. (And yes, I'm still enough of a sap to fall for the happy ending every single time.)

My favorite line? "Shut up and deal." That's what Miss Kubelik tells Baxter during their gin rummy game at the end of the film. That's my motto: Shut up and deal.

So here it is, "that time of year again," and Jamie and I are still engaged, though we were supposed to have gotten married in October. What can I tell you? Things change. You can't cry about it, you have to just shut up and deal . . .

1

We were sitting on the leather sofa in front of a dying fire, listening to George Winston's *December,* sipping our Kelso Christmas cocktails, and stringing popcorn and cranberries together, when Jamie's cell phone rang softly.

"Honey," I said, "it's Sunday night. Don't answer it."

She lifted the bowl of popcorn from her lap, handed it to me. "It's probably work related, Jack," she said, reaching over to the side table for her purse. "I *have* to take it."

Frankie, my black-and-white English field setter, and Hooch, my big orange dogue de Bordeaux—who were lying comfortably beside the still naked Christmas tree and were very sleepy, thanks to the fire and the music—lifted their heads and drooped their tired eyes open.

I put the bowl down next to the cranberries, got up, and went over to the hearth to throw another log on the fire.

Jamie clicked the phone open. "This is Dr. Cutter," she said. I pulled the fireplace screen back and turned to look at her, log in hand. She covered the mouthpiece and whispered, "Stop looking at me like that." Then into the phone she said, "Oh, no, that's terrible." She shot me an "I-told-you-so" look, listened a bit and said, "No, I know where it is. I'll be right over," and clicked the phone shut.

"A dead body?" I said, putting the log back on the stack.

"No," she joked, "I have a clandestine meeting with a secret admirer. Of *course* it's a dead body. And don't make that face. Can I help it if people don't always choose the most convenient moment to pass away? And it's not like *I'm* happy about the interruption either. I was enjoying our evening alone together *too*, you know."

I sighed an "Okay," then picked up the poker.

When they heard the word "okay" Frankie and Hooch looked up, hopefully.

I told them, "Sorry, doggies, you have to stay here," and they slowly and reluctantly put their heads back down.

Jamie hung up and said, "Especially considering how difficult it is to get *you* into the holiday spirit."

"Hey, the popcorn and cranberries were my *idea*," I said and poked at the embers to help the fire die down quicker. "I'm the one who went out and bought the tree, remember?"

She huffed at me. "Yes, after I pestered you about it for weeks. Jack, why do you hate Christmas?"

I put the poker back and said, "I don't hate Christmas. I just hate the phoniness and over commercialization of it. It used to have some meaning besides the bottom line."

"What kind of meaning do you think it should have?"

"I don't know. Wonder, magic, Christmas miracles. All that corny stuff."

"Honey, it can *still* mean that if you let it."

"Well, I just don't believe in it anymore."

"What's the matter?" She stood up and stretched her long legs. Her eyes were teasing me. "Did Santa forget to bring you what you wanted one year, and you've never forgiven him?"

"Very funny. Look, brown eyes, let me just get my shoes on and I'll go warm up the car for us."

She smiled brightly. "You're coming with me?"

"I'm your civilian advisor now, remember?" I said sourly. "Besides," I shrugged, " 'the couple that goes to crime scenes together stays together.' Isn't that how the saying goes?"

"Something like that," she chuckled. "And that right there is a Christmas miracle—you voluntarily coming with me to a crime scene, especially when there are no dogs involved."

"None that we *know* of." I shook my head. "You're having way too much fun at my expense right now, you realize that?"

She smiled sweetly. "And it might not *be* a crime scene, you know. It could have been an accident or natural causes."

"Hah! With our luck?" I said. "How much do you want to bet?"

"Well, we'll see. And don't leave the popcorn out where the dogs can get it." She nodded to the bowl.

"I wasn't going to," I lied, going back to pick it up.

"And you better put a coat on, honey, not just your

shoes. Wear that nice parka I got you last year. It's cold outside."

"What makes you think I wasn't going to wear a coat?"

"Because I know you, Jack Field." She came over, kissed me, then stroked my beard. "You're such a tough guy, you think you're immune to all kinds of freezing weather. I'll go upstairs and get out of these sweats, then meet you out front."

"I'll be waiting," I said, taking the popcorn bowl and finished strings back out to the kitchen, with the dogs up on their feet and following me, their tails *and* their butts wagging. *Mmm . . . he's going to the kitchen!*

After I'd put the bowl and strings safely on the counter, they followed me into the mudroom where I put on my boots, but no coat or parka, just my fleece-lined Levi's jacket.

Frankie's big brown eyes were soulful and searching. Hooch's, a couple shades lighter, were shining and happy.

I said to the dogs, "You know, that woman is being awfully bossy tonight."

They looked at me as if to say, "What are *you* complaining about? You tell *us* what to do all the time."

"Yeah, well, that's different," I told them then grabbed my keys. "You guys *like* being told what to do. Now go back inside and lie down."

They obediently trotted back to their place by the tree, but not without first shooting me a look over their shoulders, as if to say, "See?" Then they curled up and sighed in unison.

I went outside, where my breath clouds trailed behind me as I ran to the Suburban, got in, and started the engine.

It had just started snowing, which was nice. I looked through the windshield wipers at my Victorian two-story house, with its wide front porch. The red and green Christmas lights were glowing softly in the snow and made colored streaks on the wet windshield glass. I almost liked the way they looked. But the only reason I'd put them up in the first place was to get my groomer, Mrs. Murtaugh, off my back.

"It'll make people feel good," she'd said, while clipping a bichon frise, "and that'll be good for business."

So I gave in, like I always do, and put up the ladder, got out the hammer, and strung the lights above the porch and around the first-floor windows. It hasn't done anything to improve business that I can tell, but it makes her happy.

I looked over at the renovated carriage house where my foster son, Leon, lives. The light was on, so he was still up, watching TV, playing his Game Boy, or, hopefully, studying.

Then I looked over at my '38 Ford woody wagon, which I'd covered with a tarp a month before. The Chevy was a much better choice for winter driving anyway.

Damn, it's cold out here, I thought, waiting for the heater to warm up. Maybe I *should've* worn that stupid parka, the one Jamie got me for Christmas last year. On top of which, I could feel my yearly Christmas cold coming on. Just great. Going to a crime scene was exactly what I needed to take my mind off all this phony holiday nonsense.

The heater began to shoot warm waves from under the dash and I climbed into the passenger seat so Jamie could drive—she'd had fewer cocktails. And as I sat there, semi-contented in my own little corner of the world atop the coastal mountains of Maine, I had no idea that I was about to start an adventure that would forever change the meaning of Christmas, at least for me, anyway, and maybe for a few other people as well. But I'm getting ahead of myself.

All good stories like this start with a dead body.

2

She was lying faceup at the bottom of a set of carpeted stairs which led to the second floor of the mansion. Most of the blood that had pooled around her head had been soaked up by the Persian carpet, leaving a gruesome, satiny crust that clashed with the subtle blue and gold, and fine craftsmanship, of the rug. She was dressed in a maid's uniform with her left leg—naked from the hip to the ankle—splayed across the last two steps of the staircase, the shoe still on. From the angle of her neck in relation to her head and shoulders, it looked as if she'd snapped it in two during the fall.

Jamie and I had come up the winding, ocean drive in the snow and had checked in with the two cops sitting in Camden PD cruisers at the electronic gate, where a security guard sat inside a little booth, yawning over a Thermos of coffee. We were then escorted by the guard and his flashlight up the inner drive past dead topiaries, garlanded now with small white Christmas lights—glowing, pale as distant stars seen through mist. We walked past more lights on the pine trees and leaf-lorn oaks and maples, then past bone dry marble fountains, around a sweeping, gently sloped, snow-covered lawn, then to the flagstone steps leading to the mansion itself, which was also wrapped in twinkling lights, and then up to the broad, oaken, holly-wreathed front door, crisscrossed with wrought iron to make it feel even more like you were entering an enchanted fairy castle. The sparkling lights, the cut-stone walls, and the leaded windows—with their diamond-shaped panes—did the rest.

The brass and beveled-glass porch light, which hung over the front door, and which I assumed usually held a white bulb now held a red one. It cast what was supposed to be a jolly, Christmasy glow over the area. But red is also the color of blood, so it foreshadowed what waited for us inside the house.

We'd come in, shaken off the snow, hung up our coats next to several others on brass hooks, and had found two uniforms guarding the body. A plainclothes detective, medium height, was talking to an elderly couple in a sitting room to the left of the stairs.

The room was furnished with pink and coral tufted chairs, striped settees, and whatnot. The walls were framed with bookshelves, holding ancient-looking tomes of the type collectors favor. The couple were dressed in evening clothes, the wife in a black gown, her wrists and neck quietly shimmering with pearls.

The detective had strong features, unfortunate red hair, and wore a pair of round eyeglasses. He held a small notepad in one hand and a pen in the other. He'd nodded at us as we came past him to look at the body.

Jamie carefully set down her gray medical examiner's kit on the lace cover-cloth of a cherrywood table with curved legs, which stood next to the landing, then gestured with the backs of her hands to shoo two uniformed Camden cops away.

"I need a little room to work, here, fellas."

"Sorry, doc," said one of them, whose nametag read "D. Weist." "We were just trying to determine—"

"Shoo. Go. That's my job." She knelt down.

I took another look at the body and decided I'd seen enough. Looking at corpses is never fun, so I looked up at the stairs instead. It would have taken a very hard blow, I thought, to cause that much blood loss. If she'd hit her head as she fell, there would have been some indication of that on the runner or the banister, but I didn't see any. Just a lot of blood spatter.

I cast my eyes farther up, to the top step, and saw what might have been more spatter across a cream-colored wall and a parchment-pressed wildflower specimen, framed in black enamel and encased in glass. This indicated, at least at first glance, that she'd been struck up there and hadn't hit her head accidentally as she fell. The crime scene unit would be better able to determine the force and angle of the blows that had caused her fall and had, in all likelihood, killed her.

I noticed a lipstick-sized security camera placed where the wall and ceiling came together. It was pointed down at the staircase. Well, this'll be easy, I thought. The whole thing will be on videotape. I wondered, though, why they had security cameras placed *inside* the house, rather than just at the entrances.

I looked to the right and saw a dining room, with a large antique oak table, bare except for two large red and green foil-wrapped pots of poinsettias. The paneled walls were decorated with wreaths and garlands and other tasteful yet festive décor. To the right was a double swinging kitchen door, with round galley windows.

I went over to the sitting room to speak to the red-haired detective.

"Jack Field," I told him. "I'm with the ME's office."

He looked me over, nodded, and said to the couple, "Are you sure it was the ex-boyfriend you saw leaving the house?"

"Yes," the old gent said, nodding sadly. "She, they were having some difficul—"

"They had terrible arguments," his wife said with the trace of an Irish accent. "Amy, that's her name, Amy Frost . . ." she nodded stairward, but didn't let her eyes actually light on the body ". . . she was terribly frightened of him."

"She told you this?" I asked.

"No," she looked at her husband, "not in so many words—"

"Mmm-hmm." I nodded, but said nothing else.

The detective introduced me to Ellis and Fiona Bright, and informed them of my "official" capacity. We didn't shake hands.

"A terrible tragedy," the wife said.

The old gent patted her knee and said to the detective, "May we go upstairs now and pack?"

"Pack?" I said.

Fiona said, "We're certainly not staying *here*!"

"No," I said, "of course not. But I hope you're not thinking of leaving town."

"What?" said Ellis. "Are you telling us that—?"

The detective said, "Just be sure to notify the department of any travel plans, and provide us with contact information."

I interrupted them. "Exactly where did you see him?"

"I beg your pardon?" said Ellis.

"As he was leaving, the ex-boyfriend. What's his name?"

The detective said, "Thomas Huckabee."

I nodded then said to the couple, "Where were you?"

Ellis said, "We were in the car. Amy was here when we left, which was around seven-thirty. We attended a choral concert in Camden proper, and when we got back, Carl, that's our driver, pulled the car up to the front of the house. We already told this to the other detective." He gave a nod to my new friend.

"What time was this?"

"I don't know. Just after ten."

"So, about forty minutes ago. And that was the usual way Carl dropped you off, right in front of the door?"

"Yes."

"And where were you in relationship to the car?"

"We were inside the damn car," said Fiona. "What the hell difference does that—?"

"And where was this Huckabee, exactly?"

Still peeved, she said, "I don't know. He just rushed out the door, bolted past us, and ran off."

"Interesting. Which direction did he go?"

"I don't know," she said. "Toward the street?"

I said, "You mean toward the front gate? That's the only way out to the street, isn't it?"

"Yes. Unless you like climbing ten-foot walls."

I shrugged. "Some people do." I scratched my chin and looked over at the uniforms, who weren't doing anything. "Can you guys check the grounds for footprints or other signs of activity?" They looked at the detective and he nodded, making a sour face. They started to go. I turned back to the couple. "So, how did he get in, do you suppose?"

Ellis said, "Tom? We have no idea."

I said, "He didn't check in at the front gate?"

"No. Derek, that's our security guard, didn't see him."

The detective said, "Was there any blood on his clothes?"

I hung my head and sighed. Bad move, Detective, I thought. Never ask a suspect for any unknown, hypothetical details. That's Standard Interrogation Procedure 101.

They looked at each other and Ellis said, "I don't remember *seeing* any blood."

"Yes," said Fiona, nodding. "Ellis was on the other side of the seat. I saw him more clearly, right through my window. He had blood on his clothes, yes. A lot of blood."

I said, "What did it look like?"

"What?" asked Fiona.

"The blood," I said, "Was it smeared or spattered?"

"It was . . . I don't know."

"And what was he wearing?"

"It was smeared all over his jacket," she remembered suddenly, making a sweeping motion across her bosom.

The detective looked at his notes. "He was wearing a pair of blue jeans and a nylon parka," he told me.

"Yes," said Fiona. "It was a parka, not a jacket."

"What color was it?"

"Green," said Ellis. "I actually had a clearer view than Fiona thinks—"

"No, dear," said Fiona, "it was blue. Dark blue."

"Well," the detective said, "which was it?"

I put a hand on his shoulder. "That's not unusual. If they saw him through the window from different angles, there would be different levels of diffraction which would cause the variation in color. It's simple optics." This was partly true—depending on the light source—though I didn't tell him or the Brights that. To the couple I said, "Did Carl see him?"

They looked at each other.

The husband said, "Yes, I'm sure he did. He must have."

"You can ask him yourself," said Fiona. "He has an apartment over the garage." She pronounced it "*gare*-ojh," like they do in Britain.

"Okay," I said, "do you know what time Amy ate dinner?"

"We had *our* dinner at six-thirty. She served us, and I assume she had something in the kitchen shortly afterward."

"Do you know what she ate, exactly?"

"No. You'd have to ask the cook."

I nodded at the detective and he made a note about it. Fiona said, "Is what she had to eat important?"

"It might help pinpoint the exact time of the murder."

"But we already told you, it must have happened shortly before we arrived home. That's why Tom ran out like he did."

"We just need to double-check. You can go for now."

They stared at me. The detective handed Ellis a card, then said, "Thanks. If you think of anything else . . ."

Ellis pocketed the card then helped his wife to her feet and they started to go toward the dining room.

"Oh, one other thing," I stopped them. "Who else besides Amy was in the residence tonight?"

"I've got that," said the detective. "After the cook left, which was around seven, she was here alone."

"Was that unusual?" I asked Mr. Bright.

"Not at Christmas. We have a butler, Roger Stark, and

his wife, Glenda. She oversees the housekeeping staff. But they're in Bangor visiting their daughter tonight."

"And how many people do you have on staff?"

"Ten, in all."

I nodded. "And how many actually live in the residence?"

"Just Amy. She was my wife's personal maid. And the Starks. The cook and the rest of the housekeeping staff have their own homes. As does the grounds-keeping crew."

"Okay, we'll need their contact information," I said.

The detective said, "Yeah, I've already got that too."

"Good." Then to the couple I said, "Just one more thing. When I came in I noticed that you have an alarm system. And, of course, the security guard out front."

"That's right," Ellis said. "And we have two dogs who patrol the property when the guard leaves at night."

"Really?" I smiled. "What kind of dogs?"

"They're Doberman pinschers, trained in Germany."

I nodded, then bit my lip. "It's awful cold out there."

"Don't worry. They have down coats. And both Maxim and Fritz sleep in a heated kennel, next to the garage." He pronounced it the American way. "Carl lets them out at midnight."

"Well, you've taken a lot of security precautions. I also noticed that you have some surveillance cameras inside the house, as well. I was just wondering why they were necessary."

Fiona clutched her pearl necklace and said, "Some of my jewelry has turned up missing in the past year or so."

"I see. And you thought someone on the staff might—?"

"We just wanted to be sure," said Ellis.

The state crime scene unit—five guys and a gal—showed up. They dusted the snow off their clothes, came toward the body, and began setting up. The couple cast them an anxious look.

"Did you suspect the maid," I said, "or this Huckabee?"

"We didn't know whom to suspect," said Fiona.

I said, "Were either of them having money problems?"

"Yes," said Fiona, though Ellis shot her a look. "Tom's son has chronic kidney disease. The bills are enormous . . . then there's his violent past. He spent five years in prison."

I lifted my eyebrows. "On what charge?"

"Manslaughter," she said and raised her chin. "He killed his wife."

The detective quickly wrote that down.

Ellis said, "In all fairness, the wife's parents are paying Tim's medical bills. So it's not as if Tom has—"

"Still," Fiona said, "with his history, you have to wonder. We never found any evidence that *she* was taking things. She's a good girl. Or *was*, poor dear. And she was so attached to me. Tom was the one, I'm certain of it."

"Wait, I'm a little curious why you both call him Tom."

Ellis looked down a moment, then back at me. "He, he was working for us at one point in time." Before I could ask him in what capacity, he said, "He installed the security cameras."

"Interesting," I said, "thanks. I know how difficult this must be. Especially coming at the holidays."

They muttered in agreement then Fiona looked at

the two uniforms and the CSU team and said, "Will you tell them to be careful? There are some very valuable pieces of antique—"

"Don't worry," said the redheaded detective reassuringly, "they won't harm anything."

"Well, good," she said, with a frown. "See that they don't." Then she and her husband went through the dining room and into the kitchen where, I presumed, there was another set of stairs or an elevator leading to the upper floors.

The detective tapped his pencil and gave me a look.

I said, "Oh, sorry to butt in like that, detective . . . ?"

"It's Bailey. Brad Bailey." He grudgingly stuck out his hand and I shook it.

"So," I said, "no one else was home tonight, huh?"

"No, just the maid and the guy at the gate. Oh, and their son Christopher lives here, but he's out of town."

"Where out of town?"

"I don't know. The Bahamas."

"Where in the Bahamas?"

"Jeez, you don't quit, do you? All they told me was that he's on vacation in the Bahamas. He's a bit of a playboy."

"Un-huh. Well, we'll have to check on that, won't we?"

"You know, you're a real pain in the neck."

"For now, though," I said, "let's go have a talk with the chauffeur, what do you say, Detective?"

"Are you trying to take over this case?"

"No, I'm just a civilian advisor," I gave him a winning smile, "just trying to get a clear picture of what happened."

"Well, you could be a little less bossy about it."

"Am I being bossy? Sorry, it seems to be going around tonight."

"Huh?" He just stood there and adjusted his glasses.

I didn't have time to explain. There are certain bits of information that need to be gone into quickly at the start of an investigation, so I headed toward the kitchen, figuring there might be a side door there, leading to the garage. "I think we should go talk to Carl now," I said over my shoulder, "before they have a chance to coach him, do you mind?"

He came after me. "Wait. You think they're lying?"

I stopped. "It's been known to happen. From what I saw of the body, and the walls at the top of the stairs, I'd say that if the ex-boyfriend killed her there'd be blood spattered, not smeared, on his clothes. And blood spatter doesn't read well on a dark blue or green parka at night, even under normal lighting conditions. I don't know if you noticed, but the bulb over the front porch is currently red, I assume for the holidays. And blood doesn't read at *all* in red light. Again, it's just a matter of optics. You coming?"

He followed me into the kitchen. It was white, spacious, and fully equipped with gleaming chrome-plated appliances. There was a hallway and stairwell to the left.

"So you're saying that they *are* lying?"

"No, not lying necessarily," I said, "just being 'helpful'. They may have seen him, but you're the one who planted the thought of blood-stained clothes in their heads."

"How the heck did I do that?"

As we strode through the kitchen, I noticed two tiny red lights lit on the wall phone, meaning that someone was making a call to someone else on the property, or that two people were making calls. Or two phones were off the hook. Before I could listen in, both lights went out.

We went out the kitchen door and I stopped to check the lock, to make sure we could get back in the same way. There was a slot for a security swipe card as well as a regular keyhole. I took a training leash out of my inside jacket pocket and wedged it into the frame, then closed the door.

As we went toward the garage I explained that the proper way to interrogate a witness is to let them tell *you* what they saw, not provide them with details, like the blood. Of course it's necessary to ask what a suspect was wearing, or if he had a weapon. But when you ask something like "Did he have a gun?" or "Did you see any blood on his clothes" to someone who already thinks they've just seen a killer run by, their brains automatically fill in the blanks, and they suddenly remember that, yes, he *did* have a gun, or why yes, now that you mention it, there *was* blood on his clothes, quite a *lot* of blood.

"Once that thought is planted in the brain," I said, as we climbed a set of white wooden stairs leading to the chauffeur's apartment, "it gets stored in the memory, as if it really happened. And a good defense attorney, or a good detective, for that matter, would come to the scene at the same time of night, under the same conditions, and check to see if someone sitting in that same car could see blood spattered or smeared on a dark green or dark blue parka while someone ran past in a split second's time."

"Well," he said, "we should know more soon enough. We've got his name and description, and I've got men out looking for him now. If we find the victim's blood on his clothes . . ."

"Good. Then you'll have a solid case. Maybe."

"What do you mean 'maybe'?"

"Two things still bother me," I said, knocking sharply on the door. "First, how did Huckabee get inside the house?"

A voice with an Eastern European accent said, "Yah, yah, I'll be there in a minute." From his accent I got the feeling that his name was probably spelled Karl, not Carl.

Bailey pushed his glasses up on his nose and said. "The maid probably let him in."

"Maybe," I shook my head, "but Mrs. Bright said that Amy was frightened of this guy Huckabee, remember? 'Terribly frightened,' she said. So why would she let him inside the house when she's all alone on a Sunday night?"

He sucked on his cheek. "Maybe he broke in?"

"How? This place has a ten foot wall, guard dogs, a guarded security gate, and alarms and cameras everywhere."

"Which he installed, remember."

"Yes, if the Brights are telling the truth, he installed the cameras. But not the rest. We'll have to check the surveillance tapes and see what's on them."

"That would help," he said, then looked at my Levi's jacket. "Aren't you freezing your buns off in that thing?"

"Nah," I lied. "Cold weather doesn't affect me."

"Well, scrud," he said, "it sure as heck affects *me*. So, what's the second thing still bothering you?"

I knocked on the door again.

"Yah, yah," Karl shouted. "In a *minute*, I said."

I wondered if I should tell Bailey about the second thing, then decided it was his *case,* after all, so I told him: "The body was found around ten, which is when Huckabee supposedly ran out of the house, right? But the victim had to have been killed at least two hours before that. Maybe three."

"What? How do you know that? Did Dr. Cutter already say something to you about it?"

I shook my head. "It's obvious from the condition of the blood around her head. It takes at least a couple of hours for the blood to get like that."

"Maybe he spent that time erasing the videotapes?"

"That's a possibility. But still, two hours, even three? Anything could have happened in that amount of time."

And please don't telegraph that information to any of our witnesses, I wanted to add. But I didn't want to step on his toes any more than I already had.

Besides, just then, Karl—a shortish, though thick-bodied and thick-faced man, early thirties, with suspicious black eyes, still dressed in his chauffeur's outfit except for the hat and jacket—finally opened the door and we went inside to talk.

3

It was a tidy place for the most part, with some modest furniture of the Swedish bare wood-and-cushion style. I only caught a glance of this out of the corner of my eye, of course, due to the fact that the German-trained Dobies that Bright had mentioned weren't sleeping peacefully in their heated kennel—they were sitting at attention in Karl's kitchen, growling with serious intent at me and Bailey. They had no leashes on.

"Hello, Hunde!" I said, while I tried to remember their names and felt my testicles go into hiding. Then I slowly raised my right arm slightly at the elbow, with my palm flat and open, then made a swift movement, dropping it at my side, which is the standard hand signal for the down command, and at the same time said, "Maxim, Fritzie, *platz*!"

They just sat there.

Well, I thought, whoever trained them did a helluva job—they don't take commands from strangers.

"Scared of the dogs?" Karl sneered at me. "They wouldn't do anything to you unless I told them."

"Just being careful. Did you train them?"

"No, they were trained in Germany. What do you want?"

Bailey said, "We need to ask you a few questions about what happened tonight."

"Yah, I figured. "Mrs. Bright just called and told me you might come by. Have a seat."

As we came around the back of the couch, the dogs began growling again. Over his shoulder Karl said, *"Platz!"* and they dropped into the down position and kept quiet.

"Well trained," I said, admiringly.

Karl took a seat across from us and scowled. "What do you expect? They cost a lot of money, these dogs."

The more I got a chance to hear his accent, the more I realized that he hadn't said "Yah" earlier but *"Dah!"* Meaning that he was probably Russian, maybe Polish. I looked over at Bailey and noticed that he had his legs crossed and his hands in his lap. The dogs must've really shaken him up.

"So," I said to Karl, glancing at the things strewn on his coffee table—an open bag of potato chips, a half-empty vodka bottle, a pack of cigarettes, a lighter, and some men's magazines, "you're from Russia? Or is that a Polish accent?"

"Very good." He shrugged. "My father was Russian, my mother was Polish."

I looked at Bailey. "ID," I told him.

He gave me a blank look.

I tilted my head at Karl. "Get his ID."

"Oh." He looked at Karl. "Can I see some—" Before he could finish Karl got out his wallet and threw it to him. Bailey opened it and pulled out the man's driver's license.

I said, "How long have you worked for the Brights?"

"A while."

Bailey put the license back in the wallet. I shook my head at him and said, "Write down the number and DOB." He sighed but did as I told him. I looked back at Karl.

He said, "I thought you had questions about the murder."

There was something about him, and the way he acted so cool yet seemed a little on edge, that sparked a memory of some sort, though I couldn't put my finger on how, or if, I knew him. That was when I noticed his watch, with its two-inch wide leather strap, which sparked another memory.

"Just answer the question," Bailey said, still writing.

Karl gave him a withering glance. "I *did* answer. I've been working for them for a while. I don't know how long."

"Narrow it down a little," Bailey said.

He shrugged. "Maybe six years or so, off and on. They travel a lot. I drive them here and in Palm Beach."

"Yet they spend the winters in Maine?" I asked.

He snorted. "They like a white Christmas. They have homes here, and in Florida, New York, and Switzerland. The past few years, they spend most of their time in Maine."

Bailey finished with the man's ID and threw the wallet back to him, then we went into the details of what he'd seen earlier and he gave us a carbon copy of what we'd already gotten from the Brights, with Karl adding a nice little touch: he said he couldn't tell whether the killer's parka was green or blue.

"Karl," I said, "how do you know *he's* the killer?"

He shrugged. "It's obvious. He comes out of the house, with blood on his clothes, the boss and wife go inside, and they find the body." He snapped his fingers. "Crystal clear."

"Yeah," said Bailey, "except that the murder took place a good two hours before Huckabee ran out of the house."

I hung my head and sighed.

Karl looked down at the pack of cigarettes, as if he were about to grab one, then stopped himself, possibly thinking that it might look like he was lying and was only grabbing a smoke to cover it. He shrugged, calmly. "How do I know? I only knows what I sees. He comes out of house, has blood on parka, and rans off." Then he reached over for the pack—they were Camel unfiltered—shook one out, put it in his mouth, grabbed the lighter with his left hand, and lit up.

"Why didn't you go after him?" I said.

He blew out a puff of smoke. "Not my job. I have to park car in garage." He took another puff. "Are we done? I have told you what I knows. Can I help if this man kills her then does something else for two hours before leaves house?"

"Okay, Karl," I said, noting the sudden change in his ability to use, or misuse, English grammar and syntax, "what can you tell us about the victim?"

"Not much," another puff, "is pretty, work hard, they find her in New York. When they move here, she comes too."

"So they've moved here permanently?"

"No. Did I says that? No, my English is not too good. They stay here most of year these days. I'm not sure."

"What do you mean you're not sure, Karl? If they're in Maine, you're driving them around, right?"

"Anyway," he said, "I was with them at concert

whole night. Not insides at concert, of course, but waiting in car, you understand. So about killing, I only knows this, what I already tolds you."

"Okay, thanks. What kind of car do you drive them in?"

"Depends. If is nice out, the Town Car. If roads is bad, the Navigator."

"And their son, Christopher, what does he drive?"

He made a face. "English sports car. Is tough job, to keeps it running. All the time trouble withs transmission."

I said, "And what do you know about the missing jewelry?"

"What?" He seemed genuinely startled. "No, I don't know nothing. No missing jewelries."

"Then why did they have the video cameras installed?"

He squinted, nodded his head, thinking something over. "*Dah,* that would be good reason for cameras." He looked me in the eye. "But coulds be other reason too."

Bailey said, "Like what?"

"I can't says about it." He shrugged. "I can't says anything what I don't know for sures. I am servant. I drive car. Keep clean. Make sure engine runs good. At night, I let dogs out. What goes on inside house, I don't know. Just . . . some strange things, I think, goes on sometimes."

"What kinds of strange things?" Bailey said.

Karl put out his cigarette and picked up the vodka bottle. "I don't know what is, but I see strange lights sometimes. Okay? Give me the spooks. Like is ghosts or something." He glugged a shot, straight from the bottle, sighed, and wiped his lips. He held out the bottle for me. It was his way of being a good host, and of seeing if Bailey and I could be trusted.

I reached over and took it, then put it to my lips and took a swig. I offered it to Bailey but he put his hand up.

"Sorry," he said.

"Come on," I told him. "You're being rude to Karl."

"I'm not being rude, I just don't drink. And even if I *did*—"

"I know—you can't drink on duty." I shrugged and gave the bottle back to Karl.

He put it down and sat back, giving Bailey the eye. "I don't trusts man who won't drink with me."

"He can't drink on duty, Karl. Now, tell us about these lights. And how do you know they're ghosts?"

He shrugged. "What is, I don't know, and don't want to. Me? I don't believe in such things. But is *some*-thing, so I just pay no attention and do my job—drive car, keep engines running, let dogs out at night."

"And why do think the video cameras are connected?"

He shook his head. "As for me, I can only guess. They think they have ghosts in house? I don't know. Maybe if they thinks lights is ghosts, they want to get . . . what's the word? Proofs?"

"That's the word," I said. "Or close enough."

"Of course," he let out a dismissive laugh, "lights only happen when *he's* in town."

"And who's he, Karl?"

"The Professor. When he comes, is big deal. 'Karl, go pick up Professor from airport.' 'Karl, be careful with Professor's steamer trunks.' 'Karl, Professor wants pizza. Go to town and get.' No 'please' just 'go get.' And those steamer trunks are very big, very heavy." He blew a raspberry. "That Professor he *always* get what he wants. And when he's in town . . ." he shrugged ". . . that's when the lights come too."

"And where do you see them?"

"I already tolds you, they comes from in house."

"You've been inside the house and seen them?"

"I only goes in house to eat in kitchen. I shows you."

He got up and led me to the window, which looked out over the driveway and gave a nice view of the back of the mansion. I looked back over my shoulder at the dogs. They were very calm, but very focused. Staring at me, in fact. Damn, they were well trained. Those German Schutzhund boys really know what they're doing.

Karl said, "You sees, above second floor?"

I said I did. There were two stories, with an additional floor and a half above them.

"That part is new. Five, maybe six years ago they add on, bring in stones from Ireland." I noted that they'd tried to match the original architectural style of the house, but hadn't quite pulled it off. Karl said, "They do this all because of Professor."

"Why? Is that where he sleeps when he's here?"

"Do I know where he sleeps? Steamer trunks always goes to third floor, and is no elevator past second. But I don't think he sleeps there. Too small. Professor is big man."

"I don't suppose you know what he's a professor of?"

He looked blank. "What does mean, this 'professor of'?"

"Professor of physics, chemistry, what?"

He laughed so hard I thought he might hurt himself.

"That is very good! Very, very good! I tell you what he's professor of, he's professor of Give Me Money."

I let him laugh for a bit, then said, "And his name?"

He shook his head. "His name, I don't know. All the time they just call him Professor."

"I see. Well, Karl, thank you for your time."

"Don't worry. Is fine. You come to see me, we talk, I answer questions, yes? Is fine."

Bailey stood up, a little nervously. "Um, one more thing. I'm going to need you to bring the car around front and park it exactly where it was when the three of you saw Huckabee go by."

Karl gave him a murderous look, which he turned into a threatening smile. "You tells me what I does with car now?"

I said, "He's a police officer, investigating a murder, Karl. There's no hurry, but you have to do it."

"Just like goddamn *policja*." He spit on the floor. "Always push little guy arounds."

"Just *do* it," said Bailey.

The dogs were still staring, still in the down position. Bailey nervously followed me to the door.

"Hah!" Karl said, laughing at us. "You two still scared of little doggies?" I turned to him and saw something change in his eyes. "That's good. You *should* be afraid. Better to be afraid of something you can see than stupid ghosts, right?" Then he turned to the dogs and said, *"Wachen Sie!"* in a sharp whisper. They growled and bared their teeth.

Bailey was about to faint. He began backing toward the door, holding his hands over his crotch.

I told him, "Easy, don't make any sudden moves," then said, "Okay, Karl. Call them off."

His eyes held a cold rage. They suddenly seemed as

dangerous as the dogs' teeth. "They aren't called *on,* yet; they just on watch. They won't make move unless I says the secret word."

"Then give them the secret word to stop being on watch, would you mind?"

A looked passed over his face. I couldn't tell what was in it: Frustration? Guilt? Resignation? Then he was finally himself again. *"Mathilde,"* he said softly and the dogs relaxed, and I mean they *really* relaxed. Fritz even wagged his little stub of a tail. (I think it was Fritz.)

Karl went back to his chair, sat down, and reached out his left hand for the vodka and took another swig.

I said, "So they're not just trained for guard work, but protection as well?"

He shrugged. "Is both dogs twelve-time Schutzhund champions, trained for lot of things."

"Well," I said, "they're a couple of damn fine—"

"Enough about the dogs," Bailey said to me. Then to Karl he said. "You just committed a felony."

"What felony?" said Karl, acting innocent.

"You just threatened a police officer with bodily harm."

He gave a facial shrug. "Ah, was just a joke."

"Some joke," Bailey said, and took a deep breath. "I'll let it slide this time. But the next time, you're going to jail. And you'd better bring the car around like I told you."

Karl saluted. "Yes, *sir*! Right away, *sir*!"

"At ease, General," I said.

4

Bailey and I got safely outside, and after he'd composed himself, he said, "What do you think?"

"I think something screwy is going on. And he's right."

"About what?"

"It's better to be afraid of those dogs than of ghosts."

"No kidding. And that look he got in his eye. That was scary." He cocked his head. "Maybe *he's* our killer, Jack."

"Maybe. It's worth looking into."

He let out a breath. "What'd he say to calm them down?"

"I don't know. 'Mathilde'?" I said as we started down the stairs. The snow had stopped, leaving a white blanket on the driveway and lawns. "It's probably the trainer's mother's name or something." I explained that attack dogs are always taught a secret word that makes them attack and a safety word that makes them back off instantly, no matter who says it.

"It's never a typical sounding command," I went on, "but something that's unusual enough so that the dogs wouldn't hear it spoken very often, but not so unusual that you can't remember it."

"Well, it sure worked. I mean, that was amazing."

"Yep. Once they're off watch, they're the calmest, most sociable dogs you'd ever meet. Most cops who work with a K-9 unit have no problem bringing retired police dogs home to play with the kids. And even while they're being trained, as soon as they hear the safety word, they stop attacking the guy in the padded suit and treat him like he's their best buddy."

I stopped him at the garage and I said, "Oh, and it was nice to see you asking Karl to bring the car around."

He almost blushed. "Well, I'm not a total idiot."

"I never thought you were," I lied.

He got on the radio and asked someone to bring two parkas to the scene, a dark blue and a dark green one, while I took a quick peek inside the three-car garage, which had rectangular windows, at eye level, for each of the three doors. There was a black Lincoln Town Car, an empty space for another car, and a Lincoln Navigator. I asked to borrow his flashlight.

He gave it to me and said, "What are you looking for?"

"Clues."

I shone the flashlight through the windows and saw that the Navigator was clean, there was a transmission fluid stain on the empty space, and that the Town Car had no precipitation residue on the hood. I returned the flash to Bailey.

When he finished his call he said, "So?"

"It looks like the son's car is missing. So if he's not in the Bahamas, he's probably not here."

"Okay. The parkas are on their way. What do you think we should use to smear on them?"

"You mean to simulate blood? Weren't you ever a kid?"

"Yeah? So?"

I lifted my palms up—meaning "isn't it obvious?"

"Oh, right," he smiled. "Ketchup."

We went back to the kitchen and as I removed the leash I'd left in the door, I noticed a red light lit up on the wall phone, then another red light, right next to it, lit up too. I pointed this out. "They're now concocting a story to account for the two-hour time difference."

"What do you mean?"

I lifted the handset from its cradle then motioned to Bailey to be quiet. He nodded, then leaned in close so he could also hear what was being said. I pressed the button next to the first red light and we heard Karl, in still accented, but no longer broken, English saying, "Tell them that some of your jewelry is missing! That's what they think the cameras are for. There has to be some reason Tom was in the house for so long."

Fiona said, "Very well, Karl. Thanks. I'll tell Ellis."

The second red light went out and I put the handset back.

Bailey said, "We should go upstairs and arrest them."

"We don't want to tip our hand yet. Let's wait till they make their move." I sighed. "You know what? I think we've got a mystery on our hands, here, buddy."

"A mystery?"

I explained, "That's what we'd call a case like this back in New York. Most homicides you know pretty quickly who did it and why. It's just a matter of tracking down the perp and cuffing him. But a mystery? That's where everybody is either lying or hiding something, and there are too many clues that end up not meaning a damn thing in the end."

"Like ghosts and mysterious professors. What do you figure that was all about?"

"Good question. It sounds like it might be a scam of some sort. You know, contacting the dearly departed?"

He nodded, though I could tell he didn't agree. "Listen, we already know Karl was lying about some things. You think he was telling the truth about that?"

"I don't know. I *think* so. I have a feeling that he's got a shady past, but that it's just that—in the past. But it's also obvious he doesn't like the professor. Or hadn't you noticed that he has trouble controlling his temper?"

"Uh, yeah. I had noticed that."

I scratched my ear. "But I don't know why they'd need to build another floor and a half on top of the mansion to contact ghosts." I thought about it. "The wife has a faint brogue. Maybe the stones were brought in from her ancestral home in Ireland. But no, that wouldn't make any sense. From what little I know, ghosts tend to stay close to wherever they died. They don't wander off, chasing after a bunch of rocks."

"Wait. Are you saying you actually believe in ghosts?"

I laughed. "Not really. I'm just thinking of the popular mythology." I thought some more. "Still, it might be helpful to know where Mrs. Bright was born and where in Ireland those stones came from."

He wrote that in his notebook, then looked at something he'd already written, and hung his head. "I just wrote it under the thing you told me about the two-hour time difference. I guess I shouldn't have told Karl about—"

"No, you shouldn't." I patted his shoulder. "But that's okay. You're learning. How many homicides have you worked?"

"This'll be my third. Sort of."

"Yeah? I worked three my first week. That is, after the lieutenant thought I could be trusted, which took a year."

"Well, I'm doing my best to pick up a few things from watching you. Like the way you did your interviews."

"You were paying attention, huh? That's good. Let's see if we can find the maid's bedroom. It's probably behind the kitchen somewhere. While we're looking around I can give you a tutorial on interview techniques, if you like."

"Yeah. Yeah, I would."

We went to the hallway next to the stairwell and found a large pantry, filled with the usual supplies, then another door past that, which was unlocked. We went inside.

It was clearly a young woman's bedroom; there were some stuffed bears on the bed, and the curtains were gauzy and fringed with lace. There were also some posters on the wall of guys wearing cowboy hats, which indicated her poor taste in music. Or men.

Bailey caught my look of disapproval and said, "Maybe you're like me. You just don't like country music."

"I love country music, and none of these lameass bozos would know *real* country music if it came up and bit 'em on the ass. You check the dresser, I'll look through the closet."

"What are we looking for?"

"Letters, a diary, an address book."

We began our search and he said, "So, tell me something. Why were you so palsey with the chauffeur? You called him by name a lot when you spoke to him."

I smiled. "You noticed that, huh? Yeah, doing that makes a guy like him feel more amenable to opening up to you. You don't think I overdid it?"

"Not at all. I thought it was very subtle." He frowned. "One thing, though. Why didn't you do that with the Brights?"

"You noticed that too? Very good, Detective, very observant. I didn't use *their* first names because it would have had the opposite effect. You can't be informal with a wealthy, older couple and expect them to feel chummy. They demand more deference."

"Right." He frowned. "But you didn't show them any."

I smiled. "No, I didn't, did I?"

"Why not?"

"A couple reasons. I wanted to let them know who was in charge. If I had called them Mr. and Mrs. Bright they would have seen me as their inferior, and would've felt no need to talk to us at all, let alone feel compelled to tell the truth. So I had to take a more no-nonsense approach. I also knew they were trying to push the idea of Huckabee being the killer, but I'd had a look at the bloodstained carpet, remember? So I knew something was off about their story." I gave him another winning smile. "You think I overdid that?"

"No, I'd say it was just right, with them *and* Karl."

"Good. I was worried I might be a little rusty."

"Can I ask you something else?" I said he could. "Why didn't you confront them about the red porch light?"

I laughed. "You're really thinking this through. That's good." I explained that I couldn't be a hundred percent sure I was right about whether the blood would be visible, either by the red light, or the car's headlights, or whatever the light source was, until we did a visual test of our own. "More importantly," I said, "I wanted to get them locked in to their story before confronting them with the truth. If I'd said something about the porch light being red they might've claimed there was a regular white bulb in the lamp when they got home, but that they changed it after they found the body."

"Why in the world would they do that?"

"Lie about the bulb, or change it?"

"Why would they have changed it?"

"They wouldn't have. But it doesn't matter. With these two, once they get the lies going, and get Karl to back them up, they'll keep spinning lie on top of lie until your head explodes. You should hear some of the outlandish things people expect you to swallow. They'll stick to any fantasy they think will get them out of a jam."

"Seems like I've got a lot to learn."

"Ah, you're doing great." There was nothing in the closet, so I came over to him. "And don't worry about your little slips. They might actually help us out. Now we can get them trapped in a lie."

He nodded. "No letters or diary in the dresser. So, what's our next move?"

"Did you check under the pillows?"

He shook his head, lifted the pillows and found a pink leather diary.

"Good," I said. "Is it hers?"

He opened it. "Property of Amy Frost," he read.

"Okay, hang on to it. I'd like to nose around upstairs, take a look at that garret, maybe see if we can find where that video system is and check it out before they have a chance to erase everything and blame *that* on Huckabee too."

"You seem to think Huckabee didn't do it."

"Honestly? I don't know who did or didn't do what at this point. All I know is, someone's trying awfully hard to make him look guilty. And they're turning this from being a straight, open-and-shut homicide into—"

"A mystery. I got it."

We went to the hallway and I said, "Before we nose around upstairs, let's go back and see what Dr. Cutter has to say about the time of death and whatnot. Maybe while we're doing that the Brights will come down and tell us some facackta story about how a diamond bracelet has suddenly gone missing."

We went back into the kitchen and I said, "And what do you want to bet their doctor and lawyer are going to show up here any minute?"

"Why do you say that?"

"They're a wealthy old couple. If the lawyer can't stop us from questioning them, the doctor will step in and claim that they're under stress and that all questions will have to wait until their hearts or blood pressure can manage the shock." I pointed back at the phone. "There's the first call now." One of the two lights was lit up again.

"I take it all back," he said, smiling.

"Take what back?"

"Every bad thing I thought about you since we first met."

I nodded. "Thanks. I'll bet you had a few of them."

"Oh, yeah," he said, going toward the refrigerator. "I thought you were pulling an attitude because you're famous."

I sighed. "You mean the Gordon Beeson case?"

He nodded. "Everybody knows about it."

"Look, if I could've come up with a way to trap Beeson's killer without doing it on live TV, with international satellite feeds, I would have done it. But he'd've gotten away with it if I hadn't pulled that stunt. Anyway, I had my fifteen minutes and I'm glad to be done with it."

"Sure, you're done," he said, opening the refrigerator door, "unless you solve another high-profile case."

"Hey, as long as I don't have to solve it on live TV, I'll be fine." I looked at him. "*Now* what are you doing?"

He reached inside the fridge, pulled out a red bottle of Heinz, and put it in the bottom pocket of his jacket. "Just grabbing some ketchup before the lawyer shows up and tells me I'm violating somebody's facackta rights."

5

It wasn't a diamond bracelet, but an emerald necklace, that turned up missing. Or so Mrs. Bright claimed as she and her husband rushed into the room again, a few minutes after Bailey and I had come back to talk to Jamie about the time of death, which I'd been right about, more or less.

The couple were now dressed in casual wear of the LL Bean variety—I assume for their imminent departure from the mansion to whatever hotel they'd booked for the night.

"Oh, dear me! Oh, dear me!" Fiona cried, doing her best to look worried sick. "I was just putting away my pearls and noticed my emerald necklace is missing! Who could have taken it?" She stopped a moment then gasped as if it had suddenly come to her. "It was him! Tom Huckabee! I just know it. Poor, dear Amy must have caught him in the act and that's why he killed her. That must be it!"

I wanted to suggest that she ask Karl for some acting lessons but didn't.

All the crime scene investigators, including two

guys who were photographing and making notes about the blood spatter at the top of the stairs, stopped what they were doing to watch.

Bailey diligently wrote the information about the missing jewelry in his little notebook, then said, "Can you excuse me a minute?" and pulled me aside. "Okay, now what do I do?"

I quickly outlined a plan of action. He nodded, turned back to the couple and went to work.

How many pieces are missing? *Just the necklace.*

Where is it usually kept? *In a wall safe.*

And that's where it was tonight? *No, in the dresser.*

Why was it in the dresser? *I was going to wear it.*

You changed your mind? *Yes, I changed gowns.*

Anything missing from the safe? *I didn't check.*

Who has the combination? *Just Ellis and myself.*

Can we search your room? *I beg your pardon?*

Can we search—? *Why do you need to search—?*

Will you allow us to search your room, yes or no? *No.*

She insisted that the necklace was stolen and that there was no reason to search her room. "Do you think I wouldn't know if one of my necklaces had been stolen? I mean, really."

"The thing is, ma'am, this is a homicide investigation. We have a legal duty to search any and all parts of the premises that might hold any evidence relating to the crime."

Jamie came over to me and whispered, "What's going on?"

"I'll explain in a minute," I whispered.

Fiona huffed at the detective. "You certainly have no right to go searching through my private things."

"Actually, we do. Will you show us the way?"

She pulled a faint and collapsed on the floor.

Ellis just stood there. Jamie knelt next to Fiona and felt her pulse. She said, "Someone get her some water."

Me, I had to resist an impulse to give Fiona a little jab with my toe, to see if she was faking it.

Ellis said, "I'll go."

"Good," I said, "I'll tag along."

He halted. "There's really no need."

"Just the same, I'll come give you a hand. Everybody else stay here."

Bright and I went into the kitchen. I watched him search through the cupboards to find a water glass. He found one and took it to the sink. I thought I heard the front door of the mansion open and close, followed by some commotion in the next room, so I peeked through the galley window and saw two men—one tall and rail thin, the other short and round—hovering around Fiona. The short one held a little black bag. They were both dressed in business suits, even though it was getting close to midnight. On a Sunday night.

I turned to look at Ellis, who was just standing there, staring into space, holding the glass under the tap, with water streaming over the sides. "I think it's full, sir."

"What?" He came to, looked at the glass, and turned off the water. "Yes. I was thinking of something else."

"And I believe the family doctor and lawyer are here."

"What?" he said, coming toward me, holding the glass away from his body as if it held nitroglycerine.

"At least that's who it looks like." I jerked a thumb at the door then held it open for him. "Reinforcements, eh? And just in the nick of time."

"I don't know what you mean," he said, giving me a strong whiff of brandy as he passed by.

Fiona was on her feet now but just barely. She was being held in place by the two men in suits.

Jamie shot me a look. I raised my hands, palms up.

The two men were fawning over Fiona, telling her to calm down, that everything was under control, that no one was going to search her room. She just stood gasping and fanning her face with one hand. She saw Ellis and held her hands out for the water. He gave it to her and helped her take a long gulp.

When she came up for air, Ellis, still acting like a zombie, held onto the half-empty glass.

Bailey said, "Good. Now that that's over with, let's go search your room."

She pulled another faint, but was held in place this time, just barely, by the doctor and lawyer.

"She needs to lie down," said the short man, struggling to stay upright himself. "She's not well."

Bailey looked at me for directions.

I jerked my chin at the sitting room and said, "She can lie down on the divan while the rest of us go upstairs."

The tall one said, "No one is going anywhere without my clients' permission."

Bailey scratched the back of his neck. "From what I know about the law, counselor, we can search the entire house if we have to. It's a crime scene."

"I'm sorry, but you're wrong," said the tall man, as he and his cohort waltzed Mrs. Bright toward the divan. "Until you get a warrant, the Brights' private quarters are off limits."

They lay her down on the divan. She whispered, "Water. More water, Ellis?"

Ellis turned to go back to the kitchen and I reminded him, "There's still some in the glass, sir."

He nodded and took the glass over to Fiona.

Bailey said, "The doc can look after her, all right. The rest of us are going to search that room."

"Nobody move," said the lawyer. "I demand to speak privately with my clients before you take any more action."

Bailey looked at me.

I shrugged and nodded.

To the lawyer he said, "You've got two minutes."

"Thank you," said the lawyer, though he didn't mean it.

The doctor and lawyer huddled with Fiona and Ellis for a bit and Bailey came back over to me and Jamie.

The CSU team went back to work.

"Jack," Jamie said, "what's this about searching her room?"

"She's lying about the missing necklace."

She looked at Bailey. He shrugged.

She said, "How can you be sure?"

"That's what you pay me for, honey."

She chuckled, shook her head. "If you recall, sweetheart, I *can't* pay you or you'll lose your benefits."

True. Due to my "three-quarter" retirement package I was only allowed to earn about $15,000 a year or lose some of my benefits, and I make more than that just running my kennel.

"Okay, so you don't pay me. I'm still your criminology expert, and in my expert opinion something fishy's going on."

She shrugged and turned to a pretty, statuesque black woman who was standing next to the body, holding a camera. "Are you about done, Gretchen?"

"Yep. I've got shots of everything."

"Okay," she nodded, then said to two men from the ME's office, "Let's bag her and get her out to the van."

They brought a body bag over to where Amy lay and Jamie touched my arm, then went to supervise.

Gretchen, the photographer, gave me an appraising look, then tilted her head at Jamie. "Lucky girl," she said, rewinding her film.

"Uh, thanks," I said.

"Now what do we do?" said Bailey.

"Huh?" I said. "Oh, don't back down. We don't want them going upstairs without some police presence."

He shrugged. "You're the boss. At least for now."

The doctor and attorney came over and introduced themselves formally. The lawyer was J. J. Higginbottom, of Higginbottom, Sterling, and Fisk, the doctor was—I forget, Jennings? Fleming? I was too busy keeping an eye on Fiona to listen.

She was fanning herself and acting distraught, but she was also occasionally and, I'm sure *she* thought, artfully, peeking over at us to see how things were going.

Higginbottom renewed his objections to the search. "My client is elderly and it would be too much of a shock to her to have a gang of police thugs going through her private quarters."

Fleming (or Jennings) chimed in, "She needs to go upstairs to bed. She needs her medicine."

"Why?" I asked. "Is your little black bag empty?"

He looked at the bag, which lay on the floor where Fiona had pulled her faint. "Well, no. But I don't think I have the exact prescription and dosage. For that she needs access to her medicine cabinet. And she needs bed rest."

"We're investigating a murder," Bailey said, "and we need to search any part of the property that might be significant. She can take her medicine and lie on her bed, but not without at least one police officer in the room."

"That's totally unacceptable," said Higginbottom.

Dr. Fleming said, "How can she rest with the police all over the place, going through her belongings?"

I looked up at the CSU crew and said, "Has anyone found a murder weapon yet?"

No one had.

I nudged Bailey, and he said to the attorney, "If the killer was upstairs stealing jewelry, he may have left the murder weapon up there as well. We're making that search."

Higginbottom made a grim face. "Fine. But not until after she's had her medicine and's had a chance to calm down."

"Fine with me," said Bailey, with a shrug. "But she'll have to be supervised by at least one police officer."

"Absolutely not. Dr. Jannings and I will be in attendance. No outsiders until she's stable."

Bailey said, "We can't run the risk of evidence being tainted or tampered with."

"See here," said Higginbottom. "Is my client a suspect?"

Bailey looked at me.

I said, "Of course not. But the law is clear. The police have the right to full access without interference from interested parties." I said to the doctor, "You're free to root around in her medicine cabinet and find what she needs. Detective Bailey and I will accompany you."

"Not without a warrant," said Higginbottom.

"Fine," said Bailey, taking a cell phone from his jacket.

"Fine," said Higginbottom, doing the same.

"I'm calling a judge for a warrant," said Bailey.

"And I'm calling a judge for a stay."

"Knock it off," I said, "we're searching that room."

While they were engaged in a pissing contest, Jamie and the ME transport guys were putting the body bag onto a gurney. She put on her yellow parka and as they left two men came in.

One was Dan Coletti, an affable redhead, who's a lieutenant with the Camden PD. The other I'd never met, though I'd seen his picture in the paper. He was the Camden chief of police, a tallish, barrel-chested, pug-faced, black Irishman, with thick eyebrows and clipped, gunmetal gray hair. He was chewing on a hangnail as he walked in the door.

They came over and spoke to Bailey briefly, then took him aside, into the dining room. Coletti and Bailey seemed to be arguing the same point to the chief, who kept chewing his hangnail and looking over at the lawyer, then at the Brights, and shaking his head. When it was over, Coletti and Bailey looked grim and were both shaking their heads.

The chief came over to speak to Higginbottom. "Let us know when your client is feeling well enough to have my men search the bedroom."

"Thank you, Chief. Can she go upstairs now?"

"Yeah, in a minute." He turned to Bailey. "You're off this case as of right now. And what's that in your pocket?" he said, referring to the ketchup bottle.

Bailey hesitated.

I said, "I think he was shopping when he got the call."

Bailey nodded.

The chief scowled at me, then turned to Coletti. "Dan, you get up to speed on it, and take it from here."

Coletti said, "I think that's a mistake, Chief. Bailey's been here from the git-go. I think we should work togeth—"

"Bailey's bungled things with the Brights," he said. "He's off the case."

"Whatever you say."

The chief squinted at me. "As for you, Field, you have no business being here. I want you out of here *now*."

I shrugged and said, "Too bad. I'm an investigator for the State ME's Office."

"The ME is done here." He pointed to the door. "The body just went that way. You do the same." He turned to the Brights. "You're welcome to go upstairs now, if you like."

"Thanks, Jim," said Ellis as Fiona popped up off the divan. Then she, Ellis, the doctor, and lawyer scurried toward the kitchen and vanished.

I said, "So, you're on a first name basis, huh, Jim?"

"So? What of it?"

"Oh, nothing. But what do you want to bet they're going upstairs to fabricate, destroy, or tamper with evidence?"

"Look, Field, I told you nicely once—"

"Actually? You didn't do it nicely. And I don't want to pull rank on you, but like I said, I'm with the State ME's Office, and the state trumps local authority."

He stepped closer and his face got quiet. He was trying to intimidate me with his slight weight/height advantage. "Get out of here now before I physically throw you out."

I just laughed through my nose.

"You think I won't do it?"

"You could *try*. But it wouldn't put you in a very good light with your men if you ended up moaning into the carpet, holding on to your nuts." I looked down at his hangnail. A single drop of blood was about to fall onto the carpet. I said, "And another thing, you moron, you're about to contaminate the crime scene. Don't you know *any*thing?"

He looked at his hand, put his finger in his mouth, then turned to the cops and the CSU. "Somebody get me a Band-Aid!" He looked back at me. "You still here, jackass?"

I just shook my head and went toward the door.

"Uh," Coletti said, stopping me with one arm, "I need to have a few words with Jack first, before he goes."

The chief gave him a stare, still sucking his finger.

Coletti smiled and shrugged. "If you want me to get up to speed, I'll need to have a conversation with him."

"Fine. Do it outside. That man is not welcome in here."

So Bailey zipped up his parka—a dark blue one, I noticed—and we all went outside and had us a confab. A light mist had risen, giving the grounds an eerie, mysterious feeling. I was sure the Atlantic Ocean was out there somewhere beyond the gates, but even it had been swallowed up by the fog.

Jamie, who'd just finished with her part of the transport operation, came over to join us.

We explained to her what had happened and then stood around making breath clouds and hugging ourselves and doing the cold weather dance, and Bailey and I told Jamie and Coletti everything we knew and everything we didn't know.

When we were done he commiserated with us a bit, then went back inside the mansion, where only the big boys were allowed to play.

"Now what?" said Bailey.

"Yeah, Jack," Jamie hugged my arm. "You're shivering. Didn't I tell you to wear that parka I got you?"

"Yes, honey, and I'm coming down with a cold and I'm unwanted and unappreciated by the local authorities."

"So? I'm done with the body for now. Let's go home."

I took out my keys and held them out for her to take. "You go ahead, honey. I want to snoop around the grounds a little."

She didn't take them. "Whatever for?"

Just then the two cops I'd sent out to look for footprints came around the corner, from the back.

Bailey asked if they'd found anything. They said they'd searched the entire grounds and hadn't found a thing. Bailey thanked them and sent them inside to report to Coletti.

I said, "A mysterious killer runs out of the house, covered in blood, is unseen by the guard at the front gate—meaning he had to have escaped over the wall—and yet he didn't leave any footprints or other evidence that he was here?"

Bailey said, "They could have been covered by the snow."

"Maybe. But I don't think it's deep enough to totally cover the prints of a man running. That bears some looking into." I held out the keys to Jamie again. "You go home. I'm in the mood to snoop."

"If you're staying then I'm staying."

"No, you should go home, honey."

"Un-uh. 'The couple who snoops together,' remember? But what happens if Chief Colbern catches us?"

"So what? We have the right to be here whether that idiot likes it or not."

"I know, honey. I just don't want to make waves."

I thought it over then tossed the keys behind a column next to the front door. "Okay then," I said. "We'll just tell him I lost my keys."

6

We heard the sound of the garage door opening and a car starting up. Bailey and I looked at one another.

"Karl," I said, with a chuckle.

"Yep," said Bailey with a smile.

"Who's Karl?"

We reminded Jamie about Huckabee's parka, and whether the blood would have been visible, as Karl brought the Town Car around and parked it in front of the door. He didn't do a very elegant job of it. The left front tire ended up on the curbstone. He got out and it was clear he'd had more vodka.

I said to him, "Thanks, Karl. Is this where the car was sitting when the killer ran past?"

Karl shrugged, looking at the vehicle. "More or less."

Bailey said, "Okay. Get back in, keep quiet, and keep the headlights on and the motor running."

Karl spat on the ground then did as he was told, slamming the door to make a point.

"Well," said Bailey, "now we have to wait for the parkas to arrive." He saw me looking at *his* parka. "No. No way."

"It's the right color."

He looked at Jamie. "I hope you know how to get ketchup stains out of polyester," he said to her.

"Don't look at *me*," she said. "Jack's the culinary and cleanliness expert."

"Since when?" I asked, then explained to Bailey that I do basic New York bachelor-type cooking, strictly stove-top stuff, though I do keep a neat house.

"Yes," Jamie said, "but your 'stove-top' stuff, as you call it, is always delicious. And you taught me how to get the smell of garlic off your hands after you've been chopping it, remember?"

"Oh, that's easy."

"How do you it?" said Bailey.

"Just use a stainless steel spoon like you would a bar of soap. Can we get on with this before Karl starts honking the horn or something?"

Bailey took out the bottle of Heinz and handed it to me. I asked Jamie how the blow to the head had occurred and she told me it was a fracture to the occipital bone located in the back of the skull, meaning the victim had been struck from behind. And she said the wound was on the right side of her head. There were no defensive wounds on her hands and arms.

"So," I thought it out, "the killer was right-handed, and the blood spray would have hit him about here . . ." I indicated Bailey's right sleeve, shoulder, and chest area. I opened the cap, stood back a little, and squirted, doing my best to approximate blood spatter.

Jamie and I got into the car and we did the test several different times, with the same result every time. The ketchup "blood" wasn't visible under the porch light or in the headlights.

Jamie and I got out of the car and I said, "You can go now, Karl, but leave the car here for a bit."

"Sure, sure," he groused. "I does what you tells me, no problem. I am servant."

"And can the phony bad English, Karl. I know you can speak the language properly."

"How you knows this?"

"Never mind. I'll tell you later."

"Okay," he shrugged, "but you better watch yourself. It's almost midnight, time for dogs come out."

"Not tonight, Karl. The police will be running in and out of the house all night. If you let Maxim and Fritzie loose you'll be in even more trouble than you are now."

Karl said, "What kinds trouble I am in now?"

"It's not bad, but I'll tell you that later too. And no more vodka tonight, either. The Brights are probably going to be spending the night in a hotel and they'll need you to drive them."

He sighed and got out of the car. "Now you tells me."

We watched him stumble his way back toward the garage, cursing and spitting.

"Hey, you smell nice," I said to Bailey.

"Hah. I hope you're right about the stain." He sniffed himself. "And that smell better come out too, or I'm going to spend the rest of the winter craving french fries."

Jamie laughed then said, "So, what's next, Jack?"

"Now we snoop. Anybody got a flashlight?"

"I've got one," said Bailey, unzipping his parka. "Ah, crap. Now I've got ketchup all over my hands again."

"Grab a handful of snow," I said and he did. Then he handed me his flashlight. I wiped the excess ketchup on my jeans then said, "You two'd better stay here."

"What are you looking for, exactly?" said Jamie.

"I don't know," I said and walked down the drive a ways so I could turn and look at the house to see what lights were on upstairs and where.

There was a lustrous yellow glow coming from four windows on the left side of the house on the second floor—probably the master suite. That would be my first place to search—under those windows. I walked toward that side of the house, shining Bailey's flash on the ground and around the shrubbery.

Sometimes you're lucky, sometimes you're smart, sometimes the people you're dealing with are just stupid. It may have been a combination of all three, but I found something in less than two minutes, despite the glow from the Christmas lights. I was about fifteen yards away, but instead of going over to investigate, I called over my shoulder to Jamie and Bailey.

They came over. I shone the flash and something glittered in the bushes, right underneath one of the windows.

"What do you see?" I said.

"It looks like a necklace," Jamie said.

Bailey shook his head. "People are morons."

"Let's take a closer look," I said.

We walked over and ended up standing about ten feet away. The necklace hung by a branch on top of a snow-covered bush of some sort. The bush was of the deciduous variety and its leaves had fallen off, leaving bare branches, one of which was sticking up through the snow covering the rest of the bush.

"What do you notice?" I said to Bailey.

"It's an emerald necklace." He thought a bit. "It doesn't prove they planted it, though. They'll just argue that Huckabee left it there when he fled the scene earlier."

"Really? But they said he left the house a little after ten, right? The snowstorm started after that and it only stopped a little while ago. Now what do you see?"

He smiled. "There's no snow on the necklace, meaning it had to have been put there after they got home."

"Jack," Jamie said, looking up at the house. "They must have dropped it out the window!"

"That's right. Or *she* did. I get the feeling that this is all Mrs. Bright's bright idea."

"But why did you have us come over?"

I shrugged. "They might claim that I found it somewhere else and planted it there. You two are witnesses that I never went near these bushes." I looked down at the snow. "And our footprints are still too far away for any of us to have planted it there, either."

"I'll go tell the chief," Bailey said.

"No." I put a hand on his shoulder. "Tell Coletti. Don't tell him what we've found, just get him out here."

"You got it."

He went inside and Jamie hugged me and told me I had to take better care of myself and always wear warm clothing and not try to be such a tough guy, then handed me a tissue so I could blow my nose.

"That's a myth, you know," I said.

"What is?"

"That cold weather causes colds."

"It's not the cold weather, per se, it's the sudden change in body temperature, which lowers the body's immunoresponse to—"

"Thanks for the tissue."

Bailey came back out with Coletti. We showed him the necklace, then explained about the bloody parka. He shook his head and started back toward the house.

"Are you going to get the chief?" I asked.

"No," he said, over his shoulder, "I'm going to get a photographer and an evidence bag for the necklace."

About a minute later he came back outside with Gretchen, who, I swear, winked when she saw me. She took some photos, first with a Polaroid, then with a 35mm, then Coletti put the necklace into a ziplock bag, sealed it, and wrote on the evidence tag. Gretchen stood there for a bit, looking at me, until Coletti told her she could go back inside. She nodded, gave me a last look, then left.

Jamie punched my arm. "What was *that* all about?

"Ow! How do *I* know?" To Coletti I said, "So, now what?"

He looked at me but deliberately kept his eyes off Jamie. (They went to high school together and he's had a crush on her ever since.) "I hate to ask," he said, "but what would *you* do if you were in my position, Jack?"

I laughed. "Me? I'd go back inside, slap the cuffs on them, arrest them for obstruction, then take them down to the station house and put the scare of God into them."

He shook his head, smiling. "Well, effective as that might be, it's not going to happen."

"Granted. But why the hell not? They're guilty of planting evidence in a murder investigation aren't they?"

Coletti thought of something. "We *could* arrest the chauffeur. He's involved too, according to what you heard over the phone."

I shook my head. "That would be a bad move."

"Why?"

If Karl was who I thought he was I didn't want to spook him. "It's like a game of chess. Karl is the weak link in their defense. If you bust him you lose his usefulness."

"Jack," Jamie said.

"Okay, honey. We'll go in a minute. I just want to play one more piece on the board first."

"And what piece is that?" Coletti asked. He looked at Bailey. "What are you smiling about?"

"Nothing. I just like the way Jack's mind works. And I think we *should* slap the cuffs on the old couple."

"Not going to happen. So, Jack, what's the other piece?"

"Well, the chief is guilty of facilitating a crime by not following proper procedure. If he hadn't allowed the Brights to go upstairs without some police presence, they wouldn't have been able to plant evidence. If it were me, I'd arrest him too. Let me finish. Obviously you can't do that. But the state police can. Remember the case in a few years back, with the body buried in the garage?"

I was referring to a missing woman, who was married to a poker buddy of the chief of police of a major city in the state. The chief vouched for the husband and called off the investigation, stating that the woman had obviously run off, even though her car was parked in front of the house and her purse and all her clothes were still inside. Her daughter made a fuss in the media, the State Police finally had to come in and reopen the case, and some cadaver dogs found the woman's body, buried in the garage. The chief lost his job.

"How do you know about that case?" Coletti said. "It happened before you ever moved to Maine."

I shrugged. "There were dogs involved. If I were you I'd keep the memory of it fresh in Colbern's mind."

Coletti shook his head, but he was smiling. "I guess you're right about the way his mind works," he told Bailey. "I don't know if I'm willing to risk my job over it, but . . ." He looked at me. "You think this guy Huckabee is innocent?"

"I don't know and I don't care. All I know is if he *did* do it, a good defense attorney will use this cockamamie setup to cast enough reasonable doubt to get him off. Think about it. Let's say you find the guy and the victim's blood is all over his clothes. The defense will argue that *it* was planted, just like the necklace was. That's why you can't let people go running around a crime scene unsupervised."

He thought about it and nodded. "Maybe I should have *you* come back inside and talk to the chief."

"Me? I'd have an urge to give him a good smack between the eyes."

"Jack!" Jamie warned.

"I'm not saying I'd *do* it, but I'm coming down with a cold and my resistance is low. Besides, he wouldn't listen to me. Hell, he probably won't even listen to *you*."

Coletti nodded. "You're probably right."

"I *know* I'm right. And one other thing you might want to remind him of: for some reason the media around here like me." I shrugged. "I guess solving a couple of high-profile cases made me look good, I don't know. But they're going to be all over this case, and I'm going to have plenty to say about it if Colbern doesn't straighten up and fly right."

"Huh. I thought you didn't like being in the news," Coletti said with a grin.

"I hate it. But it can be a useful tool when necessary. Just make sure the chief remembers that."

He chewed his lip. "Maybe I can bring it up somehow."

"Good. Now I'm going home." I put my arm around Jamie.

Coletti looked away. "Funny, I thought you two were supposed to get married in October."

"Yeah, we were sup*posed* to," Jamie said, twirling her engagement ring, "but with my new position at the ME's office, and the renovations on Jack's house, we had to postpone it."

"We're still not inviting you," I said.

"Jack!" She almost hit me then said to Coletti, "It's going to be a small wedding, just close friends and family. Sorry."

"That's all right," he said to his shoes. "I'll let you know how things work out with the chief. Come on, Brad." He turned to go, stopped, reached in his pocket and pulled out a set of keys. "These yours, by any chance?"

I took them. "Yeah, I must've dropped them."

"Right," he said over his shoulder as he walked away.

We turned to walk back to the front gate and Jamie said, "Did you have to say that to him?"

"What, about not inviting him to the wedding? Sorry, but it kind of bothers me the way he looks at you all the time."

"You mean the way Gretchen was looking at *you*?"

"The photographer? I have no idea what that was about." I looked at her. "Her name's Gretchen?"

"Yes," she huffed. "You want me to get you her *phone* number? And anyway, you didn't have to be so *mean* to Danny. I'm never mean to your crazy ex-girlfriend, am I?"

"Was I being mean? I thought I was just being direct."

She shook her head and snorted.

"And I wish you *were* mean to Kristin. It might stop some of her antics."

"Then maybe you're right, maybe I *should* be mean to her."

"And she's not crazy, she has bipolar disorder."

"Well anyway, you should apologize to Danny the first chance you get. I'm serious."

"Okay. Can we talk about this later?" I sniffled. "This cold is really killing me."

"You want another tissue?"

"Yeah, thanks."

We went through the gate, where the Camden officers were still standing around and the security guard was in his booth.

I handed Jamie the keys and said, "You go ahead and warm up the car. I want to talk to the security guard first."

"Jack, I thought you wanted to go home!"

"I do. But I also need to do a part of what you're not paying me to do."

"You're impossible," she said, and went to the car.

I went to the booth, with a nod to one of the officers to come listen in, and rapped on the door. The guard opened it a crack. He had a space heater inside, keeping him toasty.

"I'm with the ME's office," I said. His nametag read, Kozak. "You're Derek?" He nodded and I said, "What did you see tonight?"

"Nothing." He shrugged. "The boss came home about ten. That's all I know."

"By 'the boss,' do you mean Mr. Bright or his wife?"

He laughed. "I was referring to the old man, but you're right. She kind of runs things around here."

"And you didn't see anyone else come in or go out?"

"No, though I took a bathroom break about eight-thirty. If someone had a swipe card, they could've come in then."

"And where were you exactly during that time?"

He shrugged. "Nowhere. I went around the back to use the bathroom next to the kitchen, then came straight back here."

"You used a card key to open the kitchen door?"

"That's right."

"Did you see anyone else while you were on your break?"

"What's this all about? You think *I* killed her?"

"We just need to exclude you by accounting for your whereabouts, that's all."

"Jesus, I barely even knew who she was. And no, no one else saw me and I didn't see anyone else, including the maid. I just went inside to take a piss, that's all."

"Un-huh. And who all has security cards?"

"Karl, the Brights, and most of the staff."

"What about the professor?"

"Him? He kind of comes and goes as he pleases. But you know, it's the strangest thing. Sometimes . . ."

"Sometimes what?"

"Well, sometimes, when I'm absolutely sure that everyone is inside the house, including the professor, he'll show up at the front gate, looking like he's been dragged through hell."

"That's interesting." I looked at the red button that operates the gate. "Is there an electronic log?"

He nodded. "Two, as a matter of fact. One here . . ." he pointed to a metal box next to the red button, ". . . and one at the security company's main office."

"Is that the same company Tom Huckabee worked for?"

He shrugged. "No. From what I understand he worked for an electronics company. Not the same outfit at all."

"I see. And does the lock on the kitchen door also show up on the log?"

"Yeah, as a matter of fact. Each card is coded to its owner, so you can check it and see that I didn't have time to run around and kill anybody. I just went inside to take—"

"A piss, I know. Okay, thanks. Make a copy of your log and have this officer get it to one of the detectives inside."

Derek said, "You got it."

I looked at the officer and he nodded a confirmation.

"Good, thanks." I turned to the Suburban and found Karl waiting with one hip planted against the fender.

"Hey, Karl," I said, "What's up?"

"You tells me now? These troubles I am in?"

"Okay, look, I overheard your phone conversation with Mrs. Bright. Where you suggested that she claim some of her jewelry was missing? So I heard you speak normally. Plus, now *she's* guilty of filing a false police report and planting evidence, which is a felony. And *you're* guilty of being an accessory."

His face shrank. "Am I goings to be arrested?"

"No. I think I talked the police out of filing charges."

He thought it over. "Why you does this for me?"

"Karl," I said, going around to the other side, "can the phony bad English, okay? And I'm only doing it because I want to learn more from you about Professor Gimme Money."

"Hah!"

I leaned across the roof. "You said you don't know his name, but how did you pick him up at the airport the first time?"

A smile slowly warmed his face. "You're a very clever man. Yes, I had a sign the first time. The Mrs. made it for me. His name is Professor Hayes. I don't know the rest."

Jamie rolled down the window and said, "Jack!"

"In a second, honey."

"Well, hurry up," she said and rolled the window back up.

To Karl I said, "Okay . . . Professor Hayes. And the strange lights. They only come when he's staying in the house?"

He shrugged. "It's the only time I see them. The damn lights come shining in my window and I can't sleep."

I had a feeling that he couldn't sleep was because he was scared there really *were* ghosts in the house.

"Has he been here this weekend?"

"Yes. I drove him to the airport this afternoon."

"What flight did he take?"

"I don't know the number. It was the four-thirty flight to LaGuardia."

"He's from New York?"

He shrugged. "How do I know where he's from?"

"But he always flies in and back from there?"

"Yes. Always LaGuardia, both ways."

"Can you give me a description of him?"

He shrugged. "Tall, like I said before." He looked me over. "A couple of inches or so taller than you."

"So, six-three, six-four?"

"Maybe a little taller. He's skinny, so maybe he just looks taller. He has long gray hair but bald on top, a long gray pointed beard, bushy eyebrows, and his face, I don't know how to say it—has blue eyes, big cheekbones, and a long nose. Always wears a three-piece woolen suit and has a big wooden walking stick."

"You mean like a cane?"

"No, like this tall." He held his up shoulder high.

"Hmmm. Well, except for the three-piece suit he sounds like a dead ringer for Gandalf."

"Who?"

"You ever see that movie, *The Lord of the Rings*?"

He said he hadn't.

"Well, it doesn't matter. All right, Karl. Thanks. If the police give you any trouble, call me." I pushed a business card across the roof of the car and he took it.

"Thank you," he said. I noticed his watch again, with its wide strap. He looked at the card, then back up at me. "Why are you on my side with the cops?"

I didn't want to get into the whole Russian mob thing and how it must've taken a lot of courage for him to leave New York and start a new life. I'd worked a few cases in Brooklyn and knew from past experience that ex-Russian mobsters aren't usually too eager to talk about their past ties, so I just said, "I have my reasons. Just tell me one thing: did you really see Huckabee?"

"If I tell you no, I have to testify in court?"

I hesitated.

"I thought so."

"Karl, you may have to testify either way, unless we

can get a confession from the killer first. And for that I need to know the truth."

He shook his head and sighed. "If it's just between us, I didn't see him. But I won't testify in court."

"Okay, thanks."

He nodded and turned away. I stood there a moment, watching him go. Then I looked up at the mansion.

With the twinkling lights and wisps of fog blowing slowly around it, it looked like maybe it actually *was* haunted. Or, if you had that kind of mentality, you might think it was inhabited by hobbits and wizards.

Jamie leaned over to my side of the car and rolled down the window. "Jack, now what are you looking for?"

"I don't know, honey," I said, "ghosts?"

"Ghosts?" she almost laughed. "*What* ghosts?"

"You know, the ghosts of Christmas past?"

She shook her head. "Just get in the car, you idiot."

7

I had a miserable night with my cold, but you don't need to know the details, except that Jamie got a good night's sleep upstairs while I camped out on the sofa with plenty of Kleenex, orange juice, garlic, vitamin C, zinc, echinacea, and goldenseal. I would have slept in the downstairs bedroom, but it and several other parts of the house are still under renovation, though the construction crew were all on vacation.

Frankie slept by the hearth, while I let Hooch share the sofa. I usually make the big lug sleep in the kennel—he snores something awful and no one can sleep when he's in the room—but whenever I'm sick, he can't bear to be away from me, hence not only the stuffy head but the cricks in my back, neck, and shoulders from trying to sleep around and under him.

Jamie came downstairs around seven. She tiptoed to the sofa, told Hooch to get off, which he did, and scooched my legs over so she could sit next to me. She was in robe and slippers and looked all clean and pretty from a shower, her long brown hair still a little wet and smelling of shampoo. She leaned down to kiss me and I held on to her neck a little too long.

"Jack," she said, giggling, "stop sniffing my hair."

"Sorry. It's about the only thing I *can* smell."

She sat up and put her hand to my forehead.

"Do I have a fever?" I asked.

"Yes, a mild one. What are you going to do today?"

"Probably just lie in bed and be miserable. You?"

"I'm performing an autopsy, remember? Since you're already up, come have breakfast with me."

"I'm not hungry," I said. "Besides, aren't you supposed to feed a cold and starve a fever? Or is it the other way around?"

She laughed. "Neither, you should eat something whether you have a cold *or* a fever. That's an old wives' tale."

"Well anyway, I'll eat later."

"Ah, sweetie, but come sit with me while *I* eat, okay?"

"Okay. I have to take the dogs out first, though."

"Okay. I'll make breakfast while you do that."

"I'll just have a blueberry muffin, I think," I said, getting up. "Or some oatmeal." Frankie and Hooch got up and stretched, then shook themselves. "And it's not just Frankie and Hooch," I went on, "I've got a dozen dogs in the kennel that need to be exercised and fed before I can eat."

She grabbed my hand. "Then you stay here and *I'll* take care of the dogs."

"Honey, it's not your job," I said, though I didn't put up much of a fight. In fact I just let her sit me back down next to the blanket.

"No, but I'm your fiancée and one of these days,

once we actually get married, if we *do,* I'll probably have to pitch in once in a while when you forget to take care of yourself."

"Not that again. I'm telling you, I get the same damn cold every Christmas whether I wear a warm coat or not."

"Which you never do, so that doesn't prove anything."

"And why do think we're never getting married?"

"I don't know. Because you keep putting off setting the date, for one thing."

"Honey, you're working two jobs until they can find a new chief of pathology at the hospital, remember? Plus the house is still being renovated. I thought we agreed to wait until—"

"I know. I'm sorry I mentioned it."

"And if you're not going to let me get out of bed and take care of the dogs, wake up Leon and have him do it."

"Hah. Have you ever tried to wake him up this early?"

"Good point," I said. (Leon's sixteen and like a lot of kids his age, he has some bizarre sleep patterns.)

She said, "Anyway, you stay here and I'll take care of the dogs. We'll worry about next year's cold next year. And we can talk about setting the date when you're feeling more up to it." She put the blanket across my lap.

"Okay," I said. "Do you know what to do?"

"Jack." She made a face. "I think I can take a few dogs down to the play yard for ten minutes or so. You or Farrell can feed them later. Or Leon can if he ever gets out of bed. It won't kill the dogs to wait an hour or so before they eat."

"Okay," I said. "I love you."

"I love you too, honey."

"Wait," I said, as she turned to go.

She turned back. "What is it?"

"Nothing. I just want to get my morning fix. You know, look at how beautiful you are."

She smiled and shook her head. "You really *do* have a fever." Then she went to the mudroom and called Frankie and Hooch. They looked at her, then at me.

"Go on, you guys. Go with Jamie."

They trotted over to her and wagged their tails.

She put on her parka, then her boots, gloves, and a knit hat. Then they all went outside while I lay down on the sofa, crawled under the blanket, and tried to get some sleep.

8

"So, how did it go?" I asked over breakfast. I was having oatmeal—with no milk or sugar, just blueberries and walnuts—and a glass of orange juice. Jamie, now dressed for work *and* the holidays, in chinos and a reindeer and snowflake sweater, was having bacon, eggs, toast, and coffee.

"You mean the dogs?" she smiled. "It was a lot of fun. It made me remember why you love being a trainer and running your kennel so much." She started to laugh.

"What's so funny?"

"Nothing. I was just remembering this one dog, you know the one who looks like a cross between a husky and a panda bear."

"Saki? She's an akita."

"Whatever. The point is it's so cute how she plays, even with that little white dog. She puts her chin on the ground—"

"You mean Susie Q? She's a Maltese. Is it cold out?"

"Not very, why?"

"Because she should wear a coat, that little one."

"Yes, I know. Which is why I put her under my parka after she started shivering."

"That's good."

Just then Leon came in, dressed in his jammies, a parka, and his Adidas high-tops, unlaced. He was half awake. "Yo," he said, rubbing his eyes, "you havin' breakfast without me?"

Jamie said, "What woke *you* up?"

"Probably the bacon," I said. "It's packed with hunger pheromones that attract male teenagers."

"Hah, hah," Leon said and sat down.

"Did you already take Magee out?" I asked.

"Yeah." We heard scratching at the door and he looked over there. "Shit." He got up, went over, and let Magee in. The little rascal had icicles on his fur. He zoomed into the kitchen, raced past us into the living room, and tore around in circles, teasing Frankie and Hooch into chasing him.

"Leon, no playing in the house. And watch your mouth."

"What'd I say?" He thought it over. "Oh, 'shit.' Sorry. Magee, come!"

The dog zoomed back into the kitchen. Frankie and Hooch followed but saw that we were eating and stood outside the entryway, wagging their tails hopefully.

"Go lie down," I told them.

They just stood there, acting like they weren't sure if I was talking to them or Magee.

"Frankie? Hooch? Go." They hung their heads then trotted back to the Christmas tree.

Leon told Magee to sit, sat himself, looked at Jamie's plate, then looked at me. "You gonna make me some?"

She said, "Jack's not feeling well. I'll do it."

"He can do it himself," I said. "Can't you Leon?"

"Aw, man," he said getting up.

Jamie said to him, "If I'd known you'd be up this early I would have made some more." Then, while he went to the refrigerator and got out the bacon and the carton of eggs, she said to me, "Why does Magee get to come in the kitchen while we're eating, and Frankie and Hooch don't?"

I explained that Leon sets Magee's rules, not me. "And besides, Magee doesn't drool and they *do*."

"Hmmm. I don't suppose you could train them not to?"

I laughed at the thought. "Pavlov conditioned dogs to salivate in response to a previously unconnected stimulus. It doesn't work so well the other way around."

Magee, who'd gotten tired of sitting, lay down and began licking himself. Then he looked up and saw Leon bringing the bacon and eggs over to the counter. He got up and went over to "help."

"So, Jack," Jamie said, "how do they train cadaver dogs?"

"What? Why on earth would you want to know that?"

"You mentioned that case in Portland. I was wondering how they can train them to find bodies."

"It's not my area, but I imagine it's similar to any scent-detection work. They teach them to play fetch with something containing the smell of decomposing flesh, then—"

"But how? What do they train them with?"

"Do you really want to discuss this over breakfast?"

"I know *I* don't," said Leon, as he put the carton and

the package of bacon on the counter. Magee watched him, wagging his tail. Leon cracked open five eggs and dropped them into the pan, then put six strips of bacon in on top of them. I shook my head and resisted an impulse to tell him to put the bacon in first, or to go over and do it for him, but it was already too late.

Jamie said, "I'm a medical examiner, remember?"

I shrugged. "Okay. Well, they either use Pseudoscents, which are an artificial version of the real thing, or in states where it's legal, they use actual human remains."

"Ooh," she grimaced, "but I guess if they have to . . . and weren't there two sets of dogs in that case in Portland?"

"Were there?"

"I think so. I think the Portland police searched the garage and their dogs didn't find anything. It was only when the state police dogs came in that they eventually found the body under the cement."

"There could be several reasons for that. The state of decomposition might have been too low during the first search, or the Portland dogs weren't well suited for detection work."

"What do you mean?"

I shrugged. "Some trainers prefer using dogs with low prey drive and no aggression, which I think is a mistake. More aggressive dogs are also more aggressive about finding things. Then there's the training paradigm. The current crop of American trainers have strayed from the European model for reasons of political correctness or because they're caught up in the latest fads with clickers and operant conditioning, when the real key to training will always be the prey drive."

"Yo, Jack," said Leon, "what's operant conditioning?"

I explained that some people believe there are four basic ways a dog learns anything: positive reinforcement, negative punishment, positive punishment, and negative reinforcement.

He said, "It sounds like a lot of mumbo-jumbo."

I agreed, then explained that despite the current belief throughout much of the dog world that all learning is based on either operant or classical conditioning, and nothing else, there are numerous examples of things dogs do every day that contradict this.

"Like what?" Jamie wanted to know.

I told her, for example, that when you bring a puppy into a new home he doesn't need to be taught over and over where the water bowl is. If he's thirsty and he drinks from it, he knows exactly where to find it from then on. But if you show it to him when he's not thirsty, and even reward him for finding it by praising him or giving him a treat, he won't have any idea how to find it when he needs a drink. "Instincts and emotions control learning naturally. There's no need for repetition, trial and error, or making associations with treats."

I told her of some things I'd taught Frankie that took place completely outside the realm of conditioning, including the "Up the stairs!" command. "I only taught it to him once, in the old walk-up where we used to live, and he's never forgotten it. In fact, I tested him a few days later on the front steps of a brownstone we passed by on a walk. This was only the second time I'd ever given him the command and he instantly obeyed it. Ran right up the strange stoop."

"How'd you teach it to him?" Leon asked.

"Good question. I put him in a sit/stay at the bottom of the stairs in our building, teased him with a toy but kept telling him to stay. Then I ran up the stairs with the toy, acting excited and full of energy, ran back down, then threw the toy up to the top of the stairs, stood straight up next to the bottom step, pointed, and said, 'Okay, up the stairs!' and he ran up as hard and as fast as he could."

"I get it," Leon said, "you stimulated his prey drive by teasing him with the toy and making him hold the stay."

"That's right."

"And he still knows the command?" Jamie said, skeptically.

"Sure." I got up. "You want to see?"

"What about my eggs?" Leon said.

"This'll only take a second."

They and Magee followed me to the living room. As we came in Frankie and Hooch looked up and I said, "Hey, Frankie! Come on, let's do a little demonstration."

He and Hooch got up, stretched, then shook themselves. Magee ran over to them. I positioned myself by the stairs, then said to Jamie, "Now how many times since we've met would you say you've heard me give Frankie this particular command?"

"I don't think I've *ever* heard you do it."

"Right. That's because I haven't given it to him in years. Not since we left New York, in fact. Now, watch." Both Frankie and Hooch were looking at me curiously. I said to Frankie, "Hey, Frankie—ready?"

His ears pricked up.

"Okay," I said, excitedly, "up the stairs!"

Without thinking he ran past me and started running up the stairs. Hooch didn't know what was going on but decided it was his business to run up the stairs too. Then Magee joined them. They all got to the top and stood there, staring at me, wagging their tails, awaiting further instructions.

"That's pretty amazing," said Jamie.

"Yep. He learned it *once*, that first time, and has never forgotten it. Okay, doggies," I said to them, "come on down."

They zoomed down the stairs, danced around me a bit, then I pointed to their place by the tree and told them to go lie down, which Frankie and Hooch did, with a little playful pawing at each other and Magee first.

"Interesting," Jamie said, as we went to the kitchen and sat back down at the table. "And he learned it just once because what you call his prey drive was highly stimulated?"

"That's right."

She thought it over. "But not all dogs *have* a prey drive, do they? I mean, how about that cute little Maltese?"

"Are you kidding? Susie Q could play fetch for hours. And yes, all dogs have prey drive, in one form or another. You just have to work a little harder with certain dogs to bring it out in them."

"How?"

"It depends on the dog, but the underlying process is always a matter of increasing the dog's emotional tension by frustrating some desire to the point that a prey object becomes the focal point of that tension, but before he becomes *so* frustrated that he shuts down and gives up."

Leon said, "Just like you did when you teased Frankie with a toy and told him to stay at the bottom of the stairs."

"Exactly. Once you reach that point, of increased tension-without-frustration, you can really heighten the learning experience. And it has nothing to do with operant conditioning." I explained that instincts trump conditioning and told her that the man who invented clicker training admitted this himself, saying that animals often prefer instinctive behaviors over conditioned ones. I said, "So why not *utilize* those instincts instead of trying to condition a dog to go against his natural way of doing things?"

"Yo, Jack, how come this bacon isn't cooking?"

"I told you, you have to move the eggs out of the way."

"I already did that."

"Just wait a little longer," I said. "It'll cook." Then I started to explain the flaw in Premack's principle—or at least in how it's worded—but Jamie had stopped listening.

"Jack," she said, "didn't you once promise not to talk about your theories on dogs with me? We agreed that if you had any interesting ideas—or at least ideas that *you* think are interesting—you'd write a book and put them in it."

"Honey, you're the one who asked me how they train detection dogs, remember? And once I get started . . ."

"I know, I know. So," she said with a wry smile as she buttered her toast, "I guess I'll just have to take the clicker I got you for Christmas back to the pet store."

"Very funny."

"So, how do you think it went last night?"

"You mean after we left? I don't know. We'll have to wait to hear from Coletti."

"Well, if I learn of any new developments," she said, putting some jam on the toast, "I'll pass them on."

"Thanks, but I think I'll survive the day without knowing anything more about the case." I sniffled a bit and thought of something. "Though I would like to know if they found Huckabee and if he has an alibi for the time of death."

"Okay, I'll let you know. Anything else?"

"Well, it's kind of obvious, but if his alibi doesn't pan out, they should check to see if he's right-handed."

"Why would they need—? Oh, right. She was struck from behind and the injury was on the right side of her head."

"Yep. So unless the killer struck her backhanded—"

Jamie chewed her toast, then said, "You want me to bring home some takeout for dinner? Chinese or something?"

"That'd be nice, but I think I'll cook tonight. It'll take my mind off this cold. Any requests?"

"It's freezing out, so anything spicy would be great."

"Okay. I've got some salmon fillets in the fridge. I could try making chili with them."

"Salmon chili? I'm not sure I like the sound of that."

"Yeah, me neither," said Leon, bringing his eggs and bacon to the table. Magee followed him.

"You'll like this, Leon. Trust me."

"You wanna bet?"

"Yeah." To Jamie I said, "I've been wanting to experiment. I was thinking I'd make the chili base with white, black, and pinto beans, mango salsa, roasted garlic and tomatoes, sweat some onions and peppers, then cube the salmon like you would a piece of chuck, rub on some Mexican chili powder, coriander, and cumin, mixed with some cilantro-infused olive oil, dip the salmon cubes in crushed cashews, pan sear them in butter, then when they're done rare, add them to the beans and salsa, and top it all off with fresh chunks of avocado, shredded ginger, and a squirt of fresh lime juice."

"I don't believe it," she said, smiling. "That actually sounds fabulous."

"See, Leon? Somebody appreciates my cooking."

"I appreciate it—when it ain't seafood."

Jamie said, "When did you think this up?"

"Last night, when I couldn't sleep."

"Well, it sounds delicious."

Magee was watching Leon eat with great interest. "No feeding Magee scraps," I reminded Leon.

"Who said I was gonna?"

"I just want to make sure you remember."

"Nah," he said, with a mouthful of eggs, "you're just trying to increase my emotional tension."

I laughed. "Good one, Leon."

Jamie stood up and I did too, but she put a hand on my shoulder. "You don't have to walk me to my car today."

"Okay," I sat back down, "I'll call you later."

"Okay. And finish your report, if you're not too sick."

"What report?"

"You're my civilian advisor, remember? I need you to write a report on the case."

I shook my head. "You want it typed or handwritten?"

She smiled. "Handwritten is fine."

"You want it in triplicate?"

She laughed. "Stop trying to annoy me. I'll call you when I get to the office."

"Okay, boss."

After Jamie left for the morgue, and Leon had finished his breakfast and he and Magee had gone back to bed, despite my reminding him that he had to go to school (he claimed it was a snow day), I realized I wouldn't be able to take Frankie and Hooch to the pediatric ward for our regular Monday afternoon visit. It's not because I felt *that* bad, though I *did*—I felt awful. But I was still in the contagious stage and that's the last thing those kids needed.

I tried to call Farrell Woods to see if he could fill in for me—he was a handler for the K-9 Corps in Vietnam and all the dogs, including Frankie and Hooch, adore him—but he wasn't home. Probably already on his way in to do the morning rounds, picking up doggies for day care. He lives just north of Belfast and has a bit of a drive to get to the kennel, which is located halfway between the mountain villages of Hope and Perseverance.

I knew Mrs. Murtaugh would be over soon, too. She lives just across the county road. We didn't have any grooming appointments scheduled, except for Frankie and Hooch—they have to be bathed the day of each hospital visit—but she likes to hang out in my kitchen and bake cookies and muffins when she doesn't have anything else to do. They're free—the cookies and muffins, along with a bottomless cup of coffee—to all my clients who come by to drop off or pick up a dog, instead of paying the five bucks extra to have the pooch picked up. I was looking forward to seeing her. I had some shopping I wanted her to do after she gave Frankie and Hooch their baths. (She also loves to do my grocery shopping.)

In fact, I was writing a list and was up to the produce—the red and yellow peppers, the Hass avocados, the fresh lime and cilantro—and had even started thinking about how I wasn't that different from Ellis and Fiona Bright in a way—sure they have servants, but I have employees—when the phone rang.

"We found Huckabee," Bailey said.

9

"He claims he wasn't there," Bailey continued. "He says he has an alibi. We're checking it out, of course. But there was one thing in his favor. He has a blue parka, but as far as we could tell, there was no blood on it. We've sent it to the lab to see what they can find."

I sniffled and said, "So you're back on the case?"

He laughed. "Yeah, the chief had to eat a little dirt, though Coletti was nice enough in how he handled it. Are you all right, Jack? You don't sound so good."

"Just this miserable cold."

"Yeah, I hear it's going arou—"

"Not *this* cold. I get it every year. Anyway, if Coletti didn't have the state cops put Colbern in jail, he was a lot nicer about it than *I* would have been."

He chuckled. "You still pissed about that?"

"Not really. I just think everyone else should be half as pissed as I am, or was."

"You must have made a lot of friends in New York."

"Very funny." (He was right, though—I did piss a few people off, from time to time.)

"So, yeah, I'm back working the case with Dan.

Anyway, after we confronted the Brights last night they admitted to planting the necklace and we were finally able to search upstairs, and get this, Jack—their safe was totally empty except for a blank piece of old parchment paper."

"You mean *all* their jewelry is missing now?"

"Yep. And some personal keepsakes. The old lady kept saying something about an irreplaceable letter from her long-lost brother. She was really distraught to find it missing."

I chuckled. "Serves them right for planting the necklace in the first place. You sure she wasn't faking?"

"If you'd been there you'd know this was different. It was strange, though. When we opened the safe, she came over and took out the piece of parchment. There was nothing on it. It was totally blank. But she just stared at it and blubbered, 'They've taken his letter, just like they took Sean.'"

"No kidding. Who's 'they' and who's Sean?"

"My guess would be Sean's the brother. I don't know who 'they' are. We weren't able to question *her* about it because that's when her doctor took over. But they're sticking to their story about seeing Huckabee and the blood on his parka."

"I suppose he could've washed it off."

"Yeah, but the guys at the lab said they'd still be able to find traces. Meanwhile, we accounted for the whereabouts of the other servants, so they're in the clear, but we can't track down the son, Christopher. But get this: his full name is Christopher Robin Bright."

"You're kidding. Well, that says a lot about this family, doesn't it? And he's not in the Bahamas?"

"We don't know yet."

"Maybe he's at Pooh Corner," I said.

He laughed. "Maybe. But like you noticed, his car isn't in the garage and it's not at the airport. His sailboat isn't in the harbor either, but that's about all we know so far."

"It'd be nice to know if he was having an affair with the deceased. You said he's a playboy, right?"

"Yeah, I've been going through her diary and some of the entries point to that. She was also apparently having a fight with Huckabee about something. I'm still not clear what."

I told him about Karl's description of Hayes.

"Well, if he looks like Gandalf he shouldn't be hard to find. We'll check that flight to LaGuardia."

"Good. What did the video surveillance tapes show?"

"Hah. What tapes? There aren't any."

"Great. What did the Brights, or *Mrs*. Bright, in particular, have to say about *that*?"

"What do you think? She claims Huckabee took them. But I'm on my way over to see the man who runs the company Huckabee worked for to get more background. Apparently he was some kind of electronics wizard. Jack? You still there?"

"Yeah, I was just thinking. And I'm starting to get the feeling that maybe Karl really *was* right about those cameras."

"You mean that they were put there to see ghosts? Maybe her brother's ghost, huh? Which might lead us back to this mysterious Professor Hayes?"

"Yep. At least that's a possibility. Did you check to see if Huckabee is right- or left-handed?"

"No. Why?"

I explained.

"Well, there you go. I knew there was a reason I called you. I'll check that out."

"Did you check the security log on the front gate and the kitchen door?"

He said he had and there was no record of anyone using the gate between the time the Brights left for the choral concert and the time they got back. The kitchen door was used around eight-fifteen, then again at eight-sixteen. Just enough time to take a piss.

"Well that probably lets out the security guard. But we still don't know how the hell Huckabee could've come and gone last night, unless of course he's Spiderman."

He laughed. "Like you said, it's a mystery."

"No kidding. And did you find out his exact height?"

"No, but I'd say he's about six feet." He paused. "Dumb question: why do we need to know exactly how tall he is?"

I explained that the ME's report would show the angle of the blows to her head, which could then be used to triangulate the exact height of the killer. "You'll get some useful information on that from the CSU, too."

There was a pause.

I said, "You need me to explain that, too?"

"A little, I guess."

So I told him that the pattern of the blood spatter could be used to determine exactly where the killer was standing in relation to his victim. "That way, there'll be no mistake about his height. Without that information, the defense could argue that either the killer or the victim had been standing on one of the stairs."

"I understand. I think."

"Don't worry, you'll get there. It sounds to me like you're doing a pretty good job. You've already narrowed it down to three potential suspects."

"I have?"

"Sure. It's either Spiderman, Gandalf, or Christopher Robin."

He laughed. "Thanks. Can I call you later if I have—?"

"Yeah, but I might be in bed with this awful cold." And don't tell me again that it's been going around, I wanted to say. It's my Christmas cold. I get it every year and it always lasts right up until the day after Christmas.

"Too bad," he said, before I could say any of this, "I hear it's been going around."

"Yeah, I think that's my other line."

"Really? I didn't hear anything."

"I'll talk to you later."

A few minutes went by then Jamie called.

"Jack, what was that you said earlier about needing your morning fix?"

"You mean, needing to look at how beautiful you are?"

"That's it. Is that true? You do that every morning?"

"Whenever you spend the night here, yeah."

"Then how come I don't know anything about it?"

"You're usually asleep."

"You mean you watch me while I'm sleeping?"

"I don't watch you, I just look at you."

"Hmmm. I'm not sure how I feel about that."

"Why? You're so beautiful when you're asleep."

"I'm sure I must look horrible."

"Not to me. To me you look adorable, like an enchanted fairy princess or something."

She laughed. "You mean like Snow White or Sleeping Beauty?"

"Sure. You're Snow White and I'm Dopey."

That got a laugh, then she said, "And what happens on the nights when I stay at my apartment?"

"Nothing. I just think about you and miss you terribly. Hey, don't you have an autopsy to perform?"

"Yeah, I just wanted to talk to you first."

"Well, now you have."

"I know. And I feel better, except for the fact that now I know you watch me while I'm asleep. I probably won't be able to sleep at *all* from now on."

"Hah!" Jamie sleeps like a log. "Anyway, like I said, I don't 'watch' you, I just like to look at you and think about how lucky I am, for a little while before I get up. Now, get back to work."

She sighed. "Okay. I'll call you when I'm done with the preliminary. And you really think about how lucky you are?"

"Every morning."

"That's nice to know. Thanks, honey."

"Welcome," I said and waited to hear her say she was lucky too, but she just said good-bye and hung up.

Well, I couldn't hold it against her. Everybody knows *I'm* the lucky one. Everybody, I thought, except that pretty photographer. What was her name again?

Oh, right—Gretchen.

10

The kids at the pediatric ward were far from being in the holiday spirit. Who could blame them? They were all stuck inside a hospital while other kids their age were out having snowball fights, sledding, or lying asleep in their own beds at night, free from pain, IV tubes, and mean doctors, and dreaming of what they'd find under the tree come Christmas morning.

Frankie and Hooch did their best to cheer them up. Hooch even agreed to wear a Santa Claus hat with a little jingle bell on the end. His huge, orange face looked almost human under it, though some people might think he looked more like a cross between an oompa-loompa and a naughty elf. Meanwhile, the most that Frankie would agree to was a red Christmas collar with silver bells and green felt pine trees on it. No hats for him. (Yes, I tried one on him but he kept trying to scratch it off with his back leg.)

I had a similar impulse with the surgical mask I'd been forced to wear. Farrell Woods had refused to fill in for me because he said he couldn't stand to be around sick kids.

"Ah, man!" he'd said. "Doesn't it break your heart?"

"I try not to think about it too much."

"So what *do* you think about?"

"How happy they are to see the dogs."

"Man! Now you're tryin' to guilt me into it."

"No. If you don't want to do it, then you shouldn't."

"All right. I feel bad, though, leavin' you in the lurch. Hey, that reminds me."

"What?"

He scratched his beard and looked off.

"Farrell, what is it?"

"Man, you know how bad I am with money."

I sighed. "You want your Christmas bonus early?"

"Yeah, and any extra hours you could throw my way."

I'd almost offered to pay him to go to the hospital for me, but knew he wouldn't be able to do it, even with the added incentive, so I'd said, "Sure. I'll see what I can do."

Then I'd called the hospital to tell them about my cold and to cancel the day's festivities, but the head nurse said, "No problem. You'll just have to scrub down and wear a surgical mask. See you at noon?"

So there I was, scrubbed till I was antiseptic, wearing a cotton mask and feeling more than a little foolish.

"Children," said Maureen (she's the head pediatric nurse), as she announced our arrival, "look who's come for a visit!"

We were in the rec room, with its red and green foil "snowflake" banners, the imitation, white flocked Christmas tree, with twinkling lights and colored ornaments shining under the bright fluorescent lights. The dogs were wagging their tails and sniffing around the wheelchairs and such. The kids were squealing with delight as always, and I was feeling foolish in my jeans and plaid shirt, with the mask and surgical gloves on.

"Can I ride Hooch?" one of the cancer girls asked. I don't remember her name. I try not to get too close to any of the kids or learn anything about their conditions, if I can help it.

"Sure, honey," I said, helping her up. "Don't pull on his ears, though. Just hold on to his collar."

Everyone squealed with delight to watch her riding the big galoot and soon the room filled with cries of "my turn!" "me next!" and the like.

I knew the girl had cancer because she was no more than six years old and she was bald. Like I said, it can really get to you, so I always focus on the dogs and their comportment, making sure that Hooch doesn't knock over any IV stands with his tail. And—since both dogs naturally have a high drool factor—I try to keep a sharp eye out on their jowls for any foam or other signs of imminent dribble. Slobbering on the kids or the medical equipment is a big no-no.

The one thing I *do* like to notice about the kids is the way they smile and laugh when the dogs arrive, as if they've totally forgotten about the unfair and frightening situation they're in.

At any rate, once we were done creating happy havoc in the rec room, a nurse's aid took us on the rounds of the intensive care unit, which contained the kids too sick or too weak to participate in the main action, and that's when we were rejoined by Maureen who introduced us to a kid named Tim Huckabee.

The room was flooded with flowers, poinsettias, Christmas cards, and lights that hung around the windows. Tim was hooked up by an IV in his arm to a dialysis machine. He looked to be about six or so, but

Maureen told me that was a side effect of renal failure. I remembered why from the two years I spent at Harvard medical school, studying to become a psychiatrist: healthy kidneys produce human growth hormone, but when they're injured or diseased they not only lose the ability to filter blood, they also stop producing HGH. So despite how young he looked, Tim Huckabee was actually twelve.

He was also very weak, although he did his best to enjoy the visit. I could tell he really loved dogs, just from the look in his sunken eyes when we first walked through the door.

"Hello, doggies!" he half whispered, then patted the side of his bed with his free arm. For some reason, the dogs always contain their energy and approach the really sick kids slowly and carefully. Hooch, whose head was about bed height, came the closest and actually nuzzled Tim's hand and arm.

Tim spent a few minutes stroking the dog's big noggin, then we left him with a tired smile on his ashen face.

When we got outside the nurse's aid took off for a lunch break but Maureen stayed by the door. Her green eyes showed an uncharacteristic, watery look. She even took a deep breath and leaned against the wall.

"Are you okay?" I said softly.

"What?" She reached out to pull my mask down.

I helped her and said, "Sorry. I thought I had to keep this on at all times."

"No, Tim's the last child today." She sighed.

"He looks pretty bad. He's not going to make it?"

She shook her head. "He's end stage. He's got two weeks, tops, unless we can find a donor. That's why he's hospitalized full-time." She explained that Tim had developed HUS—hemolytic uremic syndrome—from eating hamburger meat tainted with the *E. coli* bacteria five years earlier. The infection went untreated, due to a misdiagnosis by the pediatrician, who thought the diarrhea and vomiting were just stomach flu. When the symptoms persisted Tim was finally diagnosed properly, but by then his kidneys had become infected and he went into renal failure.

"And he's been like this for five years?" I asked.

"It's gotten worse in the past few months or so. He gets the hemodialysis three times a week." She sighed. "And that's not the half of it, Jack." She lowered her voice. "His mother was murdered around the same time that he was first infected, poor kid. He's been under the care of his grandparents for the past five years because his father has been in prison." She shook her head. "He was convicted of—"

"I know," I said. "I heard about the case."

"At any rate, it gets even worse." She looked at me. "But you don't want to know all the details."

"I *do*, actually." I put Frankie and Hooch in a down/stay.

"The thing is," she went on, "he's on a waiting list for a transplant, but there aren't enough donors to go around. But his father is an eight-point match. You only need six to be accepted. *And* he's willing to give up one of his kidneys."

"So? What's the problem?"

She shook her head angrily. "The grandparents won't allow it. They're still furious at Tom Huckabee for killing their daughter, and I guess they feel that having a kidney from his mother's killer would be . . . I don't know, some sort of betrayal to her memory or something."

"And they know Tim's only got a few weeks to live?"

She nodded, looking down at the floor. "They can't accept that it's the only alternative."

"Can't the father or the hospital take legal action?"

"Oh, the case has been in family court for months." She explained that Tim was legally declared an orphan so he qualified for Medicaid and SSI, and that both the hospital and Medicaid had filed a joint legal action to make him a ward of the state to facilitate surgery. "Tim's father lost legal control when he was convicted of murder. He isn't even allowed to visit the boy."

I gave a sour laugh. "Let alone drop off a kidney?"

She glared at me. "I'm glad you find this so amusing."

"Gallows humor," I said, making an apologetic face.

She touched my arm. "I'm sorry. I know the feeling. We do it all the time here, me and the other nurses." She unleaned herself from the wall, put on another face, and said, "And now, I have other kids to take care of. Thanks, as always, Jack, for brightening their week a little."

"No problem. If there's anything I can do for Tim . . ."

She shook her head. "Unless you've got a Christmas miracle up your sleeve?"

I shook my head. "I wish I *did,* but I'm all out." I looked down at the dogs. They looked back at me, expectantly, wagging their tails a little. "Though, come to think of it, these dogs can be pretty miraculous. Would it be too much trouble if I brought them back by to see Tim tomorrow?"

She touched my arm again. "No trouble at all. You know the ropes by now, so you won't need a nurse or nurse's aid to accompany you. Are you sure you're up to it?"

"No, but a little cold is nothing compared to . . ."

"Good, then. Just be careful he doesn't talk you into giving him anything to drink when you visit."

"Okay. Why?"

"His fluid intake has to be carefully controlled and monitored. Same with his diet."

"Poor kid."

She nodded. "Tell me about it."

"Oh, one other thing," I said. "Do you know if the mother was infected with *E. coli* at the same time he was?"

She gave me a quizzical look.

"You said she died around the same time that Tim first came down with it, so I was just wondering—"

"Sorry, I don't know. But she didn't die from *E. coli*, Jack, she was killed by her husband."

"I know."

She squeezed my arm. "See you tomorrow." She turned and walked back toward the nurse's station, then over her shoulder she said, "And just remember what they say . . ."

"What's that?"

She turned to face me. "You said you wished you had a Christmas miracle up your sleeve, right?"

"Yeah?"

She shrugged. "Be careful what you wish for."

11

What I wished for was to go home and lie down and see if I could find an old *Rockford Files* on the dish to numb my brain and forget about my cold, but since I was already up and around I decided to take the dogs home, then drive into Camden and drop by the library, and maybe to the offices of the *Camden Herald*, to see what I could find out about the Bright family's history and the original Huckabee murder case.

On the drive down I used the cell phone that Jamie had given me for Christmas the year before to call Otis Barnes at the *Herald*. I told him what I was interested in and he said he'd be glad to help me with my research as long as I gave him some inside information on the investigation.

"The usual quid pro quo, eh, Otis?"

"Yes, Jack. And it's nice to hear you speaking Latin. It reminds me of that friend of yours—what's his name?"

"Lou Kelso?"

"That's right." He laughed. "I'll never forget what he said outside the county jail the day you were released."

He was referring to the Gordon Beeson case and my unjust incarceration at the hands of Jamie's old boss, Dr. Reiner. " '*Res ipsa loquitor,*' he said. 'The thing speaks for itself.' I really like that expression. *Res ipsa loquitor.*"

"Well, the stuffed-up sound of my voice and the occasional sniffles you hear also speak for themselves, so—"

"Got a cold, huh?"

"Yes, thanks for noticing."

"I hear it's going around."

No, it's not going around, I wanted to say, it's my own personal Christmas cold, etc., but said, "So I don't want to spend any more time on this research than I have to."

"I gotcha, Jack. I'll start pulling articles from the morgue and have them ready for you when you get here."

I got to Camden, which is a different place in winter than in summer. I had always thought the town would shut down completely after the first frost, but it's inhabited by die-hard locals, and a fine bunch of folks they are too (though don't tell them I said so). There's always a place to park, and if you should wander into any of the bars or restaurants, you wouldn't find them full by any stretch, but neither would you lack for pleasant, though not overfriendly, company.

I wasn't hungry, though, so I drove to the inland end of the harbor and parked in the lot next to the Camden Public Library, which was built in the 1920s and sits on a hill overlooking the harbor, a fact the architects weren't unmindful of. They included tall, arched windows in the plans for the building, giving the main room of the library one of the best views along the Maine coast. I wasn't interested in the view, though. I went straight to the front desk.

"Hi," I said quietly, to the small woman with white hair who was busy with a crossword puzzle in a book of them. She looked up at me over her reading glasses. I said, "Do you know where I could find any information about the Bright family and their little house overlooking the ocean?"

She looked off in the distance though she wasn't really looking at anything. She was thinking.

"Well," she said softly, "we have a local history section, but I don't know if there'll be anything useful in it. What did you want to know?"

I shrugged. "Anything. There was an unfortunate incident out at the mansion last night and I'm—"

"The murder?" she said, her eyes bright.

"Yes. And I'm looking into—"

"You're Jack Field!" she said, with happy surprise.

"Yes."

"My, my. It's not often we get a real live celebrity in here. There was that Mel Gibson movie that they shot in town, but that was years ago. He came in to look at the library as a possible location. He played a teacher, you know." She looked at me. "You sort of remind me of him."

"Yeah, I get that a lot," I lied. "Him and Tom Cruise. Now could you direct me to the local history section?"

My sarcasm went right over her head. "Tom Cruise? Sorry, I don't see that. Here, let me take you there."

So she took me to the local history section and I eventually got her to leave me alone. I found a couple of slim, dusty, locally printed books, took them to a table, pulled out a chair, sat down, and basically found out that the Bright Mansion had been built in the 1920s on the site of the old First Congregational Church. I also found out that Ellis Bright's grandfather, Cullen

Bright, had been a Wall Street tycoon in the teens and twenties, and that he'd been moneyed enough to build a mansion along the coast, but not enough to buy property in Bar Harbor or on Mt. Desert Isle.

It was nice, though, to sit in the library and look out the windows. It reminded me of a certain period in high school when I spent my lunch hours just reading in the school library instead of hanging out in the halls with my pals, or skateboarding around the parking lot. My friends didn't understand why I'd waste my time reading anything that wasn't part of a homework assignment or that wouldn't get me extra credit in class. And *I* didn't understand why they didn't enjoy reading just for the sake of reading as I did.

I thanked the woman at the front desk and endured another mention of Mel Gibson and a happy "Merry Christmas," then walked, sniffling, the five or six blocks from the library to the *Camden Herald* and waited at the front desk for about five seconds before Otis Barnes came bounding out of his office, all smiles and glad to see me.

I was glad to see him, too. The receptionist's radio was all wound up and ready to play "Jingle Bell Rock," which would've really ruined my day.

Tall, lanky, mid-sixties, with hair the color of French bread, Otis stuck a bony hand out for me to shake and invited me into his inner sanctum, where some old, though unyellowed, clippings were spread out across his desk.

"So," he said, taking a seat. "I've been going back over our coverage of the Huckabee murder case and it's very interesting. I remember I had the impression at the time that he might've been innocent. Now I'm not so sure. Is Huckabee a suspect in last night's killing?"

"Otis," I said, "you know I can't comment on any aspect of an ongoing investigation except to say that, yes, he is, for now. But that's completely off the record."

"Good. I thought so."

"Besides, the medical examiner has yet to determine the cause and manner of death."

"But you saw the body?"

I sighed a yes then gave him a precis of the night's events and discoveries.

"They actually planted a necklace to implicate Huckabee?"

"It would seem so."

He gave me a piercing look. "What are they like?" he said. "The Brights?"

"I was hoping you could tell *me*."

He shook his head. "They're a bit mysterious. In fact, more than a just a bit. I wouldn't go so far as to say that they're Howard Hughes–mysterious, but there's certainly a lingering air of something strange about them."

"You don't say. What do *you* know about them?"

He sighed, shook his head, then gave me a little background on the Bright family and their lonely mansion overlooking the ocean. It turns out he knew quite a bit.

Ellis and Fiona Bright weren't true Camdenites, or even true Mainers, for that matter. They lived in New York City for the most part, though, as I'd already learned from Karl, they had homes in Florida and Switzerland as well. The mansion was supposed to be a summer home. But about five years ago they stopped living anywhere else and seemed to hunker down on their little cliff overlooking the sea and town. They rarely went out, just the occasional concert or movie, no parties or other events, and their serving staff began to dwindle until it was just the maid, a butler and his wife, a chauffeur, and a cook.

"What about the old man's background?" I asked.

He told me that Ellis Bright's parents died early, left him and his young bride an enormous fortune, but not much else was known about them. There was said to have been a child, born in the late 1940s or early '50s who died as an infant under mysterious circumstances. "Though from what we know now about SIDS," he said, "that may have been what caused the young girl's sudden death, if the rumor is true."

Ellis Bright's salad days landed him squarely, and some might say luckily, between WWII and the Korean conflict, so he had no military record and no battle scars, not that there was much chance of him being drafted in either of those wars. There had been talk among some of the older townspeople of a youthful indiscretion of some kind that had taken place between the wars and that still tainted him in some distant way. As for Fiona, she had the air of British aristocracy, but no one could say for sure if she really as an aristocrat or even really British.

"She's Irish," I said.

"Really?"

I shrugged. "I'm going by a faint accent I detected while I was interviewing her last night."

Then there was the son, Christopher. Chris was in his mid-forties, yet still lived with his parents, off and on. It was mostly *on* lately due to some financial reverses that ate up the better part of his own inheritance. And to say that Chris Bright "lived" anywhere would be painting things with too broad a stroke. He had a sailboat, he often stayed at a hotel in New York, he had many, many friends of the female persuasion and so had no real permanent address.

"And he was their second child?"

Otis nodded. "That's right."

"They're an odd family, aren't they?" He nodded. "And what did you find out about Tom Huckabee and his wife's murder?"

"I covered the case so I remember that one pretty well."

He told me that it had seemed like the usual domestic dispute gone bad: he'd grabbed hold of his wife's arms and shaken her too hard during some kind of argument and when he realized she wasn't breathing he called 911. The paramedics found him trying to revive her, but she was already dead.

"And what was *his* story about what happened?"

"That he'd come home, found her unconscious, shook her to wake her up, called 911, and that there was no fight."

He told me that Huckabee had grown up in Philadelphia, had spent seven or eight years traveling around the country, and in Europe, had settled eventually in New York and had come to Camden around the same time that the Brights decided to settle somewhat permanently in their summer home.

I said, "The murder victim, this maid, was supposedly his ex-girlfriend, but from the timeline I'm wondering . . ."

"What?"

"Did the relationship with Amy Frost start while he was still married? Did it start after he got out of prison?" I thought of something. "How long has he been out?"

He looked over some things he'd written on a yellow legal pad. "He was paroled about six months ago."

I nodded. "I suppose that's enough time for two people to hook up, then break up, and start having fights. Still, I don't know. Something's not right about the timeline." I sniffled a bit, yawned, then stretched and stood up. "I can't think about it anymore right now, though. I need to get home and get some rest." I went to the door. "Thanks, Otis."

"Oh," he smiled, "you'll pay me back. I'm not worried. And take care of that cold!"

I got safely outside without too much trouble: the receptionist's radio was now tuned to the news.

12

I got back to the house, said hello to the doggies, built a fire, and then "ffwd"ed through and erased all the calls from the local media on my answering machine. Then I sat down on the sofa to write my report for Jamie, in pencil, on a yellow legal pad. It turned out not to be such a bad idea—or such a pain in the ass—as I'd first thought.

TIMELINE

@ 7:30–8:30 P.M. Amy Frost is struck a hard blow on the back of the head while standing at the top of the stairs, dies shortly thereafter (see ME's report for actual TOD).

@ 10:15 P.M. Mr. and Mrs. Bright return home and find the body. They claim to have seen suspect Thomas Huckabee leaving the house just as they arrived. They immediately call 911. (Note: check tape of 911 call to see if they mentioned seeing the suspect.)

<u>11:05–11:35</u> Dr. Cutter and I arrive at the scene and observe the body, etc. During this time I conducted interviews with Mr. and Mrs. Bright and their driver, Karl Petrovich. I found both of the Brights to be evasive and untruthful in their answers. They seemed intent on pointing the blame at Thomas Huckabee, but were clearly lying about key points. In my opinion, they're either covering for the real killer or are convinced Huckabee committed the murder and are trying to frame him for it, based on their belief that he's guilty. Meanwhile, Petrovich, though <u>also</u> evasive, confirmed my suspicion about the Brights' lies, and Detective Bailey and I overheard a telephone conversation in which the Brights spoke about fabricating a report about stolen jewelry to further implicate Huckabee.

<u>11:36</u> The Brights are allowed by Chief Colbern to go upstairs unattended, in violation of proper procedure, and despite protestations from Detective Bailey and me. Colbern pulls Bailey off the case and orders me to leave the scene, even though he's not authorized to do so.

<u>11:42</u> A gold and emerald necklace is found outside the house, beneath the Bright's bedroom window, hanging from a snow-covered bush, but with no snow on the necklace. It had clearly

been dropped out the window while the Brights were upstairs with no police presence. (They admitted this to police the next day.)

<u>11:47</u> I conduct a further interview with Karl Petrovich and learn that a "Professor Hayes" was in the house earlier that day, and that he's known to always carry a large wooden walking stick (possible murder weapon). Hayes may be involved in a con of some sort, involving "ghosts" or strange lights and other phenomena, coming from the third story of the mansion. These phenomena, according to Petrovich, only occur when Hayes is in the residence. Petrovich also reported to me that he drove Hayes to the Portland airport on the afternoon of the murder to catch a 4:30 flight to LaGuardia. However, a police investigation cannot confirm yet whether Hayes was actually on that flight.

POSSIBLE SUSPECTS
~~Spiderman, Gandalf, Christopher Robin.~~

Huckabee
Has a possible alibi, which is still being checked out. Supposedly had a prior relationship with the victim, and was convicted of murdering his wife 5 yrs. ago. He installed the video cameras and may have knowledge of ways to get around the security system on the premises.

Professor Hayes
Identity and whereabouts at the time of the murder are unknown. Possible motive is uncertain. Kozak, the security guard, reported that Hayes sometimes appeared outside the front gate, when to all intents and purposes he <u>should</u> have been inside the house.

Christopher Bright
Whereabouts at the time of the murder are also unknown. Possible sexual relationship with victim. Possibly had the ability to leave the premises without being seen. May have been hiding in the house when the police arrived, though his car was not in the garage at 11:30 P.M.

Derek Kozak
Admits to being in the house at roughly the same time the murder took place, though the security log on the kitchen door shows he was inside for less than two minutes. No relationship has been established between Kozak and the murder victim.

Conclusion
The three most crucial factors, in my view, are determining a possible motive for the killing, locating the murder weapon, and finding out how the killer was able to come and go at will with-

out setting off the security alarms. Either the killer had special skills and equipment available, or there's an unknown point of exit somewhere on the grounds.

I had just finished writing this all down when the front doorbell rang, which is a fairly rare occurrence. Even the UPS guy never rings the bell—I always get a postcard saying they "attempted delivery." The dogs, who had been sound asleep, jumped up in a storm of barking.

"Good dogs!" You always want to praise a dog for barking at the doorbell, it makes them quiet down faster.

I stood up and said, "It's probably just the Jehovah's Witnesses," but it wasn't. When the dogs and I got to the door we found Kristin Downey, an ex-girlfriend of mine from my grad school days at Columbia, and her college-age stepdaughter Jen, whose father, Sonny Vreeland, is the heir to the Sun-Vee vitamin fortune. They were standing on the porch, both wrapped up in casual winter wear—Kristin's of the Michael Kors variety, Jen's more in the Michael Stipe mold. Kristin was smiling. Jen's pale face—with her black eyeliner and lipstick—looked shy, bored, and hopeful at the same time, an interesting combination.

"Hi, Jack," said Kristin, her pretty brown eyes flashing. "I hope we're not disturbing you."

"Uh, not at all," I said, holding the door open.

Frankie immediately ran outside and jumped up on Jen. Her dour face broke into about a million smiles. Hooch, whose rear end was wiggling in a shared excitement with Frankie's emotions, went after him for a moment, then quickly decided the door wasn't for him and came back inside.

Kristin stepped through the storm door, right behind Hooch, and said, "I'm flying Jen home for the holidays and she wanted to come play with your dog before we go, if that's all right with you."

I glanced at Jen. She was leaning over Frankie. She tilted her head up to give me a hopeful look. I said, "I think that's a great idea. Frankie would love it."

"Thanks, Jack," she said, shyly.

"Good," said Kristin, as Jen and Frankie ran off the porch and out into the snow. When they were gone she said, "And I have some things I want to discuss with you in private."

Uh-oh, I thought, but said, "Okay . . . ?"

"Don't worry," she half whispered, taking off her coat, "it's about Jen's Christmas present. She's getting a dog."

We went to the sofa, while Hooch lumbered back to his cozy spot by the Christmas tree.

"A dog?" I said, moving my case notes so she could sit down. She threw her coat over the arm of the sofa. I sat down next to her and said, "Isn't owning a puppy a little impractical for someone living in a dorm room?"

"Oh, we're planning on keeping the dog at the house in Short Hills. That way we might get Jen to come home and visit more often. And we're not getting a puppy. Daisy is a year old—she was a show dog but didn't quite have what it takes."

"I see," I said and wanted to add, so it's not a present for Jennifer as much as it's a way to exert parental control over her, but I didn't. "And where do I come in?"

"Well, you know Sonny has several Dalmatians, all

show dogs, and all of whom Jennifer adores. I thought she might like to have one of her very own. And I thought we should ask you about the trainer we've hired."

She told me the man's name, saying that he came highly recommended by their veterinarian and several of their friends.

"Then you not only need to find another dog trainer, you need to find a new vet and a whole new set of friends. I mean it, Kristin, that man is evil incarnate where dogs are concerned. I wouldn't even let him in the same room with a puppy, let alone trust him to do any *kind* of training."

Shocked, Kristin kind of shook her head and said, "Don't hold back, Jack. Tell me what you really think of him."

"Have you *met* the guy?"

"No. I just spoke to him briefly on the phone. He seemed very qualified, if somewhat expensive."

I shook my head and tried to calm myself down. "Look, if you want a dog who only obeys because she's been scared within an inch of her life, then by all means hire that rat bastard. But I could give you the names of a couple of trainers who would cost you a quarter of what he charges and their training wouldn't leave the dog a nervous wreck. I'm telling you, this guy is the poster child for everything that's wrong with dog training in this country."

"Okay, okay. So who should I get?"

I gave her Jason Herman's name and the name of another trainer I knew, but added, "I don't know if he's still training or not. I think he's mostly writing novels now."

"He's a novelist and a dog trainer?"

"Yeah," I shook my head. "He writes some stupid series of mystery novels with dogs written into the story lines."

"Huh. That sounds right up your alley."

"Not really. I hate mysteries."

"Well anyway, thanks. I'll try calling them."

"Good. And I'm sorry I blew up. I'm just battling this awful Christmas cold and dealing with a real-life mystery."

Her face brightened in an ah-hah look. "Of course, your yearly Christmas cold. I'd forgotten about that."

I shrugged. "Some things never change."

She tilted her head and said, "I don't suppose you'd be coming down to the city for Christmas, would you?"

"Yeah, I have to drive Leon down to spend the holidays with his grandmother in Harlem. Why?"

"Well, we'll be at the apartment on Park. Maybe you could come meet Jen's new dog and give us some pointers."

"Sorry, I'm taking him down this weekend. Jamie and I'll be spending Christmas Eve with her dad, and Christmas Day at her mom's house. And my dad and my sister Annabelle are flying in from California with her husband and four kids."

"You didn't used to be so family-oriented."

I nodded. "I know. That was before I met Jamie."

"I see." She smiled. "But if Jen has any questions, she can call you?"

I sighed. "Jen can call me anytime for anything."

"Wow. I didn't know you liked her that much."

I shrugged. "Well, I do. She's kind of screwy, but it's mostly a teenage affectation kind of thing, I think."

"She certainly has that, in spades. Like running off and disappearing this summer."

Yeah, I thought, and I'd been the one to find her when she'd run off back in July. And both women, Jen and her stepmom, had tried to kiss me in the kennel that summer. Kristin did it during the engagement party Jamie and I had a few days after the Fourth. Jen tried it a few days later.

I haven't said anything to Jamie about either incident, and wasn't about to tell Kristin about Jen's kiss, but I did mention it to Kelso once and he'd said not to worry too much, that it was just a "chick thing."

I laughed and said, "Oh, really?"

"Sure. Once you're engaged, some members of the sisterhood feel it's their duty to flirt with you to see if you stand muster as true husband material. Though the girl probably only did it because her stepmother did."

I laughed again. "Kelso, Where do you come up with this stuff?"

"Don't get me wrong. It's not like they have meetings and decide what to do. It's unconscious. They just can't help themselves. You have a master's in psychology, right, Jack? I'm surprised you don't know about it."

"That's because it's a figment of your imagination."

"Is it? And whatever you do, don't tell Jamie."

"Of course I'm going to tell her," I said. "We don't have any secrets from each other."

He snorted. "That's your second mistake."

"Yeah? And what's my first?"

"Letting Kristin come around at all. Past girlfriends need to stay just that—in the past. That goes double for their horny young stepdaughters."

I sighed then said, "Well all the same, I have to tell Jamie what happened."

"Jack?" Kristin said. "What are you thinking about?"

"Huh?" I said, coming back to the present. "Oh, I was just thinking about Jen. She's a good kid with a good heart. And she's great with dogs. I wish she hadn't made the basketball team so I could have her working for me, you know?"

She smoothed her woolen skirt. "Are your feelings for her something Jamie should be made aware of?"

"It's not like that. And Jamie knows exactly how I feel about Jen." I gave her a look. "Why? Are you jealous?"

She smoothed her skirt again. "Hardly." She looked up at me. "Well, maybe a little, but not in the way you think." She gave me a look then sighed. "I'm jealous because I wish Jen looked up to me the way she does you."

This was news to me. "She looks up to me?"

She nodded. "A lot. Of course, she would never come out and say it, but I can tell by the way she talks about you."

"Well, I'll be darned. She talks about me?"

"All the time, actually."

"I would've never guessed. I asked her once if I could come see one of her games, but she gave me the brush-off."

"Well, at least we're alike on that score." She sighed. "I don't know, maybe it's an independence thing. She's even worse with Sonny, but there are other reasons for that."

"Such as?"

"Such as past history that I'm not going to get into."

We sat there for a moment. I knew there was something else I wanted to ask her but couldn't remember what it was.

"What are you thinking about now?" she said finally.

"This facackta case I'm working on. There was something I wanted to—oh, you once worked with Lance Burton, right?"

"Well, I designed the sets for his Broadway show, yes."

"So you might know some tricks or illusions somebody could use to convince people they've got ghosts in their house?"

"Sorry," she said, smiling. "I know a few secrets but I'd be in big trouble with the magician's union if I divulged any of them."

"But you could hook me up with someone who could give me some ideas?"

"Seriously?"

"Yes. I think it may be an important part of this murder case. If I could figure out what the scam is exactly . . ."

"I could call Lance, I guess, and maybe he'll agree to talk to you, if it'll help solve the case." She stood up. "Well, thanks again for the information." She picked up her coat then looked at me. "If this idiot trainer is so bad, why does he come so highly recommended from so many people?"

I shook my head and stood up. "The thing about dogs is that roughly forty percent of them can be well-trained no matter kind of training method you use. They're just incredibly adaptable to learning. They want to align their behavior to fit whatever structural dynamic they're met with. So almost all trainers are successful at least forty percent of the time. It's only with the other sixty percent that you get problems. When most trainers fail they tend to blame the owner or the breeder or the dog, never themselves or their training method. It's a sad fact of human nature."

I began walking her to the door. "Think about it, there are thousands and thousands of dog trainers in this country, there are hundreds of books on the subject, they teach courses on behavior in all the veterinary schools, and yet the shelters are still full of unwanted dogs. And most adult dogs are abandoned because of training problems. I think that every time a dog trainer or a vet fails a dog, he should blame himself and question the validity of his methods."

We got to the door and she said, "Really? Have you ever failed at training a dog?"

"Of course, a few times—at least initially. And it always forced me to rethink my approach."

"You don't need to save every dog in the world, do you?"

"No," I said, unconvincingly. "But I can still *try*."

She chuckled. "I don't think you've ever admitted to failing at anything before, Jack. At least not to me."

"Of course I have. You were there, remember?"

"You mean us? Columbia?" She touched my chest. "That whole mess?"

"What else?"

I opened the door and we stood there a moment.

She shook her head. "We were both so young. We were Jen's age, for god's sake. What the hell did we know?"

"That doesn't change the fact that—"

"I forgive you, Jack. You don't need to feel guilty about what happened anymore."

"Thanks. I wish it were that easy."

"Besides, I was sick, remember?"

"I know," I said, and felt my eyes getting wet. "It's just that I should have known how to—"

"Sshh." She put her hand to my lips. "It's okay." She looked into my eyes. "Now I get what this is about, at least part of it. You still *love* me and worry about me, don't you?"

"Of course I do. Just not in the same—"

"I know." She leaned into me. "It's okay. I don't expect that from you. And I'm sorry I kissed you that day."

"That's all right."

"No, it isn't." She pulled back. "And you don't need to worry about me. Though you were right, when you asked me if I'd gone off my meds that day in the kennel. I hadn't, but I *did* have to switch them suddenly and didn't have the new dosage right."

"Why did you have to switch medications?"

"It doesn't matter. I'm fine now. And I appreciate everything you did for me when we were just kids."

"Huh. What did *I* do?"

"For one thing, if it weren't for you I would have never been diagnosed. I might have gone on trying to kill myself, all because of some stupid chemical imbalance in my brain."

"I guess that's true. And you might have even succeeded at some point."

"Yes. And that's one reason I feel so close to Jen."

"Why? Is she—?"

"No. But her mother—"

"Can we go now?" Jen shouted impatiently.

She was standing by Kristin's silver Mercedes, with Frankie at her side. Kristin and I pulled apart, embarrassed at having been caught standing together in a tender moment. It had been platonic, mostly, though it probably didn't look that way to Jen. She stood there with arms akimbo, staring holes in us.

"Keep your shirt on, young lady!" Kristin shouted. "I thought you wanted to play with the dog."

"Well, I'm done now, so can we go?"

"All right. I'm coming." She turned to me and smiled a tired smile. "Kids. Take care of your cold, Jack."

"I will."

She walked down the steps toward her stepdaughter. Frankie danced around the car. Kristin stopped outside her door and shouted, "And I'm not your mother, Jack!"

Then she got in, did a K-turn, and drove up the drive, with Frankie chasing them up all the way up to the county road, barking as they drove off.

"I'm not your mother," she'd said. I wondered what she'd meant by that, then figured she was referring to the fact that my mother also suffered from manic-depression, which is what they called it then, and had tried to kill herself repeatedly, eventually succeeding several years after Kristin and I broke up, right in the middle of my second year at Harvard.

Finally, when I got my voice back, I called Frankie and he came running back to me full speed, wagging his tail. "Good boy!" I said and we went back inside the house, where he and Hooch roughhoused for a bit before I told them to settle.

Then I sat down on the sofa, stared at the fire, and began to cry over a distant memory that had suddenly surfaced:

It was Christmas. I was nine or ten at the time, and had come down with a cold so I went into my mother's room to see if she could take care of me, and found her sitting on the edge of the bed with a huge handful of pills in one hand and a glass of water in the other. An empty pill bottle sat next to her on the nightstand.

"Mom?" I'd said.

"What is it?" she'd said, annoyed at me.

"I don't feel well. Can you take my temperature?"

She shook her head and gave me a dark gray stare. "Why do *I* always have to take care of you?"

"I don't know."

"Can't you ever take care of yourself? Just *once*?"

"I don't know."

"Why do you have to get sick *now*, of all times?"

"I don't know."

She sat there a moment, sighed, put the water glass on the nightstand, then funneled the pills back in the bottle, and said, "I'm sorry, honey. Come here. Let me feel your forehead."

I sat next to her and felt her cool hand on my hot skin.

"Okay. You're a little feverish. Go back to bed. I'll be in in a little while."

"Thanks," I said, and trotted off to my room, got under the covers and waited and prayed that she'd really come in and take care of me.

That was the year of my mother's first suicide attempt.

It was also the year of my first Christmas cold.

13

The salmon chili turned out great. Leon even asked for seconds. Then thirds. Jamie, who'd read my case notes, said, "How do you think the killer escaped undetected?"

"Well," I said, "those security logs for the gate need to be looked into for any anomalies, or else—"

"Yo, Jack," said Leon, with a mouthful of chili, "what's 'anomaly' mean?"

"It means something that doesn't fit a pattern."

Jamie said, "It means we need more information."

"Yes," I agreed, "but in a case like this, a blatant *lack* of information moves you in the right direction. For one thing, I think the house, the garage, and the grounds need to be researched. There may be an exit hidden somewhere."

She laughed. "Like a secret tunnel or something?"

"Well, it does sound kind of farfetched, but—"

"Yo, Jack," said Leon. "Check it! Maybe that house was part of the underground railroad."

I smiled. "You know what? That's brilliant, Leon."

Jamie said, "But wait. Wasn't the mansion built sometime in the 1920s?"

"1925," I said. "But it was built on the site of an old First Congregational Church, so Leon could really be on to something. It would certainly explain what the security guard told me about the mysterious professor, and how sometimes, when he's supposed to be inside the house, he'll appear at the front gate, looking dirty and disheveled."

"See?" Leon said, "I ain't no dummy. Maine was a major stopping point for runaway slaves on their way to Canada."

"How do you know that?" I asked.

He shrugged and spooned some more chili. "I may sleep through geometry, but I like my history teacher."

Jamie said, "That could be worth looking into."

After dinner I took the dogs out for their final play in the snow, then the three of us—me, Jamie, and Leon—finished decorating the tree and stood around admiring its beauty and feeling the glow of its twinkling lights. Then, when Leon and Magee had gone back to the guest cottage, Jamie insisted I go upstairs to bed with her instead of sleeping on the couch.

"What'll I do with Hooch? He can't stand to be away from me when I'm sick, and he'll keep you up all night."

"I wasn't thinking of having you stay all night. Or Hooch, for that matter. I just need you for half an hour."

"Ah-hah. And you don't mind catching my cold?"

She laughed and grabbed my hand. "It's not infectious, Jack, remember? It's your own personal Christmas cold, having nothing to do with the general laws of science or medicine."

"That's it, make fun of me."

"Get over it. At least till I'm through with you."

When she was satisfied and we were cuddled up in the spoons position, with Hooch snoring loudly in the corner of the room, and Frankie lying at the foot of the bed, she said:

"Jack?"

"Um-hum?"

"What are you getting me for Christmas?"

I laughed. "Nice try. Get me hot and bothered then sneak a question like that in afterward. Un-uh."

"Okay. What are you getting Leon?"

"I don't know. I think I'll get him an iPod."

She chuckled. "Do you even know what that is?"

"I think so. It's like a digital walkman or something. He can download music from the Internet on it. Right?"

I could feel her chest moving, as she laughed some more. Then she said, "Jack, do you even know what the Internet is?"

"Sure. It's the World Wide Web. Everybody knows that."

She laughed again. "Very good. So, where's Leon spending Christmas this year? At his grandmother's?"

"That's the plan."

"That'll be nice for him. And I was thinking, if you get this cold every Christmas, like clockwork, as you like to claim, how come you weren't sick last Christmas?"

"I was."

"No you weren't. Remember? All through the Allison DeMarco case, and even after we went to the Bahamas, you were fine. It's only when we got back that you came down with it."

I thought it over. "You know, you're right."

"Of course I'm right. So why didn't you get sick?"

I said nothing. I wanted to tell her about Kristin's visit and the memory I'd had about my mother, but I didn't know how to do it without the tears sneaking up on me again. And I don't like to cry in front of Jamie if I can help it.

"Jack? Are you asleep?"

"No, I'm thinking. The only thing I can think of is that last year I was falling in love with you."

"What, and you're not in love with me anymore?"

"No, of course I am. It's just that last year I was still in the *process* of falling in love. You're a doctor. You know the positive effects that has on the immune system."

"That's true." She squeezed herself against me.

"So," I said, feeling the emotional tension in my chest ease off a little, "there's a rational, medical explanation after all."

"Un-uh. Which means next year I'll just have to make you fall in love with me all over again. Starting at Thanksgiving. Or maybe Halloween."

"Thanks, honey. But I don't think that'll work."

"Why not?" She sounded hurt.

"Because I don't see how I could possibly be any more in love with you than I am right now."

She turned to kiss me then, once her lips were no longer busy, she said, "Okay, that's it, take Hooch out right now."

"Why? Is his snoring bothering you?"

"Not *now,* it isn't it. I'm thinking of later. The snoring, on top of the thought of you staring at me while I'm asleep, I don't think I could get a wink."

"Honey, I told you I don't *stare,* I just like to look."

"Okay, then," she said, pulling the covers back to show me her gorgeous naked body. "How's this?"

I shot out of bed and said, "Come on, Hooch. You've

got to sleep outside." I opened the door and he obediently trotted over and walked through it, but just stood
there, refusing to move any farther. I turned to Jamie.
"Will it be okay if he just sleeps by the door?"

"Just shut the damn door and get back over here."

I did as I was instructed and she climbed on top of
me, grabbed my hands and put them where she wanted
them, and gave me a victorious smile. "So, Jack, I
guess if I want to train *you* I have to what, increase
your emotional tension?"

"It would certainly heighten the experience," I said,
"but I already know how to fetch."

14

A few days passed, with me still battling my cold when Jamie wasn't around—when she *was,* my symptoms mysteriously disappeared—and me and the dogs visiting Tim Huckabee at the hospital every afternoon. On Tuesday Jamie finished the autopsy on the maid, Amy Frost. She called to tell me that, as suspected, she'd died from the head wound. The information from the cook about when she'd had dinner (6:30), and the condition of her stomach contents, put the time of death at roughly 7:40, but definitely before eight. This let Derek Kozak off as a possible suspect.

Brad Bailey would call a couple of times a day to keep me up on the latest developments from his standpoint, even when there weren't any. In fact, he called me on Tuesday, right after Jamie did. He told me that a complete background search on Karl—whose last name was Petrovich—came up negative.

"Well," I sniffled, "that's good to know."

"No, Jack. Not just negative, there's absolutely nothing on the guy, anywhere. It's like he didn't exist until a few years ago."

"Interesting. That might explain the size of his watch band." I explained what I'd noticed earlier, and why. "Some Russian gang members wear tattoos inside their wrists." Then I speculated that either Karl still had the tattoo or had a scar where he'd had it removed.

"Interesting. But let me finish: so we called him in for questioning and he never showed."

"You mean he's gone, left town?"

"Put it this way, the Brights have already got ads in all the local papers, looking for a new chauffeur. That might make him look good for the murder if his alibi didn't check out."

"Yeah, plus he's left-handed. *Did* his alibi check?"

"Yep. He was definitely seen driving the Brights to the concert at seven-thirty, so he's in the clear."

I thought it over. "He's probably been hiding out from the Russian mob. Those guys are ruthless. And now that the story is in the news, maybe Karl figured it was time to find a new hideout.

"How's *Huckabee's* alibi holding up?"

"He claims he was driving back from New York that night. We're still trying to track down his witness, a Donna Moore. She lives on West 46th Street in New York. I faxed the info to the NYPD and they're going to talk to her. I *also* found out he's right-handed. And he's five-eleven."

"That's good. I'd like to have a talk with him myself and get his side of the story."

"Okay. I'll try to set it up."

"Any news on the killer's height yet?"

"No, they haven't found the murder weapon, and they have to factor in its size. We had some dogs in looking for it." He sighed. "I know you're a dog lover, Jack, but . . ."

"What?"

"Well, it just seemed to me like the damn dogs didn't know what the hell they were doing, that's all."

I laughed. "That's entirely possible. Jamie and I were talking about this just the other day. Who trained them?"

"I don't know. Someone here in Maine, I think."

"Well, it could be that the murder weapon isn't inside the house. Did they search the grounds?"

"Yeah, and the whole damn neighborhood. Nothing."

"Any luck on finding a hidden exit from the property?"

"No. I still think there's a problem with the security system. And I'm puzzled about the murder weapon."

"So, the killer probably took it with him. Unless the dogs weren't trained or handled properly."

"What do you mean?"

I explained and asked, "Were they on or off lead?"

"They were all leashed."

"Well, being on lead can cause a dog to be influenced, inadvertently, by the handler. They may stop looking in a certain area if the handler thinks there's nothing there." I told him of a case I'd once worked in New York, where a gunman escaped through an empty apartment in the building where the shooting had taken place, then disappeared. Some police dogs were brought in and one of them kept going to an abandoned gas range in the kitchen, but the handler kept trying to pull him away. Finally, someone with some sense decided to check inside the oven and found the killer's gun, with his prints all over it. The shooter's prints were in the system and he was quickly located and apprehended.

"You have to learn to trust the dogs and not try to influence them too much. The handler had the idea that the dogs should be looking in a closet for the perp and never considered that there might be a crucial piece of evidence inside that oven."

"Maybe that was it here, too. But I had a look around that third story, you know, the one with the ghosts in it?"

I chuckled again. "Yeah?"

"Something's not right up there. I can't put my finger on what it is exactly, but something feels off to me."

"Hmmm. Did you get any info on the construction plans?"

"Yeah, it was done by an outfit from New York City. And here's another thing, there's no bathroom, no sinks, no plumbing of any kind up there. At least none that *I* could see, but when I went to the county clerk's office to requisition the plans I noticed that another set of blueprints had been sent to a plumbing company in Belfast."

"Hmm. Do you think you could get *their* copy? If that upstairs addition is part of a scam, there might be two sets of plans. They may have built some false walls or something."

"Makes sense, because the only time those dogs seemed to be on the scent of anything was when they sniffed one of the walls upstairs. And now that you mention it, the handlers, as you call them, kept trying to pull the dogs away from there. I'll go visit the plumbers today and ask to see their copy. But wouldn't the building inspector have noticed the false walls? They have to drop by the site every so often to make sure things are being done on the up-and-up."

"That's true. But the inspector could've been bribed. That kind of thing happens all the time in New York, especially if you're rich. I'd imagine that some of the inspectors in Maine are no different."

"Good point. And listen, I asked Dr. Cutter to look into the autopsy of Huckabee's wife, you know the first murder, to see if there were any similarities in the MO."

"Really? She didn't tell me about it."

"She probably hasn't had time to get to it yet." He paused. "Are you two really getting married?"

I told him that was the plan.

"You're a lucky guy. She's quite a babe." He stopped. "Or do you mind me saying that?"

I laughed. "No, it's true. She's a *total* babe."

"Sorry I brought it up. I just got the impression from the way you spoke to Coletti that—"

"Look, I don't mind discussing Jamie's babe-itude with anyone who doesn't have a personal interest in her, and he *does*. So, have you dug up anything on Professor Hayes yet?"

"Nope. Nada. He had a flight booked, but we don't know for sure yet if he took it. Beyond that, he's a total cipher. It might help if we knew his first name."

"You didn't get that from the passenger list?"

"Just his first initials: J.K. We don't know what they stand for, but we're searching databases for a J.K. Hayes."

I thought of something. "You might subpoena the Brights' financial records, see if they wrote any checks to him."

"Good idea," he scoffed. "Now all I have to figure out is how to do it."

"You think you can't subpoena their bank records?"

"Sure, we could get a dozen judges to sign a dozen subpoenas and they'd get a dozen more to countermand them."

"Well, you *could* just ask them," I said.

"The Brights? Just ask them, just like that?"

"Why not? All they can do is say no."

I could hear him thinking it over. "You've got something up your sleeve, don't you?"

"Maybe. Just be sure to make it a written request."

"Okay," he said skeptically, "I'll give it a shot."

I thanked him then called Otis Barnes to give him a few more scoops on the case, particularly the fact that the Brights were "fleeing the jurisdiction" and refusing to release their bank statements to the police.

On Wednesday I got more calls from the local press and a call from an old client—a news producer in New York named Vanessa Martin, whose cocker spaniel, Caroline, I'd trained. She wanted to do a feature story on me for one of her network's weekly newsmagazines.

"Why would I want to be on *Nightline*?" I asked her.

"It's not *Nightline*, Jack, it's *Dateline*."

"Either way."

She tried to convince me that my story would make a good segment on the show—a retired NYPD detective solving homicides in Maine while running a kennel and training dogs full-time. "The viewers would *love* a story like this."

"I'm sure *they* would, Vanessa, but I *wouldn't*."

"If you change your mind, let me know. And whatever you do, don't go on *Nightline* or *Sixty Minutes* before calling me."

"Like that'll happen. How's Caroline?"

"Caroline's great, as always."

Jamie called and told me she'd checked the autopsy report on Tim's mother, Rhoda Huckabee, whose maiden name was Grant. She'd also died of a head injury, though her death was caused by cerebral edema, not a fractured skull.

"And what would cause that?" I asked her.

"The edema? Apparently she'd been shaken really hard by her husband. There were bruises on her upper arms."

"So it definitely wasn't from an *E. coli* infection?"

"It certainly doesn't look that way, no. Why?"

"No reason. Just a wild idea on my part."

After the paper came out on Thursday, I got a threatening phone call from Chief Colbern, which I ignored, but I also got a call from Bailey. He told me the Brights had miraculously agreed to release their bank statements. He also told me they were leaving for Switzerland on Sunday.

"Are they taking the dogs with them?"

"What dogs?"

"The two Dobermans who had their eyes on your testicles the other night."

"Oh, them. I have no idea. Why?"

"I run a boarding kennel."

"You'd want to board their dogs?"

"I'd love to. Those are some damn fine animals. And the department is going to let the Brights go, just like that?"

"To Switzerland? The chief says we can't stop them."

"After all the lying they've done? What's wrong with him? Where are they staying?"

"The Lodge at Camden Hills. Anyway, I just wanted to say about the bank statements: nice goin', Jack. Oh, and I got the blueprints from the plumbing company, like you suggested."

"Good. Let me know what you find out."

That afternoon, things took kind of a nasty turn, thanks to both Chief Colbern and Karl, or at least, thanks to some former "friends" of his from Sheepshead Bay, Brooklyn.

* * *

I normally take 17 past Perseverance to West Rockport, then 90 to its junction with U.S. 1, and drive south to Glen Cove, where the hospital is located. Camden is a little out of the way, to the north. But my cold had migrated from my head down to my throat, which was now feeling too sore and tight to swallow, so I hadn't had breakfast, just some juice and a lot of water, and decided to go to Mariner's Restaurant in Camden to see what kind of soup they had.

When I got to the city limits, though, I was stopped for a "routine" traffic check by Officer D. Weist. He not only checked my license and registration he practically did a full vehicle inspection, checking under the hood, even crawling under the car to look at the muffler.

Then, after he'd finished, it took him twenty minutes to write a ticket for having unsecured dogs in the vehicle.

He finally handed me the hundred-dollar ticket, had me sign it, and said, "The chief wants you to know that you're not welcome inside the Camden city limits."

"That's what this was all about? The fact that I called him a moron the other night in front of his men?"

He tore off my copy and made an apologetic face. "Just doing what I'm told. That part about the message from the chief? I gave you that for free, on account of I like you."

"Great. Next time, could you like me a little less?"

I parked in the lot outside the hospital's emergency entrance, and as I got out of the car, I was stopped by what at first glance seemed to be a very attractive woman. But as she came up to me I realized it was an illusion, created mostly by makeup and hair: she wasn't "born-pretty," but "porn-pretty," as my pal Lou Kelso likes to say.

"Are you Mr. Jack Field?" she said, with the trace of a Russian accent.

I said I was.

"You have beautiful dogs," she pet Frankie and smiled, and I noticed that her teeth were capped.

"Thanks," I said.

"So well-behaved. You must be a very good trainer." She had a little trouble hiding her accent on the *v* and *r* in "very good." "I bet you could do wonders with *my* dog."

I asked her what kind she had and she told me he was a Pomeranian. "His name is Jimmy. He's very affectionate, but he barks a lot."

I shrugged. "It's a characteristic of the breed."

"So there's nothing I can do?"

"Sure there is. Do you scold him when he barks?"

"Yes, all the time, but it doesn't work."

"No, that's because from his point of view you're only joining in on the barking, or barking *at* him."

"Really? Can you teach me how to control him?"

"Probably," I said, and gave her my card. "Call me. I don't have time to discuss it right now, though."

She put a hand on my arm. "Just one thing." She bit her lower lip. "I'm looking for someone. My brother."

Okay, here it comes, I thought. She's going to ask me about Karl. Besides being ruthless, those Russian mobsters are very tricky. This is one of their tactics—sending out a call girl to play the damsel in distress. "What's his name?"

"Karl Petrovich."

I nodded and said, "Yeah, I think he works as a chauffeur for the Bright family. I could give you directions."

She shook her head sadly. "No, he quit his job and I have to locate him right away. It's terribly important."

"Really?" I faked concern. "Did he inherit some money, or is one of your relatives dying?"

"But how did you know this? Our mother is very sick."

"Oh, I'm sorry to hear that. But tell your bosses back in Brooklyn I have no idea where he is."

"But, Mr. Field, our mother—"

"Can it, Natasha."

She huffed. "My name is Ivana."

"Whatever. I was with the NYPD for fifteen years. I know the drill." I grabbed her wrist and twisted it to reveal a tattoo, which was a diamond, and next to it, a letter from the Russian alphabet—a Cyrillic *P*, which looks like an *R*. "So, even if I did know where Karl's gone, I wouldn't give you that information. You can tell your bosses I said so."

She pulled her wrist away and her face hardened. "Are you sure that's what you want me to tell them?"

"It doesn't matter, sweetheart. Like I said, I have no idea where he is."

She smiled a wicked smile. "If you says so. But if you changes your mind . . ." She handed me *her* business card.

"Doubtful," I said, but took the card and walked the dogs into the hospital where I dropped it in the nearest trash can.

15

A couple, in their mid-fifties, were coming out of Tim's room just as Frankie, Hooch, and I were walking down the hall. I assumed they were Tim's grandparents and my assumption was borne out by the way the woman beamed when she saw the dogs.

"Oh," she said coming toward us, with arms outstretched, "you must be the man with the dogs."

"That's me," I grinned. I pulled my surgical mask down, but tried not to let my face show the anger I felt toward her for not letting Tim's father donate one of his kidneys.

"And these are your doggies!" She leaned down to smother them with kisses. They obliged her. "What good doggies!"

The husband followed her the way some husbands do.

She said, "I don't know how to thank you for what you've done for Tim. That boy is so in love with your dogs. And I can see why now. They're just the sweetest things."

The husband came up with feigned casualness; wanting to shake my hand but not wanting to make it into a big deal. He finally shrugged and stuck his hand out for me to take. I didn't particularly want to, but I shook it anyway.

He said, "Wendell Grant. This is my wife, Connie."

"Nice to meet you," I said with a straight face, and introduced myself.

"I wish there was something we could do for you, Mr. Field," he said, acting like it was no big deal or anything. "Tim really loves these visits."

Mrs. Grant, still huddled over Frankie and Hooch, said, "All he ever talks about is these dogs!"

Before I knew what I was doing I said, "If you really want to do something for me, you could let Tim's father donate one of his kidneys to the poor kid."

Wendell said, "How do you know about that?"

Connie stood up and tsked. "It's all over town by now." She looked at me. "I'm afraid that's impossible."

"No it's not," I said, unable to stop myself from butting in. "Look, I admit I have no idea what it's been like for you to lose your daughter the way you did, but—"

"No, you don't."

"Right. And I admit it. And I admit that it's none of my business. But I would imagine you'd want to think twice about this. It's one thing to lose your daughter, but it's another to be responsible for letting Tim die, when you could very easily—"

"You don't understand," she said. "He's very high on the waiting list. There'll be a donor soon, I just know it."

"Yeah? And what happens if there's no match?"

"Okay," said the husband, "that's it. We're not going to discuss this with you or allow you to visit Tim anymore."

I was dumbstruck. "You can't be serious."

"He's our responsibility. I can't have you interfer—"

"Okay, okay." I put my hands up. "Sorry I mentioned it. But don't keep him from seeing the dogs."

We all stood there fuming—all except Frankie and Hooch, of course, who were wagging their tails.

"Look," I said, "I know this must be a sore spot, so I'm sorry I brought it up. I won't mention it again."

A look passed between them and then Connie said, "Okay, you can bring the dogs. But please don't mention that man to us or to Timmy ever again."

"Fine, I won't. I'm sorry I said anything."

He said, "We love our grandson, Mr. Field."

"Of course you do," I lied.

We shook hands again then he put his arm around his wife's shoulder and she leaned against him, and they walked away. I watched for a moment, feeling like a creep for sticking it to them, and like an even worse creep for not sticking it to them harder.

Then I pulled my mask back up and went to see Tim.

Despite the bad feelings I carried into the room, we'd come on a good day. He was between appointments on his dialysis calendar and his face had a little color. He brightened up even more when he saw Frankie and Hooch.

"Hello, doggies!" he said, beaming. "I've been wondering when you'd come!" He looked at me. "Hi, Mr. Field."

"You can call me Jack. And it's too bad you don't like these dogs very much."

"Don't like them?" He looked at me and realized I'd been kidding. "I *love* these dogs, though I think I like Hooch the best," he said, smiling at the big boy. "Sorry, Frankie."

"He doesn't mind. So why do you like Hooch the best?"

"Because he's not like a dog at all, but a real person."

"Well," I said, "that's because he's *not* a dog, actually. He just puts on a dog suit for our visits."

"A dog suit?"

"You know, like at Christmas some grown-ups put on a Santa suit to thrill the little kids."

"No, they do it to fool them." He scowled. "That's because there really is no Santa Claus."

"You're kidding! Really? You know, I heard that rumor too, but I don't know if I believe it."

He chuckled and shook his head. "You keep forgetting I'm twelve. Just because I look like I'm six doesn't mean I *am.*"

"I know the feeling," I said, smiling, though he could only see my eyes. "I'm not really twelve even though I act like it most of the time."

"I believe you," he said laughing. His face changed to that of a child who wants something. He said, "I'm awfully thirsty. Could you get me a glass of water?"

"I'd like to, Tim, but you know the rules. I can't."

"But I'm really thirsty and the nurse forgot to leave me anything to drink."

"Nice try. Maureen told me about how your daily intake of water has to be carefully monitored."

"Figures," he said sadly.

"Hey, you want to see Frankie do a trick?"

His face brightened a little. "What does he do?"

"He can count to five by barking out the numbers."

"That's impossible," he said, skeptically. "Dogs can't count."

"Frankie can. Just give me any number between one and five."

"Okay, six."

I laughed and said, "Seriously."

"Okay then, two. That should be an easy one."

I looked at Frankie and he barked twice and I praised him.

"No way!" said Tim. "Get him to do it again! Three."

I looked at Frankie. He barked three times and I praised him. Then we went through all the numbers, from one to five.

"Whoa! How did you teach him to do that?"

"I can't tell you. It's a secret. Now you want to see Hooch's big trick?"

"Sure. Does he count too?"

"Hooch? No, he's terrible at math. He can stand on his head, though."

He laughed. "No, sir." He looked at me. "Can he really?"

"Sure, watch." I turned to Hooch. "Stand on your head."

Hooch just looked at me.

"Come on, Hooch—stand on your head."

He just stared at me and wagged his tail.

"Sorry," I said. "I guess he's not in the mood."

"I knew he couldn't do it." He gave me a look. "So, if he's not a dog, what is he under his dog suit?"

"An elf," I said.

He giggled. "He looks like an elf. Or an oompa-loompa."

"Very good. In fact, he's part-elf, part-oompa-loompa. So he's actually an elfa-loompa."

He was still giggling. "I almost believe you, that's what's so sad," he said, though he didn't seem sad. In fact, he seemed to be having fun, but then his face changed and he said, "But I don't believe in elves."

"No elves and no Santa Claus for you, huh, kid?"

"No. And I don't believe in Christmas either. The whole thing sucks."

"I know. You're in kind of a tough spot, aren't ya?"

"What would you know?"

"You're right, I wouldn't. Want to tell me about it?"

"Not really."

"I bet you feel like you're missing out on a lot of cool things that all the other kids your age do."

"You mean 'normal' kids."

"That's one way of looking at it." I pulled out a chair and sat down. "I bet you don't miss school much, though."

He smiled. "That's true. I have a tutor. She comes every morning, and it's a lot nicer than when I had to go to school every day. The other kids used to give me a hard time because I was littler than everybody else. I guess they figured it was fun to pick on me. Sometimes . . ."

"What?"

"Nothing. It's just that sometimes I think I'd be better off dead than having to face that again. I mean, even if I *do* get better, I still won't have any friends."

"Sure, that's one way of looking at it."

"What other way is there?"

"You think being sick has put you at a disadvantage, don't you?"

"That's putting it a bit mildly, don't you think?"

He was right, I thought, he wasn't six, or even twelve. He was pretty damn grown up in some ways. "Well, here's the thing: have you ever read any stories about knights in armor, King Arthur, and that sort of thing?"

"Yeah?"

"Well, those stories are all about what's called 'the hero's journey.' Lots of bad things happen to the hero along the way, and he always comes through in the end, right?"

"Yeah, but I'm not a hero."

"*I* think you are."

"But I don't *want* to be. I just want to be a regular kid, like everybody else."

"Yeah, that's understandable. But the thing is, you're not. It sucks, but there's nothing you can do about that now. You're stuck being on a hero's journey. And that means that whatever obstacles you come across, the ones that make you feel like you're at a disadvantage, all the things that happen on your journey will actually make you stronger than the other kids, once you get well. Then you'll have an advantage over *them*. Do you know why the other kids gave you a hard time in the first place?"

"'Cause they're a bunch of jerks."

"No. Because they're afraid."

"Afraid? Afraid of what?"

"Afraid that what happened to you could happen to them and they wouldn't be able to handle it. So, here's the cool part: once you actually *do* get better, they're going to stop being afraid and start looking up to you, even if just a little, because you came through something that none of them thought they'd be able to. Don't get me wrong. Some of them will still be jerks. Life's full of them. But most kids will know that you're a real hero and they'll admire you for it."

"Maybe." He thought it over and said, "But how do I know I'll even get well? And why did I have to get picked for this stupid journey in the first place?"

"I can't answer that. That's part of what makes people keep reading those stories, to find out how the hero deals with his obstacles and to see how it turns out in the end."

"And how's *my* story going to turn out?"

"I don't know. But I do know one thing . . ."

"What's that?"

I shrugged. "Things change."

He shook his head. "*Some* things don't."

"Maybe it doesn't feel like it now, but things always change one way or another. You just have to keep battling your obstacles, and keep hoping things'll get better."

"But I'm tired of hoping." A tear formed in his eye. "And I don't want to have any more obstacles."

"No real hero does," I said, feeling my throat tighten. "But that's part of the story. So, let's make a deal. If you keep hoping that things'll get better, I'll try to teach Hooch to stand on his head. Deal?"

He thought it over. "Deal. But I don't think you can do it," he said sadly, then his eyes filled with hope. "Can you?"

"Probably not," I agreed.

"That's what I thought," he grumped. "It's impossible."

"Maybe. But that's what you thought when I told you Frankie could count. Remember?"

He shrugged. "That's true."

"And even if it *is* impossible, I can still try, can't I? And maybe if I try hard enough I *can*. You may not know this, Tim, but I'm the bestest dog trainer in the whole wide world."

He laughed. "Sure you are. And I keep telling you, I'm not six, so don't talk to me like I am."

"Sorry. But listen, maybe I could at least get him to stand on his front paws, how would that be?"

"I'd like to see that. I think he's too big, though."

"Too big for a dog, maybe, but not for an elfa-loompa."

He laughed. "You mean, oompan-elfa."

"Or maybe he's part vampire, so he's a vamp-aloofa."

"Or an elfa-loompire!" he said, laughing.

We riffed like that for a while and when the hilarity died down I said, "You see, that's another thing that'll help you make friends with the other kids, once you get better. Having a sense of humor, being silly if you feel like it. Kids love to laugh. Here's another thing about kids your age: they hate school but they love to learn things. And most of them are going to want to learn how you got through your journey. You can teach them about what it's like to be a hero and they can teach you how to play baseball and tease girls."

"Sounds cool."

"Yep." I stood up. "Okay, Tim, we've got to go. You keep hoping, and I'll keep trying to teach this big elfa-loompire to stand on his head. We've got a deal, remember?"

He nodded. "I remember."

"Good. We'll see you tomorrow. Okay?"

"I hope so," he said. "See? I said 'I hope so.' That means I'm already keeping my part of the bargain."

"That's good, Tim. And I'll keep mine," I said, leashing the dogs up and wondering how the hell I was going to do it.

"You better try really hard, Jack," he said.

"I will. I promise. And speaking of oompa-loompas, remember what Willy Wonka told Charley about what happened to the boy who suddenly got everything he ever wanted?" He waited expectantly to hear. "He lived happily ever after."

He smiled momentarily then his face got hopeless again and he said, "That was just a movie."

"Yeah, but it was based on a true story."

He shook his head. "No, it wasn't."

"Really? Remember what else Willy Wonka said? He said, 'We are the music makers, we are the dreamers of dreams,' remember? So you keep dreaming and we'll see ya tomorrow."

"Okay," he said as a happy tear formed in his eye.

Great, I thought as we went out to the hall, I'm turning into the White Queen in *Alice in Wonderland:* I've just set out to do two impossible things before breakfast.

The first impossible thing was teaching the lumbering mastiff to stand on his head, which actually *was* impossible, and I knew it, though I intended to give it my best shot. And maybe it wouldn't be totally impossible after all. Dogs can really surprise you sometimes, and Hooch will do almost anything I ask him to, if he *can.* The second impossible thing was keeping Tim Huckabee's hopes and dreams—not to mention his body—alive long enough for a miracle to happen and bring him a new kidney. I hoped that maybe, just maybe, I could do that by giving him something to look forward to—the thought of seeing Hooch standing on his big noggin.

But the new kidney? That was totally out of my hands. Or so I thought.

But like I'd told the kid, things change.

16

I was feeling a little light-headed as I took the doggies out to the hall. Probably from spending so much time in the hospital, I thought. So I went to the drinking fountain and had a long drink of water. It helped a little but not much.

Then, as we came out the back entrance of the hospital, and I saw the black Lincoln parked sideways, ten feet in front of my Suburban, my brain came back alive. The first thing I noticed was that the tailpipe was emitting blue smoke. I thought, briefly, that maybe they were waiting for a parking space, but I'd worked enough cases in Sheepshead Bay to have developed a sixth sense for situations like this.

There was a security guard, stationed in a booth at the entrance to the hospital, reading a newspaper.

"Call the police," I told him.

"What?"

"There may be a little trouble, maybe even some gunfire taking place here any minute. Call 911 now!"

He dropped his paper and picked up the phone.

As I went to the car a rush of things went through my mind:

First, were they actually Ivana's backup goons? If so, I would know soon enough. Second, if they *were,* what was the best way to deal with them? They usually operate with force and a complete lack of compunction about using it. I could either try to escape, which would only piss them off and make them come back even stronger, maybe dropping by the kennel and shooting a couple of dogs just to get revenge for making them work so hard. Or I could just tell them that I didn't know anything, which was still no guarantee that they wouldn't shoot Frankie or Hooch to see if I was lying. This thought made my blood boil, but I didn't have time for anger, or fear, for that matter. I had to stay on balance emotionally in order to think clearly. My last choice, which looked like my only real one, was to immediately and permanently disable them, and do it in a way that brought shame on them and their boss. They would probably never stop otherwise.

I'd backed into my space, with a few feet of room to let the dogs jump out the back, so there was no way out but straight ahead. When I got to the car, I opened the tailgate to let them in. As I did, three men in overcoats leisurely got out of the Town Car.

Yep—they were Russian mafia, all right. At least they looked like it. To prove that point even further, one of them casually shouted something about wanting to ask me some questions about Karl Petrovich. I ignored him, had the dogs jump inside, then went in after them and closed and locked the tailgate behind me, then crawled to the front of the car.

By the time I got there all three men had weapons

drawn, though they held them easily at their sides, still giving the appearance of being regular guys, just casually strolling through the parking lot. I wasn't fooled. Those guns could come up and shoot in a fraction of a second. I started the engine and, sure enough, the guns came up. Too bad, fellas, I thought. Two of them were standing between the hood of my car and the side of the Lincoln, while the other one was coming around toward my window, his gun now back down at his side.

I put it in gear and stomped on the gas. The one on my left jumped back to get out of the way, raised his Glock and fired wildly, but missed the car entirely. The others got off a couple of shots that starred my windshield, but quickly had to stop firing because they suffered some minor fractures in the collision. Or not so minor, how do I know? I'm not an orthopedist; I'm a dog trainer.

Once the air bag deflated, I put the car in reverse, twisted the wheel tight, stomped on the gas, and took a good hard swipe at the other one, who was still shooting. I caught him good in the hip with my left fender. He spilled across my hood, the steam from my ruptured radiator blasted his face, and his weapon scooted out of his hand, up the hood toward me. It landed in the windshield wiper well. I felt a quick bump, put the car in park, jumped out, reached across the hood to the wiper well and grabbed his gun.

I gave a quick look toward the others, in case they still had ideas about shooting me. They did, or seemed to, but had no ability to act on their impulses. They had both lost the use of their extremities.

The driver was still inside the car and was trying to open his door, but the frame had been crunched in in the collision, so he scooted over to the passenger side door, opened it, got out, and ran off.

I came around the front of my car to see the one I'd just hit, lying on the frozen pavement. He seemed to be going for his ankle, and I thought he might have another weapon holstered there, but then realized that one of my tires had run over his leg (hence the bump I'd felt) and he was assessing the damage. I told him to lie facedown, which he refused to do, so I showed him his gun, which left a bit of a mark on his cheek, I'm afraid, probably due to the forceful way I showed it to him. Then I made a move to stomp on his ankle and he finally turned over and put his hands behind his neck. I crouched down, put a knee in his back, set his gun aside, then took off my belt and used it to secure his wrists.

Two sheriff's Jeeps arrived, sirens blaring. Sheriff Flynn, with his big mustache and potbelly, got out of one. I didn't recognize the youngish deputy who got out of the other.

I lifted the Russian to his feet and said, "You know, if you had questions about Petrovich, you could have just called me on the phone and asked me. I'm in the book."

His topaz eyes tried to penetrate mine, though it was tough work trying to see through his tears, brought on by the radiator steam. "And what would you have told me?"

"Same thing I told Ivana. I don't know where he is. And even if I did, I wouldn't give you the information."

Sheriff Horace Flynn, Jamie's ex-uncle-in-law, came over to me, while one of his deputies went over to the orthopedic cases. Meanwhile, two paramedics were wheeling a gurney their way too.

My prisoner winced as he tried to put a little weight on his bad leg, and said to me, "You are in serious trouble, my friend." To Flynn he said, "I want to speak to my attorney."

I said, "You're the one in serious trouble, my friend. I'm an investigator for the ME's office, which means I'm law enforcement. When your boss learns how you and your pals botched this job, you'll want to go into hiding yourself, the way Karl did. I'll bet your boss is scratching your names off his list of active employees as we speak."

"I want a lawyer."

"You okay, Jack?" Flynn said, twitching his salt-and-pepper mustache.

"Yeah," I lied, "just a little thirsty. And I need to check on my dogs. They're probably more shaken-up about this than I am."

"If you say so, but you're white as a sheet."

I ignored him, went to front of the car where there was a Poland Spring bottle in the cup holder. I reached inside, grabbed it and opened it, then took a long draught. It eased my thirst but I was still feeling a little light-headed. And the funny thing is, the more I drank, the worse I felt. Still, I drank the bottle dry, then went around to the back and let the dogs out, and they jumped on me and danced around, wagging their tails. My face and hands felt clammy and I was a little queasy, so I sat on the back bumper and put my head between my legs.

The dogs took this as another invitation for jumping and licking. Then Hooch's gaze wandered, off to my right, he stopped his happy dance, and began to growl. I followed his stare and saw the three injured gunmen being wheeled into the hospital and I felt both a wave of relief and a strong urge to throw up.

So I put my head back between my legs again, but it was too late. I hurled onto the asphalt, barely missing my boots, and both dogs immediately started licking up the mess.

"Thanks, you guys," I said. "You're a big help."

Flynn came around and said, "You okay?"

"I'll be fine in a minute. Too much adrenaline, I guess."

"Well, I'm going to try and get some statements. Join me when you're up to it. Jesus, what's wrong with these dogs?"

"Nothing," I said. "They're just being dogs."

"Well, Jesus, can't you stop them?"

"Probably. If I wasn't using all my strength to keep from passing out, or answering your damn questions."

He looked at me more closely. "Jack, you're sweating and you're white as a ghost. You're really scaring me. I think I'll go grab a nurse."

"Good," I quipped, "grab me one while you're at it."

Then I felt Flynn's big hands on my shoulders, helping to guide me as I fell over on my face and passed out.

17

I hate hospitals.

I know, she said.

What am I doing here?

You passed out. Did you eat anything today?

No. Just some orange juice. And I drank a lot of water.

Well, your electrolyte balance is out of whack.

But water and juice are good for you.

Not if you drink too *much* water.

I opened my eyes. "Can you do that? Drink too much water?"

She nodded. "You have a mild case of hyponatremia."

"Is that bad?"

"It *can* be. It basically means water intoxication. Now go back to sleep."

"What's in my arm?"

"They just put in a saline IV to make you feel better."

"I want to go home. Where are Frankie and Hooch?"

"They're right here. Just rest a bit and feel better, Jack, then you can come home with me. Okay?"

"Okay." I closed my eyes.

She said, I love you.
I love you too.
Go to sleep.
I will.

18

On the drive up U.S.1 toward Rockport Jamie said, "How come you never told me that you were visiting Tim Huckabee?"

"Why would I? You know I hate to talk about stuff like that with anybody."

"Well, I'm not just anybody, Jack."

"I didn't mean it like that. So is it serious?"

"What?"

"Hyponutremia."

"You mean hypo*na*tremia, with an *na*, as in sodium. Yes, you could've died from it or gone into a coma."

"Really?" I thought it over. "How does it kill you, exactly?"

"It lowers the sodium levels in your blood and eventually causes cerebral and pulmonary edema."

"Edema. That's what killed Tim's mother, wasn't it?"

"Yes, but her edema was caused by head trauma. Remember? She didn't have hyponatremia or pulmonary edema."

"Are you sure? Did you look at the entire autopsy report?"

She looked at me. "Well, no. Just the death certificate." She thought it over. "I thought you were hot on the idea that she was killed by an *E. coli* infection."

"I wasn't 'hot' on it. It just a wild idea I had, based on the fact that she died around the same time Tim got infected. Could someone with an *E. coli* infection die from cerebral edema?"

"Usually it's kidney failure." She shook her head and sighed. "Which, now that I think about it, would also cause swelling of the brain tissue. All right, I'll go back and look over the entire report. Then will you be satisfied?"

"Me? Probably not." I looked out the side-view mirror and saw a couple of cars behind us. It was hard to make out what kind of cars they were because it was snowing again.

"Is someone tailing us?" I said.

She looked in the rearview. "It's probably Uncle Horace. He said he's going to put some men on the kennel to make sure they don't try anything again."

"Who, the Russians? I thought they were all under arrest or in intensive care."

"They are, thanks to you."

"So, what's the problem?"

"Flynn's worried that their boss might send some more muscle up from New York."

"I think I took care of that possibility. If they'd known I was a law-enforcement official they never would have tried anything. They have a strict rule about not going after cops or DAs and the like."

"Well, that's a relief. I hope they stick to their rules."

I tried to remember something. "Honey, I know you told me this, but what are we planning to do about my car?"

She sighed. "I called a tow company to take it to the Chevy dealership in Rockland. You busted your radiator, among other things, remember?"

"Oh, yeah. When will it be fixed?"

"They said it would take a couple of days at least."

"Crap. I hate driving the woody in this weather."

"It isn't very practical, is it? Oh, and we found something interesting in the victim's hair and inside her wound, some sort of microorganism that I didn't recognize. So I sent some samples to a forensic biologist and they turned out to be what's called bioluminescent dinoflagellates."

"Sounds strange. What are they?"

She shrugged. "Some type of marine plankton that emit light when the water around them is disturbed. They produce photons through some sort of biochemical process."

"Huh. And where do they live?"

She looked at me. "In the ocean. I told you they were—"

"Marine plankton, I know. But what part of the ocean? What's their natural habitat?"

"Oh. Well, there are some in the waters off the coast of Maine. There's an outfit in Castine that offers kayak tours in Penobscot Bay to see them."

"Sounds fun. Maybe we should do that, after I get over my cold."

"Okay, but I don't think they're active in the winter months, though there *are* species in the Caribbean that are."

"So they're not just in Maine?"

"No. They have them in San Diego, Maryland— they come from all over. The biologist is still trying to narrow down the source of our specimens."

We got to the junction of 90 in Rockport, but before Jamie could make the turn a siren went off behind us. Jamie looked in her rearview and said, "Now what?"

She pulled off to the side of the road. I looked back and saw Officer Weist getting out of his Camden PD cruiser.

"Oh boy," I said. "Here we go again."

As Jamie rolled down her window I explained what had happened earlier. She was furious.

Before Weist could ask for her license and registration she began a tirade against him and the chief, ending with the, I thought, reasonable point that Rockport wasn't the chief's jurisdiction in the first place.

"Well, technically speaking," said Weist, standing patiently in the falling snow, "it is. I'll need you to keep the engine running and switch on your turn signals."

Two County Sheriff's Jeeps pulled up to a stop behind Weist's vehicle.

Jamie said, "This is police harassment."

Weist nodded, kind of sadly. "It sure is. *I* think you should file a complaint against the department."

"Don't think I *won't*."

"I think you *should*. Now, your turn signals?"

Flynn came up to the car, wanting to know what the hell was going on.

"Routine traffic check," said Weist.

"Police intimidation from Chief Colbern," said Jamie.

Jamie and I got out of the car. Flynn threatened Weist with the same treatment he'd been giving me and Jamie if he didn't back off.

Weist said, "Look, this is the chief's idea, not mine. If I don't do what I'm told, I'll lose my job."

"Fine," said Flynn. "Colbern lives outside the Camden city limits, so his house and property are under *my* jurisdiction. I'll make it the Sheriff's Department's priority to bust *his* ass for any little infraction we find."

Weist chuckled. "I'd like to see that."

"You think I won't do it?"

"No, I think you *should* give him a taste of his own medicine. But that's not going to stop me from writing Dr. Cutter a ticket or impounding her vehicle if I have to."

I said, "You're going to do *what,* now?"

Jamie huffed. "You've *got* to be kidding."

Weist shrugged. "Any lack of cooperation from either of these two and I'm supposed to call for a tow."

"That's it," said Flynn, "you're under arrest."

"For what?" said Weist in disbelief.

"I'll think of something on the way to the county jail."

"You can't put me in jail!"

"The hell I can't." Flynn went for his cuffs. "Put your hands behind your back."

Weist put a finger to Flynn's chest. Flynn grabbed it, twisted his arm behind his back, and pushed him up against Jamie's car. A deputy came running over from the other car.

"I got it," said Flynn over his shoulder. The deputy stopped in his tracks and just stood there. Flynn put the cuffs on Weist and said, "We're going for a little ride."

"Uncle Horace," said Jamie, "I'll pay the damn ticket."

"The hell you will." To Weist he said, "Don't worry. As soon as she and Jack are outside the city limits I'll let you go. Till then, you're mine. Got it?"

"This is a mistake, Sheriff."

"No, the city council appointing a Chief of Police with no background in law enforcement is the mistake."

"I agree with you, but what can *I* do about it?"

"You don't have to do anything but leave these two alone."

"Fine, arrest me. But this is going in my report."

Flynn told him what he could do with his report. Then the deputy asked Flynn what they were going to do next and he said, "Just follow me till they're outside the city limits."

They both got back in their Jeeps, leaving Weist's vehicle—with the front door standing open and the lights still flashing—by the side of the road. Flynn put Weist in the back of his Jeep. He even pushed down on the top of his head as if he were an actual perp, then called out to Jamie, "You can take off now, honey. We'll be right behind you."

"Uncle Horace," she said, exasperated, "don't do this! They'll only arrest Jack next."

"Don't worry, I'm not arresting anybody. Just go!"

She shook her head and we got back in the car where the dogs were highly agitated by all the negative emotion.

"It's okay, boys," I said. "Everything's fine."

We drove off, with the escort behind us. When we got to West Rockport, about five miles or so, Flynn's siren went off, signaling Jamie to pull over. She did. We looked behind us and saw Flynn help Weist out of the back of his Jeep, unlock the handcuffs, and send him walking back to his cruiser.

Jamie shook her head. "This is nuts."

I said, "You're telling me? So if Colbern has no experience in law enforcement, what the hell did he do before he became chief?"

She shook her head sadly. "He was head of the Chamber of Commerce. You know what? I'm filing a complaint with the city council. And the state police."

"Don't do that yet, honey. We have to wait until another Camden cop does something similar."

The sheriff's siren gave a quick burst, telling us to get moving, so Jamie put the Jag in gear and we drove off. Jamie went on and on about what had just happened, and it wasn't until we were well outside West Rockport that the conversation turned away from Colbern and back to the case.

"So," I said, finally, "these dinoflagamacallems were on the murder weapon, and that's how they got in her hair?"

"What? Oh. That's what it looks like."

"Any idea yet on what type of weapon was used?"

"Jack, I'm really worried about this harassment."

"Don't worry. He's only doing it to get under my skin."

"But, Jack, what if he comes out to the kennel and tries to arrest you at gunpoint?"

"Simple. I'll just take his gun away and shoot him in the nuts."

She laughed. "Be serious."

"Accidentally, of course. Look, can we stop worrying about Colbern's stupid vendetta and get back to discussing the case? He'll either get over it or make some dumbass mistake and lose his job. What kind of weapon was used?"

"Probably a wooden club of some kind. Maybe the wrong end of a baseball bat. I couldn't say for sure."

"Or an oar, maybe? That might have traces of marine life on it. A baseball bat or a club wouldn't, necessarily."

"That's true. But because of the size and shape of the wound, it couldn't have been the flat end of the oar she was struck with. It would have to have been the handle."

I thought it over. "Yeah, and it would be kind of clumsy trying to kill someone with an oar if you're holding it by the big end. Same with the big end of a baseball bat."

"That's true. It's still a mystery."

"There's that word again." She asked me what I was referring to and I explained what I'd told Bailey.

"Funny," she said, "I thought *all* cases were mysteries."

"Not from a cop's standpoint. Only the weird ones are."

She drove for a while, still steaming about the incident, then thought of something else and said, "You know, Jack, an *E. coli* infection reduces levels of ADH, or anti-diuretic hormone, and that would increase thirst . . ."

"Ah-hah! And that would make someone drink too much water. So I could be right about how she died?"

She shook her head. "It's a remote possibility."

"You know, I still can't believe that drinking too much water can kill you."

"Well, it can. So be more careful. If you feel dehydrated, try a sports drink. Do you have any at home?"

"I have some Gatorade."

"Good."

I promised that I would drink some once I got home, mostly to ease her mind—I didn't have any intention of actually doing it, since I don't like Gatorade. Then I told her about my promise to Tim Huckabee.

"Why did you do that?"

"I don't know," I sighed. "I was just trying to think of some way to keep him from losing all hope, you know?"

"That's good." She looked at me. "You don't usually get so attached to these kids."

"I know," I grumped.

"Maureen Todd, she's the head pediatric nurse—"

"I know who she is."

"Anyway, she came downstairs to see you while you were unconscious. She also asked me to do a blood and tissue typing on you."

"That's odd. Why would she do that?"

"Why do you think? To see if you're a possible match for Tim Huckabee's new kidney."

I shook my head. "I'm not *that* attached to him."

"Well," she tossed it aside, "it's probably a moot point anyway. The likelihood of you being—"

"Honey, I like that kid a lot and I feel bad for him, but his father's an eight-point match already. Besides, I can't go around giving away my internal organs to every little kid who needs them, no matter how attached I am."

"I know." She patted my knee. "And you're already doing your part. I mean, come on, if anyone can teach a dog like Hooch to stand on his head, it'd have to be you, Jack."

"You seem to have a lot of faith in my abilities."

She nodded. "I do."

"Really? You could have fooled me."

"Well, don't get me wrong, when it comes to dog training and crime solving, I think you're the most brilliant man there is. But when it comes to taking care of yourself . . ."

"Then I'm a dummy, huh?"

"A big one." She drove a bit.

"And isn't it illegal for Maureen to do that?"

"Yes, but I'm your fiancée. I can do whatever I want."

I laughed. "No, you can't."

"True. But what are you going to do, sue me?"

I had to laugh some more. She had me there.

We came to the four-way, and Jamie slowed down to look around. No one was coming so she drove through.

"And speaking of tissue matches and such," she went on, "we compared the samples found under our victim's fingernails with the semen inside her uterine—"

"Hold on, go back a second. You did a rape kit on Amy Frost?"

"Sort of. It's standard procedure with any young woman who's murdered. You know that."

"I guess I forgot. It seems so invasive and degrading."

"Believe me, I know. But it's not as degrading as ignoring evidence that might lead to catching whoever might have killed her."

"No, I guess you're right. So what did you find out?"

"The samples came from two different sources, both male."

"Hmm. So the person she slept with probably isn't the one who killed her."

"Probably not."

I sighed. "I hate this damn cold. It's kept me home too much to be of any use on this case."

"What do you mean? You've been a lot of help."

"Thanks, but that's not true. I haven't even met any of the three prime suspects. I should at least be out there interviewing these three guys, you know? It seems like I'm either home in bed or at the hospital."

"I suppose, but you have to take care of yourself when you're sick, Jack. And I know you don't think this is important, but it is. You could have died today."

"Hey, I was the one getting shot at, remember?"

She snorted. "I'm not talking about that and you

know it. You've been shot at before and you always manage to come through. Not that I approve of you putting yourself in the line of fire the way you do. But this is different."

"Okay, okay. Anyway, I already told you that I'd have some Gatorade when I get home."

"Un-huh," she said, skeptically, then made a quick left at the Perseverance general store and filling station, but drove past the pumps and up to the store entrance.

I looked at the gas gauge. "Why are we stopping?" I asked. "You've got a full tank."

She parked and said, "I'm going to stock up on Gatorade. You stay here with the dogs and relax."

"Yes, mommy," I said.

19

I made spaghetti and meatballs that night. It's Leon's favorite, and it was just me and him for dinner. Jamie had called earlier to say she wouldn't be back till after ten—she's a busy lady these days. At any rate, I had just finished doing the dishes when Brad Bailey called.

"So," he said, "you want a look at that third floor?"

"Yes, but I'm supposed to be a good boy and go to bed early tonight. I nearly died today, supposedly."

"Yeah, I heard. I also heard you did some damage to a couple of Russian goons. So, if it's too much for you—"

"Never mind that; what time are you picking me up?"

He laughed. "I'm on my way."

"Good. And bring a UV lamp. I want to get a good look at that blood trail."

We spent a little time going over the first floor. There was a large, in fact huge, sunken living room just past the sitting room where Fiona had fanned herself silly on the divan. There was an enormous fireplace on the south wall, and floor-to-ceiling windows on both the east and west sides of the room.

We'd already toured the kitchen and Amy Frost's bedroom so when I finished nosing around the living room, we went up to the second story.

We got to the top of the landing and I just stood there, stuck to the carpet and lost in thought.

"What are you doing?" Bailey said.

"Putting myself in the killer's shoes."

"How do they fit?"

"I don't know," I said. "They're a little tight."

I envisioned myself coming at Amy Frost from behind, holding an oar or a walking stick or a baseball bat and swinging it at the back of her head hard enough to crack her skull open and kill her. After the shock of it passed I said, "This was no accident or a sudden fit of rage. It was cold-blooded murder. He intended to kill her."

"How can you tell?"

I let out a deep breath. "You don't want to know. Can we look around the master bedroom, or is that off limits?"

"Well," he looked uncomfortable, "they haven't locked it, but their attorney says—"

"Attorneys say a lot of things. Let's go have a look."

The master suite—bedroom and bath—sat right over the living room and was almost as big. The walls and even the ceiling were paneled in dark walnut. There were floor-to-ceiling windows on the east wall, which gave its own view of the ocean. It also had its own fireplace, almost as big as the one downstairs. I'm not an expert on antiques, so I don't know what era the bedroom décor was from, but it looked to be a couple hundred years old and was probably French or English.

I asked Bailey to show me where the safe was located and he took me to what looked to be a Gainsborough, hanging to the right of the king-sized four-poster. He swung the painting back to reveal a wall safe with a black combination dial and a chrome-plated steel handle.

"Nice and secure," I said, then turned around and scanned the wall and ceiling behind me. There was what looked like a lipstick camera in the corner of one of the wooden ceiling panels. I went to the window, where there were two stuffed antique chairs; pulled one of them under the camera, got up on it and examined the surveillance device more closely.

"Another camera?"

"Yep. And it's aimed right at the safe."

"Interesting."

"Well," I said, getting down, "since Huckabee put the cameras in, this makes it look like he's our thief, and probably our killer."

Bailey wrote that down in his notebook.

"Still," I said, taking the chair back to its original position, "someone else could have *known* about the camera."

He wrote that down too.

I said, "What's on the other side of this floor?"

"A guest bedroom and bathroom, and Chris Bright's suite, I guess you'd call it. He's got his own bathroom with a Jacuzzi, plus a bar and a mini-kitchen."

"Let's have a look."

As we went through Chris Bright's quarters—where the furnishings were more modern, and the color scheme was gray, green, and purple—I asked Bailey if the Brights had given up any information about the mysterious professor—his name, his address, his field of study, anything? He told me that the Brights weren't talking to the police, except through their lawyers.

"And let me guess," I said, "the chief is actually *letting* them stonewall you?"

He sighed. "That's right."

I looked around the room. "This has been searched thoroughly, I take it?"

He nodded. "With a fine-tooth—"

"Really?" I said, noticing a framed painting that seemed a little askew. "You even looked behind all the artwork?"

He seemed confused. "You think there's another safe in *this* room?"

"Why not?" I went over to the suspicious painting and pulled on it. It came back easily, revealing another, smaller and less secure safe.

"Well, I'll be."

"Yes, you will." I fiddled with the dial and pulled the handle, but it was nothing doing. "Well," I said, "I stupidly left my safe-cracking tools at home, so I guess you'll have to contact the lawyers and get the combination."

He wrote that down in his notebook.

"Okay," I said, "now for the real show. Let's have a look at that third floor. Have you got the UV light?"

He handed me what looked like a flashlight. We went into the hall and I said, "Okay, let's turn off the lights."

He did and I turned on the UV flashlight and splashed it across the carpet near the top of the stairs.

The CSU had luminoled the area and a clear blood trail showed up under the ultraviolet light as bright spots.

"Wow," said Bailey, "that's really cool."

"You've never seen it before, huh?"

"No. It's kind of amazing. How does it work?"

"I don't know, exactly. I think it has something to do with the proteins in the blood. The luminol makes them glow under ultraviolet light. Let's see where they lead."

We followed the drops to a staircase at the north end of the hall. The spatter became sparse as we climbed the treads, disappearing entirely after the first two steps. But when we got to the third floor it reappeared again.

Bailey said, "That's odd. I thought all the blood had dripped off the murder weapon by the time he got to the stairs. How could it reappear again?"

"It's probably a matter of how the killer was holding the weapon. If it was a long wooden object, like an oar or a baseball bat, the killer might have been running down the hall, holding it like this . . ." I demonstrated, using the UV flashlight, holding it horizontally at my side, parallel to the floor. "The blood would drip more than it would if the killer were holding the weapon like this . . ." I held the flashlight vertically. "Which is how you'd hold it while climbing the stairs. Then the blood would drip down the sides of the bat and possibly onto the killer's hand."

"Wow, that's amazing that you can know all that from the pattern of the blood drops."

"Oh, there's a lot more to it than that. You can tell how fast someone is moving, what direction they're going, a lot of things, just from the shape of the droplets."

He shook his head. "I've got a lot to learn."

"Yes, you do," I said as we followed the blood drops to a door, opened it and went inside. We were in a library and the drops were no longer visible at all. I handed Bailey his UV flashlight and said, "Let's hit the lights."

He hit the switch and I saw that we were in a spacious library, with a fireplace, a double-paned window, the kind where each pane opens with a hand crank, and a full-length mirror, all on the west wall. The other three walls were covered in books.

Bailey pointed to the mirror and said, "That's where the dogs wanted to go the other day."

I went over to take a look. "Huh. Maybe it's two-way glass and there's a hidden room behind it."

He shrugged. "I don't see how. This whole wall is flush with the exterior of the building."

I went to the window and looked out. "I see your point." I opened one of the panes, poked my head through and looked down to the backyard. "Yep." Then I looked over toward the part of the exterior that aligned with where the mirror hung. There was an architectural detail—I don't know what it's called, it was like an abutment of some sort—that stuck out from the rest of the building. I turned to Bailey and said, "Take a look at this."

He came over, poked his head out, looked at the abutment and said, "Well, that's just there for decoration, I think. It's not structural."

"Maybe not," I said, then looked at the room we were in and said, "Is it just me, or is the geometry of this room a little off?"

Bailey looked carefully around the room but didn't see anything out of the ordinary. "It looks square to me."

"It's rectangular, actually. But isn't the whole thing kind of set at an off-angle to the rest of the building?"

"I don't see it."

I couldn't put my finger on exactly what seemed off either so I let it go. "What else is there on this floor? I mean, this is a little strange—a room that just sits here and there's no door to any other rooms."

"Yeah, I know. There's an empty room at the other end of the hall. It's a lot bigger than this one."

"And what's in between?"

"Nothing. I measured it and the sizes of the two rooms, and there's about a ten to twelve foot difference, which I assume contains wiring, plumbing fixtures, and the like. In fact, according to the plumber's schematic, that's where all the pipes lead."

"Well," I said, "we've got to find out what's inside that space between these two rooms." I looked at him. "Have you discussed this with Coletti?"

He shrugged. "As far as he's concerned Huckabee's the prime suspect, and the third floor has nothing to do with him."

I shook my head. "Doesn't he get how important it is that the killer brought the murder weapon up here?"

"Oh, yeah. But the blood trail ends in the hall. So he thinks Huckabee came up here, threw the murder weapon out the window, went back to the second floor to rob the safe, then went downstairs, out the back way, retrieved the weapon, and took it with him when he left the premises."

"That makes very little sense to me."

"People do strange things under stress."

I sighed and laughed at the same time. "You're talking to a supposed expert in criminal psychology. If he wanted to ditch the murder weapon, why wouldn't he just throw it out a window on the second floor? But he didn't, meaning he had to have come up here for a specific reason."

"Maybe he'd stashed the combination to the safe up here."

"Okay, that's good thinking." I paused. "Are the monitors and VCRs for the surveillance cameras up here?"

"No. They're down in the basement."

"Well, let's go have a look at the basement."

We went downstairs and when we got to the kitchen, I felt a little woozy so I sat down at the kitchen table—the one where the staff has to eat their lonely meals.

"Are you okay, Jack?"

"Not really. Check the fridge for Gatorade, would you?"

He went over and opened it up. There wasn't any. "How about some water?"

"That's the last thing I need." I could feel my hands and arms vibrating. I said, "Tell you what, find some salt and get me a glass of water. Quick."

He did as I'd asked and I took the top off the salt shaker, shook about a half a teaspoonful onto my tongue, then drank a little water. I felt a little better, but only just a little, so I had another shot of salt and another sip of water. I was still not quite right.

"All right," I said, "the trip to the basement is off—for tonight, anyway. Give me your cell phone." He did. I handed it back to him and said, "I don't know his number."

"Whose number?"

"Coletti's."

He sighed, flipped it open, speed-dialed Coletti, and handed the phone back to me.

"Hey, Dan," I said, after he'd picked up, "it's Jack. First of all, Jamie tells me I need to apologize for the crack I made the other night."

"What crack is that?"

"About not inviting you to the wedding."

"Oh. Well, that's okay."

"Good. Anyway, I'm here at the crime scene with your young inspector Bailey . . ."

"Uh, Jack," Coletti said, "did you stop and think to ask first if you'd called me at a bad time?"

"Oh. I guess not. Did I call you at a bad time?"

"Yes. I'm with my kids."

"Huh. I didn't even know you were married."

"Divorced," he said, as Bailey mouthed the word for me. "And you'd know things like that about people, Jack, if you weren't such a self-absorbed—"

"Whatever, listen, sorry. I have to talk fast before I pass out or something. Look, there are some huge holes in your investigation and I wanted to let you know what they are. First of all . . ."

"Tell the kid. I'm busy at the moment."

"Okay, but now Jamie and I are *definitely* not inviting you to—"

He hung up on me.

I gave Bailey his phone and said, "I think you'd better take me home. I need to boost my electrolytes. I don't know, maybe it's just this damn cold. No, don't help me up . . ."

On the ride home I asked him if the dogs had searched the first floor and the basement, or just the two upper stories.

"Well, the handlers—as you called them—said there was too much blood on the main floor, and that would throw them off, so they didn't do a search of it. And since the blood trail led upstairs, they didn't think it was necessary to take the dogs all the way down to the basement."

"Well, that could end up being a huge mistake." I told him what needed to be done to ensure that the investigation was as thorough and complete as possible, and to pass the information along to Coletti.

"Those dogs need to be brought back in to search the basement, the kitchen, and the rest of the first floor. And you're going to have to tear down some of those walls on the third floor to see what's behind them. I especially want to know what's behind that mirror."

"I'll tell Dan. How are you feeling?"

I sighed. "I feel okay now. It was probably just congestion from this damn cold. I can't breathe properly so maybe I'm not getting enough oxygen."

"I hope that's what it is."

"Can I ask you something?" I looked at him and he nodded. "Do *you* think I'm self-absorbed?"

"Hah!" he laughed. "Is that a trick question?"

20

The next morning the cold migrated to my chest. Still, hacking cough and all, I took Hooch down to the play yard to see if I could figure out a way to get him to stand on his head, or teach him *some* kind of new trick to impress Tim.

The first step in doing *any* form of training is to know all the steps you need to go through to get from A to G. As I'd told Jamie, sometimes, if you build a dog's prey drive to a high enough level, you can teach a command once, just once, and the dog never forgets it—he'll go straight from A to G in one step. That's how I'd taught Frankie several of his commands. But teaching tricks is often a slow, painstaking process for both the dog and the trainer, involving a lot of repetition and usually food rewards. Circus dogs—who are often American Eskimos, bichons, or poodles, or mutts with the same body type—are often trained to walk on their front legs. And I think I recall seeing a beagle or Jack Russell do it on Letterman once. But those are all small breeds and have a less elongated body shape than a dogue de Bordeaux.

What was I going to do?

Hooch looked at me curiously. I seldom take him down to the play yard alone. In fact, now that I thought about it, I don't think I'd *ever* done it before. So he was wondering what we were doing or what we were *going* to do. One of the great things about dogs—maybe the *best* thing about them—is their desire to engage in something that involves a group purpose. This is often mistaken for a "desire to please," when it's really nothing more than a manifestation of the prey drive, which they inherited from wolves. When wolves hunt together each member of the pack puts his individual needs and desires second to the overall group purpose. Hooch had that look in his eye now, as if to say, "Well? What are we going to do together? Let's do *some*thing!"

I thought back to a strange incident that happened when Frankie was younger, and we still lived in New York. I had him out in Central Park one winter day and was talking to a pleasant young woman, the owner of a springer spaniel named Brandy. Brandy had gotten bored with our conversation and her nose took her off in search of interesting smells. Brandy's owner and I continued our conversation and paid little attention to the dog until she eventually went down a hill toward the park drive and was about a hundred yards or so away.

Her owner began to call the dog excitedly, "Brandy! Come! Brandy get back here now!"

Brandy didn't come back and didn't even turn around to look at us. So I said, "Frankie, go grab Brandy's leash and bring her back here." I made it sound important.

He looked at me a moment, then ran over to the other dog, took her leash in his mouth, and brought her back. Brandy's owner was amazed, but no more than I. I'd never trained Frankie to do such a thing and had only been kidding around when I'd told him to do it. But he did it. (I told this story once to a science fiction fan and she said, "He probably just grokked what you wanted him to do.")

"Thank you," Brandy's owner said to me, taking hold of her dog's leash. "You really must be an incredible trainer."

However true that might have been (and I'm not saying it *is* true, Jamie and Tim Huckabee's faith in me notwithstanding), Frankie never did anything like that again. But I wondered if Hooch, who was showing signs of getting tired of waiting around for me to give him something to do, might *grok* that I wanted him to stand on his head.

"Hooch," I said, "stand on your head."

He looked at me, tilted his head, then went into a play bow—his front paws hugging the ground and his rump sticking up in the air. Ah-hah, I thought, he grokked step A.

"Good boy, Hooch!" Then I produced a tennis ball from my down jacket and threw it for him to chase. I repeated this game four or five times, then took a break and played with him a while, getting him to chase me around and jump up on me. I ended the game by falling down in the snow, acting "submissive," and letting him jump all over me and around me.

"Oh, no," I cried. "You got me! You're alpha! You're the *king* dog!" This made him incredibly happy, and I recommend that anyone with almost any kind of dog try it at least once (unless the dog doesn't know it's a game).

I got to my feet, stood up straight, and said, "Hooch,

stand on your head." He did the play bow again, rocketing into position this time, and I threw the ball for him to chase.

I repeated the process three times, taking a break between giving the command and just playing with him, then said, "Okay, big fella, let's go eat. You hungry?"

He smiled and wagged his tail.

As we went up toward the house a Camden PD cruiser pulled into the drive and a young uniformed officer got out.

"You Jack Field?" he asked, all business.

I stopped about twenty yards away, had a coughing fit, and when I was done I said, "Yeah? What do *you* want?"

"Chief Colbern wants to talk to you. I'm going to need you to come with me."

I laughed, which started me coughing again. When I stopped I told him to go do something biologically impossible.

"You said what?"

"You heard me. And get off my property. This is private land. You're trespassing."

His forehead wrinkled with disbelief. "Um, uh," he said, "but I'm *telling* you to come with me. You *have* to do it."

I started walking up to the house again. "What are you, twelve? Go home. Get out of here."

"Then I'm going to have to take you into custody."

"You and what scout troop? Scat!"

He reached for his holster, saw the look in my eye, slid back inside the cruiser, and got on the radio.

I heard him say, "He told me to get off his property. What do I do?"

"Hey, cubby, what's your name?"

"Why?"

"I'll need to know it for my harassment complaint against the department."

"It's Fowler. Roy Fowler."

"Good boy, Roy. Now get off my property."

"But I have to—"

I said, "I asked you to leave, which means you have to go. That's the law. So, do your whining to the chief from somewhere else." Then I took Hooch up to the house.

We got to the kitchen, with Frankie dancing around the two of us, and as I was about to put the food in Hooch's bowl I heard the police car crunching back up the drive. I shook my head again at the lunacy of it all.

The phone rang. I filled Hooch's bowl then went to the phone and picked it up.

"Mr. Field?" a Russian-accented voice said.

"Who is this?" I said, taking a seat. "Is this Karl?"

"*Da.* Are you okay? You sound like you've got a—"

"Cold. Yeah, I do. Where in the world are you?"

"That, I can't say. You understand, I hope."

"I think I do. Just give me a hint about your location."

He laughed. "Why? So you come looks for me?"

"Can the phony bad English, Karl. Remember?"

"*Da,* I remember. I also remember what you does for me—that is, what you did for me yesterday."

"How do you know what I did yesterday?"

"I have friends who have friends. So, thank you."

"I didn't do it for you; I did it to save my own skin. If you'd been there I probably would've thrown *you* to the wolves."

"Hmm. I think probably *not.*"

"Yeah, I think you're probably right."

"Why, though? Why do you take my side on things?"

"I don't know, Karl. You just seem like a decent guy who got caught up in something bad for a while and then got out."

He paused. "It's hard being decent guy in this town."

"Yeah, what town is that?"

"Okay, since you keeps asking," he said, "I gives you one clue, but don't tell anybody: it's a nice town, where I am. In fact, it's so nice they named it twice."

"Really? You're in Walla Walla?"

He laughed. "Other side of map."

"Boy, you've got some balls to go back there, Karl."

"What choice do I have? I have to fix things now or die, don't you think? These people of mine, they never quit."

"I know. And how exactly are you planning to fix things? I hope you aren't—"

"If I fix them, we'll meet again. *Then* I'll tell you."

"Okay. *Why* are you trying to fix them?"

"Stupid reason. I'm in love with a girl back in Camden. She's a waitress in the coffee shop."

"That's the best reason in the world, Karl. Do you need any help? Is that why you called?"

"No, I called to say apology for trouble and to say thank you for what you've done for me."

"Okay, now maybe you can do something for *me*."

There was a pause. "Sure. Just name it."

It was my turn to pause. "Well, I don't know what it is yet, Karl. It has to do with this case. Give me your phone number or a way to contact you and if I need something, I'll call you. Okay?" Silence. "Karl, are you still there?"

"*Da.* Just thinking." He gave me a contact number and I wrote it down. "But this number, don't give it to anyone else."

"Don't worry, I won't."

He hung up, Hooch finished eating, and I wondered what Karl's life was like before he became a chauffeur. I also had to wonder a bit if my good opinion of him was misguided.

They say Russians are famous for two things besides vodka—guilt and guile. Was he being devious? I didn't think so. But if he *was*, I thought, what can I do about it?

So my mind went back to the training I'd done with Hooch: had he learned to do a play bow well enough to do it on cue at the hospital so I could at least show Tim that I was making progress? I hoped I had enough time to work him on it again before our trip to visit Tim. Unfortunately, I never got the chance.

Things change.

21

I was about to jump in the shower when the phone rang. It was Maureen.

"You won't need to come to the hospital today," she said. "Tim Huckabee's in surgery."

I immediately thought a matching donor had been found. "Wow, that's great news."

"Sorry, no, it's not the transplant. He had a vascular thrombosis and needs a new dialysis graft."

My knees got weak. She told me that Tim's dialysis tubes had been hooked up to a synthetic graft, located in his arm, and a blood clot had formed in the vein, blocking the flow of clean blood back to his body from the dialysis machine.

"Is he going to be all right?"

She took a deep breath. "Let's hope so. The doctors are working on him now. They're inserting a catheter in his neck, which should solve the problem, at least until a new kidney arrives. If it does."

"Ah, poor kid. What rotten luck."

"Yeah. If he makes it through the surgery, he'll be

kind of out of it for a few days. When he's feeling well enough for you to bring the dogs by, I'll let you know."

"Okay, thanks. Send him our best wishes."

" '*Our*' best wishes?"

"Yeah, from me and the dogs."

She laughed. "Okay, I'll do that."

Bailey called and asked me if I felt up to going with him to interview Christopher Bright. The harbormaster had informed the Camden PD that his sailboat, *The Andilar* was back in its slip, and that his English sports car was parked at Sharp's Wharf.

I said, "Good. I've been itching to interview somebody. And his boat is named after a Townes Van Zandt song?"

"What?"

"It's from a song called 'The Silver Ships of Andilar,' by Townes Van Zandt, one of the best songwriters of all time."

"Never heard of him. You want me to come pick you up?"

"Sure."

Bailey let me drive his car—a crappy gray Plymouth, circa 1980—so he could go over his notes and catch me up on the case. As we pulled onto the county road he said, "So, you're feeling better today?"

"Depends on your definition." I coughed. "The cold's worse, but at least I don't feel loopy like I did last night."

"That's good."

I coughed a little more then told him about the call from Karl, though I didn't tell him that Karl was back in New York, just that he was trying to make amends with his bosses.

"No kidding. I wonder what he did to peeve them off."

"It might be worth finding out."

"Do you think Karl could be the killer?"

"Sure, except for the fact that he's left-handed and he has an airtight alibi."

"Oh, yeah. I forgot."

"So what's going on from your end?"

He explained what he'd looked into. The first item was that Tom Huckabee had been working on the addition to the Bright mansion at the time of his wife's murder.

"No kidding. Doing what?"

"I'd like to know that myself. All I know is he was working for an electronics outfit from New York."

I said, "So Huckabee's somehow connected to the professor and the construction of that third floor, huh?"

"Yep. Which makes him look even better than ever for the murder, especially since his alibi witness still hasn't been found. And if there were false walls or hidden doors, like you suggested, there'd need to be some kind of electronic gizmos to open and close them, right?"

"Maybe, maybe not. But if Huckabee was working with the professor, that might explain his involvement with the construction. But then again, he could have just been an independent contractor. Anything on Amy Frost's background?"

He said no, there was nothing in the system except for a driver's license, which gave them her D.O.B. and driving record, which was clean.

"We talked to the Bright's staff and her landlord in New York. She was a waitress-slash-actress and lived on Ninth Avenue and 46th Street before becoming the

Brights' maid. We've got the NYPD checking into it but they've probably got more important things to do."

"It's a murder case, so they'll put all the manpower they can on it. Don't worry about that."

"Still, I'd like to go down there myself."

"Good idea. What's stopping you?"

" 'Budgetary considerations' is the story I got."

"Probably true. Did you get the combination to Chris Bright's safe?"

"Not yet, but we will."

"Good. What *do* you know about Chris Bright's relationship with the victim?"

"We got a hint from some of the staff that there was a sexual thing going on between them."

"Yeah? And what's *his* story? It's a bit unusual for a grown man to be living with mummy and daddy. I heard that he spent all his inheritance."

"Most of it. He had a drug problem, maybe still does. He also likes to gamble and buy expensive toys, like cars and boats. And then there's his penchant for young women."

"Including our murder victim?"

"Seems like it. That's what I'm hoping he'll tell us when we see him. Or at least we can get him to volunteer to give us a DNA sample."

"So young Christopher Robin was sleeping with the maid."

"Yep, like father like son, I guess."

"What? The old man was sleeping with her *too*?"

"No. Sorry, I guess I forgot to mention, that's how he and *Mrs*. Bright hooked up. She was a housemaid for *his* family, and he, uh, got her pregnant."

"And he actually married her? Rich families in those kinds of cases usually have the mother 'taken care of,' in some nice way, of course. They don't let the kid *marry* her."

He shrugged. "I guess he must have really loved her."

"Yeah, or maybe she was the type to see an opportunity and not let it go. She seems very determined to have things her way, that woman." I thought of something. "Didn't Ellis Bright's parents die shortly after he married Fiona?"

"Yep."

"Anything there? Some kind of questionable circumstances surrounding their deaths?"

"No, they died in a plane crash. So did a lot of other people." He riffed through his notes. "Here's another thing. She grew up in Ireland, then the family moved to Boston when she was about nine. But her younger brother Sean disappeared about a year before that and was never found."

"So that's the missing brother. Interesting, but I—"

"And get this, Jack," he said, "according to the local newspaper, the townspeople were all convinced that the boy had been kidnapped by elves."

I roared with laughter. "You've got to be kidding."

"Nope. Though the newspaper referred to them as the 'wee folk.'" He shrugged. "Well, it was sixty years ago."

I said, "People still believe in some strange things." By way of example, I explained the alpha theory to him.

"There are people who actually believe that about dogs?"

"*Believe* it?" I said. "Some people think it's a science. It's even taught at universities. And it's like a religion to some dog trainers."

"Well, that's weird." He shrugged. "But some people

still believe in elves, believe it or not. I know a lot of people up in Iceland still do."

"Really? How do you know that?"

"I spent two years there on a mission for my church."

I looked at him. "You're a Mormon?"

"Yep."

"Well, that explains a lot. And talk about strange beliefs. I mean, I don't want to put down your religion, Detective, but don't your people believe that God lives on a huge planet somewhere, in a galaxy far, far away?"

"Yes," he said defensively. "It's called Kolob."

"Well, doesn't that strike you as a little more like science fiction than religion?"

"I guess, if you take it out of context. But you have to remember, there was no such thing as science fiction when the church was founded."

"But you still believe that an angel came to Joseph Smith while he was asleep in his bedroom?"

"That's right. So? What religion are you?"

"I'm a lapsed Catholic. And don't tell me about some of the things *Catholics* believe. I know all about them. That's one reason I'm lapsed. And if you want to talk about strange beliefs, let's discuss the whole Mormon underwear thing, and how it supposedly keeps you safe from danger."

He smiled. "We prefer the word 'garments.' And they've actually protected *me* in the past." He shrugged. "But I guess everyone thinks everybody else's beliefs are strange."

"Yep. It's human nature."

"Still, you have to wonder if Mrs. Bright still believes that her brother was actually kidnapped by elves."

I laughed again. "Come on. She was eight years old

when it happened, right? Kids believe in a lot of things at that age."

"Yeah, but I was baptized when I was eight."

"Yeah, and I was baptized when I was in diapers. So?"

"So, I still believe in the Mormon Church."

"Good for you. I seriously doubt that any sane person, with the kind of money and background Mrs. Bright has—"

"Sure, but her *original* background—"

"Okay, it's possible she still believes in elves and fairies and leprechauns, and that's what the professor's scam is all about. But come on—that's *very* unlikely."

"Yeah, but didn't Sherlock Holmes say that when you remove the impossible, whatever's left, no matter how unlikely, is the truth?"

"Yeah, except that Sherlock Holmes never actually said *any*thing because he wasn't a real person. He was created by a British medical doctor named Arthur Conan Doyle. Still, you're right—or *Doyle* was—the process of deductive reasoning involves removing untruths to uncover what's *actually* true. And that brings up an interesting story about Doyle and his own belief in certain mythical beings . . ."

I told him about some photographs supposedly taken of fairies by two English girls in their back garden around the time of World War I, and how the Kodak Company vouched for their authenticity, as did Doyle—quite vigorously and very publicly.

"The photos were real?" Bailey asked, surprised.

"No," I laughed as we came to the three-way intersection in the middle of Camden. "I've seen the pictures—or copies of them in a book—and they're as fake as can be. It's *one* case where Doyle's reasoning let him down."

He shook his head. "It's hard to picture Sherlock Holmes believing in elves and fairies."

I laughed. "Like I said, Holmes isn't a real person. And like I also said, people have some strange beliefs. That includes you and your underwear, Detective."

He laughed. "Which brings us back to the possibility of people believing in elves?"

"Extremely doubtful," I said.

"But possible?"

"Sure, in Iceland, maybe. But then, it *is* kind of close to the North Pole."

"The North Pole?"

"Yeah. Where Santa Claus lives?"

I turned off Bayview into the empty parking lot at Sharp's Wharf, empty except for some ducks and gulls, and a bright red Triumph two-seater, circa mid-fifties—probably young Bright's car. The parking lot was covered in snow, but there was none on the car. I immediately liked Chris Bright, or at least his taste in cars and the names he gives his boats.

I parked next to the roadster and said, "Anyway, we've got better things to worry about here in the real world than some elfin kidnappers from Ireland. The most likely scenario is that Hayes has conned Mrs. Bright into believing he can contact her dead brother's ghost."

"Yeah, I guess you're right."

I opened the door and got out. There were a couple of big schooners—the kind they use to take summer tourists out on tours of the harbor. They were all fast asleep and bundled up in plastic tarps.

"Huh," I said, "it looks like Christo's been here." Bailey gave me a blank look. "You know," I said, "the artist who likes to put wrapping paper on buildings and bridges, and turned Central Park into an eyesore?"

I think he made some sort of reply, but I couldn't tell you exactly what he said because the next thing I remember is gasping for air as if my life depended on it.

22

I also remember I was cold and I was wet and I was underwater. Salt water. And the back of my head was on fire with pain. Oh, did I mention? I couldn't breathe.

Slippery hands were reaching for me and voices were saying something I barely remember:

"Grab his hands," I think someone said.

"Help me get him up on the dock," said someone else.

I was pulled out of the water and found Bailey and an old man in a yellow rain slicker hauling me up onto the slippery planks. I lay there and coughed and sputtered and tried to catch my breath.

There were other words, of the "are you all right, Jack?" variety, which I didn't focus on. All I could think about was how cold I was and my confusion as to what the hell happened.

"What the hell happened?" I said, looking up at Bailey.

"You don't remember?"

I told him the last thing I remembered was getting

out of the car. He was puzzled, but explained that we'd gone down to the *Andilar* together. That he had identified himself as a police officer and asked for permission to come aboard. There was no answer so we boarded the boat, heard some noise coming from the hold, went down the stairs, looked around, didn't find anything, then heard footsteps up on deck, went back up the stairs, with me in the lead, and I was hit from behind.

"You don't remember *any* of this?"

"Nope." I rubbed the back of my head. "He must have hit me pretty hard. God my head hurts. What'd he use?"

"An oar."

"Interesting. So then what happened?"

"You went down like a stone, though you scratched his face as you fell. I drew my weapon and then a woman hit *me*. I don't know what with. And I didn't totally lose consciousness when I got hit, though you apparently did."

"Yeah," I said. "That would explain why I don't remember anything. So then what happened?"

"Then they dumped us overboard."

"Did you get a look at either of them?"

"Just the one who hit you. It was definitely Chris Bright. I didn't see the woman, though I remember thinking it might've been another friend of Karl's."

"Why do you say that?"

"She had a Russian accent."

"Really? That might've been Ivana." I explained that maybe, since the Russians had no luck finding Karl through me, they might have sent her after Chris Bright.

"Sounds reasonable. Anyway, I did manage to grab

the oar out of Bright's hand." He pointed to an oar on the dock.

"Good. It might be evidence."

"Of course it's evidence."

"No, I mean it may be the murder weapon. Ugh!"

"No kidding? Don't try to stand up yet, Jack."

"I'm freezing my ass off down here."

"Okay," he said to the older man as he gripped me under one arm, "help me get him to the car."

"I don't need any help walking . . ." I said as they pulled me up, ". . . Jesus, it's cold . . . just getting to my feet."

"Are you sure you can make it to the car?"

"Yeah." I turned to the old man, still a little wobbly. "Did you see any of this happen?"

He shook his head. "I was doing some work on my engine." He pointed back down the dock toward the waterfall and the stream that feeds into the harbor. They were laced with ice. "I heard some shouting, came up on deck, and saw the two of you in the water and the *Andilar* heading toward the open water."

"Great. Did you call the Coast Guard?"

"Not yet. I wanted to get you out of the water first."

"Good thinking."

"I'll call them now, though, if you want."

"I'll use my cell phone," said Bailey.

I said, "Really? Your cell phone's waterproof?"

He pulled it out of his pocket. It was dripping wet. He shrugged. "Good point." He said to the old man, "Be sure to mention that they just assaulted two police officers."

"Screw that," I said. "Tell them it was attempted murder."

"You got it," said the old man. "Jeez, you're really shivering. You want me to get you a blanket?"

Bailey said, "There's one in the car."

I said to the old man, "I don't su-su-ppose you'd want to take us out after them, w-w-would you?"

He shook his head sadly. "Engine's not running."

"Th-th-that's okay. B-b-bad idea anyway."

"Even if it weren't," he explained unnecessarily, "we'd never catch them in my tub."

"Just c-c-call the Coast Guard," I said. "And give Detective Bailey your name and contact information." I looked at Bailey. "Aren't you c-c-cold?"

"A little. But I'm wearing Mormon underwear, remember? It keeps you safe from all *kinds* of danger."

"Apparently not *all* kinds or we'd have those b-b-bastards in custody now. And where's your g-g-gun?"

"One of them threw it overboard after us."

"Great. Okay, I'll be in the c-c-car."

"Shouldn't we secure the crime scene first?"

I shook my head. "The dock is secondary. The primary scene is that boat. But, yeah, call the department and have someone come out and take a look around." I turned to the old man. "You're going to have to stay until they get here and t-t-tell them what you know."

"Fine with me," he said. "It'll take a couple of hours at least before I can get my carburetor fixed."

"Okay," Bailey said. "We'd better go back to the station and tell Coletti what just—"

"The hell we w-w-will. We're g-g-going straight to the hospital."

"Scrud, Jack. Are you that bad off?"

"I don't know. But I *do* know that if I don't get myself checked out by an ER doctor, Jamie's going to k-kill me."

"We could commandeer a speed boat and go after them."

I shook my head. "We're not Holmes and Watson. We can't go running around, chasing after every p-possible suspect. Let the Coast Guard handle it." I turned back. "And next time you want me in on an interview? Let's do it at the station house where we won't get mugged."

He laughed. "You got it."

"Crap," I said to no one in particular as I walked away, "this is why I hate solving crimes."

"Jack?" Bailey said, stopping me. He pointed. "The car's over that way."

"Yeah, yeah. I would've found it eventually—there's only one other c-car in the lot." I turned. "Which reminds me—"

"Yeah, I'll have it impounded."

"Right. And what the hell does 'scrud' mean?"

He shrugged. "It's a Mormon swear word."

I laughed. "You people even have your own swear words?"

He smiled. "Flippin'-A, man." Then he told me what flip and scrud stood for.

"Interesting," I said. "Well, thanks for letting me in on the lingo. If you need me, I'll be in the f-flippin' car."

23

Bailey took me to the ER but got a call from the chief, who ordered him back to the scene, breaking yet another rule of police procedure: the first order of business, before doing any evidence gathering, or even securing the crime scene, is to provide medical attention to anyone who needs it.

A nice young nurse took me to a room with four curtained areas, gave me a gown and a robe and a blanket, and told me to undress. When I was done, she told me to wait for the doctor while she put my things in the dryer.

After about twenty minutes of sitting around trying not to think about the other patients or what was wrong with them, the doctor—a slim young intern who looked to be about Leon's age—showed up, made some irrelevant comment about my cough, then insisted on a CT scan, which I grudgingly put up with.

It wasn't long before Jamie showed up, closed the curtain behind her, and sat next to me on the bed and held my hand.

There were the usual exchanges about how I felt,

then she started asking me some, I thought, very odd questions.

"Jack? Who's the President of the United States?"

"What? What is this, current events?"

"Just answer the question."

She had a serious, medical look in her eye, which is when I realized the purpose of her interrogation.

I furrowed my brow. "Now let me think. I know this, but I just can't . . . You know, that reminds me of a joke . . ." I started to tell her the one about the three plastic surgeons who'd each worked miracles on an accident victim.

"Jack, just answer the question."

"Wait. You'll like this one, trust me."

I told her that the first surgeon bragged that he'd once had a patient who'd been disfigured when she went through a windshield in a car accident. He said, "There was nothing left but shredded skin and bone. Now she's a top model."

The second doctor said he could top that. His patient was a young farm boy who had been scouted by the Yankees as a starting pitcher until his throwing arm got torn off by a thresher. "I had nothing to work with but an empty shirtsleeve, some connective tissue, and a lot of heart. Last year that kid won the Cy Young Award."

The third doctor said he could top them both. His patient had been a dim-witted Texas rancher who one day rode his horse straight into an oncoming freight train. "I had nothing left to work with but three brain cells, a sphincter muscle, and a cowboy hat. Now he's the President of the United States."

She laughed then said, "So, I guess you *do* know who the President is, though you don't seem to care for him much."

"It's just a joke."

She said, "Okay. What are your dogs' names?"

"Are you kidding me?"

"No. Answer the question."

I hesitated. "That's funny. I can't seem to . . ."

"Jack, you seriously don't remember?"

"Well, I know one of them is bigger than the other, and he's kind of the color of old scotch, but their names . . ."

"Try to think."

"Oh, I know: Scotch and Soda? No, that's not it."

"Jack, this is important."

"I'm trying! Is it Frankie and . . ."

"Frankie and what?"

"Frankie and Johnny? No, I know, it's Turner and Hooch. Or is it Starsky and Hutch?" That's when I lost it.

"Very funny," she said.

"Well anyway, I'm not 'altered,' so don't worry. What have *you* been up to while I was getting conked?"

"Well, for one thing I went over the entire autopsy report on Rhoda Huckabee, and hang on to your hat, Jack—"

"What hat?"

"Just shut up and listen. She had pulmonary edema."

"So Huckabee *didn't* kill her."

"I didn't say that. I have no way of knowing what caused her pulmonary edema. It may have been related to the cerebral edema, which was the cause of death, it may not."

"Meaning?"

"If it was cardiogenic, meaning it was caused by a heart condition, then it could be unrelated to the cerebral edema. I can't say for sure. But due to the low levels of ADH in her blood I'd say that the pulmonary edema *may* have been caused by hyponatremic encephalopathy."

"In English, please."

She explained that the swelling, or edema, of the brain might have been the result of hyponatremia, based on higher or lower than normal levels of some things found in her blood at the time of death—ketones, ADH, and sodium—and said that this showed she had undiagnosed diabetes, which can cause thirst, and which could have been a causative factor for hyponatremia.

"And that could've all been precipitated by the *E. coli*?"

"I have no way of knowing that. I'd have to do another autopsy and look at her kidney tissue under a microscope and do a tissue section on her hypothalamus as well. The low ADH levels could have been caused by some pathology in the brain."

I shook my head. "Why wasn't any of that done at the first autopsy? I mean, why didn't anybody catch this?"

"Who knows? Maybe the ME was overworked."

"Like you're *not* overworked?"

She laughed. "Yes, but then *I* have three jobs."

I thought that over. "I know of two, what's the third?"

"Taking care of you. Anyway, the couple had a history of domestic violence complaints, there was bruising on her arms. Remember, Huckabee admitted that he shook her, though he claimed he was trying to wake her up. My guess is that the M.E. and the police felt the case was a slam dunk."

I kissed her. "Well, I'm glad you took another look at it. Have you told the victim's parents yet?"

"No, I've been busy worrying about you. But I *did*

inform the district attorney's office and they're discussing it."

"Discussing it? What does that mean?"

"You know exactly what it means."

I did. If the case were still at trial, the DA would have the options of either dropping the charges, or turning over this new, possibly exculpatory evidence to the defense. If Huckabee were still in prison, the evidence would give him grounds for a new trial, which wouldn't be automatic; it would require going through a long, possibly drawn-out appeals process. But having a jury verdict set aside after Huckabee had already done his time was more complicated, legally speaking, even if Jamie could say with a medical certainty that the murder charge was unwarranted in the first place.

I said, "How certain are you that she wasn't murdered?"

"I already told you, Jack, I can't tell. Not without doing a complete new autopsy, which would probably mean exhuming the body. But given the evidence I *do* have, all I can say is that it's quite possible that her death was due to medical reasons, not an act of homicide."

"So that's your expert medical opinion?"

She laughed. "For the third and last time—"

"Fine. Maybe it'll be enough to convince the Grants to let Tim's father donate a kidney." I thought it over. "I suppose a public apology from the DA is out of the question."

She shook her head. "It's possible, but very unlikely, especially with this new murder charge looming over his head. The NYPD was unable to locate his alibi witness, and now the DA says they just need one more piece of evidence to swear out an arrest warrant on him for the murder of Amy Frost."

"Which is another case of slam-dunkitis, if you ask me."

"Could be. Personally, I don't think they'll do much of anything about the old case until the current one is resolved. Now, what happened this morning at the harbor?"

I told her everything.

"Let me see your fingernails." I let her take my hands. "Well, whatever blood and tissue may have been under there has been removed by the detersive effect of the salt water."

"That figures," I said.

"Do you think that oar might be the murder weapon?"

"It's a possibility, but we'll have to see if the forensics lab can find anything that connects it to the victim. Though I imagine the water in the harbor would've 'detersed' that, too."

"Probably, though I can compare the size and shape of the oar to the head wound."

"That's a good idea, but the fact that Bright tried to escape indicates that he's guilty of something. Then again, if he has a drug habit, he could've just been trying to hide the fact that there were drugs on board the vessel. Still, he's a possible suspect. Has the Coast Guard found him yet?"

"I don't know. I've been too busy worrying about you."

"Well, don't worry," I said, coughing a little, "I'm fine. And how do you know it was undiagnosed?"

"How do I know *what* was undiagnosed?"

"Her diabetes."

"Oh, I checked her medical records. There was no mention of it. Plus, there was no insulin or syringes found at the scene. And you're not fine. First there's your Christmas cold, which defies medical science . . ." (I almost interrupted her to relate the memory I'd had about my mother, but didn't get the chance.) ". . . then there was your little demolition derby in the hospital parking lot, followed by hyponatremia, and now a case of hypo*therm*ia and a possible concussion. Jack, you may think you're impervious to danger, but—"

"I know I'm not, honey."

"Do you?"

"Yes, Doctor. I'm just as pervious as the next guy. That's one reason I hate getting involved in these facackta murder cases."

"Well, as far as this case goes, I think you're right. Maybe you should just let the police handle it from now on."

"Hah! With Chief Colbern at the helm? Fat chance. Isn't there some way you could convince the State Police to run interference and—?"

"Believe me, if I had any influence I'd use it. But I'm an ME, remember? Not a chief of detectives."

"Well, we'll just have to muddle through, then, I guess. Are the Russians still around?"

"One is in the state prison's hospital ward. The other two are in intensive care, under police guard. One of them even asked for a Polish priest to give him the last rites."

"Why a Polish priest? And is he really that bad off?"

She shrugged. "He *thinks* he is, and he's part-Polish."

"Huh. So's Karl. Maybe they're related."

"Probably. Why did you ask about the Russians?"

"I got a call from Karl today." I told her that he

might be in the Big Apple, and was trying to make things right with the Russian mob.

"Hmm. Do you think he's telling the truth?"

"You doubt my inner lie detector?"

"Sometimes. You did quite a job on them, you know."

"What was I supposed to do? They were shooting at me."

She squeezed my hand. "I know. But I hope you're not getting any more bright ideas. You think they might somehow be connected to the murder?"

"Who knows? They seem awfully interested in Karl."

"Yeah, why is that?" She wrinkled her brow.

"I don't know. He did *some*thing to piss them off. I'd love to find out what it was and if it's connected to this case. But like I said, I don't particularly like getting shot at and sapped, which is one reason I hate these facackta—"

"What's another reason? And what does facackta mean, exactly?"

I told her the other reason was that I just wanted to run my kennel and play with my dogs, and that facackta was a Yiddish word, which was a nicer way of saying that something was crappy or fouled up. Then I added, "Though Bailey would probably call the case 'scruddy' or 'flipped' up."

"I like your word a lot better. And where the hell do Bailey's words come from?"

"They're Mormon swear words."

She laughed. "You've got to be kidding."

"Apparently not."

She held my hand. "I think Bailey is pretty funny. He kind of reminds me of a puppy dog around you."

"He does?"

"Yeah, like he'd follow you anywhere and do anything for you. And since when do you speak Yiddish?"

"What? Oh, I *don't*. But when you live in New York for a while, you tend to pick up a few words here and there."

"Such as?"

"Schlep, shpritz, shtup, schmooze. When can I leave?"

"When Dr. Kaplan says you can. Not before. And how are you planning on getting home, anyway?"

"I'll just ask Flynn or Bailey to give me a ride."

She shook her head then smiled. "They've got better things to do than to keep shlepping you around."

I chuckled. "See? Everybody knows *that* one."

She nodded, thought of something, and laughed. "Three brain cells, a sphincter muscle, and a cowboy hat, huh?"

"That's right."

"Good one. Anyway, I've got a few things to do first, then I can drive you. But I have to come right back here."

"You work too much. Are you going to talk to the Grants? They're probably visiting Tim, or *will* be."

"I'll try."

"You want me to come talk to them with you?"

She tilted her head. "If I thought you wouldn't piss them off, I might, but I think you're too attached to—"

"You're probably right."

Her face got serious—very serious. "That reminds me. The lab work just came back and you're a six-point blood and tissue match."

I huffed at her. "Honey, I told you I'm not going to donate one of my—"

"I know, I know."

"I mean what happens if, God forbid, you or Annabelle or Leon needed a new kidney? Or one of my nieces or my nephew?"

"So you *have* thought about it."

"Yeah," I grumped. "I've thought about it."

"Really?"

"Yes. Thanks to you and Maureen. It's going to be even worse now that I know I'm a six-point match for that poor kid. How'd his surgery go?"

She hesitated. "The new graft is in, and there were no complications with *that,* but the pediatric nephrologist thinks Tim won't be able to survive another surgery, which puts his chances of survival pretty low."

"Oh no."

She took my hand. "It's pretty serious."

"Don't tell me."

She took a deep breath. "They put him in a medically induced coma."

"Oh *no.*"

Her eyes got a little wet. "It looks like the only way he'll be stable enough to survive the transplant."

"And we had such a good talk the last time I was here."

"I'm sorry."

"You have to convince his grandparents to—"

"I know, Jack." She stood up. "Meanwhile, I have to take care of *you.* Are you hungry?"

"Yeah, I'm starving, actually. Bailey roped me into this debacle before I had a chance to eat breakfast."

"Well, you have to eat, Jack. Do you want me to have one of the nurses bring you something?"

"What, like some hospital Jell-O or a cardboard-flavored chicken sandwich? No thanks. What I really need right now is a rare T-bone steak and a shot of Macallan's with one cube of ice."

She smiled. "Would you settle for a burrito supreme?"

I smiled. "You're going to send a nurse to Taco Bell?"

"It's right around the corner. You love Mexican food. I'm sure Maureen would be happy to go."

"Right. She'll butter me up with tacos so I'll change my mind about giving up one of my kidneys. How long has he got?"

"A few days, maybe a week."

"Aw, Jesus."

She knew what I was thinking. As she went to the door she said, "It's *your* decision, honey. Take your time to think it over."

"Okay," I said. "And make it two soft taco supremes and a chalupa, with Baja sauce. Oh, and a small Dr. Pepper, no ice, and have her bring me some of those packets of hot sauce. The hot kind, not the mild ones."

"And you'll drink some Gatorade with your tacos, not just the Dr. Pepper?"

"Yeah, I'll drink some flippin' Gatorade."

After she left my mind wasn't on the tacos and Gatorade. I was thinking about how attached I was to my kidneys. I couldn't just sit and stew over it, though. I had to hope that Jamie could get the Grants to see the light, which would let me off the hook.

I took a deep breath and forced my mind back on the case. I wondered how I could get my hands on a cassock and collar, and—since the patient/prisoner would probably recognize *me*—I was wondering whom I could talk into impersonating a Polish father. And no good Catholic would be likely to volunteer.

Hmmm, I thought, maybe I should ask a Mormon.

24

Jamie dropped me off at the kennel then went back to the hospital, which gave me ample opportunity to go through her new closet, looking for her long, black Donna Karan coat. I was in the middle of my search when I got a call from someone who claimed *not* to be Lance Burton. Several times.

"Yeah, I get it," I said, sitting on the bed. "You're not Lance Burton, you just play him on TV."

He laughed. "Just so you know that anything I say should not be attributed to Mr. Burton. Now, what's the situation?"

I explained the basic premise and he thought it over.

"Well," he said, "there are any number of ways to open hidden doors electronically. The basic idea is to do it while the audience is looking somewhere else. For instance, there might be a flat panel on the floor, with a copper electrode wired to activate the door mechanism. You might have another electrode on the sole of your shoe so no one could open the door accidentally by simply stepping on the panel."

"I think I got you. How would a person come by two such electrodes?"

He laughed. "You'd have to talk to an actual magician."

"You mean like the real Lance Burton."

"That's right. And he's supposed to be onstage in a few minutes. Or you could talk to an electronics expert."

Like Tom Huckabee, I thought, then I asked him how to make ghosts appear and disappear, and he gave me a brief explanation, involving mirrors, lasers, and fog machines.

"That may work on stage," I said, "but we're talking about the third story of a mansion on the coast of Maine."

"Same-same," he said, "just on a smaller scale."

"And I guess I'd have to talk to the real Lance Burton to get any info on where such equipment could be had, right?"

"Yeah," he chuckled, "but the real Lance Burton is doing a dress rehearsal right now, and is locked inside a tank of water. Plus, he would never talk to you about it or he'd be drummed out of the magician's union."

"Wait. You mean there really *is* a magician's union?"

"Figure of speech," he said. "It's more like a secret brotherhood. And we prefer the term, illusionists. Anyway, I'm supposed to emerge from that tank in about two minutes, so we'll have to save the rest of our discussion for later."

"So, you're not in the tank now?"

He laughed. "No, I'm in my dressing room."

"Well, thanks, Lance."

"You're welcome. And I'm not Lance Burton."

"Sorry, I forgot."

"Jack," said Mrs. Murtaugh, appearing in the doorway as I hung up, "there's someone here to drop off some dogs."

"Okay. What dogs?"

"I don't know. Two Doberman pinschers?"

"Holy cow!" I said, leaping to my feet. "They're going to be staying here?"

"Yes, but you have to be careful. They were staying with Kirk Collins and one of the dogs bit him."

"Serves him right," I said, going past her. "That Nazi bastard deserves to get bit by every dog he meets."

"I know, but Jack!"

I danced down the stairs and raced through the living room. Frankie and Hooch jumped up and followed me as I grabbed my parka and ran outside.

The blond Nazi, with a choirboy face, stood beside his green van, holding a bandaged hand against his chest.

I shook my head and said, "What you'd try on them this time, the baseball bat or the alpha rollover?"

"I retired the bat, if it's any of your business. One of them growled at me, so I gave him a leash correction."

"Okay," I said with a sigh, "that was your first mistake. What was your second?"

"It's no mistake, Field. I threw him on his back and yelled 'No!' in his face. He needed to learn a lesson."

"Looks to me like you're the one who got the lesson. You're lucky he didn't bite your nose off. And didn't I once tell you that the alpha theory is false, which makes the alpha rollover not just abusive but insane?"

"Yeah, but you're full of crap."

"I may be full of crap," I said, "but I'm not the one who needs a tetanus shot."

"Look, do you want to keep these dogs here or not? Because my next stop is the local shelter."

"Of course I'll keep them here. And what do you want to bet I don't get bit?"

"Sure," he said with a scowl, "you're all peace and love and moonbeams. Good luck."

"No," I said, "I'm someone who respects a dog's true nature, which has nothing to do with—"

"Just take the dogs, do you mind? Spare me another lecture on your stupid moonbeam philosophy, okay?"

"Okay," I said, "get in the car."

He was shocked. "But you're gonna need help getting them out of the back and keeping them under control."

"Maybe so, but you'll just antagonize them, so butt out."

"Okay by me," he said, going to the door.

"And, don't worry. I'll be fine."

The truth is, I was in a tough spot. I didn't know the dogs and they didn't know me. I could certainly have used some help, but Farrell was on the afternoon rounds and Leon was late getting home from school. And there was no way I'd trust Kirk Collins with these dogs. They'd just been through an emotional ordeal with him, which meant I was dealing with a couple of well-tuned, high-energy, German-engineered biting machines—with black and tan fur and huge teeth—who were in a state of intense emotional tension. Translation: they were extremely ready, willing, and able to bite anything that moved, namely me. On top of all that, they were both unneutered males, as were Starsky and Hutch. The kennel grounds was *their* turf and they were already starting to get wound up about meeting two potential rivals. Male canine harmones and pheromones can be very potent.

I said, "Are they loose back there or in crates?"

"You think I'm crazy? They're crated. I'd have put muzzles on 'em too, but I've only got one good hand."

"As long as they're crated I'm not worried," I lied.

"What's the matter, Field," said Collins, smiling over the doorframe, "your theories don't hold water in the real world? You can talk the talk but you can't walk the walk?"

I'll be walking over your face in a minute, I wanted to say but didn't. "Just shut up and get in the car."

"It's your funeral."

I put Frankie and Hooch in a down/stay, then went around to the back of the van. I opened the door and was met with some pretty terrifying sounds. The two Dobies were in steel crates in the back. Their leashes were on, but they weren't muzzled. In fact, their teeth were itching for my flesh.

What had Karl said to call them off? I couldn't remember the safety word. I knew it was a woman's name and it started with a *T*, or was it a *D*? Great. This has to happen just when I'd been putting off making a payment on my life insurance.

I climbed in the back, sat cross-legged on the floor and said, *"Guten Hunde! Ja! Ja!* Such *guten Hunde!"*

Rrrrrrr. They weren't buying it.

Most aggression is based on fear. Even Collins's aggression toward the Dobies was fear-based. So to make the boys less fearful I rolled over on my back, and scooched my butt closer to their crates, continuing to praise them in German. They didn't know what to make of it or me.

Neither did Kirk Collins, who was watching me from the safety of the front seat.

"What the flip are you doing?" he said (though he didn't use the word "flip"). "You *want* them to think they're alpha?"

"Shut up and play with the radio or something, okay?"

I got close to their crates and just lay there for a little while, praising them in their native tongue. This calmed them down a little, but not enough for me to feel safe. I tried a few women's names on them, Trixie, Dolores, Thelma, but it had no effect. Maybe it didn't start with a T or a D. Maybe it just had a T or a D in it. What was it?

I put my hands up to, but not inside, their crates and they snarled and tried to bite my fingers off through the bars. Damnit! *What was that name?*

Oh, well, I thought, I'll have to just keep praising them and hope I remember it. Then for some strange reason a song started running through my head. No, not a song, just a tune. A nice, catchy tune. What was it called? Part of the lyric came to me, something about a jolly swagman. What was that from? "Once a jolly swagman sat beside a . . ." something.

"I've got it," I said, " 'Waltzing Matilda!' " As soon as I said it the dogs stopped growling. Then I used the German pronunciation, saying it softly so Collins couldn't hear me. I put my fingers up to the bars again and instead of trying to bite them they began licking me. "Mathilde, *Guten Hunde!!*"

"Hey, how'd you calm them down like that?" Collins asked.

"Easy. They like Australian folk songs."

"You're nuts, you know that?"

The dogs growled again when they heard his voice.

"Yeah, I'm nuts, all right. Nuts about these magnificent doggies. And keep your mouth shut. Your voice is aggravating them."

"Fine."

"And I don't suppose you have any tennis balls up there?"

I heard him shuffling around up front and then two tennis balls arced over the front seat, bounced off the crates, then landed on top of my parka.

I grabbed them and said, "Thanks." Collins wasn't a total idiot after all, just a mean-spirited, gutless wonder.

I put each tennis ball through the bars and let the dogs take them with their mouths, which they were happy to do—their jaws had been aching to bite something. Then I slowly and deliberately got onto my knees, continuing to praise the boys, and continuing to keep a sharp eye on their body language. They bit their tennis balls a little harder as I moved around, but they didn't drop them or start growling at me.

I stood up, hunched over so I didn't knock my head on the van's ceiling, then opened both crates at the same time and the dogs came shooting out, wagging their stubby tails.

This was the moment of truth. I was trapped inside a small space with two supposedly vicious dogs, with nothing between their teeth and my hands, testicles, and kidneys but a couple of used tennis balls and a woman's name.

"Mathilde! *Guten Hunde!*" I said, slowly reaching for their leashes. *"Ja! Ja! Guten!"*

I got hold of the leashes and backed toward the door, praising them. They followed me.

"Pure luck," I heard from up front.

"No talking," I said, in a silly, singsong voice.

"Yeah, whatever," he muttered. Then I heard the engine start as I led the dogs out the door and onto the snowy driveway. Maxim and Fritz were leaping around, so happy and proud of their tennis balls I almost had to laugh.

I came around the passenger side of the van, reminded Starsky and Hutch to stay, even though they couldn't see me from where they were lying in the snow, then rapped on the passenger side window.

Collins leaned over and rolled it down.

I said, "You got some paperwork for me to sign?"

"What paperwork?" he snapped.

"I know it's hard, but try to keep the tone of your voice light and happy, would you mind?"

"Fine, Mr. Moonbeam!" he said in a Sesame Street tone. "There's no paperwork! But if you need me to write something up for you! I can have it delivered by UPS tomorrow!" He scooted back to the driver's seat and put the van in gear.

"Don't send it UPS," I groaned.

Before I could finish he started backing up the van, which meant I had to remind Starsky and Hutch to stay again.

Their butts were wiggling, and Frankie was whining a little, but they held the stay. When I turned back, the van was halfway up the drive.

I looked down at Max and Fritz and said, "I never get anything when people send it UPS."

They just looked up at me, wagging their stubs, happy as hell with their tennis balls.

I love dogs.

I ran them in a fast heel down to the play yard. I didn't know the German word for heel, so I just got them on my left side, patted my left leg excitedly, and started running. They ran right next to me the whole way.

I left them there and got Frankie and Hooch back up to the house and settled by the hearth. Then I grabbed my cell phone, and went back down to the play yard to see if I could get the Dobermans to play fetch with me.

When I came through the gate they were happy to see me, as though I were their new best friend, so I patted my chest and said, "Hup!" and they both jumped up on me, still holding the tennis balls with their teeth and wagging their stubs.

"Guten Hunde!" I said, then twisted sideways and they jumped off. Then I made a quick downward motion with my right hand and said, *"Aus!"* and they spit out their tennis balls.

That's when I realized this was going to be easier than I'd thought. Tennis balls, the universal language of dogs.

I reached down, picked up the balls and they backed away, happily waiting for me to throw one. I made a few feints with one of the balls, saying, "Wait! Wait!" Then I threw it and said, "Okay!" and they raced after it, trailing their leashes. Like I'd told Bailey, these were some damn fine animals. Their muscles were like coiled springs and their movements and reflexes reminded you not of their wild cousin the wolf as much as a gazelle or a cheetah, or both.

I took turns, tying one up for a few minutes while I played fetch with the other, periodically trying out a few commands in English, using standard training body language and hand signals, and throwing in the few commands I actually knew in German, like *"aus!"* and *"platz."*

In less than twenty minutes I had them obeying all the basic commands in English. And not just obeying them, I had them loving it. This was just a bridge, mind you. And I had no illusions that I was actually doing any training. All I was doing was conditioning them to take commands from me, and not because I cared anything about getting them to sit or lie down or stay. What I really wanted was to get them to the point where, after I let them sniff a sample of the victim's blood, they'd obey my command to go find more of that smell, which would hopefully lead me to the murder weapon.

I finished the session and let them run around on their own for a while, then I stood by the gate and called Jamie.

"Can you get me a sample of the victim's blood?"

"I suppose so."

"Tonight?"

"Okay."

"Did you talk to the Grants?

"Of course."

"And?"

"They're thinking it over."

"Well, that's a step in the right direction."

"Is that all?"

I took a moment. "Are you pissed off about something?"

"You mean other than the fact that you're barking commands at me?"

"Sorry about that. I was just in the middle of—"

"Oh, and let me think," she said with an icy tone. "Is there anything else? I know there was *some*thing . . ."

"Jamie, just spill it, okay?"

"There you go, barking at me again."

"Jamie, sweetheart," I said, softening my tone, "please tell me what you're upset about?"

"Oh, nothing. Just the fact that you're having secret meetings with your ex-girlfriend and not telling me."

I started to laugh but squelched myself, realizing it wouldn't go over very well at that exact moment, so I turned it into what I thought was a convincing cough.

She said, "Are you *laughing* at me?"

"Honey, I have a cold. I was just coughing."

"Sounded like you were laughing to me."

"Anyway, yes, Kristin and Jen came by the other day, but I wasn't hiding anything from you. It just slipped my mind. And who told you they were here?"

"Mrs. Murtaugh. And how could it slip your mind?"

"I don't know. It just did. In fact, I was about to tell you in bed the other night, then other things happened."

She huffed. "Well, it'll be a while before those other things happen again if you keep hiding things from me."

"I wasn't hiding anything. I told you, it slipped—"

"Forget it. We can talk more about it on our way to my mom's house tonight for dinner."

"We're having dinner at your mom's tonight?"

Oops. There was a stony silence.

"You mean *that* slipped your mind too?"

"I've got a cold," I offered again, "a lot of things have been slipping my—"

"What? Like the fact that we're engaged? Has that been slipping your mind too, Jack?"

This again? I wanted to say. "Things have been hectic, you know that. We're doing it sometime in October, right?"

" 'Doing it?' Is it some kind of chore to you?"

"No, of course not. Honey, I thought we were going to discuss this later."

"Sometimes I wonder if you really want to marry me."

I took a deep breath and switched out of defensive mode into apologetic. "Please don't be upset with me, sweetheart. I'm sorry I forgot to tell you about Kristin and Jen dropping by. And I'll be happy to set an exact date anytime you want. And, yes, I really want to marry you. More than anything."

"Really?"

"Yes."

"Okay," she said. "And we'll set the new date to-night? Because we have to do it soon."

"Yes. By the way, where's that black Donna Karan coat of yours? The one that buttons all the way up with no collar?"

"In the downstairs closet. Why?"

I told her what I had in mind.

She laughed. That was a good sign. "Fine," she said, still laughing, "and I wish I could be there to see how this *comes* out."

"I have to find out why these guys are after Karl, and whether it's connected to the case. He won't talk to the cops but he'll confess to a priest."

"Even a fake one. Fine, you can use my coat. But what are you going to do about the collar and rosary?"

"We'll think of something. There's my other line."

"Okay, we'll talk more later though, right?"

"Yes, honey. I love you."

"I love you too. But don't forget, we're setting the date tonight."

"I won't forget."

Bailey was on the other line.

"Jack, I've got good news and some bad news." He sounded deadly serious.

"Okay, what's the good news? Is your siren on?"

"Yeah. I'll explain about that when I get to the bad news. The good news is Huckabee's agreed to talk to you."

"Cool. When and where?"

"Tonight at the Whale's Tooth Pub. He agreed to let Jamie come, but he doesn't want me or any other cops there. It has to be totally off the record."

"Oh, man." I explained about dinner with Jamie's mom then said, "That's okay. She'll understand."

"Are you sure? I can try to set up another time."

"Don't worry about it. What's the bad news?"

"Leon's been arrested."

"What?" I yelled. "What the hell for?" When Max and Fritz heard the sound in my voice they stopped what they were doing, came running back to me, and immediately sat, staring at me. It was almost as if they were waiting for instructions on who I wanted them to kill. *Good boys!*

"You'd have to ask the chief."

"Chief *Colbern* had Leon arrested?"

"Yep. I'm on my way now to pick you up and drive you down there. That's why I've got the siren going—"

"He's really crossed the line this time."

"No shit."

"Wait a minute, Detective, did you just say what I *think* you said?"

He let out a breath. "Yeah. Some things need stronger language and this is one of them."

"Okay," I laughed, "take it easy. It'll be fine. I think I hear your siren now."

"I should be there in two minutes. Oh, and we got the combination to Chris Bright's safe. Finally."

"Good. Anything probative in it?"

"Yeah. A letter from Amy Frost, telling him she was pregnant, and hinting that she wanted a lot of money to make the whole thing go away."

"Wow. Except she wasn't pregnant. The autopsy report—"

"I know," he said, "I read it. Seems like the professor wasn't the only one running a con on the Bright family."

"Well, that's a pretty good motive for murder."

"Yep. Let's hope the Coast Guard can track him down."

"Okay. Let me get these dogs put into the kennel and I'll be ready to roll when you get here. Oh, and don't let me forget to grab Jamie's Donna Karan coat before we go."

"What?"

"I'll explain on the way."

25

On the way to Camden I called Greg Sinclair, a State Police detective I'd worked with, and told him what was going on with Colbern's mishandling of the case, and his harassment campaign against me, Jamie, and now Leon.

"Ah, that's a bitch, Jack. I'm sorry. I can present it to the brass, but they probably won't be able to decide anything until Monday."

"Screw that," I said, "I want you to come to Camden and put the bastard in handcuffs right now."

He laughed. "I'd love to but I like my job too much."

"Fine," I said, "I'll get Flynn to do it."

"Sounds good to me."

"And you'll pass this on?"

"Oh, yeah. It'd help if the state medical examiner could express her doubts about Colbern's handling of the case."

"You mean 'mishandling,'" I said. "And don't worry, Jamie's already on board, or will be as soon as she hears about Colbern's latest tactic."

"All right, Jack. I'll see what I can do."

I hung up then called Jamie to tell her I couldn't come to dinner with her because I had to meet with Huckabee, but got her voice mail and left a message about what was going on with Leon and my meeting at the Whale's Tooth Pub.

At the same time Bailey was on his phone, getting information on Leon's whereabouts and the status of his case.

While he was doing that I called Flynn, told him about the situation, and he agreed to meet us at the station house.

"Okay, you're not going to believe this," Bailey said, once he'd finished his call. "I just spoke to Steve Thomas, he's the arresting officer, and he's a good friend of mine. Leon was arrested for having an open container."

"Container of what?"

"Beer."

"That's ridiculous."

"Yeah. Apparently Steve was told by the chief to keep a certain 'underage Negro' under surveillance."

"He referred to Leon as an underage Negro?"

"I'm afraid so."

"Who *talks* like that?" I took a deep breath. "Go on."

"And Steve was told to bust him for the slightest infraction, crossing the street against the light, smoking, roughhousing, anything. So Steve was sitting on the high school parking lot, watching Leon to see what, if anything, he might do wrong. Leon's waiting for the school bus and he apparently decides to be a good citizen and pick up some empty cans by the side of the road and drop them in the trash."

"And one of them was an empty beer can?"

"It gets better. Steve's a good guy, and a good cop,

so he's not going to arrest Leon for picking up trash. But he gets a radio call from the chief, who's in another car down the road, watching this through binoculars. He tells Steve to bust Leon, Steve puts up a fuss, the chief threatens to fire him, and your kid's in a jail cell as we speak."

I blew my lid. "He's in a jail cell? He's sixteen and they put him in a cell? Doesn't the Camden PD have a juvenile holding area?"

"Sure, we do. The illegal incarceration came as a result of direct orders from the chief. Apparently he doesn't know the proper procedure for holding juvenile suspects."

I smiled. "Tough. Ignorance of the law is no excuse. We've got him now. If a New York cop did that to a juvie suspect he'd lose his job in a heartbeat."

He sighed. "We can only hope . . ."

"Speaking of hope, I hope you have a Polaroid."

"Of course," he smiled. "And lots of film."

"Good. The more evidence the better. Plus the photos will make a nice keepsake for Leon."

"A keepsake? Wouldn't he rather forget the whole thing?"

"Nah," I smiled. "He's going to get a lot of mileage out of this. He'll milk it for all it's worth. The only one I'm really worried about is *moi*."

"Why? What did you do?"

"Nothing. It's what I *want* to do." I looked at him. "You promise to keep an eye on me? Because all I can think of right now is how good Colbern's fat head is going to look when I'm done with it."

"Flippin'-A, man," he said, with his eyes burning. (And he didn't say "flippin.'")

* * *

Flynn met us outside the building for a brief confab, then he drove off, promising to set up the frame we were planning for the chief.

Bailey and I went inside, past the front desk, and took Polaroids of Leon inside his jail cell.

"Yo, Jack!" he said, holding the bars. "You gotta get me outta here!"

"Don't worry, Leon. I just have to sign some paperwork and you'll be released in ten minutes, tops."

"Yo, but I didn't do nothin.' "

"I know you didn't. This is all my fault."

"Your fault? Aw, man! So *you're* responsible?"

"In a way, yeah. Sorry." I looked at Bailey. "I told you he was going to milk this." To Leon I said, "Just sit tight for a few minutes and I'll get you released."

We went out front, where there were a few civilians sitting in plastic chairs, waiting for information, or to release friends or loved ones. One of them looked familiar, though he was hunched over as if asleep. His hair, the color of French bread, gave him away.

I signed the release form, promised to make sure Leon made his court appearance, and in a few minutes another officer brought Leon out and returned his backpack.

"Yo, this is police brutality, man!"

I smiled but said, "Knock it off, Leon. They were only doing what they were told."

My words had no effect. He stood glaring around the station. "It's because I'm black, ain't it? That's why you all did this to me! You wouldn'ta done nothing like this to no white kid!"

"Leon," I said, patiently, trying not to laugh, "relax. I told you it's not their fault."

"Relax? How am I suppose to relax when there ain't no justice in this world for the black man? A'ight?"

"Leon, you're absolutely right. It's a rotten system. Just shut up now, or you'll ruin our chances at a lawsuit."

His eyes brightened. "Yo, that's it, yo!" He looked around and said, "I'm gonna sue all your asses for this!"

"Okay, let's talk about it in the car."

It was at this moment that Chief Colbern decided to show his grotesque face. He strolled into the room and said, "What's all the commotion in here?"

"It's nothing, Chief," said the desk sergeant.

"I thought I heard someone yelling." He looked at Leon, then back at the sergeant. "Is this Negro causing trouble?"

The room was suddenly still. I could feel my blood boil. Then I felt Bailey grab my arm. "Easy, Jack," he said.

Leon stared at the chief. "What? What did you just call me, you mother—?"

I put a hand over his mouth.

The chief said, "You giving me lip, boy?" He looked around the room. "You all saw this Negro sassing me."

"Uh, no, Chief," said the desk sergeant. "None of us saw anything like that, sir."

Someone said, "All I see is an asshole in a cheap suit."

The chief whirled around. "Who said that?"

No one spoke.

"If no one tells me who said that, you're all fired."

Bailey raised his hand. "It was me, Chief."

Before Colbern could say anything, someone else raised a hand and said, "No, it was me."

"No, Chief," said the desk sergeant, raising his hand. "I said it."

In short order everyone in the room, including all

the civilians except me and Leon, had a hand in the air, claiming to be the one who'd made the crack.

"The thing is, Chief," Bailey said sadly, "besides not following proper procedure in how the kid was incarcerated, and besides detaining him on a made-up charge, you simply don't refer to a black kid as a Negro these days."

Colbern's face went red. "I want your badge. Now!"

Bailey pulled his jacket back, unhooked his badge from his belt, and threw it on the floor at the chief's feet.

Before the chief could reach down to pick it up, Bailey's badge was joined by those of every other cop there. A few of the civilians even threw their driver's licenses at him.

Leon was smiling now. "That's what *I'm* talkin' about!"

The chief took a moment, then picked up Bailey's badge. He left the others on the floor. "I'm going to overlook this from the rest of you. But let me tell you people one thing, there are gonna be some changes made around here."

The hunched over man stood up and held out a miniature tape recorder. "You've got *that* right, Chief," he said.

"Hey, Otis," I said to him. "I *thought* that was you."

"Yeah, a friend of yours gave me a call."

Good old Sheriff Flynn, I thought.

The chief glared at Otis. "You don't scare me, Barnes," he said, "with your piddling little weekly rag."

Otis shrugged. "This is one time when I'll be happy to let the rest of the state's media out-scoop me. It might even make the AP wire."

Leon said, "That's what *I'm* talkin' about!" He

looked around the room. "I'm chill with you all." He looked at the chief. "Except this fool."

"Thanks, kid," said the sergeant, smiling. "Sorry we had to put you through this."

"That's a'ight," he smiled. "Now I got me plenty of ammo for a million dollar lawsuit!"

"Don't get ahead of yourself, Leon," I said.

"Nah, you can't bring me down now, Pops. I'm sittin' on top of the world."

Bailey and I took Leon with us to the hospital. He was smiling the whole way, though I still had a sour feeling in the pit of my stomach. That feeling went away the next morning when I made a phone call to Flynn.

I don't know all the details, but here's what he told me:

As Chief Colbern got in his car to go home that evening he didn't notice the open bottle of whiskey that was sitting in the back seat of his car, in open view.

When he got to the city limits he was pulled over by a Rockland County Sheriff's vehicle. The deputy who stopped him—a young black woman named Trudy Compton—saw the open container and wrote him a ticket for the violation.

The chief became incensed, used some foul language, including some racial slurs and some inappropriate, gender-related comments, and Trudy called for back up, the chief was handcuffed, taken to Rockland County Jail, where he had to spend the night because his paperwork was "lost" until the next morning. He had to share a cell with a Negro.

Now, that's what *I'm* talking about.

And just so you know? The man he shared the cell with was Trudy Compton's brother, a law student who thought it would be fun to get an up close look at the American justice system in action.

But I'm getting ahead of myself again. Here's what happened at the hospital:

26

Jamie's Donna Karan coat was a little loose on Detective Bailey, though I thought it made him look even more like a priest. He put it on in the parking lot and buttoned it all the way up to hide the fact that we didn't have a priest's collar for him. I asked him if he had a Bible handy.

He said, "No. I've got a Triple-Combination, though." He explained that it was three books of Mormon scripture, put into one volume, and was bound in Corinthian leather. He got it out of the glove box and showed it to me.

"Well, it doesn't have a cross embossed on the cover, but it'll have to do. Let's go inside."

Leon had his schoolbooks with him so we left him in the waiting room to do his homework. Or tried to.

"Yo, Jack," he complained, "I ain't got no homework."

"Real English, please. You're not unjustly incarcerated anymore, so you can knock off the Ebonics."

"Yes, sir," he said, putting on a phony "white" accent. "I was just saying that I don't actually have any homework to do, sir, and that—shit, I forgot! I got me a book on the underground railroad from the liberry today."

"Good, read that. And watch your language."

"Yes, sir," he said. "I should have said the 'library.' " Then he threw himself into one of the plastic chairs and started digging through his backpack.

While Bailey and I made our way toward the doctors' lounge I explained Leon's theory about a possible tunnel under the Bright mansion.

He shook his head. "That sounds pretty unlikely."

"Maybe. But every other explanation for how the killer escaped undetected is *more* than unlikely, it's impossible."

"Sherlock Holmes again," he said, nodding. "Why are we going to the doctors' lounge?"

"Because I want to be in the room with you when you talk to the patient. He's seen me before, but I figure with a doctor's smock, a surgical mask, and your glasses on, he won't recognize me. I was thinking I might even shave my beard off while you get into character. It's right over here."

I got out a credit card and picked the lock.

He sighed. "I hesitate to ask, but how do you know your way around so well?"

I popped the door open and said, "I wouldn't want to disturb your Mormon moral values, Detective, but yes—Jamie and I have fooled around in here a few times."

We went inside and he said, "My Mormon moral values don't apply to Gentiles, so don't worry."

"Gentiles?"

"That's how we refer to non-Mormons."

"Even Jews are referred to us Gentiles?"

"Yep."

"Wow. That Joseph Smith was pretty creative. He not only makes up his own Bible he—"

"He didn't make it up, he translated it. Look, can we not have a religious debate, please? I'm already feeling a little awkward about impersonating a Catholic priest. How do you know so much about our church?"

I explained that I spent my childhood summers at my grandmother's farm in Eagle, Idaho. "I also dated a Mormon girl in college for a while. She used to flip my brains out, if you know what I mean."

"I really don't want to."

"Why? She was a lot of fun."

"Can you stop trying to piss me off and just get this over with? I don't even know what I'm supposed to do."

I opened Jamie's locker, found a smock, a Lady Schick, and some aloe vera, went to the sink, and while I shaved I gave Bailey the lowdown on how the last rites are performed.

"I think I can fake the confession," he said, "but there's no way I can fake the last rites."

"Don't worry," I said, splashing water on my face to rinse off the aloe vera. "It'll never get that far." I grabbed a paper towel and dried my face. "While you're conning him into telling us about Karl, I'll pretend to look at his chart. Once we've got the information," I said, putting on the smock, "I'll give you a signal, you tell him he's going to be fine and God forgives him, and we get the hell out of there. How do I look?"

He tilted his head. "I think you're going to need to try again later with a real razor. But the surgical mask ought to hide most of the damage. And I would've never guessed you had a cleft chin. Why do you wear a beard when you've got a Cary Grant chin like that?"

"More like Robert Mitchum," I corrected him. "And it's a bitch to shave."

He laughed. "Now I'm pissing *you* off."

"A little."

"I'll have to file that for future reference when I want to get under *your* skin." He made a notation mark in the air. "Sensitive about his chin."

"Sure," I said. "You want me to tell you some more about that Mormon girl? She had these really big—"

"No! I've had enough locker room talk."

"Yeah, me too. All right, let's do this thing."

He looked back at the sink. "Aren't you going to clean Jamie's razor and put it back?"

"Hah! You should get a look at what she does to *my* razors." We went to the door. "And I was about to say she had 'really big eyes.' Here, give me your glasses."

We went up to intensive care where we found a young uniformed cop, sitting in a metal chair with padded arms and seat, guarding the room and reading a gun magazine. He recognized Bailey, who asked him if a priest had come to visit yet. He said no they hadn't found one who could speak Polish. He let us go right in, with minimal conversation.

"Nice coat," was all he said as Bailey went past.

"It's a Donna Karan," I said.

Bailey turned around. "You can't see it under his mask, but he's got a rugged, cleft chin."

"Un-huh," said the cop.

Then, before I closed the door I heard him say to himself, "Cheese, seems like you can just never predict who's gonna turn out to be gay these days."

The room was dark and quiet except for the sounds of dual respirators and heart monitors.

Bailey leaned over to me and whispered, "How do I know which of them asked for the priest?"

"Just stand between the beds, cross yourself, say a *pax vobiscum* and see who looks up and grabs your hand."

He shook his head. "You're a very mean man."

"These guys are both killers, Detective. I save all my pity for the families of their victims."

I have to admit, though, seeing the damage I'd done to these two guys, and worrying that one or both of them might actually croak because of me, even though they wouldn't have hesitated to kill me, and, in fact, had tried to do just that, brought my Catholic guilt back in spades and made me want to tug on Bailey's sleeve and say, "Forgive me father, for I have sinned."

He went to the beds and crossed himself. The patient on the right opened his eyes and reached out his hand as far as the police restraints and the IV tube would let him. Bailey leaned over and pulled the man's oxygen mask down.

"Ksiadz?" said the patient.

"Um . . . yes, my son?"

"You are nots Polish?"

"No, sorry, we couldn't, there wasn't a Polish priest available. Are you ready to confess your sins before God?"

"Yes, *Ksiadz.*" He prepared himself to confess. "When I was fifteen my father dieds and our family needed moneys."

I coughed and Bailey looked at me, then back at the patient and said, "Excuse me just a minute, my son."

Bailey came back to me and whispered, "What?"

"Tell him God knows all his sins and that if he renounces them all now he'll be forgiven. Otherwise we'll be here in time for a real priest to show up."

He looked down at the chart I was holding. "Is he serious? What's his chart say?"

"How do I know? I can't see anything with these damn glasses of yours."

"Yeah, and I can't see anything with*out* them. How do I get him to talk about Karl?"

"Improvise! And hurry it up!"

He shook his head, sighed, and went back into character. "It's very serious, my son." He looked back at me. "The doctor says you could go at any moment." Then he encouraged him to renounce all his sins at once.

The patient said he did renounce them.

"Good, my son. Now, who did you come here to kill and why?"

"His name is Andreyev Gregori. He was a . . . I don't know the word in English. In Polish we say *'paser.'* In Russian, is *'spekulant.'* "

"And what does a *paser* or *spekulant* do?"

"He finds a buyer for stolens property."

Bailey nodded. "Like jewels, diamonds?"

The patient nodded.

Bailey said, "We call that a 'fence' in English. Was this man Gregori supposed to fence the jewels that were stolen from his employers?"

He shook his head. "Don't know. He stole moneys from boss six years ago. When boss hears about murder in news and sees Andreyev's picture, he thinks is up to old tricks and wants him dead." He sighed. "Now *I* die instead."

I coughed.

Bailey said, "Just a moment, my son." He came back over to me. "Now what?"

"Tell him I was looking at the wrong chart, that he's going to be fine, and his *friend* is going to die. Then let's get the hell out of here. These glasses are killing my eyes."

He shook his head. "Like I said before, Jack—you're a very mean man."

"Just do it."

He went back to the patient, crossed himself, muttered some fake Latin, and left the man with a smile on his face.

On the way out I told the uniformed cop that the patient wouldn't be needing a priest after all, then gave Bailey his glasses back and we scooted down the hall.

"Real nice, Jack," he said while we waited for the elevator. "What if that man actually dies without getting a chance to confess to a real priest?"

"What do you care? He's going to hell anyway unless he gets baptized in a Mormon temple, right?"

He shook his head. "You don't know anything about it."

The elevator door opened, we got on, and I said. "Besides, if he dies, *I'm* the one in trouble. So remember *me* in your prayers tonight."

"Believe me, you're gonna need all the prayers you can get. And you were wrong about Karl, after all."

"It sure looks that way, doesn't it?"

Leon had to drive because neither Bailey's eyes nor mine would stay in focus. Leon told us about the book he'd checked out of the liberry. He was convinced that he could lead us straight to the underground railroad tunnel.

"Good," I said from the backseat, "we'll take Maxie

and Fritz there tomorrow night and have them help us look for it."

"But, yo, Jack, I think I know exactly where it is."

"Okay, Leon. But we'll take the dogs anyway. They're going to help us find the murder weapon. If it's still in the house or on the property somewhere, that is."

"Maybe the killer took it with him," Bailey said. "You said the same thing yourself the other day."

"I say a lot of things," I shrugged, thinking of Karl.

"You think the professor is the killer now?"

"It's looking like a real possibility."

"Well, now that I'm off the force, I don't know exactly what to do with this anymore." He lifted a file folder off the dashboard. "I guess it's yours, Jack."

"Thanks," I said, taking it from him.

"Just one thing," he said, but his cell phone rang. He answered it, spoke a few brief words, including, "You're kidding! He confessed?" then hung up and said, "That was Dan. A friend of Huckabee says he confessed to the killing."

I sat there stunned for a moment then said, "Jesus, I didn't see that coming. Everything is falling apart. Well, I really need to talk to him myself now, as soon as possible." I sighed. "And Jamie's not going to take my missing dinner at her mother's very well." I stopped. "I wonder why the hell she hasn't returned my phone call."

When I got home I found her upstairs, packing.

I just stood in the doorway. "What's going on?"

"What does it look like? I'm moving out. What did you do to your beard?"

"I shaved it. Look, Jamie, sweetheart, stop packing."

"No, I've made up my mind. Why'd you shave it?"

"To go undercover. I'll explain later. Can't we talk about this?"

"Can we? It seems like you're always looking for an excuse to avoid the subject of our supposed wedding."

I clenched my fists and took a deep breath. "I'm not trying to avoid it, sweetheart. Things have just come up."

"Things . . ." she threw some sweaters into the suitcase ". . . are always coming up."

I knew she was getting her period because I've learned to keep track. I've also learned not to mention that fact when she gets like this. And I know enough not to use the words emotional, irrational, or hormonal, even though she likes to blame some of *my* behavior on excess testosterone.

"Look," I said, "I'm sorry about tonight and I'm sorry if I've seemed . . ." I stopped to rephrase. "That is, I'm sorry I've been negligent about the wedding plans, but I have to meet with Huckabee tonight. It can't wait. Can't you call your mom and cancel dinner and come with me?"

She glared at me. "You can't be serious. It's Christmas, Jack. I know that doesn't mean anything to you, but spending time with family is important to me."

"It's important to me too. But so is finding Amy Frost's killer. Speaking of family, don't you at least want to know what happened to Leon this afternoon?"

"What happened?" She stopped packing.

I told her about Colbern's latest escapade. She expressed genuine concern and outrage then went right back to packing. "I'll be staying at my mom's tonight. I'll be back for the rest of my things tomorrow."

"Honey, you've been under a lot of stress lately," I

said, knowing that nothing *I* could say at that moment would really change things. I also knew that if she went to her mom's it would work in my favor. Laura would talk to her, woman to woman, mother to daughter, and maybe calm her down. "Think about it, it's the holidays, you're working two jobs, trying to help me solve a murder—"

"It's more than that. I should've known you weren't serious about getting married from the way you proposed."

"What?" It's true, though. It wasn't a traditional proposal, down on one knee, and all that. "I thought you liked the way I proposed to you."

"Hah! Setting off my car alarm in the middle of the night and waking up the neighbors? Then making me search through the dresser drawer to find the ring? Which reminds me . . . you can have the damn thing . . . if I can just . . ." She couldn't get it off her finger.

See? I wanted to say, you're retaining water. "Keep it," I told her. "And you *did* say yes to me that night, remember? Several times, if you recall. And you seemed very happy."

"That was before I realized that everything is just a game to you. The way you proposed, our whole relationship, even solving a murder case is just a game."

"No, it's not."

"Sure it is. It's a game of chess, remember?"

I hung my head. "Look, can we talk about this later? I've got dogs to take care of and I'm hungry as hell. On top of which, my Christmas cold is—"

"Go play with your dogs. That's what you're good at."

"Okay, but I'm applying the 72-hour rule."

"The 72-hour rule?"

"That's where we both treat this as a temporary glitch and not a real break up until Monday night."

She shook her head. "Treat it any way you want, Jack. As far as I'm concerned it's over. Oh, and I got you a vial of the victim's blood, like you asked. It's in an envelope in the refrigerator. I also got you some more Gatorade."

"Thank you."

"And I think I like you better with a beard."

"Me too."

"So? What are you just standing there for? Your dogs are more important than I am. Go take care of them."

"Okay," I said. "But *no* one is more important to me than you are, Jamie—it's just that the dogs and Huckabee can't wait. And I'm still imposing the 72-hour rule."

"Do what you want." She went back to the closet for more clothes to throw at the suitcase.

27

I was starving so I got to the Whale's Tooth Pub half an hour early. It was a nice, homey joint, with tall windows overlooking the ocean and a huge fireplace with a big stack of logs next to the hearth, which was decorated with pine boughs and Christmas lights and the like.

It was between the dinner hour and serious drinking time, and the piano player was just setting up his fake sheets on top of the upright grand.

I took a seat at the bar and ordered an Andrew's Brown Ale from the slim young redheaded bartender.

"Nice choice," he said, wiping the bar with a towel.

A waitress came by and gave me a menu, but I didn't look at it. I just asked about the fish and chips.

"Are they the real deal?" I said. "Because I lived in England when I was a teenager, so—"

"I think you'll like 'em," she said.

"And you have real malt vinegar for the chips?"

"Yep. Imported." She pointed to the brown bottles sitting on the tables, so I said I'd try them.

She went to the kitchen to place my order and my

mind went back to the trouble with Jamie. I probably don't need to do anything, I thought. She'll get over it by Monday night. She has to. I felt someone taking the barstool next to me.

A pleasant female voice said, "So, Jack, we meet again."

I turned and saw Gretchen, the photographer, looking more than a little sexy in a tight red turtleneck sweater and blue jeans. Her black hair was pulled back in a black bandeau, offsetting her coffee-colored skin and high cheekbones.

"Hi, Gretchen," I said.

She smiled a happy smile. "You know my name."

"Uh, yeah. Jamie mentioned it."

"Really?" She put a glass on the bar. It was empty except for the memory of a single ice cube. "I need another of these babies," she told the bartender.

He said, "Johnny Black, with one ice cube."

"That's right." She turned back to me and shrugged. "I prefer Macallan's but . . . the only single malts they serve here are Glenlivet or Glenfiddich."

I shook my head. "Why does anyone drink those?"

"I know," she smiled. "It's gotta be either Macallan's, Glenmorangie, or, at the very least, Aberlour."

"How about Cardhu?"

"I *love* Cardhu, but it's hard to find." She gave me a shy shrug and said, "So, where *is* the lucky girl?"

"Jamie? She's busy with a few things."

"Too bad," she said, but didn't mean it. "But that's the way it crumbles sometimes, huh?"

" 'That's the way it crumbles?' "

She shrugged. "Cookie-wise."

"Hey," I chuckled. "That's a line from *The Apartment.*"

"Yeah. It was on last night. It's a lot better than those inane Christmas flicks they show every year." She leaned a little toward me. "Can I make a confession?" She looked around at the holiday décor and wrinkled her nose. "I hate Christmas."

"No kidding. I kind of share the sentiment."

"Really?" The bartender returned with her drink. She held it up to make a toast. "To hating Christmas."

I lifted my beer. "I'll drink to that."

She squinted at me. "You look different."

"I do? Oh, yeah. I shaved my beard."

She got an ah-hah look in her eye as we drank our toast. "So, there's trouble on the Jamie front, huh?"

"No." I almost blushed. "What makes you say that?"

She shrugged. "When a woman is thinking of breaking up with a man, she cuts her hair or changes her hairdo. When a man is looking to change partners, he grows a mustache or a beard, or else he shaves them off."

"Well, it's nothing like that, trust me."

"Un-huh. Are you *sure* you're not out looking for a little fun tonight, sans Jamie?"

"Um, no. I'm here to meet someone."

"Really? Well, you just did." She let her arm fall over my shoulder and twirled a finger around the hair curling over my turtleneck. Her perfume was marvelous. It reminded me of Kristin Downey and a red scarf she always wore. She left it in my apartment once, shortly after we first met, and I sniffed the damn thing for three days.

"Is that Opium?" I said, feeling my jeans get tight.

She flashed her eyes. "Yes, it is. Thanks for noticing." She sipped her drink. "I guess that must be what Jamie wears, huh?"

"No. She's allergic to perfume, actually."

"Too bad." She tilted her head back, exposing her long, lovely neck. "Want another free sample?"

Yes, I thought, but said, "No thanks. I'm fine."

She smiled and put the palm of her hand to my chest. "Why? Jamie's probably slaving over a dead body. We could dance a little, maybe take a drive down the coast."

"A drive down the coast? Is that a euphemism for . . . ?"

"It could be." She smiled. God, she had a killer smile. "You could take it to mean anything you want it to."

"Well, thanks for the offer," I said, trying not to think what I was thinking. "It's awfully tempting, really. You're very pretty, Gretchen. And you have a killer smile. But a) I'm engaged, b) I'm engaged, c) I'm engaged, and d)—"

"Let me guess, you're engaged."

No, d) is you're a little drunk, I wanted to say, but said, "No, d) I've got a miserable cold. Besides, I only trade euphemisms with one girl at a time." I lifted my beer to my lips. "I'm sure you're very good at it, but—"

"Oh," she smiled, "I could rock your world, Jack Field. You have no idea. I could grind you like fresh coffee."

Ah, screw the case, I thought. Screw the 72-hour rule. Let Jamie and Huckabee fend for themselves.

So I said, "okay let's go," and paid for our drinks, took her hand and we went out to the parking lot where we smashed our lips and faces and bodies together in the cold night air, then hopped hurriedly into the car, spitting gravel as we hauled ass out of the parking lot and took off down the road.

I asked her where she lived and she said, "Later, just find a place to pull over, quick." So I did, next to the old mill, and we steamed up the windows for a while then went to her place and I took all her clothes off, and she took off mine, and we blended our bodies together on the rug in front of her fireplace, then foraged in the fridge for a while, ended up doing it on the kitchen floor, then dragged ourselves to the bedroom and kept at it like minks until sunrise.

I didn't feel a damn bit guilty about it afterward, either, because none of this actually happened. It was just a brief fantasy that took about a fraction of a second.

"Freshly ground coffee, huh?" I said. "Sounds delicious. But I'm meeting someone here. It's connected to the murder case."

"I see," she twirled her ice cube. "On the clock, huh?"

I chuckled. "Yeah. Kind of."

"Well," she held her drink out for a toast, "if you change your mind, I'll be around. Here's to euphemisms."

"Sure." I clinked my bottle against her glass. "They're what makes the world go 'round."

"Funny . . . I thought there was another word for *that*."

"Uh, yeah," I explained, as if to a dummy, or a drunk, "that's what euphemism means."

"I *know* what it *means*," she said. "I was making a *joke*, which I guess went over your head." She batted her eyes.

I laughed. It's hard to resist a girl who can make you feel like a fool and make you laugh at the same time. (Jamie does it to me all the time.)

"Good one," I said, then saw Tom Huckabee behind

her. I caught my breath. "And you almost had me there for a second. But the guy I'm here to talk to just came in."

She picked up her drink and handbag, leaned in close and whispered, "If you change your mind, I'll be over by the fire." She glanced at Huckabee, who seemed a little desperate as he looked around the place. Then she let her eyes circle the room, leaned in close, giving me another shock of her perfume, and said. "My *problem* is, you're the most interesting guy *in* here."

I nodded. "My problem is I'm the most interesting guy everywhere I go."

She laughed. "I hate to admit it but you're probably right. When you're done with Gomer, maybe we could sit by the fire, request the "Theme from *The Apartment*," and make out a little. Technically that wouldn't be cheating, would it?"

"It sounds nice but, yeah—technically, it would. Look, Gretchen, you're smart and sexy and I'd love to get to know you. If it weren't for Jamie, Gomer would be here alone right now and I'd probably be somewhere down the coast with you. Maybe Mexico. Just don't tell Jamie I said that."

She drew her fingers across her lips. "What happens in the Whale's Tooth stays in the Whale's Tooth."

"See? You really *are* smart. You can quote Moby Dick."

She laughed. Damn, she had a nice laugh.

Huckabee came up to us and said, "Um, Jack Field?"

"That's me."

Gretchen said to him, "He's the most interesting guy in the place. Just ask him. He thinks I read Melville."

"Mel *who*?" said Huckabee.

Then came that laugh again and I wondered—just for a second, no make that a millisecond—if I could run to the phone, call Jamie, tell her about my golden opportunity, and ask her if I could temporarily suspend the 72-hour rule.

No, it doesn't work that way, I thought. Then I realized I was still mad at her, furious, in fact, and *that* was part of what made the thing with Gretchen seem so appealing. Damn, it's tough being faithful. Especially since, according to Jamie, we were no longer a couple.

I raised my glass to her. "Nice flirting with you. If Jamie and I ever split up, I'll give you a call."

"You promise?" she said,

"Oh, I promise. Within seventy-two hours, on the dot. In fact"—I got out a notebook and a pen and handed them to her—"why don't you write down your name and number, just in case it happens."

"I think I will," she said with a smile. She wrote down her name and phone number, gave the pen and notebook back, then walked over to the fire.

I was a good boy. I didn't watch her go. Not much.

The bartender wiped the bar again and said, "Ain't you the lucky devil?"

"Me?" I said.

He nodded. "She comes in once or twice a week, never talks to anyone. Won't even let a guy buy her a drink."

"No kidding."

He shrugged. "And I've never seen her come on to anybody before tonight, let alone get shot down."

Huckabee took her barstool. "You wanted to talk to me?"

"Huh," I said, feeling a little happy with myself.

"Mr. Field?" Huckabee said.

"Yeah, call me Jack," I said, as the waitress brought my fish and chips, wrapped in newspaper, just like they do in England, "let's get a table by the window." To the waitress I said, "Wow! These look almost perfect."

Huckabee said, "It's nicer by the fire."

The waitress said, "Almost?"

"Well," I said, grousing, "these are technically just big french fries," I held one up, "not actual chips. The ones I used to get in England were round like potato chips, only a lot thicker. But the newspaper wrapping is a nice touch. And they smell great."

"I *told* you. And I'll tell the cook about the chips."

"I said, it's nicer by the fire," Huckabee said.

"Yeah, I heard you," I said, picking up my beer and food, "but I'm feeling a little feverish. I need a window."

"First of all," he said after we settled by the window, "I want to thank you for what you've been doing for Tim. I appreciate it. A lot. Second, everything I'm going to tell you tonight has to be totally off the record. Okay?"

"Okay. Have you spoken to Tim's grandparents recently?"

"No," he scowled. "Legally I can't contact them."

"Well, that may change soon." I told him about Jamie's opinion on his wife's death.

He was too shocked to smile at the news. He just said, "You mean I'll be exonerated, finally?"

"Maybe, maybe not. But at least the Grants are thinking about letting you save Tim's life now."

He shook his head sadly. "God, I would give anything—"

"The trouble is," I said, taking a bite of fish, "the cops think you confessed to killing Amy Frost."

"What? No, I didn't. I didn't kill her *or* my wife."

I savored the fish. It was damn good. "That's not what your boss says. He says you told him you did it."

"No, I said I felt responsible. But that's because if I hadn't gotten Amy mixed up in all this she'd still be alive. And why on earth would I want to kill my own sister?"

"Your sister?" I nearly choked on my haddock.

28

"Amy Frost was your *sister*?" I said, washing the fish down with some beer.

He nodded. "The thing about us being exes was her idea, to keep the Brights from being suspicious."

"So how come no one's found out about this till now?"

"You mean like that first detective I spoke to?"

"Bailey, yeah."

"He didn't really ask me very many questions except did I have an alibi and someone who could corroborate it."

"And *was* there someone?"

"Yes. Her name is Donna Moore. She and I were in New York, at her apartment, that weekend. I drove back that night. I don't know why the police haven't talked to her."

"And you gave Detective Bailey all her contact information?"

"Yeah, I gave him everything. He seemed a little strange, though, if you ask me."

"How so?"

"I don't know. He called me by my first name a lot—Tom this, and Tom that. It was a little odd."

I shook my head. "He's still a bit new at the game. But you *were* having fights with your sister Amy?"

"Yes, because I wanted to get her out of there before something like this happened. Maybe I should explain."

I doused a french fry with malt vinegar and said, "Yeah, maybe you should."

The piano player started in on "Jolly Old Saint Nick," a horrible choice. I looked over at Gretchen. She shook her head sadly at me and mouthed, "Christmas sucks."

I nodded in agreement, then saw her hold out an empty glass for the waitress to take for a refill.

"Well, the whole thing started," Huckabee told me sadly, "when I was fifteen . . ."

He saw a nightclub magician, Magnus the Magnificent, in his hometown of Philadelphia when his high school had an assembly in the auditorium and Magnus did his act for the kids. Huckabee loved it and was hooked on magic.

He started sneaking into the nightclub where Magnus was performing and would hang around after the shows, pestering the magician with questions about how he did his tricks.

"They're not tricks, young man," Magnus told him, "they're illusions."

It turned out that Magnus was a mediocre, low-rent magician by night but a very successful con artist by day. He saw Huckabee as a potential partner in crime. Magnus promised to teach him everything he knew about magic if Huckabee would help him run cons on unsuspecting suckers.

I said, "So, Professor Hayes and Magnus the Magnificent are one and the same?"

"Yes. And he'd kill me if I told you this, but his real name is Harold Peterman."

I laughed. "Go on."

At eighteen Huckabee began traveling with Magnus and his female assistant—the Wonderful Wanda, real name Shirley Schwartzbaum. They traveled across the country and even toured Europe, doing magic shows and running con games, always one step ahead of the law. Magnus and Wanda fought constantly and soon it was just Magnus and Huckabee.

"I think he may have killed her," Huckabee said. "At least I thought so at the time. He told me she ran off, but if she did she left a lot of her things behind."

Huckabee grew tired of the life, Magnus grew tired of "nickel-and-dime marks," so they settled in New York City, where they could fade into the background and at the same time find more well-to-do victims.

"So you liked being a con artist at first?"

"When I was young, yeah. It was kind of fun. Magnus was a great teacher. After a while, though, the fun kind of wore off and the magic—no pun intended—was gone."

Huckabee, who'd been taking correspondence courses in electronics, got a job with an outfit specializing in security systems, which Magnus approved of, for his own reasons. Huckabee also married an actress wannabe named Rhoda Grant, who was his sister Amy's roommate. Magnus didn't approve of the marriage.

Meanwhile, Amy, now married and quickly divorced from an actor named Albert Frost, was working as a waitress but was determined to become an actress herself. She and Tom and Rhoda saw each other quite a bit, and Huckabee occasionally helped out with Amy's rent and utilities.

A few years passed and the company Huckabee worked for got a contract installing electronic security systems for the Brights' Park Avenue apartment. It was there that he overheard a conversation between Mr. and Mrs. Bright, involving the story of Fiona's lost brother, and how he was supposedly kidnapped by elves many years earlier. One day he related the story to Magnus who quickly developed a plan to fleece the Brights out of as much money as possible.

"You've got to be kidding," I said. "All this time I thought it was the ghosts in the attic scam. But elves?"

"I know." He smiled sadly. "But it *was* kind of brilliant in a way. Who would ever suspect such a thing? And Magnus always said you work with whatever's important to the mark, no matter how ridiculous it seems to anyone else."

I smiled. "That's kind of the way dog training works, actually. You find out what's important to the dog, then you con him into thinking that obeying your commands is exactly what he wanted to do all along."

He stared. "That's brilliant."

"*I* think so. Anyway, go on."

Magnus renamed himself Dr. Jonathan Kensington Hayes, did a lot of research on elfin mythology, and set up a phony foundation: The Institute for Second World Studies.

He built a persona for himself, making appearances at parties and benefits as a mysterious Stanford-educated figure who had a knowledge of secret worlds, always refusing to discuss his work, hinting politely that his research was too dangerous and arcane for small minds, all aimed to capture Mrs. Bright's attention, which it eventually did.

At first Hayes refused to return her phone calls, even

though he'd left his business card with Ellis and several of her friends. She persisted and he finally agreed to meet her at his humble office on West 33rd Street. The office was designed to show his total lack of interest in monetary gain, as was the meeting. He refused his usual fee when the meeting was over, though he promised to look into her brother's case to see if it would aid his own research.

A few weeks later he called her, both excited and in despair. During one of his journeys into the mystical realms he'd found evidence that her brother was still alive. But, he told her, he couldn't afford to take it any further. Would she be satisfied by just seeing a letter Sean had written from his prison cell inside the elfin kingdoms?

I shook my head at the absurdity of it, but said nothing.

Fiona was on the hook. Of course she wanted to see the letter. But why stop there? Why not find Sean, free him, and bring him back from wherever he was being held?

It couldn't be done, the professor told her. It would take more time and money than he could afford and he simply wouldn't feel right having her foot the bill since there was no guarantee that he could bring Sean safely back to her.

Fiona said she didn't care about the money. If the letter were authentic she'd pay anything.

Magnus hesitated, then told her that the letter itself was tricky; the elves weren't happy about artifacts from their world showing up in human hands and they have spells to guard against it. He explained that he didn't know what would happen to the letter once he showed it to her. He said it might turn to dust before she could read it, it might burn up in her hands, it might even kill them both.

"But I *must* see that letter!"

He sighed. "I'll need to do some more research. There are certain spells—hidden in very secret places—that may protect us. We'll have to wait, though, until my grant comes through from the Irish government."

"I'll pay you for your research. Do it as soon as possible."

"You don't understand, Fiona. I can't take any money from you."

Of course she talked him into it and the research went on for two years, with telegrams coming from places like Dublin, London, Zurich. There was always some museum curator who wanted a bribe, an expert who wouldn't talk without getting a fat stipend. And the money always came. Lots and lots of it.

Then the day arrived when the professor had finally learned all the spells that would keep Fiona safe when she was allowed to see the letter.

The lights in the study of the Park Avenue apartment were kept low because the professor warned that too much light, especially from electric bulbs, would cause the writing on the letter to disappear. Sunlight or candlelight would cause it to burst into flames.

He took an ancient-looking piece of parchment from an old leather folder, embossed with a green Celtic letter F, and allowed Fiona to hold it and look at it. She gasped, immediately recognizing her brother's childhood hand, which Hayes had copied from a real letter that Huckabee had "borrowed." Before she could read the entire missive, the writing on it disappeared.

I laughed in disbelief. "Disappearing ink? That's a beginner's magic trick."

"Yep," said Huckabee, "but with the build-up and the way the letter looked, it must've been convincing."

"You don't seem to feel guilty about all this."

He shrugged. "I never liked Mrs. Bright."

"I know the feeling, but still . . ."

Huckabee went on: Hayes learned of an NYU professor named Dr. Hiraki Einstein, who was doing legitimate research into elfin folklore, and the possibility that certain sacred or magical places in the world might contain energy fields that provide actual portals into other dimensions. That's when Hayes got the idea of building just such a portal in the Brights' mansion in Maine.

"So that's what's upstairs? A make-believe portal into the elfin kingdom?"

He nodded and softly sang, " 'We're off to see the wizard . . .' "

Hayes handled the construction, meaning that any "cost overruns" would go into his pocket, and certain items, like genuine stone from Ireland, would actually come from Indiana, at one-tenth the price, with the difference, again, going into his pocket.

I heard the pianist playing a familiar tune I couldn't quite place, then realized it was the "Theme from *The Apartment*." I looked over at Gretchen. She had another scotch in her hand, held it up, and gave me one of her killer smiles.

I smiled at her then turned back to Huckabee. "I'm sorry, you were saying the granite came from Indiana."

"Right. That's when we moved to Maine, me and Rhoda and Tim. I worked on the construction, setting up hidden walls and doors in the game room . . ."

"With an electrode in the floor? Oh, and the lasers and fog machines?"

Surprised, he said, "How do you know all that?"

"I spoke to someone who isn't Lance Burton. So do you think the game room, as you call it, is still operational?"

"Sure. It's set to be ready go for about two, three weeks at a time with no maintenance. Anyway, before the construction was finished is when Tim got sick and Rhoda died and that whole mess happened." He took a deep breath. "I can't go back to prison, Mr. Field."

"Call me Jack."

"I just can't. That's why when I got out a few months ago I tried to talk Amy into leaving the game. But she said Magnus had a big score coming and she wanted her piece of it or she'd blow the whistle."

I nodded. "That would be a motive for him to kill her. How did she get involved in the first place?"

"She had trouble paying her rent and needed money, so I got her a job as the Bright's maid. Initially she was the skeptic who tried to talk Mrs. Bright out of spending all her money on this hoax."

I was puzzled. "And Magnus went for that?"

"It was his *idea*. Look, everybody has doubts about stuff like this, even Fiona Bright. The idea is to plant someone on the inside to voice those doubts. This makes the mark defensive about what she wants to believe; she becomes more locked in. But the skeptic has to be careful not to go too far, or they'll get fired. In fact, Fiona threatened to fire Amy several times. Then, at a critical point, the skeptic sees something or tells the mark she's seen something that makes her a believer after all. All doubt is gone from the mark's mind and they're totally hooked."

I said, "Hayes knows a hell of a lot about psychology."

"That's what makes a good con man. Then, after the

mansion was built, the plan for Amy's part was to take care of the equipment upstairs, keep the magic pool and fountain operational, and to feed the dwarves."

I started laughing. "Feed the dwarves?"

"Yeah, midgets, little people, whatever you're supposed to call them these days. They had to eat."

I nodded. "I get it. They were supposed to impersonate elves who appeared in the magic portal or something. And I bet there were two of them hiding somewhere upstairs."

"Yes, a male and a female. How did you know that?"

I told him about the professor's two steamer trunks and the fact that he always wore the same outfit every day. I said, "Obviously, the trunks weren't for his clothes."

"Well," he said, "I was in prison when all that started, so I don't know how the midgets were supposed to get in and out of the mansion, but that makes sense."

"Little people," I said. "I think that's what they like to be called, not midgets. Do you know how the *professor* got in and out of the house without being seen?"

"No. There was a secret elevator that went from the third floor to the basement. But other than that . . ."

"How many others were involved?"

"There's no way to answer that. Someone could be added at a moment's notice to set up a second party to unwittingly influence a mark, or draw attention away from the game."

He explained there might be several people, never two the same, who would pop up, perhaps at a party or benefit, and say hello to Hayes, Haven't seen you since that lecture you gave at the Sorbonne or I hear your daughter's at Stanford now, following in the old man's footsteps, eh?

"He can't print it on his business cards or even *say* he went to Stanford or lectured in Paris. That's fraud. So he sets up these things over a period of months, pays the other artists for their time, and they move on to another game.

"Soon all the marks believe in a fabricated résumé the professor supposedly has that they've never seen. There might've been thirty people, each playing a different role and none of whom knew what the actual con was. The idea is that if someone comes along and says, 'So-and-so said you went to Stanford,' Hayes can just say, 'I can't comment on what other people believe about me,' and that's that."

"Very clever." I thought of something. "Listen, if Hayes killed your sister, it had something to do with the jewel heist, since the two things happened the same night."

"Probably. I guess that was the 'big score' Magnus was talking about."

"Just one thing, though. You were the one who installed the video cameras inside the mansion, right?" He nodded. "And there was a camera in the bedroom that gave a good view of the safe right?" He nodded again. "And you didn't know what it was there for?"

He sighed. "I had my ideas but by that point I couldn't say anything to anyone."

"But that's how he got the combination to the safe, though, right? You had to have been suspicious."

"Of course, but I had to take the job if for no other reason than to see Amy and talk some sense into her."

"All right. Here's another thing I don't understand.

Maybe you can help me. If Hayes was planning a jewel heist, would he just do it on the fly and improvise, or would he have every angle of it—including fencing the stolen items afterward—figured out in advance?"

"Are you kidding? He figures some of these things out two or three *years* in advance."

"And I imagine before the con even started he would've done a lot of research into the household staff?"

"What are you getting at?"

"How much do you know about the chauffeur?"

"Karl? I don't know anything about him, and don't want to know. He has very scary eyes."

"I guess he does sometimes. But he was working for the Brights in New York?"

"No. He only worked in Florida and Maine, not in New York. I think they used cabs or a car service there."

"But Hayes would've done a thorough investigation into Karl's background at some point?"

"Of course." He bit his lip. "It was probably more thorough than the one the Brights did themselves."

"How does he do his research?"

"Magnus? How *doesn't* he? He has hidden cameras, hidden microphones, sometimes he hires other con artists to follow someone around for weeks to find out their daily schedules, sometimes he intercepts the mark's mail, steams it open, then redelivers it. The idea is to know everything you possibly can before making your first move."

"Okay. So how did the portal operate?"

He explained the basic setup: the main room on the third floor was a fairly large library with a fireplace on the east wall.

"Yeah, I've seen that much. And the mirror next to the fireplace. It's made of two-way glass?"

"That's right." He said there was a switch hidden in a modillion on the left side of the mantel, which when twisted clockwise caused the mirror and the wall around it to rise into the ceiling. That's what the half-floor above the third story was for, a place for the various moving walls to disappear to, though the Brights were told that it was necessary to provide protection from excess elfin energy.

I laughed. "I still can't believe they bought all this. And why the two-way glass?"

"So Magnus could stand behind it and watch Fiona and Ellis and listen in on their conversations."

He said that behind the mirror was a semicircular hallway, which curved to the left and led back to a triangular-shaped room on the right; the "backstage" area, including a dressing room for the midgets—

"Little people."

"Whatever." In the dressing room were two beds, a closet with their wardrobe, a makeup desk and mirror, and a TV. Beyond that was a bathroom and the secret elevator.

To the left of all this was the game room—a fairly large, circular room with a saltwater pool in the center. The walls were made of plaster, though they were painted to look like solid granite, with chunks of costume jewelry emeralds and veins of gold leaf running through the rock. The room came equipped with various mirrors, placed at angles so as to make the room seem much larger than it was.

When it was time to "open" the portal, the Professor would stand near the hearth in the library and wave his staff in the air while stepping on a copper switch hid-

den between two of the hearthstones. The switch acti-
vated a computer program that caused the air to fill
with CO_2 fog, green lights to flood the room, a sudden
flash, during which the south wall rose silently and unseen on hydraulic rails to that half-floor above. The fog
lifted and the elfin chamber was revealed.

Then the professor stepped into the chamber, never
letting the Brights enter it themselves—

"I thought you said you weren't around for this
part."

"Well, I *wasn't,* but I was in on the planning."

The reason, obviously, that Hayes didn't want them
coming into the chamber themselves was because the
mirrors were placed to make it look twice as big as it really was, not to mention the fact that up close it was obvious that the walls were made of plaster, not granite.
Magnus likened this to the way The Great and Powerful
Oz didn't want Dorothy to peek behind his little curtain.

"Yeah, I get it."

He went on, "The next step was to dip his walking
stick into the pool, which was filled with some kind of
plankton—"

"Bioluminescent dinoflagellates—"

"Which caused the pool—"

"Wait, why use the magic plankton and not just
some kind of lighting trick?"

"Have you ever seen them? Oh, there's nothing quite
like them in the world. The water actually comes alive
with light. You couldn't get that effect with stage lights.
And Hayes always had a flair for the dramatic."

"But why go with a pool in the first place?"

"Ah, yeah. That goes back to the way Fiona's
brother disappeared. I think he fell down a well, be-

cause the story she told was that he was taken down a well by the elves."

"Makes sense. The poor kid's bones are probably still down that well somewhere in Ireland. Can you describe Hayes's walking stick?"

"His wizard's staff? Sure. It was hand-carved, with a knobbed end on top. They sell them at a shop in Camden."

"Huh. Did it have secret electrodes hidden inside?"

"No, he just used it for effect. It's one of the rules of magic—misdirection. You wave a wand or a scarf or a big staff around and people don't notice what you're doing with your other hand, or with your feet."

"Okay, go on."

The plankton caused the pool to light up with an eerie blue-green light, setting off the next effect, more CO_2 fog, more lasers, then a door opened in the back of the chamber, where there was another small room with mirrors placed in such a way as to make it seem that the little people, in costume, were far off in the distance, even though they were inside the house.

The professor would go confer with them, importune them in their native tongue, pleading to let Fiona to see her long-lost brother. They would remain implacable, giving just a glimmer of hope that maybe with enough time, and enough money in the professor's pocket, they would relent.

Then came another burst of CO_2, some more lasers, and the portal would close and the library would be as still and silent as it was before.

"Sounds like quite a production."

"It was supposed to be. It probably was. I never got a chance to see it."

"And why go to all that trouble? I mean, one of the rules of a con game is do it quick and get out, isn't it?"

"Yeah, it was just supposed to be like that—take the construction money and run. But Magnus got caught up and wanted to see how far he could take it."

I thought about the whole idea of it and wanted to laugh but it was too sad and too silly.

"You don't feel guilty about fleecing these people out of their money?"

He shrugged. "What'd *they* ever do to earn it? Besides, I had troubles of my own, remember? My wife died, my son got sick, and I was sent to prison for a crime I didn't commit."

"So, I guess that lets your conscience off the hook?"

"A little. Look, if you want to see how it works for yourself, I can write down how to do it and you can go up there and fool around when no one's home. It's not that tough. *I* did all the hard work, programming everything."

"It might come in handy." I looked him over. "Okay, listen, the Camden PD is after you—"

He stared. "I can't go to prison again, Mr. Field."

"I told you to call me Jack." I also told him not to worry about prison, that I would take care of things. He didn't believe me.

He put his head in his hands. "I can't spend another minute behind bars. I just can't."

"You can, if you have to. You have to keep thinking about Tim. He needs you, Tom. Do you understand?"

He nodded.

"Good. Now, I'm going to need you to write down the professor's real name, his office address and home address and phone numbers and anything you can think of that'll help us find and nail him." I reached into my Levi's jacket and gave him a notepad and pen.

"Okay. I should probably give you Dr. Einstein's number too. She's a professor of comparative mythology at NYU and has a whole dossier on the professor. The Brights aren't the only people he's been scamming, and it's been driving her nuts for years."

"Other people have fallen for this crap?"

"Yeah." He shrugged. "Tolkien fans, mostly. Or rich hippies from California. Most of the marks donate money for his so-called research. The game he set up on Mrs. Bright was the only one this elaborate."

"What are the man's weaknesses, predilections? Long time female companions, drinking or drug habits?"

"He doesn't drink or do drugs and he hasn't had a steady girlfriend since Wanda. He uses call girls."

"This is in New York?"

"Yeah."

"You know which agencies or girls he likes?"

"I do, actually." He told me the name of the agency and the names of the two girls he liked best.

"Write it down."

"He's probably not in New York," he said, writing. "The way I figure it, with the stolen jewels and my sister's murder, he's long gone to Switzerland. He has a numbered account in Zurich. From there, who knows? He could be practically anywhere. His motto was always, 'If the heat is on, drop the con.' You can't make money in jail."

"Maybe, but he'll have to fence the jewels before he can leave the country. Write the town where you last saw Shirley Schwarzbaum alive, and any information about what she looked like, what she was wearing, etc. I'll contact the local authorities there. If Hayes killed her too, and we can prove it, he'll go away for two murders."

He began to write, stopped and said, "I want you to get him, Mr. Field. Amy should've been smarter than to try to blackmail him for more money. That was her mistake. But he killed her. I'm sure of it."

I wanted to tell him that his sister had also tried to blackmail Chris Bright, but I didn't. "Well," I said, "nobody's hands seem to be clean in this, but the professor's have the most blood on them."

He nodded and went back to writing. The waitress, seeing that we were no longer huddled in conversation, came over and asked if I needed another beer or some coffee.

"Yeah, I take mine black." Then I nodded over at Gretchen, who was making love to another scotch. "And one for my friend. I don't know how she takes hers."

She said, "Neither do I, but the girl sure needs it."

"She probably needs someone to drive her home too."

She smiled. "And you're gonna volunteer?"

I shrugged. "How long would it take to get a cab?"

"Who knows?" She looked at Gretchen and said, "Poor thing. She never gets drunk like this."

"It's the holidays," I said. "Some people can't cope."

"Why?" she said, frowning. "I *love* Christmas."

"Yeah, me too," I lied.

Huckabee finished writing and handed me the pad.

"I guess you're sorry you ever met him, huh, Tom?"

"Magnus? Yeah. It was my choice, though. That's what he says about the marks, too. 'It's a binary universe,' he says. 'We all have choices, even the suckers. They either fall for the con or they don't.' " He sighed and looked me in the eye. "And much as I wish you could, I don't think you'll be able to catch him or out-wit him."

I thought it over and said, "Then I guess I have to let him outsmart him*self*."

He laughed. "You know, that just might work."

29

I got Gretchen into a cab without too much trouble, though she did insist on putting her arms all the way around me and nuzzling my chest as we walked across the gravel. It was kind of nice, actually, to feel her body next to mine, though I tried not to enjoy it too much. Then, once I got the cab door open, and poured her inside, she tried to kiss me. That was also nice. I tried not to enjoy it either.

I got her all the way in, helped her move her legs out of the way of the door, and said, "Tell the man where you're going, honey."

She looked up front and told him, then turned back to me. "And you'll call me if you and Jamie—?"

I patted my chest where the notebook was. "You'll be the first to know. But the thing is, I have this rule . . ." I explained the 72-hour rule to her.

She glared at me with heavy eyelids. "I hate your rules."

"Me too," I said then tapped on the roof of the cab.

* * *

My mind was in a daze all the way home, thinking about Gretchen, her perfume. I took the dogs out for a midnight play, more for my benefit then theirs.

When I got upstairs I found a message on my cell phone. I sat on the mattress, kicked my shoes off, and listened to it, loving the sound of her voice:

"Hi," she said. "I'm sorry. Call me. *Please?* I'm at my mom's. It doesn't matter how late." There was a long pause, then she said, "I'm sorry. I miss you."

I sat there for a while, then made a phone call to New York. It rang a few times before Kelso picked up.

"What?" he said, sourly.

"It's Jack."

"I know it's Jack, Jack. I have four hundred different kinds of caller ID. What do you want?"

"I've got a couple things I need you to look into for me." I told him about Karl Petrovich/AKA Andreyev Gregori, and his troubles with the Russian gang in Brooklyn whose specialty is diamond heists and the fencing of stolen jewelry, gave him the number of Karl's cell phone, then told him about Harold Peterman/AKA Professor J.K. Hayes, and gave him the addresses and phone numbers that Huckabee had given me.

"Anything else? And why the hell don't you get some kind of internet service and send me this crap via e-mail instead of waking me up at—what time is it?"

"It's only twelve-thirty. And do you know who *reads* all those e-mails?"

"Good point." He chuckled. "Come to think of it, wasn't *I* the one who told you about the government's surveillance of all private e-mails?"

"Maybe. I forget. Maybe it was your pal. You know, that weird surveillance expert of yours, Dr. Lunch?"

"Yeah, that makes sense." There was a pause. "Something else on your mind?"

"No."

"Come on, Jack. It's me. Something to do with Jamie?"

"No. Forget it. I'll talk to you tomorrow."

"Okay. And look, Jack, whatever's going on, it feels worse now than it really *is* because it's Christmas. I'm going back to sleep."

"Okay. Call you tomorrow."

I got out my appointment book, looked on the page that had next year's calendar on it, found a date, then called her.

"October fifteenth," I said as soon as she picked up.

"What? Hello?" She sounded like she'd just fallen asleep. "Jack?" She yawned. "Did you get my message?"

"Yes, darling. I miss you too. October fifteenth."

"Okay," she said confused. "What about it?"

"It's a Saturday. We can have the reception in your mother's yard. The trees will be at their peak color."

She laughed low and deep. "Oh, honey. I love you."

"I love you too."

"I'm sorry about earlier."

"Me too. But listen . . ."

"What?" She yawned.

"Don't do that anymore, okay? It really stresses me out when you break up with me like that."

"What, honey? I didn't hear you. I was yawning."

I sighed. "Nothing. Never mind."

She yawned again and said, "How'd it go with Huckabee?"

"Go back to sleep. I'll tell you all about it tomorrow."

"Okay." She yawned another I love you then hung up.

I put the phone down, put the pad back in my jacket, got undressed, patted the bed for Frankie to jump up, then got under the covers and cuddled up next to him and waited for sleep to arrive and carry me into oblivion.

It took a long time to come.

30

On Saturday morning I made several phone calls to see if I could get someone to track down and detain Professor Hayes. I was worried that he might be about to skip the country, if he hadn't done so already, but no one seemed interested. The arrest warrant had already gone out for Huckabee, but he couldn't be found. There was an APB out on him.

Great, I thought. Here I was hoping he'd stick it out for Tim, no matter what, and he has to pull this stunt.

I got this information from Dan Coletti, who sympathized about Hayes—or so he said—but explained that until there was a warrant on him for something, anything, there was nothing he could do. He also told me that Hayes didn't make a good suspect because they'd confirmed that he'd used the ticket on the flight to La-Guardia the afternoon of the murder.

"You're sure it was actually him that boarded the plane?"

"It was either him or someone using his ID."

"Yeah, well, you should double-check to see if the

person who used the ticket actually matched his description."

"That's a stretch," he said. "Besides, we already know who the killer is—it's Huckabee. And what exactly is the con game this Hayes was supposed to be running on the Brights?"

I sighed. "I can't explain. It's way too wacky. Besides I promised Huckabee it would be off the record. But I'm telling you, Huckabee's not the guy. And Hayes could have taken the flight to LaGuardia then come right back to Maine."

"There's no record of him taking another flight."

"Of course not. If he's coming back to steal their jewels he's going to use a fake ID."

"Sorry, Jack, but with Huckabee fleeing, he looks better than ever for the murder. The case is closed."

"Thanks for nothing," I said.

Next I called the local police in Paducah, Kentucky, and explained about Shirley Schwarzbaum's disappearance ten years earlier. If they had any open cases for that time, they'd want to look at the magician she'd been traveling with. I faxed them all the information I got from Huckabee about Magnus/Hayes/Peterman's current whereabouts.

I went on to call an old pal of mine, Kevin O'Reilly, a detective out of Midtown South. Hayes's office was in his precinct.

He said, "I'd love to help you, Jack, but without some kind of paper on Hayes, there's nothing I can do."

"I can't get the locals to swear out a warrant, not even a material witness order. And I don't think the Brights will file a complaint on the con game he's been running. With the wife's background as a former maid, the scandal of this would ruin them socially. Can't you, I don't know, pick him up for jaywalking or spitting on the sidewalk?"

He laughed. "I suppose I could, if you faxed me a description or a photo of the guy and I happened to catch him in the act. So, how are things in Maine? You miss New York?"

"Like crazy sometimes and not at all at others."

"Well, call me the next time you're in town and we'll grab a beer and you can tell me all about it."

"Will do," I said.

Then I called Flynn and Sinclair. They each said they'd pass on their objections about Colbern, but it still didn't look like anything would be done about it until after the weekend.

Jamie called and I caught her up, and she promised to voice her own objections about Colbern again. She asked about Leon and how'd I sleep last night and that she couldn't wait to see me but had work to do at the hospital and wouldn't be able to sneak home until later. I liked the way she referred to my place as home.

I didn't say a word to her about Gretchen.

After we hung up I called the TV station and spoke to Lily Chow, who produces my biweekly dog training segments for the Saturday morning show. I wanted to spend the day working with the Dobermans—using their pretrained Schutzhund skills to get them to focus on the scent of Amy Frost's blood—and suggested that she videotape me doing it.

"It sounds interesting, Jack, but our viewers want real-life tips about how to train their own dogs."

"I know, but the murder is a big story right now and

I think the viewers will enjoy seeing some working dogs in action."

"Jack, the segment won't air until next Saturday. The story may be old news by then."

"I hope you're right. But it'll still be news. Plus, if you come out here you can also tape an interview of me talking about the case and put that on the air to*night*."

"You'll actually go on camera and talk about the case?"

"Yep. I've got a lot of inside dirt on it."

"I'll get the crew and be there as soon as possible."

I didn't have any PVC pipe, which is what's normally used for training detection dogs, so I smeared a tiny amount of Amy Frost's blood on the inside of a Kong—a hollow, cone-shaped, thick rubber, chew toy—and took Maxim and Fritz out to the play yard and had them play fetch for about half an hour.

Mrs. Murtaugh and D'Linda, her assistant groomer, arrived about ten. Saturday is a big day for the salon. With Christmas just a few days away, people want their dogs looking spiffy for when the relatives arrive, and for the cute little pictures they want to take of the doggie posing under the tree or by the fireplace or ripping up the wrapping paper after the presents have been opened.

I took care of some kennel business, schmoozed with a few of the dog owners who brought their dogs by, and was having a light lunch of three-bean and avocado salad, with a tall glass of red Gatorade—I don't remember what flavor it was supposed to be—when the phone rang. It was Kelso.

He'd been unable to track down Hayes, but had a

contact number for Dmitri Russevsky, the head of the Russian diamond- and jewel-fencing mob, and did I want it.

"Sure, he's going to be real glad to hear from me. I nearly killed two of his goons."

"Fine. *I'll* talk to him. What do you want to know?"

"Hayes stole some jewelry and I want to know if he's fenced it yet. The Russians might have heard something." I flipped through the file that Bailey had handed over to me and gave Kelso a description of the stolen items.

"Okay, I'll ask around discreetly and check back with you."

After he hung up I thought of something and called Ellis Bright's attorney, J. J Higginbottom and asked him how much Bright or his insurance company would be willing to pay to get the stolen jewels back.

"Why? Do you have them?"

"That's not an answer to the question I just asked."

"Look, do you have them or not?"

"Do you know how to answer a direct question or not?"

"What the hell kind of question is that?"

"I didn't think so. Call me when you have an answer."

As soon as I hung up I heard the sound of tires crunching through snow. I was expecting Lily and her crew, so I woke up Frankie and Hooch, put on my parka, and went outside.

It wasn't Lily. There were two vehicles parked in the drive, Chief Colbern's car and an animal-control van. Colbern was wearing his usual cheap suit and a wool coat. The animal-control guy, short, with dark eyes and a curly beard, wore a light green uniform and dark green parka.

Colbern said, "I got a report you're harboring two vicious dogs on your premises."

I said, "They're not vicious. Now get off my property."

He said, "Their owner, Ellis Bright is a Camden resident, so it *is* my business. I'm confiscating those dogs."

"You can't do that. Don't you know *anything* about the law?" I looked him over. "You look awfully spry today."

"What's that supposed to mean?"

"Nothing. I just heard that you spent the night in the county jail. It doesn't seem to have affected you much."

He scowled. "I'll deal with you and Flynn on that later. In court. Right now, I want you to produce those dogs."

I looked at the animal-control officer. He seemed like a reasonable guy. "Get in your van and leave."

He put his hands palm up. "I'm just responding to an emergency call."

"There's no emergency. The dogs are fine, they're legally in my care, and you have no jurisdiction."

He hesitated, looked at the chief, then said, "Do you have documentation showing they're here legally?"

"I don't need any. Do you have a warrant or a written complaint about the dogs?"

"No, but I *will* have to take a look at the animals."

"Fine. Follow me." To Colbern I said, "You can't come. And if you're not off my property by the time I get back, I'll have you arrested and thrown in jail again. You got it?"

"Tough talk," he said.

The animal-control officer, who told me his name was John Charchallis, followed me into the kennel, as did Frankie and Hooch. He looked the Dobies over. They were acting a little tense so I lied a little and said, "That's Max and Mathilde." The dogs became relaxed and happy. He rattled the gate to see if he could get them riled up and they just wagged their stubby tails.

He looked back at me, nodded, and said, "Fine. Sorry to have interrupted your day."

Colbern was still standing in front of his car when we got back outside. I said, "That's it, Chief. I warned you."

Charchallis went back toward his van and the chief stepped in front of him, and put his hand on the man's chest.

"Where do you think you're going?"

"Don't put your hands on me, sir."

"But those dogs are dangerous. They've already bit someone. You've got to do something about them."

Charchallis looked back at me.

I said, "They were staying with Kirk Collins."

He shook his head. "Serves him right. That idiot is always getting bit by some dog or another." He looked at Colbern. "I'm writing this up as a false report. You've wasted my time and the taxpayers' money."

Hooch came over to try to soothe the situation.

The chief looked down at him and took a black cylinder with a nozzle on top out of his coat pocket.

"Okay," I said, "hold on. What the hell is that?"

"Pepper spray. Get your dog back or I'll use it!"

Charchallis said, "You use it and I'll have you arrested for animal cruelty. That dog is just being friendly."

I stepped closer to him and said, "Hooch, stay!"

The chief said, "And I'm just protecting myself."

Hooch obeyed the stay command, but Colbern put his finger on the nozzle and aimed it. I ran in to take it from him, we wrestled with it for a moment, I twisted it around so the nozzle faced Colbern, and it went off, spraying him in the crotch and dousing both our hands with the fiery liquid.

He made a coarse and uncalled for comment about my mother. I wrested the bottle away from him then threw it as far as I could. Hooch held the stay but Frankie, thinking it was a toy, raced after it.

"Heyo, Frankie, come!" I shouted and he spun around, came running back to me and sat. "Good boy!" I said, then leaned down to grab some snow, which I then used to clean the pepper spray off my hand. I did this about ten times or so.

Charchallis got out his ticket pad and said, "I warned you, sir. I'm writing you up."

Colbern was looking at his pants. They were soaked, making it look like he'd pissed himself.

"This ain't over, Field."

"You're right it's not. I give that stuff about twenty seconds to soak all the way through to your skin."

He thought it over. "I gotta use your restroom."

"Sorry," I said, noticing that Lily Chow's remote van was just pulling off the county road onto the property. "That's for employees and guests only."

"Screw that," said Colbern. "I gotta wash it off."

"Not here you don't. I want you off my property. Now."

"Shit!" he said, which was followed by him grabbing his crotch. "Ow! Have a heart, Field."

While he scratched himself I said, "Like I didn't already have a heart when I refrained from spraying *you* in the face?"

Charchallis shook his head and kept writing.

"Ow! God, it burns!"

He tried to go past me, but I stepped in front of him and put a hand on his chest. He couldn't fight back because his hands were busy scratching his crotch. "Ow! Jesus! I'm sorry, okay? Let me use the can. Please?"

"Use the snow like I did."

Lily and her crew were getting out of the van. "Jack," she said, "what's going on?"

"Never mind," I shouted. "Turn the camera on!"

She put her arms in the air as if to say, "Why?"

Meanwhile Kenny, the cameraman, did as I instructed.

The chief, unable to get past me or stop the burning sensation, reached down for a handful of snow and stuffed it down his pants. It didn't help much. He was sweating now.

I told Frankie and Hooch, "Go back up to the house."

They thought about that a moment, then obeyed, trotting all the way up to the front porch.

Kenny came in for a closer shot. Charchallis stopped writing his ticket to watch. And to laugh.

The chief was stuffing more snow into his pants, which were now soaked from the belt to the knees.

"Oh, mother!" he shouted, then undid his belt, dropped his pants around his ankles and began shoveling snow onto himself, totally naked from the waist down to his black knee socks. He turned and saw Kenny. "Turn that off!" he shouted.

"Keep it running," said Lily. "This is good."

Kenny—holding the camera with one hand—gave a thumbs up.

Charchallis was doubling over with laughter.

"Crap!" Colbern tried to pull his pants up but the burning was still too intense, so he dropped to his knees, then thrust his hips into the snow, with his hairy white ass sticking up in the air.

Charchallis fell against the side of his van; laughing so hard he couldn't stand up straight.

Colbern began twisting around, thrusting his hips into the snow, doing anything he could to stop the burning.

Lily Chow came up next to me, holding a Thermos of coffee with mittened hands. She took a sip, looked at the chief, shook her head and said, "Funny way to make snow angels."

"Well, he soaked himself with pepper spray."

"Ouch, that's gotta hurt."

"Yep. A lot of Scoville units there."

She looked over at Kenny. "You realize," she said to me, "we won't be able to actually air any of this footage."

"Sure you will. You'll just have to electronically blur out the naughty bits."

She nodded, considering it. "That's true. But what's the caption? Camden Police Chief Humps Snow Bank?"

"Works for me. Plus, you can always leak it to some Internet site or something. They'll run it uncut."

"The hell!" said the chief, whose crotch had to be both freezing and burning by now. He got to his knees, tried to pull his pants up, but fell over, which is when Kenny had to put the camera down. He was laughing too hard.

Come to think of it, so were the rest of us.

"You think this is funny?" Colbern said, falling over again. "I'm filing charges against all of you!"

Kenny, under control now, went back to shooting.

Chuckling I said, "Good luck with that, Chief."

Colbern stood up, bent over, pulled his pants up, and said, "I want that videotape! It's an invasion of privacy."

I said, "It's an invasion of *lunacy*. Besides, you moron, you're on *my* property, remember? Illegally, I might add."

"Sorry," Lily said to Colbern, "but when a chief of police loses his marbles, that's news."

I said to him, "Think of the upside. Maybe the Chamber of Commerce will let you have your old job back."

Lily Chow shook her head. "After this airs? Doubtful."

Colbern stumbled to his car, got in, and drove off, fishtailing the whole way up the drive.

Charchallis smiled at me and said, "Seems like the day wasn't a total waste after all. It's not often you get to see something like that."

Just then, Mrs. Murtaugh came out of the kennel building and called, "Jack! There's a phone call from New York!"

"Who is it? Lou Kelso?"

"No, a Dmitri somebody or other. He sounds Russian."

31

Dmitri Russevsky had a softly gruff voice, matching the counterpoint of his words, which were both sweetly apologetic and darkly threatening. After I'd had enough of his hide-and-seek, conversational approach I said, "Listen, Dmitri—may I call you Dmitri?"

"Please do, my friend." He even made the word "friend" sound like a threat.

"Okay, Dmitri, you want to find Andreyev Gregori and I know where he is—sort of. As for me—I want to know anything you can tell me about some stolen jewels, and whether the thief, whose name is Hayes, has been trying to fence them in New York."

"And you will tell me where Andreyev is?"

"I'll do better than that. I'll see to it that he returns the money he took from you, and doubles it."

He made a sound that could have been a laugh. "And why would that interest me more than punishing him?"

"I don't know what interests you, Dmitri. I just think it might be more advantageous to get your money back than it would be to add another dead Russian to the pile."

"Okay, I think about it. Anything else?"

"Yeah. Hayes doesn't get to fence his jewels in New York. Whatever arrangement he had going, whether with you or with Gregori, is out for the time being."

"What a guy. You tells me what to do with my business now? What else you offer me?"

"I won't file a complaint against your three enforcers for trying to kill me."

"That shouldn't have happened. I didn't realize you was law enforcement." He thought it over. "How do you know I can contact this Professor Hayes?"

"How do you know he's a professor? Did I say he was a professor?" Another laugh. "And the truth is, I thought it over, Dmitri. Gregori's photo wasn't in the local papers or on the local news like one of your goons claimed, and if it *had* been, you're in New York, so how did your goons show up on his doorstep so quickly? You had to have inside information on his whereabouts. Who else could have gotten you that information except Professor Hayes?"

"What a guy. You're right. The only trouble is, if him and me makes a deal, it will happen this evening."

"Not if you stall him."

He grunted then said, "Why should I puts off what could be wery lucrative arrangement? If I were involved in such things, that is?"

"Because those jewels are part of a murder investigation. Fencing them would make you an accessory after the fact."

"*Da,* okay. Makes sense. How long till I get my money?"

"It'll take me a day or two to get it together. Today's Saturday, give me till Wednesday."

"Very well. You have till Tuesday, Mr. Field."

After I got off the phone, I took a deep breath, and then took Maxim and Fritzie outside and started working with them, again, this time for the cameras.

"This is kind of gruesome, isn't it?" said Lily. "Having them racing around, searching for the victim's blood?"

"I never thought about it before, but I guess you're right. Unfortunately, it's the only way to get them to find evidence in a murder investigation."

Then I leashed up the dogs, took them up to the kennel building, and told Mrs. Murtaugh and D'Linda to take a lunch break, that we were going to be using the kennel for taping.

I put the dogs in their kennel, got out a pair of Pliofilm gloves, put them on, and went to one of the rawhide bins—there are three of them, small, medium, and large. I placed a tiny drop of the victim's blood on a brand new rawhide retriever in the medium bin. I put it back with about twelve others. I also touched each of the rawhides in all of the bins to make sure they all had the same exact scent except for the one with the blood drop.

I let Max out, and said, "Okay, find!" He raced around, his toenails clattering on the concrete floor. Then he stopped, lifted his nose in the air, raced to the rawhide bins, sniffed the medium bin, then sat and barked once.

"Good boy, Max!"

Lily said, "That is so amazing."

"Ain't it. And don't give me any credit. I barely know what I'm doing here. I'm just reminding the dogs of something they already learned from a German master trainer."

I put Max back in the kennel and repeated the process with Fritz and he was just as successful as his "brother."

Lily said, "It's not like they're being taught anything at all. It's like they're just having fun."

"No kidding. They *live* for this kind of stuff."

I took Max out of his kennel again and gave both dogs a bone and let them lie on the floor and chew them.

"Now," I said to Lily, "watch this. Maxim, Fritzie!" They looked up. I pointed to Lily. *"Wachen Sie."*

They dropped their bones, stood up, and bared their teeth and growled at her menacingly.

(Don't try this at home.)

Lily gripped her clipboard tightly. "Uh, Jack? Could you make them stop before I pee my pants?"

"Sure." To the dogs I said, "Mathilde," and they relaxed, shook themselves in unison, and wagged their tails.

"You want to go over there and pet them?" I asked Lily.

"No way," she said.

"Go ahead," I laughed. "They're the sweetest doggies."

"Uh, I believe you, but no thanks."

"Come on," I said. "It'll look good on camera."

"Yeah, but won't they bite me?"

"Nope."

"Are you sure?"

"Yep. I guarantee it. They are superbly trained animals."

"That's what Siegfried and Roy said about their tigers." She took a deep breath. "Okay. Here goes nothing."

She walked carefully over, put one hand out for the

dogs to sniff, and they wagged their tails and licked her hand.

"Amazing," she said and breathed a sigh of relief.

(And don't try *this* at home either.)

Once playtime was over, and the Dobermans were put back in their kennel, I did the interview about "the case of the murdered maid" and made no bones about the fact that the police were after the wrong man, that there was another, unnamed suspect who was the real killer, and that the whole case had been botched from the beginning by Chief Colbern.

"In fact," I said, ending the interview, "recent events suggest that the chief may be suffering from a severe mental illness or emotional breakdown."

I made the "cut" sign, zipping my hand across my throat, and Lily said, "Perfect! Great tag line, Jack! We'll cut directly to the shots of Colbern humping the snowbank!"

Everyone started laughing. While we were all doubled over I heard another car coming down the driveway.

I went to the door and saw Jamie's green Jaguar sedan.

"Okay, everybody. Jamie's here. And I haven't seen my sweetie since we had a big fight last night, so it's time for you all to hit the road."

Lily nodded and said, "Makeup sex, huh?"

"That's what I'm hoping."

Kenny said, "Can we videotape that too?"

"What do you think?"

Tenderness, longing, guilt, anger, the desire to be in control, the willingness to give it up, the fear that you can never make things work no matter how hard you try, the need to keep trying anyway, all these things went into it, and when it was over all I could say was, "We oughta break up more often."

Jamie laughed.

"I'm serious."

"And I'd agree with you except I couldn't stand it if we were ever apart again, for whatever reason."

"Good point," I said, then sighed. "I don't suppose we could just *pretend* to break up once in a while?"

"It wouldn't be the same." She clutched me. "And let's not even pretend, ever again."

"Hey, I won't if you won't."

She nodded. "I think I learned my lesson."

"Good. Are you ready to come with me to the mansion and look for the murder weapon?"

"We can't. The case is closed, the crime scene has been processed out. We'd need a warrant, which we won't get."

"You've got to be kidding me. I spent the whole day working with Maxim and Fritz, and for what?"

"That's the way the cookie crumbles sometimes."

I wondered, briefly, if I should tell her about Gretchen but decided not to.

"But we're so close to catching the killer," I said.

"Anyway, it's Christmas. There are other things to think about now."

"I know," I said, just going along. "Like what?"

"Like the fact that the Coast Guard picked up Chris Bright today and they've got him in custody. So now we have his DNA."

"I don't suppose the results are back yet?"

"It takes a while, Jack. And I hope they find Tim Huckabee's idiot father before it's too late."

"He's probably in New York."

"Really?"

"I think so. He's got a girlfriend there."

"I almost had his grandparents talked into okaying the surgery, but now that he's disappeared . . . oh, and did I tell you about the bioluminescent dinoflagellates? They're from a company in Michigan that supplies college biology labs."

"That's interesting." I told her about the "magic pool" on the third floor of the mansion.

"So that's how the plankton got on the murder weapon, and from there into the victim's wound. What a strange . . ."

"Setup?"

"Something. Who in a million years?"

"I know." I thought about it. "She was eight. Maybe she was supposed to be watching him when he fell into the well, and's been in denial ever since."

"Poor Ellis."

"Yeah, poor Ellis, except some people thrive on taking care of women like Fiona."

We lay there, holding each other, listening to the sparrows chirp their evening song and Starsky and Hutch snore, and I finally said, "What if we could find access to the Brights' property without going through the front gate?"

"What do you mean?"

"Leon thinks he knows how to find the exit to the underground tunnel, if there *is* one."

She nodded. "That would work."

"Good. I'll get the dogs while you get dressed."

"Okay," she said, kissing me. "But it can wait just a few minutes longer, can't it?"

I wanted to say no, I really did. But my mouth wasn't in a position to argue.

32

The fog was back and wafting around the front gate as we arrived at the mansion. There was no light coming from inside the house. I parked the woody next to a heavy wooden guardrail that stood idealistically between the slush-gray edge of the winding road and the rocky cliff overlooking the ocean.

Leon looked down at a map he'd printed out from a web page and said, "Well, the house was built on the site of an old First Congregational Church. That's where the escaped slaves stayed before moving on to the next leg of the journey to Canada. I think they went by boat, though there's no record of it. It was all secret."

"Hey, you *do* pay attention in history class. So if the tunnel started inside the house, where did it lead to?"

He pointed to a wooden stairway, wending to the rocky beach. "I think it's at the bottom of the cliff."

"Okay," I said, opening the car door, "here goes nothing." I went around to the back and opened the tailgate. "Come on Maxie, Fritz!"

Jamie got out her side. She was carrying her ME's

bag and a large flashlight. Leon got out of the back seat, carrying his maps, another flashlight, and a knapsack.

We went to the top of the stairway and I stepped on the first tread. It creaked and wobbled. Jamie expressed concern about whether the dogs—let alone the rest of us—would be able to negotiate the stairs, but Max and Fritz saw where I was headed and scampered ahead of me and down the steps like a couple of old pros, though Fritz did slip on the bottom step. I love those dogs, I thought. In fact, I want to *be* like them: brave, focused, and never off track.

The rest of the safari maneuvered slowly down the stairs, and got to the rocky, snow-covered beach. The hard part of the adventure was keeping our balance on the slippery rocks, while we looked for the hidden entrance to the tunnel.

Jamie asked, "How are we going to find it?"

It wasn't that hard, as long as you know how to trust a dog's instincts. Maxim and Fritz went straight to a boulder, about three feet in diameter, and started barking.

Hmmm, I thought, an egret's nest, a badger hole? A hidden stash of liver treats? Or the secret way out of the elfin kingdoms, a la Magnus the Magnevolent?

I told them to back off, which they did, and noticed that there was about a one-foot crack of empty space above the boulder. I pulled the big rock to the side, surprised at how easily it moved.

"How did you do that?" Jamie asked.

"I don't know," I said, shining my flash around the bottom of it. "It seems to be on some sort of track that's been carved under the rock."

I pulled it back all the way and behind it was a

squarish tunnel entrance, about four feet high and wide, with tool marks on the floor and walls.

"This is amazing," said Jamie.

"It sure is."

"Damn, I'm good," Leon said from behind me.

"Yeah, you and the doggies."

"Six of one," he said, as the dogs went through the entrance. "I wonder if they left anything behind."

"Who, the elves?"

"No, my peeps" he said as he began to crawl forward.

"I get it," I said, going after him. "That's why you brought the knapsack? To bring back some of the things the freed slaves might've left behind?"

"That's right, Pops," he said. "I'm hoping to find some artifacts. A museum would love to get their hands on some authentic stuff from the underground railroad."

"He's right," Jamie said from behind us. "If it can be authenticated, this tunnel will become a historical landmark."

"Yeah," I said. "I bet a museum would pay you pretty good, too."

Leon stopped crawling. "I never thought of that. But it ain't about money, it's about preserving the history of the struggle. You realize that the underground railroad is one of the greatest civil rights movements in history?"

"I never thought about it, Leon, but you're right."

"Of course I'm right. I'm always right, didn't you know that? I get it from *you.*"

Jamie said, "Can we not talk so much and just get to the other end as quickly as possible?"

"What's the matter, sweetheart? You sound unhappy."

"The tunnel could collapse on us, okay?"

"Honey, it's been here for over a hundred years."

"Like that's an argument for safety?"

The three flashlights threw their beams at odd angles as we crawled up a fairly steep incline. The dogs raced ahead, then raced back to make sure we were still following them.

I said, "It must've taken a lot of work to build this."

"It makes you think, doesn't it?" Jamie panted. "Slavery was abolished, what? A hundred and fifty years ago? And—"

"A hundred and forty," Leon corrected.

"Right. And I don't think I've ever really stopped to consider what it was like for—Jack watch your foot!"

"Sorry."

"Or looked at it from anything but a historical or maybe a legal perspective. This tunnel really makes you stop and think about the humanity involved."

"It sure does," I said.

Leon gave us a history lesson on when slavery was abolished in other countries: 1791 in France, though they didn't even have slaves at the time, 1821 in Spain, 1823 in Chile, 1824 in Central America, 1829 in Mexico, 1831 in Bolivia, 1838 in Great Britain, 1854 in Venezuela, etc.

I said, "And *we* didn't get around to it until 1865."

Jamie said, "Right. And we still refer to most of those other countries as backward."

We crawled along, and after a bit Jamie sneezed

"I guess the dust is getting to you, huh?"

"I don't think so," she said. "I think I smell perfume on your parka."

"It couldn't be. How did—oh, wait a minute."

"Yes?"

"Well, there was a woman at the bar where I met

Huckabee last night. She'd had a little too much to drink so I got her a cab."

"That doesn't explain how her perfume—"

"She put her arms around me while I was walking her out to the parking lot. She was having trouble standing up."

"Did you know her?"

I made a noise in my throat.

"What does that mean?"

"It means that I didn't know her, exactly. Can we not talk about this right now?"

"There's a good idea," said Leon.

"Fine," Jamie huffed.

We came to a narrow opening in the rock and squeezed our way through. The dogs were waiting inside a small chamber made of solid rock and dirt shored up by very old timbers. There was a cast-iron ladder at the far end.

Leon shone his flashlight around the room, looking for artifacts. Jamie and I used ours to look for evidence. The dogs kept running over to us, then back to the ladder. They really wanted to go upstairs.

Leon said, "Yo, check it." He was pointing his flash at the wall next to the tunnel door. Carved in the rock was the word "Freedom" with an arrow pointing toward the exit.

Leon put his hand up to feel the letters, then threw his backpack down, turned around, sat down with his back against the wall, put his head between his knees, and began to cry.

Jamie took my hand. The Dobies sat next to our feet.

"It really brings it home, doesn't it?" she said.

I said, "Jesus, the things these people went through for something we all take for granted."

"And not just the slaves. The people who cared for them. They could have been put in jail for what they did." She looked at Leon sympathetically and said, "I guess you got a little taste of that this afternoon, didn't you, Leon?"

"Yeah," he said, wiping his eyes, "and I didn't like it. But yo, bein' a slave? That had to be a million times worse." He sniffled a bit, then said, "And even if I found something here, you know? I don't think I could take it and give it to no museum. It oughta stay in this room."

"You're right, Leon," I said. "Everything should stay just as it is." Then a glint of metal caught my eye. It was a steel key. "Except this." I went over, picked it up by its edges, and showed it to Jamie. "Maybe the key to a safety deposit box? See those numbers and the ID? It's from a Swiss bank."

She nodded. "I'll bet it fell out of the professor's coat when he was trying to squeeze his way out of here."

"Yeah, and he can't get into that safe deposit box without it. Which means he's got to come back for it."

"So we've got him?"

"If he figures out that it's here. But we've also got to find that walking stick first. It's got to be the murder weapon. I'll bet it's up wherever that ladder leads."

"How do you know?"

"That's what Maxim and Fritz are trying to tell us. And dogs are never wrong, especially *these* dogs."

Jamie opened her kit, got out a small evidence bag, and I put the key in it, gave it back to her, and she wrote KEY on the bag with a Sharpie, followed by the date and location, then put it in the kit.

I shone my flash on the ladder. "If he didn't take the

murder weapon with him, or leave it inside the tunnel, that's where it's gotta be. And these dogs know it."

"How do we get them up the ladder?"

I laughed. "If I know these two, they'd figure out a way to shinny up a rope if it got them closer to the smell of the victim's blood. But we'll only need to take Max up. You go first, and we'll follow you."

"Okay," she said. "But I don't see how this is going to work."

She put her flashlight in the pocket of her parka and began climbing the iron rungs. I held my flash on the ladder so she could see. She got to the top, where there was a trapdoor. She pushed up on it. Nothing happened.

"Push harder," I suggested.

"I'm pushing as hard as I can."

"Come back down and *I'll* do it."

"Wait a second, there's a lever. It looks new. I couldn't see it before because your flashlight keeps moving."

She pushed it and it didn't move. Then she pulled it and we heard something scraping and moving.

"It didn't do anything," she said.

"It did *some*thing. Push on the door again."

She did and it opened right up.

"Okay," I said. "I'm bringing the dog up. I turned to Leon. "You coming?"

"Yeah, I'll be up in a minute," he said, staring at his feet. Then he looked up at me and said, "You know, I'm not that different from you and Jamie. I never thought about slavery much before this. But when I go home for Christmas I'm gonna ask my grams about my family history."

"I bet you come from some brave and strong people."

"Seems like I gotta lot to live up to, huh?"

"And you *will*. Hell, son, you already *are*."

"Thanks, Pops."

I turned and saw that Jamie had switched on the lights in the room above us. "Where are you, honey?"

"It's the basement and laundry room," she called down. "I don't see the murder weapon anywhere."

"Don't worry. If it's up there Max'll find it." I turned to him. "Won't you boy?" He wagged his stub.

We went to the ladder and I picked Max up, holding him under his chest with my right arm and steadying him under the chin and throat with my left hand. Fritz barked at me and I praised him then suggested he keep quiet. He did. I hoisted Max's back paws onto the third rung, then placed his front paws on the fifth. With my left hand I moved his left front paw onto the sixth rung, and his right rear paw onto the fourth, holding his body steady with my right hand.

I began climbing, helping Max manage the rungs as best he could. "Come on, Max!" I said. "You want to find the blood? Huh? You're a good boy!" My words, and the emotion in my voice motivated him to climb higher on his own.

Jamie was waiting at the top, sitting with her legs spraddling the entrance—I sometimes forget how limber she is from yoga class. She reached down to help the dog up the last leg of the trip and fell backward. He must've been licking her face because she was giggling and saying, "Max, stop it! Stop!" in a happy voice.

I got through the entrance and we sat there a moment. Max went back and forth between us, licking our faces.

I stood up, looked around, and saw a clothes dryer,

which had been pulled away from the wall. Its "footprint" was roughly the same size as the trapdoor.

"That's how the door was hidden," Jamie said, "underneath the dryer. The lever pulls it out of the way."

"Very clever. I wonder what they hid it under, back in the 1800s." I went back to the trapdoor and called down to Leon. "You okay, down there?"

"Yeah. I'm coming up in a second."

"Bring Jamie's kit with you."

"Okay."

Max lifted his nose in the air and began barking. Fritz joined in from downstairs.

"Okay, boy! Where is it?"

He went straight to the washing machine and barked at the wall behind it. I pulled the washer back and didn't see anything. He maneuvered around the big metal obstacle and renewed his barking at the wall itself. I noticed a loose board, pulled it back, and saw the top, knobbed end, of a hand-carved wooden walking stick, or wizard's staff.

"Good boy, Max!" I said and reached into one of my pockets and gave him a Kong to chew.

"I need some gloves," I told Jamie.

Leon had arrived with Jamie's kit, pushing it through the trap door ahead of him.

"Coming right up," Jamie said.

Fritz, poor guy, was now wailing from downstairs. He wanted so badly to climb up and join us.

"What if someone's home?" Jamie said. "Won't they come down to see what the noise is about?"

"Good point." To Leon I said, "Go back downstairs and keep Fritz occupied."

"How?"

I reached into the other pocket of my parka and tossed him a second Kong. (I have big pockets.)

Jamie put on a pair of Pliofilm gloves, went past me toward the wall and said, "Let me take care of the evidence."

She reached down into the space between the studs, pulled the walking stick up, holding it gingerly beneath the knobbed end with one hand and guiding it away from the boards with the other. She placed it gently on top of the washing machine and peered at the knobbed end. "Looks like blood and hair," she said. "I'll do a presumptive test."

I could hear Leon playing fetch with Fritz, while Max lay happily on the basement floor and chewed his own Kong.

Jamie got out a cotton swab and did her presumptive test. "It's definitely human blood," she said, when she was done.

Then she dusted the rest of the staff for fingerprints. None were visible.

"Now what, Jack?"

"Good question. Without fingerprints we can't definitely prove that Hayes is the killer, unless his DNA matches the tissue under her nails. For that we have to catch him, and he's going to be hard to catch."

"That sucks. If the DNA's a match, we'd have a solid case. But, Jack, it's *his* walking stick, right?"

"Yes, but anybody could've used it—Huckabee, Chris Bright, even the old lady."

She laughed. "She's a suspect now, too?"

"I can dream, can't I?" I thought it over and said, "The thing about a con game is you need to have something the mark wants or *thinks* he wants. With Fiona

Bright it was contacting her brother. I'll bet Professor Hayes wants what's inside his safe deposit box just as much, if not more. I think our best choice is to use that key to run a con game on him."

"But, Jack, we could definitely get an arrest warrant based on this new evidence."

"Maybe," I agreed, "but an arrest warrant or a grand jury indictment are a far cry from a murder conviction, which is what we *really* want. Plus, my feeling is that as soon as a warrant is issued, he'll be on his way to Brazil or Tahiti or somewhere. After all, he started out as a magician, honey. If he knows anything, it's how to disappear."

"So what do we do?"

"We have to bag the evidence—the staff and the key—but we can't tell anybody about it. We have to put it in a secure place, preferably at the morgue. Then we go to New York."

"What's in New York?"

"Didn't you know? Just about everything."

33

Around ten on Sunday morning I called Kristin Downey and told her I was coming to New York after all and would be happy to spend a little time with Jen, teaching her how to train her Christmas-present doggie. She was happy to hear it and said she'd take care of our travel arrangements and hotel accommodations, but told me, "The thing is, Jen doesn't know about Daisy yet. We're sort of hiding her in the maid's room downstairs until Christmas morning."

"Okay, well—"

"But you could meet Daisy and do a little work with her yourself, maybe give me and Marta a few pointers."

"Marta?"

"Our housekeeper. She walks Daisy every day. Oh, and Jack, the dog pulls on the leash something awful."

"That's easy. Does she like to play games?"

"How do I know? We've only had her a few days."

She arranged for Sonny's private jet to fly up to the Belfast airport. On the drive there Jamie and I were on our cell phones. I called Kelso, my pal Kevin O'Reilly from the NYPD, and Vanessa Martin, who said she'd try to get me a two-minute spot on the *Today* show the next morning.

I said to Jamie, "Honey, could you look in my notebook and find Professor Hayes's number for me?" I pointed to the carry-on bag between her feet. "It's in the side pocket."

She found the notepad, opened it and said, "Jack?" She looked at me accusingly. "What is Gretchen's phone number doing in here?"

My face fell. I'd forgotten about that. "Oh. Well, the thing is, Gretchen was the woman in the bar the other night."

"She was?"

I sighed. "You broke up with me, remember? But I was still following the 72-hour rule, so I had Gretchen give me her number in case you were really serious, so I could call her on Monday night."

She sighed and handed me the notepad. "I'm never breaking up with you again."

"I certainly hope not."

She patted my knee and said, "Make your phone call."

I called Hayes, got a machine, and left a message saying that we were coming to New York and would love to see him, and that he could catch us on the *Today* show on Monday morning. Then we got to the airport, got on the jet and the five of us—me, Leon, Jamie, Frankie, and Hooch—took a ride south.

Once we were airborne, and Leon started breathing again, Jamie said, "Jack? I was just thinking, about the way the third floor of the mansion is set up?"

"Yeah?"

"Well, it just occurred to me that it sounds like something a Broadway set designer might have designed."

"Wow. You're probably right. I'll talk to Kristin. But that would be one hell of a coincidence, wouldn't it?"

"Stranger things have happened in this case."

"That's true."

One of the great things about flying to New York in a private jet is that you can ask the pilot to take a little ride along the Hudson before making the final approach at Teterboro, which gives you a nice view of the skyline, especially if you arrive a little before sunset, with rain clouds just starting to gather, which we did.

"It looks so pretty," Jamie said, looking out the window at the slanted, peach-colored light falling on the buildings, which stood in stark contrast to the silver-gray clouds behind them. "And it seems so calm from up here."

A limo met us at Teterboro and we got the luggage into the trunk and the dogs inside the car, dropped Leon off in Harlem, with an awkward kiss on the cheek from his grandma McMurfree, and a happy dance around him from his little sister Althea, who's seven, then had the driver take us to the Carlyle. They allow dogs, and it's located two blocks from the Vreeland's Park Avenue apartment.

"Any ideas yet, Columbo?" Jamie said after we'd unpacked. She was lounging in an arm chair and flipping through the "Arts & Leisure" section. The dogs were curled up on the king-size bed. Frankie was sound asleep, but Hooch looked around the suite with a happy grin on his face, as if he'd finally made the big time.

Jamie said, "Hey, Tierney Sutton is playing."

"No kidding? On a Sunday night?"

"Yes, according to the *New York Times*," she said. "And they rarely lie."

I laughed and said, "You want to go hear her?"

"Sure, after we eat. I'm starrrving. What's *your* plan?"

"I'm not sure. I have the inkling of something, but I don't know if I'm smart enough to pull it off."

"I find that hard to believe."

"Yeah, well, it involves conning a master con man."

"Now that sounds interesting. Do you want to call room service or is there some place good to eat around here?"

"You mean good, or *good* because Boulud is kitty-corner across the street, though we'd probably need a reservation a month or so in advance."

"The thing is, I'm just kind of in the mood for a greasy cheeseburger."

"Okay, Soup Joint it is, then. It's just down the street. And I'll have Kelso meet us there."

So we were sitting at the counter eating cheeseburgers, watching the December rain start to come down hard on Madison Avenue, when Kelso showed up, full of information, which he delivered, off center, Kelso-style, in the form of a question, though he had to make a commentary about my naked face first.

"What happened to your beard?" he said, taking off his fedora and loosening the belt of his Burberry trench coat.

"I shaved it." I tilted my head at Jamie. "She's not too happy about it, either."

She shrugged. "I'm getting used to it."

"Well, *don't*," I said. "I'm growing it back."

"That's the thing about beards," Kelso said, getting the counterman's attention, "you can always grow them back." He ordered a cheddar cheeseburger deluxe, rare, with a side of mayo then said, "So, how was your recent trip to Switzerland?"

"Okay, I'll bite. What trip did I make to Switzerland?"

"Well, I did some checking on the passenger manifests for all flights to Zurich in the past few days and found out that a man named Jack Field flew to Zurich on Wednesday, stayed for two hours and flew straight back to Kennedy."

"You mean Hayes has stolen my identity?"

"Pretty funny, huh?"

"No. And it's a good thing I don't own a credit card."

"Well, you do now, my friend. Several, in fact."

"Oh, that's just great."

Jamie said, "Oh, Jack," and squeezed my hand.

"He's got your social security number, access to your bank account, your mother's maiden name, the whole nine—"

"Can we prove it?"

"Nope. Not unless we catch him in the act."

I thought it over. He spent only two hours in Zurich; maybe he lost his safe deposit key and didn't realize it until after he got to the bank.

I said, "This guy is awfully tricky, isn't he?"

"Yep. And slippery as an elf."

Jamie said, "How does he do it? Find out so much about people, like you and the Brights?"

I recounted what Huckabee had told me concerning how Hayes uses surveillance techniques to learn all he can about his marks.

Jamie said, "I still can't believe he went through all that, just to bilk her out of some money."

"Yeah, and it's all just a game to him," I said.

"No, it's a science," Kelso said. "He's a failed scientist, Hayes. I think that's what he really is."

"You mean he could have found a cure for cancer instead of screwing up people's lives? And let's stop calling him Hayes. His name is Harold Peterman, and he's a killer and he's probably using credit cards with my name on them right now to pay for a couple of hookers."

Kelso nodded. "Yep. He's got a bad bone."

Jamie smiled. "What does that mean?"

"You've heard the saying, 'so-and-so doesn't have a bad bone in his body'? Well, this guy's got a bad bone in his body."

She nodded in agreement. "He sure does," she said.

We called Brad Bailey, gave him what we knew. He gave us what *he* knew, which is that the State Police had finally decided to take over the case, Bailey got his job back, Colbern was out as chief, Coletti was now the acting chief, and Bailey was working with the State Police to put Professor Hayes into custody.

"You mean 'Jack Field,' " I said, "since that's what he's going by now. And the warrant on Huckabee is off the books?"

"Yep. And there's an arrest order going out tonight on Harold Peterman/AKA Professor Hayes. I'm coming to New—"

"No, hold off on that for twenty-four hours. And keep the warrant out on Huckabee." He wanted to know why. "Just trust me, okay?" I sighed. "I hope he hasn't got into my retirement account or Leon's college fund. The checking account doesn't have much in it right now."

"But why take *your* money," Bailey asked, "when he's got all those jewels?"

"Two reasons: he knows I'm after him and wants to taunt me, and he hasn't been able to fence them yet."

He said, "Which brings us back to Karl?"

"Sort of." I sighed. I didn't want to explain about my conversation with Dmitri Russevsky, or that Karl was somewhere in New York. I didn't want to put him on the official radar, just in case it also put a Karl-sized blip on Dmitri's screen, so I said, "Were you about to say you're coming to New York?"

"Yeah, tomorrow morning."

"All right. Call us when you get in."

"Will do," he said and hung up.

Kelso dipped his french fry into some ketchup mixed with mayonnaise and said, "You were being a little light on some of the information with this Bailey, weren't you?"

I shrugged. "He's not a bad guy, but he's a little green. I don't entirely trust him to keep his mouth shut."

"So, what's our next step?" Jamie said.

"Two things: we want to find Huckabee and get him on a plane back to Rockland Memorial for the damn kidney transplant, and we want to smoke out Peterman. I have an old client who's a producer for Matt Lauer." I told Kelso about Vanessa Martin. "She's giving us a few minutes on the *Today* show tomorrow morning to talk about Huckabee and make a Christmas pitch for the little boy's kidney. That kind of thing goes over big this time of year. Jamie can state that in her medical opinion Huckabee was wrongfully convicted—"

"*May* have been wrongfully convicted—"

"Of his wife's murder five years ago, yada, yada, yada. And since we now know Peterman has stolen my identity, though I doubt if he's still using it—"

Kelso said, "Nothing's showed up since that plane flight on Wednesday. I'll check on those hookers, though."

"Thanks," I said with a sour laugh. "Anyway, he obviously knows I'm working the case. And *I* know he's missing something valuable—that safe deposit key. If I can make him think I've got it, he may be willing to deal." I left some money on the counter. "Are you coming with us?"

"To where?" Kelso said.

"To hear Tierney Sutton. She's playing at Le Jazz au Bar."

Kelso scowled. "I would, but I don't feel like being your chaperone."

My cell phone rang. I clicked it open. It was Dmitri and he wanted to meet with me. Alone. Now.

I hung up and told Jamie and Kelso what he wanted.

"A late-night meeting under the Brooklyn Bridge?" Kelso said. "Maybe I *should* chaperone."

34

The gothic arches of the Brooklyn Bridge hung above the black water of the East River: water so black that only the ghost-blue lights of the bridge and the Christmas lights strung around the River Café, perched on a small pier just across the estuary, with their reflections dancing and rippling with the movement of the current, were all that delineated the river from the rest of the night.

Jamie said, "It's very picturesque, but a bit smelly, isn't it?"

I shrugged. "It's the fish market," I said. "You wait here. I'll go see what Dmitri wants."

"Okay, Jack. But be careful."

"Don't worry, Kelso's hiding out there somewhere, keeping an eye on me, probably lurking behind a bluefin tuna."

I told the cabbie to keep the motor running, got out, and went over to the long, shiny black limousine.

A door opened silently and I got in. I was surprised to find myself alone with Russevsky. I had imagined at least two synthetic steroid-enhanced goons, one on either side of him, ready to smack some sense into me if I got sarcastic.

"Mr. Field," he said, putting a very large hand—with jeweled rings flashing from all ten fingers—on my knee, "thank you for meetings me here. Sorry for the inconvenience, but I live in Brooklyn, you're at Carlyle . . . is meetings you halfway here under bridge, yes?"

"I suppose."

"Where is your lovely fiancée?"

"I left her in the cab."

He laughed and his double chin jiggled. "What a guy. You were afraid there might be violence?"

"Afraid? No. Just cautious."

I rolled down my window and motioned to Jamie to join me. Dmitri and I waited silently as she came over and got in.

She sat down, then leaned over and shook his hand, which meant I had to follow suit. I didn't particularly want to do it, but I did anyway. When his big mitt let go of my hand he said, "I don't think I apologize before, on phone."

"Apologize for what?" I said, genuinely puzzled.

"The littles misunderstanding you had with some friends of mine in hospital parking lot up north."

"I thought you did. Well, apology accepted."

"Good. Now, something to drink? Vodka, scotch?"

"Sure, I'll have a scotch, neat," I said.

"Nothing for me," said Jamie.

He poured our drinks—his and mine—handed me my glass and said, "I did a little checkings into you, Mr. Field."

"Yeah?" I said, and thought for a second that he had a dog-training problem and that's why he wanted our meeting to be private. It wouldn't have been the first time I'd given free training advice to an underworld figure.

"I speaks personally to Hayes last night. He wasn't happy about postponings sale of certain items in his possession, but he agreed to another meeting on Tuesday."

"Did you meet with him in person?"

He gave me a look. "He's too careful for that."

"I see."

He took a sip of vodka then said, "You're not just here in New York to findings this Professor Hayes, though are you? You're searchings for man with a sick son."

Jamie and I looked at each other. "That's right," I said. "What does that have to do—?"

He gave a careless shrug. "I'm father, myself." He tilted his head again, slightly. "And it's Christmas . . ."

"I still don't follow."

He sat there, smiling and drinking his vodka. I sipped my scotch and puzzled it out. Then I got it: he was offering to help us find Huckabee—out of the goodness of his heart, not for any quid pro quo. He was a sentimental sap and didn't want his underlings to know it. That's why he was meeting us in private.

What a guy.

"So," I said, "you have information on his whereabouts?"

"This Hucklebee? Not yet. I have mens working on it." He shrugged. "If there's anythings else you need, let me know." He gave me a card. "My private cell number."

I handed him back my empty glass. "Thanks."

We got out of the limo and it drove off.

We went back to our cab and Kelso appeared from

behind one of the bridge supports. I started to tell him what happened but he shook his head and said, "Just call me when you get back to the hotel."

"Okay . . ."

"Just call me."

"If you say so. Can we give you a ride?"

He gave me a look. "Don't worry, I think I can grab a cab around the corner."

Jamie and I went back to our cab, told the driver to take the FDR uptown, and as we sped off Jamie said, "Why's Kelso acting strange?"

"I don't know. He may have seen something."

She sighed. "He seems like such a nice guy, in a way."

"Who, Russevsky? Yeah, unless you cross him."

She leaned back, put her head on my shoulder, and said, "One thing I don't understand: if he's willing to help us with the case, why not just have him set up a fake buy from Hayes—I mean, Peterman—and have the NYPD waiting to grab him?"

"First of all, Dmitri isn't going to admit to the NYPD or any other law enforcement agency that he actually runs a fencing operation. The second thing is, it would be bad for his business. No one would ever try to fence anything with him ever again."

She sighed and nodded. "That makes sense. There's another thing I don't understand, though. I mean, he's obviously a bad guy, whether he intended to have his goons kill you or not."

"He probably didn't care one way or another until he found out I was one of your investigators."

"So my question is: Why is he so willing to cooperate with our investigation?"

"It's in his best interest to help us nail Hayes. As to why he's willing to help us find Huckabee? You got me."

"But, Jack, why are you asking him for help solving this murder case and not doing anything to put him in jail for being a fence and a mob boss and nearly getting you killed and putting a contract out on Karl?"

"I don't know how to explain that exactly, except to say that sometimes you have to do a kind of legal triage—decide which case is the most important and let any other criminal activities kind of slide until you solve the homicide."

She nodded and yawned. "This is why I like working with dead bodies. It's more cut and dried, if you'll excuse the expression. It's all about the evidence and nothing else."

"Yeah, I envy that about what you do," I lied.

"You do not," she hit me softly. "You hate what I do."

"I don't *hate* it. It just gives me the serious willies."

"And getting into a Russian mobster's limo late at night under the Brooklyn Bridge doesn't give you the willies?"

"No," I said, "I kind of like doing stuff like that."

"Why?"

I shrugged. "It makes life interesting."

She laughed. "Now I get it. That's why you like working with dogs so much, isn't it?"

"What do you mean?"

She lifted her head up. "Come on, Jack. You've never once thought that Hooch or those Dobermans could very easily snap your head in two with one bite, if they ever got the urge?"

"Yeah, I suppose that thought had crossed my mind."

"So? You like the fact that there's this hidden danger right under your nose—that a lot of these animals, like Max and Fritz, could kill you if they felt like it."

I sighed. "It's part of it."

"And it's why you like using the dog's prey drive so much, because of the danger of it."

"I really don't think it's dangerous at all, in fact, just the opposite. It's a dog's predatory nature that makes him sociable and civilized. But yes, working with the prey drive *does* put you in touch with a kind of wild, primal energy that can be extremely exhilarating."

She put her head back on my shoulder. "I thought so. You're an adrenaline junkie. Maybe that's part of why you like *me* so much."

"No, I like you because you're the only person who can stimulate me and relax me at the same time."

"Whatever that means. And my occasional emotional outbursts don't thrill and fascinate you on some level?"

"You mean these facackta moods you get into every twenty-eight days or so?"

"Wait," she huffed, "did you just imply that it's a premenstrual thing?"

"Well, *isn't* it?"

"Okay," she formed a fist, "now you're *really* in danger."

When we got back to the hotel Jamie took a shower and I called Kelso. He told me that he'd seen what looked like someone in a van, keeping an eye on Dmitri's limo.

"Why didn't you say anything while we were there?"

"Like I said, it was a van. The kind that usually comes equipped with parabolic mics."

"Huh. So feds or the NYPD are watching Russevsky?"

"Well, I know for a fact it's not the local cops. I'll run the plates to see if it's the feds. But you said that Peterman likes to keep tabs on people, right?"

"Ah-hah."

He laughed. "Oh, you like that idea, huh?"

"I sure do. If it wasn't the feds then it means we've got Peterman on the hook."

"It also means you have to be careful."

"Okay." Just then Jamie came back in, wearing nothing but a robe, courtesy of the Carlyle. "I've got to go," I said. "Jamie just got out of the shower and I want to sniff her hair."

"That's something," he laughed. "I didn't need to know."

35

On Monday morning we did our two-minute spot with Matt Lauer and I let the viewers know that we were staying at the Carlyle, in case they had any information about Huckabee for us. We also told them they could contact Detective Kevin O'Reilly at the Midtown South Precinct, and gave the phone number.

Matt asked me about the case and I said, "Well, Matt, we now have the *key* to solving the murder."

"Are you going to tell us what it is?"

"Nope, just that it's the *key* to everything."

"Okay . . ." Then he said, "So, Jack, a lot of dog lovers watch the show. Before you go, what is the one thing you could tell them about their pets?"

"Well, I'd say it amounts to the fact that there is absolutely no such thing as an alpha dog, that the alpha theory is false, and that there's no need to act tough, or mean, or be dominant with your dog because all he or she really wants to do is find harmony by playing hunting games."

"Really?"

"Yep. The pack is solely about hunting large prey,

which means that playing hunting games like fetch or tug-of-war is usually the quickest way to solve all your training problems, if you have any."

"Interesting. And we'll be right back after this."

As soon as Jamie and I got back to the hotel I got a phone call from someone calling himself Professor Hayes, which wasn't surprising given the fact that he'd been tailing us.

Once he'd introduced himself I said, "How do I know it's actually *you* I'm talking to, Peterman, and not myself?"

He laughed and his voice was rich and resonant and I wondered if he'd ever incorporated hypnosis into his act—he certainly had the pipes for it.

"I have no idea what you're talking about, though it is *possible,* you know, for there to be two Jack Fields speaking on the phone to one another at the same time. Or aren't you familiar with string theory?"

"I am, actually. But that stuff's got nothing to do with con games and false IDs, except maybe as part of the con you ran on Mrs. Bright—making her believe in alternate realities."

"I can't comment on what she does or doesn't believe."

"I wish you *would* comment on it. I wish you'd comment on a lot of things. Like how you killed Amy Frost and where you left the damn murder weapon."

"You want me to confess and clear the whole thing up for you? I thought you already had the key to the case."

"You caught the *Today* show, huh? Well, that was TV. People say a lot of things on TV. And yes, it would make my life a whole helluva lot easier if you confessed. Maybe you hit her with your walking stick. Is that what you used?"

"But I wasn't *there* that night. I took a plane back to New York. *Surely* the police have some proof of that?"

"Maybe it was an accident—and don't call me Shirley—that's understandable. You'd only get manslaughter."

Jamie said, "Let me have the phone."

Peterman said, "Is that your lovely fiancée?"

"Yes, it's her. She wants to speak to you."

"Fine, put her on the speaker, if you have one."

I said I did have one—we were in a business suite. I put the handpiece back in the cradle, and pressed the button.

"Listen," she said, "we're going to find that walking stick sooner or later, with the victim's blood on it and the bioluminescent plankton and bits of her hair and other trace evidence, like your DNA under her finger-nails, that'll make the jury stand up and go *Wow!* guilty, right on the spot."

"How do you know she was killed by a walking stick?"

Jamie stuttered for a moment then said, "Hello? I'm the state medical examiner. It's what I do."

"Yes, dear, but the police have searched the entire premises, from what I've been told, and—"

I said, "Wait, who's been telling you things?"

"You probably think it was Fiona Bright, but it wasn't. It was a detective named Brad Bailey."

I almost believed him for a fraction of a second. "Chief Colbern I'd buy, but Bailey? I don't think so."

"Why? Because of his Mormon upbringing? Like Mormons aren't capable of sin? Don't you remember the salamander murder case in Salt Lake City? And let me ask you this—Bailey made quite a convincing Polish priest, didn't he?"

"How the hell could you know about that? And no, he didn't make a very convincing Polish priest. Now let's change the subject and talk about those jewels for a second."

"If you doubt that Bailey has been on my payroll, why not run a check on his financial records?"

"Fine. I'll do that. Now about those jewels . . ."

"What jewels?"

"The ones you stole from Fiona Bright's safe."

"How on earth would I steal anything from her safe?"

"It's not a question of how, but why it took you so long to get the combination. Oh, that's right . . . then Tom Huckabee got out of jail and you had him install video cameras throughout the house, including inside the Brights' bedroom."

"I'm sure this is going somewhere."

"You told the Brights the cameras were there to catch mischievous elves, doing naughty things at night. The truth is, you wanted just that one camera planted in the bedroom so you could watch Ellis Bright dialing the combination."

"You have a lively imagination. You must have done well in school. Is there a point to all this?"

"Absolutely. You think you're smarter than I am, but I'm not like one of your marks. I'm on to your tricks."

He laughed. "Attaboy, keep that positive attitude! It'll take you a long way." There was a pause as his laughter subsided. "Here's what I'm thinking. I have things to take care of this afternoon, but I can meet the two of you—you and Dr. Cutter, that is, not you and your imagination, though feel free to bring it along if you like—at five."

Shocked, I said, "Okay. Where and for what purpose?"

"At my office. I'm sure you know where it is. And my purpose? I want to find out how smart you really are."

"How do you know I won't show up with the state troopers, put the cuffs on you, and dance your ass back to Maine?"

"Okay, then don't come. Oh, and by the way, I'm missing a key. You haven't found it, by any chance?"

"Nope. No key, no murder weapon either. But we will, just as soon as we figure out how you got off the property without being seen that night." I stopped. "Wait, is that what you thought when I said we had the key to the case?"

"Just a hypothetical."

"Really? What kind of key was it, Mr. Peterman?"

"Nothing. It's of minor importance, really."

"Well then, maybe I *do* have it, or if I don't I will soon enough. Just like I'm going to find that murder weapon." I paused. "Hey, maybe you left the two of them in the same place, the key and the murder weapon. Like to tell me where? I'd be happy to retrieve both items for you."

"Hmmm, tempting offer. So . . . you'll be there at five?"

"I guess I have no choice, do I?"

"It's a binary universe, Mr. Field. You always have a choice, no matter what happens."

"Yeah, I heard that somewhere. See you at five," I said and hung up. I turned to Jamie. "I think we've got him."

"Are you sure?"

"No, but he wants that key."

"Do you believe what he said about Brad Bailey?"

"No. Not in this binary universe or any other. Still, how did he know about the Polish priest act?" I thought it over. "Maybe Dmitri found out about it and told him?"

"Maybe that's it. So what'll we do till five, Jack?"

"Well, I guess we can meet with this Dr. Einstein and see if she has any information that'll be useful. And of course we'll need Bailey or someone to come stay here and man the phones, in case anyone calls in about Huckabee."

"Do you think Hayes will really be there at five?"

"You mean Peterman. Of course not, but he wants *us* to be there because he wants us to *not* be somewhere else we might normally be at five."

"I'm not following."

"If we're at his office we're not somewhere else, right?"

"So?"

"So, there's something he's going to be doing at five and he doesn't want us there. It's called misdirection."

"Okay. Well what do people usually do at five, Jack?"

"I don't know. Get off work, come home, make dinner—"

"Walk the dogs!"

I looked down at Starsky and Hutch. They wagged their tails: *Did somebody say 'walk the dogs'?*

She said, "He wants to kidnap Frankie and Hooch!"

"That's brilliant, Jamie. That might be it. And the ransom to free the dogs would be that safe deposit box key."

"It makes sense. Jack, we can't go to his office."

"No, honey, we have to. We have to play his game, up to a point, so he thinks he's conning us."

"But what'll we do about Frankie and Hooch? If that's his reason for getting us to go to his office tonight—"

"That's easy. We'll just take them with us."

36

After I walked the dogs, and since we weren't "meeting" Peterman until five, Jamie had a little time for Christmas shopping, while I called NYU and set up an appointment with Dr. Hiraki Einstein, who said she could meet us at noon.

Bailey called when I got back. He'd just got into town. He agreed to man the phones while Jamie and I were downtown, though he expressed dissatisfaction about not knowing more about the case. I told him it would be better if he didn't know all the details yet.

"Just trust me on this," I said, "okay?"

He sighed. "I do, Jack. But that only goes so far."

I called Kristin and she agreed to bring Daisy and Marta, the maid, and meet me in the park for a little training.

My heart sank when I saw the poor thing walking on 76th, coming toward Fifth Avenue, stopping occasionally to paw desperately at the "gentle" halter she'd been forced to wear. Why do people believe the hype about this torture device and not pay attention to what the dog is trying to tell them?

Fortunately, Daisy also had a regular collar for her doggie ID tags. Good. Now all I had to do was teach her how much fun it is to walk next to me, or Marta, or Kristin, or Jen, the latter being the easiest because I knew that Jen had a way of making everything she did with a dog seem fun. And that's the key to training— make it as fun for the dog as possible.

"Jack," Kristin called out, as the three of them crossed the curb. "Are you lost in space again?"

"What? Oh, sorry. Yeah, I was just thinking that whoever invented that thing you've wrapped around Daisy's face should be forced to wear it themselves for a few days and see how *they* like it."

She shook her head. "I guess you disapprove."

Daisy was trying to remove the harness from her face. She rubbed her paw against the halter.

I pointed at her and said, "What does Daisy think?"

Kristin sighed and said, "But, Jack, she pulls and pulls, and the woman at the pet store said this was the most humane—"

"Really? Why not just ask Daisy how humane it is. Here, let me have the leash."

I took the leash—a six foot latigo leather model, they'd got at least one thing right—and hooked it to Daisy's collar as Kristin introduced me to Marta.

"Nice to meet you," I said. "So, you take care of her and walk her every day?"

She looked at Kristin then said, with a heavy Spanish accent, "Sometimes the Mrs. walks her, but I do mos'ly."

"And you don't mind?"

"Jes—I like doing it. I really like Daisy." She crouched down and cooed and pet the dog. She also took the "gentle" harness off the poor animal's face. I immediately liked Marta a lot.

I said, "And how often does she get walked?"

"Four times a day. At sefen, twelf, five, and ten."

"Good," I said then asked Kristin, "What does she eat?" She gave me the name of a dog food commonly recommended by vets and I said, "Well, you need to switch foods right away." I told her to call Whiskers, a holistic pet store in the East Village. "They deliver and they also have a catalogue."

"Okay. Can we get on with the training?"

"Yeah, let's do it. Come on Daisy! Let's play!"

We went into the park and I found a stick and teased her with it, got her to jump on me and play tug-of-war. I let her win and praised her for winning, then I picked up another stick and teased her with that.

She dropped the first stick, I almost let her grab the second one, but ran away instead, encouraging her to chase me and try to grab it, giving her some quick pops on the collar, as a way of goading her into chasing me, not as a correction, following each pop by saying "Heel!" in a happy, inviting voice. Then I changed my pace, going from double-time to half-time and back to a regular pace, forcing her to match my pace or lose focus on the stick.

In a fairly short time I had her walking or running next to me, matching my pace and responding to the "heel" command every time she lost focus.

"That's amazing," said Kristin.

"It's only the first step. It probably won't carry over to her next walk." I turned to Marta. "Do you think you could play these games with her the next time you walk her?"

She made a facial shrug. "I could try. It looks fun."

"Yep." I said to Kristin, "The thing is, Daisy's not really pulling on the leash. She's actually *being pulled* by things in the environment that stimulate and attract her instincts and emotions."

"Oh, I think I get it." She nodded. "All this crazy running around you've been doing is designed to have more of a pull on her instincts than the things in the environment do."

"That's exactly right. Very good."

I gave Marta the leash and coached her through the exercises. While she and Daisy were playing I asked Kristin if she'd ever done a set design for someone named Professor J. K. Hayes. She said she'd never heard of him and asked what kind of design it was. I described the game room to her.

"Oh, yes," she said, "I was asked to design something like that once. But it wasn't for anyone named Hayes."

"Who was it for?"

"A Professor Einstein, as I recall. From NYU."

Surprised, I said, "You mean Hiraki Einstein?"

"You know her?"

"No, but oddly enough I'm meeting her in a little while. So? Did you *do* it?"

"The design? No, it didn't sound legitimate."

"You were definitely approached by Dr. Einstein?"

"Approached? I don't know. She called me and described what she wanted. I told her I wasn't interested. Why?"

I explained a little about what was going on, thanked

her, by the way, for contacting Lance Burton—he'd been a big help, even though it wasn't really him who'd called or helped—then gave her some instructions for later in the evening.

Daisy was walking next to Marta, looking up at her. Then when she saw me her butt wiggled, she pulled straight over to me, jumped up, and licked my face. *I* think she was thanking me for rescuing her from the dreaded "gentle" halter.

I twisted sideways and at the same time said, "Okay, off!" in an inviting voice, and she jumped down but kept wagging her tail and wiggling her butt. I turned to Kristin and said, "See? She's happy she doesn't have to wear that damn halter thing anymore."

"Okay, I get it."

"Oh, and by the way, see if your vet can put one of those electronic dog finder things in Daisy this afternoon, just in case things go haywire with tonight's game plan."

"Okay, Jack. But I hope you know what you're doing."

"Yeah," I said, "me too."

37

Jamie and I took a cab to the Village, checking in with various people on our cell phones, getting together the players for the con on Peterman. We met Dr. Hiraki Einstein at her office at NYU a little after noon.

She was an attractive Eurasian woman, with a quirky way of blinking and playing with her glasses at the same time. She showed us in, sat behind a rather messy desk, and said, "Okay, I understand you have some questions for me."

I asked if she'd ever worked for or with Professor Hayes. She hadn't. In fact, she'd been trying to run him out of business for seven years.

"Really?" I said, "because we got a report that someone named Dr. Einstein had approached a well-known Broadway set designer to do some work on one of Hayes's scams."

She asked if this had taken place about five or six years ago. I said that it had. She shook her head and said that he'd had someone impersonating her back then.

"Well," I said, "he seems to like stealing people's

identities so that's probably it." Then I told her how he'd stolen mine recently.

She shook her head. "He's a menace. Part of the reason people don't take my work seriously is because of him. His entire approach to the subject is all wrong." She adjusted her glasses. "The first thing you need to understand about elves is they're not miniature beings, like Keebler elves or the ones you see on TV at this time of year, working in Santa's Workshop. They're human size, or a little smaller. Fairies *are* miniature beings, yes. But elves aren't."

I said, "This is from a mythological perspective?"

"No, it's from a physical perspective. The thing is, you can't physically see them. Or most people can't. They exist in a different dimension of reality."

"Wait, you think that elves and fairies really exist?"

"Well, I am studying the subject, and I'm currently working on the scientific proof. Yes."

Jamie said, "Dr. Einstein, we only want to know anything you can tell us about Professor Hayes—"

"But that's the thing," Einstein said. "Hayes doesn't even pretend to use real elves in his scam, he uses midgets."

"Little people," I said.

"Whatever. Oh, and by the way, is that really true about dogs? What you said to Matt Lauer this morning?"

"Yeah, so?"

"So, you realize that what you're saying goes totally against the scientific reality that's studied in colleges and universities and veterinary schools all over the world?"

"I guess."

She smiled. "So, what I'm saying about elves and fairies and Santa Claus goes against the reality of what everyone over the age of five or six believes about them. Okay?"

"Now you're saying that you also believe in Santa Claus?" Jamie asked, trying not to laugh.

"All myths are grounded in some form of reality, Dr. Cutter. Santa Claus is actually a real person, a Greek shepherd named Mickelhos who one day—this was in about AD 535—went after a lost sheep and accidentally wandered through a portal into the elfin kingdom. And while there he was transformed into—"

"I'm sorry," I said, standing up. "We thought you were an accredited scientist—"

Jamie said, "Jack, sit down. This is fascinating. Loony, but fascinating."

"I know I come across as kind of strange," said Dr. Einstein, adjusting her glasses, "but the truth is, elves really do exist, just in a different dimension of reality. There's even an elfin island off the coast of Maine, which can only be seen on Christmas Eve, which is when the two dimensions of magic and ordinary reality intersect."

I said, "This happens on Christmas Eve?"

"Yes," she replied. "That's why Christmas is such a magical time of year."

I laughed. "Because these two dimensions intersect?"

"Yes," she said earnestly.

"Okay," Jamie said, "now that's a little too weird."

"I know my ideas seem strange to you, but some people, a lot of people in fact, believe in angels or ghosts or aliens or elemental nature spirits and the like. There are many different dimensions and forms of reality."

"You're talking about people's beliefs, though," I said, "not scientific reality."

"In most cases, yes. But I actually have firsthand

knowledge of the subject, but haven't found a way to prove my experiences empirically. I'm still working on the math."

Jamie chuckled, turned to me, and said, "You know, Jack, she sounds exactly like you."

"What does *that* mean?"

"You know. Your little project with Tulips?"

"Oh, that." I looked at Dr. Einstein. "I have someone trying to work out the computer algorithms to prove that the canine pack is not a top-down, hierarchical system, but a bottom-up, self-emergent *heter*archy."

"See?" she said. "We're not that different." She paused and looked right at me. "You're ex-NYPD, right?"

"Yeah?"

"Do you remember the Charley Maine case?"

"No," I lied.

"Well, I do. And I went to Ireland with Mr. Maine, and helped him bring his daughter back from the elfin kingdom. Nothing can ever change that fact."

"And that's how you met this Greek sailor?"

"Shepherd, not sailor. And yes. He has a sleigh— though there aren't any reindeer—and he magically travels around the world every year on Christmas Eve and brings presents to—"

I laughed and said, "Do you actually say these kinds of things to your students?"

"Of course not. I'm paid to teach comparative mythology. I'm only telling *you* these things because . . ."

"Because why?"

"I don't *know* why, exactly. When I saw you on the *Today* show, I had the feeling that you might be open to an alternate view of reality."

I shook my head. "Sorry. Reality is reality."

"Is it? Are you familiar with information theory? The idea that the universe is a three-dimensional hologram?"

"Four-dimensional," Jamie said. "You're forgetting about time. There are three dimensions of space and one of time."

"Right," Dr. Einstein said, nodding, "four. But there's also a fifth dimension—the beliefs or point of view of the observer—where you can create an observer-determined reality."

"If you say so," I scoffed.

She looked at me for a moment. "Mr. Field, there's another reason I'm saying things to you that I would never say to my students."

"And that is?"

"I don't know how to put it. You strike me as someone who needs to believe in the magic of Christmas."

I said, "The magic of Christmas, if there is such a thing, comes from changes in human psychology during the holidays. It has nothing to do with a fat man in a red suit or two dimensions intersecting."

"He's really not that fat in person," she said sadly.

"Okay," I stood up, laughing. "Thanks for your time."

"Mr. Field," she said, "you will see that magic elfin isle if you stand off the coast of Maine on Christmas Eve, because it's real, though you might not believe what you see."

"Yeah, okay, whatever," I said.

Jamie said, "Don't take it personally, Doctor."

I added, "We thought you were going to give us some useful information about Peterman."

She sighed. "All I can tell you is that he has no idea

where the real elfin portals are. But he gets away with it because he's smart and he's got a team of lawyers to insulate him. They even filed an injunction against *me* once."

I sat back down. "Do you have their phone number?"

"I certainly do." She flipped through her Rolodex and gave me the information.

I stood up again. "Thanks. Something useful at last."

She sighed. "I'm sorry I couldn't be of more help. And I've really met Mickelhos. I really do know him personally."

"That's nice," I said, shaking my head. "If you're still in contact with Santa, let him know we're looking for Tim Huckabee's father, would you? That'd make a nice present, Christmaswise, for a lot of people."

"Well, I'm not in contact with him anymore—I wish I *were*—but best of luck."

"Same to you," I said, holding the door open for Jamie.

38

"Wow," Jamie said as we got on the elevator. "Where in the world did *she* come from?"

"Yes, honey. She's totally wacko." I paused. "The only thing is—and this is kind of weird—I remember that case."

"What case?"

"Charley Maine, his missing daughter."

"You worked on it?"

I shook my head. "No, it was before my time. When you're first starting out as a detective, they like to send you down to the records room to look through cold files, straighten up the folders, anything they can think of to get you out of their hair."

She tsked. "I can't imagine anyone doing that with *you*."

"Very funny." We got off the elevator and went through the lobby. "You want to walk through the park?"

"Sure," she said, as I held the door open for her and we went outside. "What park is this?"

"Washington Square. It used to be a hangout for

drug dealers and the like. Now it's not half bad. Anyway," I went on, "there was this case of a little girl who was brought to the emergency room by her parents one Halloween. She died in the ER. The parents wouldn't allow an autopsy, but the blood work showed nothing wrong with her."

"She wasn't poisoned?"

"Nope. And nothing was found in the candy her siblings had brought home. After a thorough investigation, the case was closed under what's called 'extraordinary circumstances,' which basically means that no one could figure it out. Especially when the girl was found to be alive and well a year later."

She stared at me. "Jack! That's impossible."

"That's why it's called extraordinary circumstances. It's impossible to explain. These cases don't happen very often but often enough that there's a name for them."

We found a park bench and sat down to admire the quiet tenor of the neighborhood, although part of my mind was focused on the guy who'd been following us since we left the faculty building, and was he really following us or not. Meanwhile, a couple of squirrels got the idea that we had some pretzels or peanuts or something and came over to stare at us.

"And that's the case she was referring to?"

"Yep. The name Charley Maine jarred my memory."

"That's so bizarre."

"Yep," I nodded. "It's a mystery."

The squirrels wandered off, though the guy who'd followed us found another park bench to sit on and kind of deliberately didn't stare or even quite look exactly in our direction, but didn't quite exactly look away from us entirely either.

Jamie said, "Well, Dr. Einstein was a total dead end."

"Not a total one," I said, getting out my cell phone. "We have a phone number . . ." I leaned over and whispered in her ear, "Did I mention how Hayes has people followed, uses hidden microphones, surveillance cameras, things like that?"

"You mean Peterman," she said.

"Him too," I said softly. "I'm going to make a couple of phone calls and I need you to call Bailey, or anyone for that matter, and talk to them in a loud voice, and stand between me and that guy on the bench over there. He's been following us. Just don't be obvious."

"Okay," she said, without looking.

"When I start dialing, you dial too."

So she stood up and dialed Bailey while I cupped my hand around my phone and called J. J. Higginbottom's office. I got the runaround from a secretary but told her it involved the return of the Bright family jewels, which she found amusing, thinking, I guess, that I'd made an anatomical reference.

Finally, Higginbottom came on the line. "Are you serious about this?"

"Yeah. And it'll also help us solve the murder."

"This firm has no legal interest in—"

"Sure you do. If you remember, your clients planted evidence at a crime scene and lied to the police."

"Now, see here—"

"Never mind the legal tactics, just get Ellis on the line for a conference call. *Now*. We don't have much time."

"I really don't think you have the right to tell me—"

"Fine. I'll call the insurance company and tell them you're holding up the return of the jewels."

There was a pause. "I'll see what I can do."

While I was on hold I overheard Jamie say to Bailey, "You mean Jack never asked you about your family?" Pause. "Three kids, at your age?" Pause. "How old's your oldest?"

Higginbottom came back on the line. "I have Ellis Bright on the line with me."

"What's this all about," said Ellis.

I gave him a capsule version, including the scam.

I heard a deep intake of breath. "I was afraid it was something like that. This is going to kill Fiona."

"Maybe not. Do you want to see Hayes put behind bars?"

"For the murder, absolutely. But I won't file charges on the confidence scheme. No one must know about that."

I kind of figured he'd say that. "I understand. But that means we have to be able to make an airtight case and force him to confess. Otherwise, the way he scammed you and Fiona is going to come out at trial in open court."

He sighed. "It's bound to come out one way or another."

"Maybe so, but if you do it my way it'll cause minimal damage to your social reputations."

"Very well."

I gave them the number of Peterman's attorney and told them what I wanted: an offer should be made to Peterman that if the jewels were returned within twenty-four hours no questions would be asked, no charges would be filed, and that he would be paid a quarter of their worth, with an ironclad guarantee that he gets the money if he follows these terms exactly. "If the lawyers ask why you think Peterman has them, you say the idea came from a known fence who worked for the Bright family."

I also asked Ellis if he would be willing to give Karl his job back, as well as loan him a portion of the finder's fee to pay a debt to a former employer.

"Wait a second," said the lawyer, "if there's an iron-clad guarantee, how in the world—?"

"Because I would assume, legally speaking, that it's only ironclad if the money is collected by Professor Jonathan Kensington Hayes, who doesn't really exist. Harold Peterman wouldn't be entitled to any such guarantee."

"Hmm. Interesting angle."

"Why give the money to Karl?" asked Ellis.

"Well, let's say that in order to set up this trap I had to make a deal with Karl's former employer. Karl owes him a lot of money, which is why he ran off suddenly."

"I don't understand, but yes. I will pay Karl, or his former employer, and give him his job back. He's a good man."

"Okay, let me know what Peterman's attorneys say."

I clicked my cell phone shut and heard Jamie say, "Well, we haven't talked about it much. But Jack's so good with Leon, I'm sure he'll make a terrific father if we decide to."

"You can hang up now," I said.

She nodded and said, "Well, nice talking to you, Detective, but I've got to go." She clicked her phone shut. "All set?" she said to me.

"Yeah, let's grab some lunch. There's a great little French spot a couple of blocks from here."

"Lead on, Columbo."

39

The sun came out but the temperature actually went down, so we were on our way to Chez Brigitte on Greenwich Avenue to get warm and have some chicken, but Kelso called to say he'd located a credit card purchase made by someone named Thomas Huckabee, or actually, Thomas Hucklebee, because that's the way it showed up on the receipt at the Smiler's deli on Ninth Avenue, right around the corner from the walkup apartment of Huckabee's supposed alibi witness, Donna Moore.

Jamie and I got in a cab and headed for Hell's Kitchen, followed at a respectful distance by that nice man from the park. He was in a cab also.

I said, "I think there's a van following us now too."

"We must be very popular."

"Yeah, or Peterman's very worried."

I opened my cell phone and called Bailey, told him where we were headed, but didn't explain what was going on or what I wanted him to do. He agreed to meet us.

We arrived at 46th and Ninth and met Kelso and two

cops, Kevin O'Reilly and Eddie Dwyer. O'Reilly and Dwyer said they'd just checked and there was no one home in Donna Moore's apartment, and since it was lunchtime, we got a booth in the Film Center Cafe, ordered burgers and such, and had a confab.

It seems that someone on the Camden PD had screwed up the address and phone number of Huckabee's alibi witness when that information was faxed to the NYPD. The address was listed as being on East 64th, not West 46th. As for the phone number, two of the digits had been accidentally reversed. So when New York's finest had tried to contact her, they weren't able to. The person that screwed up was Brad Bailey.

"I hate to bring it up," I said, "but Peterman told me this morning that Bailey's working for *him*."

Eddie said, "Wait, this Camden cop, Bailey, has been on the take with this con man you're after?"

"It's starting to look like it. Pass the salt."

"Jack!" said Jamie. "You don't believe that."

"I'm starting to. Wasn't Bailey supposed to bring the warrant on Peterman down from Camden today? Where is he?"

"Now that you mention it," Jamie said, "that day in the harbor—you have no way of knowing if it was Chris Bright or Brad Bailey who knocked you out, do you?"

"That's right. I have no memory of what actually happened, just what Bailey told me happened."

"He could've been the one who cracked you over the head."

"Yep. And there's probably a dozen more things that he's been screwing up, whether intentionally or not. For one thing, we didn't even know until a few days ago that Amy Frost was Huckabee's sister, and not his ex-girlfriend. Bailey should have known that at the first interview. Something's not right here. Either he's incompetent, or he's dyslexic, or he's on the take. Or all three. Now, don't get me wrong," I said, wanting to sound reasonable to anyone who might be listening in, "I'm not saying I actually believe what Peterman told me, but it bears looking into."

"I think you're right," Jamie said.

"So," I changed the subject, "how dumb is this Huckabee character? He's on the run from the law and he buys a can of beer and a pack of donuts with his credit card?"

"Criminals," said Kelso. "They never use their brains."

Then the talk turned to other topics while we all silently wrote notes to each other, mapping out a strategy.

O'Reilly's cell phone rang. He spoke briefly then closed the phone and said, "We ran a check on Bailey's financials, and he's received a total of twenty-five thousand dollars by direct deposit into his checking account since the day after the murder."

I said, "Looks like Peterman was telling the truth."

"That's right."

"I can't believe it. So, what do we do now?"

O'Reilly said, "We arrest him."

"Good. He should be arriving any minute."

"Oh, by the way," O'Reilly said, "we also got word that Dmitri Russevsky has put a contract out on you and Jamie."

"You're kidding," said Jamie.

I shook my head no at her, then said to O'Reilly, "I'm not sure I know who that is."

"He's the head of one of the Russian gangs out in

Brooklyn. Apparently he's not happy about you interfering with his business. So be careful while you're in town."

Once again the conversation turned to other topics, we finished our meal, paid the check, then went out to the sidewalk to wait for Bailey so my NYPD pals could put the cuffs on him, right out in public for everyone to see.

As he got out of the cab I felt bad for him. He had such a bright smile, like he was glad to see me and have a chance to meet some "real" cops from New York, but he just couldn't be trusted. It wasn't his fault, really, but there was no way around it.

"Hey, Brad," I said. "How's it going?"

"Okay," he said, as O'Reilly patted him down and Dwyer reached for his cuffs. "Hey! What's going on?"

Dwyer said, "Brad Bailey, you're under arrest for felony murder and conspiracy to commit murder."

"What?" He looked at me. "Jack? What is this?"

"Sorry, buddy," I said. "And don't say anything until you've talked to a lawyer."

They got him in the car and drove him away.

40

Jamie, Kelso, and I got in a cab and were heading up Eighth Avenue when Kevin O'Reilly called with news about Huckabee.

He told me they'd just gotten a report from someone in midtown who'd seen him walking south on Fifth Avenue, then he said, "Hang on. There's a second report coming in. It sounds like he's heading for Rockefeller Center."

"Well, his girlfriend works behind the Clinique counter at Sak's Fifth Avenue, so maybe that's where he's going." I told him where *we* were and that we'd go check it out.

"Sorry I can't put any of my men on it, but since there's technically no warrant out on the idiot—"

"You don't have to apologize to me."

I told the driver to take us up to 50th then across, and explained to Jamie and Kelso what we were doing.

"Finding one idiot in midtown, at Christmas," Kelso groused, "sounds like a major crapshoot."

"Didn't you once say that *life* is a crapshoot?"

"Did I? I may have been drunk."

"Huh," I said, "I've forgotten to ask how the sobriety thing is going. Apparently okay, or I would have noticed."

"Oh, you'd have *noticed*. I can't believe I drank so much and I'm still alive. Hey, this feels like a quick trip."

True—it would have been a very slow one if our driver weren't so good at his job. He weaved in and around the pokier cars, missed several collisions by inches, and it took us less than a minute to get from Eighth to Sixth.

We had to stop at the light across from Radio City Music Hall, with the cab idling at the crosswalk and shoppers and tourists clogging the sidewalks. There was a falafel stand and a guy roasting chestnuts to the right of us. I saw Jamie looking out the window at one of the towering buildings that line Sixth. They're all set well back from the avenue, supplying them with spacious plazas, and all the plazas wear their own brand of holiday decorations every year. The one just off to our right had an artfully placed stack of giant red Christmas ball ornaments, each one about ten feet tall, making the whole pile forty feet high.

Jamie said, "This city can be pretty spectacular."

"Yep," I said as the light changed and we continued our drive. We quickly passed the Rockefeller Center skating rink and the giant pine tree and more tourists than you'd see in Yellowstone during an entire summer. We kept our eyes peeled for Huckabee but didn't see him.

Kelso shrugged and said, "Like I told you."

"Maybe we'll get lucky."

I had the cabbie cross Fifth and drop us off between Sak's and St. Patrick's Cathedral. I paid him and we went inside.

The store's main floor is something at any time of year. The ceilings are tall and there are sedate yet comfortingly sturdy columns every ten feet or so, giving you the feeling that even when the store is too crowded—as it was now—the usual cramped experience that is so much a part of New York life has vanished, lifting spirits a little. It's nice to have high ceilings. Nearly everything is white—the walls, the ceilings, the columns. Add to that the pale white Christmas lights wrapped around the columns and, well, it puts you in the mood to spend money and feel good about it.

Unfortunately the main floor is also where all the perfume counters are, which meant that as soon as we came inside, Jamie started sneezing.

She touched my arm. "Oh, Jack, I'm sorry. I don't know if I'll be of much help."

"You want to wait outside?"

"I think I'd better."

She went out to wait on the sidewalk while Kelso and I tried to locate the Clinique counter. I cast my eyes around the room looking for the pale green logo. It was just to the right of the Louis Vuitton boutique.

What else did I see? Dumbass Huckabee, leaning on the glass and talking in what seemed to be a desperate manner to a dark-haired girl in her mid-twenties.

Like I said before, sometimes you're smart, sometimes you're lucky, and sometimes people are just dumb. He looked up, made eye contact, then got a scared yet resigned look in his eyes.

I tapped Kelso. "There he is." Then I called out,

"Hey, Tom, Merry Christmas. For everyone except your boy, Tim, huh?"

He took a deep breath. "I can't go back to prison," he said in a voice that was a little too loud for the room, and definitely too full of details concerning the kind of life experience most of the shoppers weren't expecting to hear about while buying perfume.

He started toward the side entrance but balked when he realized we were blocking his way. He turned and ran toward the elevator bank, shoving some people out of the way, ignoring the "heys" and "watch-its," which he provoked.

We ran toward him, trying not to knock anyone over, which in a popular store at Christmastime was quite a task. Unfortunately he got on the elevator car just before the door closed, so I didn't get a chance to catch him and wring his neck. I started banging on the door, yelling, "He's your son, you bastard!"

A voice said, "What's going on here?"

We turned to see a security guard with an unpleasant face. I got out my wallet, showed him my official New York Police Department ID, being careful to place my thumb over the part that read RETIRED.

"He's wanted for murder up in Maine," I said, with a tilt of my head toward the elevator. "Do you think you could get some guards together to help us search the store?"

He sucked a tooth in a way that indicated he didn't like cops or that he'd just had corn beef. "We're kind of busy right now, the holidays and all. You should call the cops."

"I thought I mentioned: I *am* the cops." Then I sighed and asked if there was any way out of the building besides the four main entrances. He said there wasn't, at least not unless you knew how to get down to the basement and out the service area. "Fine," I said. "Thanks a lot."

Kelso looked at the main elevators and said, "I guess it wouldn't make much sense to go upstairs and look around for him on our own."

"With eleven floors?" I went back to the Clinique counter and asked the girl if she was Donna Moore.

"No," she said, "I just work with her. Did he really go to prison?"

"Yeah, for a few years. So, where is she?"

"Donna? She likes to go ice skating on her lunch hour."

"Un-huh. And the guy that was just here," I said, "does he know where Donna is right now?"

"Tom? Yes. That's what I was telling him when you showed up. What was he in prison for?"

"Killing his wife, but he got a bum rap. Thanks for your help." I turned to Kelso and suggested we go outside and sit on those exits. Huckabee had to come out one of them, and if we were outside, he wouldn't know we were waiting for him until it was too late.

I left Jamie on the 50th Street exit, while Kelso covered the two entrances on Fifth, and I took the 49th Street exit. We had our cell phones ready to regroup if we saw anything. I also called Kevin O'Reilly and told him what was going on.

"You've located him?"

"Yeah, and he's just assaulted a couple of Christmas shoppers at Sak's Fifth Avenue."

He laughed and said, "For that I can get you a couple of uniformed officers." He stopped. "Sak's Fifth Avenue," he said as if scratching his head, "what street is that on again?"

I laughed at the old joke and five minutes later three guys and two women in uniform showed up. (You gotta love the NYPD.) I explained what was going on and gave them a description of Huckabee. The cops tried to take their share of surveillance duty, but weren't too good at: you have to pay close attention, not stand around and BS or try to answer a tourist's questions. Three of the officers stayed at 49th Street, two more went to 50th, which left me, Jamie, and Kelso on the front doors.

Nothing much happened for about twenty minutes except that the number of people who were lined up—and these were long lines, mind you—to gawk at the Christmas window continued to grow and get in the way of our view of the exits. What finally did happen surprised me and maybe Huckabee as well.

One of the job requirements for being a good con man is the ability to blend into any crowd. I think Huckabee would've gotten away if he hadn't looked back over his shoulder at me just as he started across the street.

Of course he happened to do it just as the stop light changed, so it took me a few more seconds than I would've liked to get across and follow him down the Plaza Promenade—which was decorated with white wicker angels with gold sashes, white lace wings with gold-veined wings, holding white wicker trumpets, and all wrapped up in tiny gold and white lights.

During the holidays the Rockefeller Plaza Promenade's the most crowded spot in New York. People like to come gaze at the giant Christmas tree, goggle at the skaters, and wait in line for their chance to get out on the ice themselves. The point is, it was very crowded, so Huckabee had to work hard to push his way through. As he did he got a lot more of those "heys" and "watch-its" with a few added "this-is-a-lines" for good measure.

I was shouting, "Police coming through! Make a path!"

People *did* make a path, which enabled me to almost catch up with him before he could get to the front of the line, which goes down a set of twelve steps to the right, and leads directly to the rink. But when he got to the gaggle of tourists at the top of the landing, he turned left and ducked under a chain, then went down the other twelve steps. He got to the bottom level and came to a three-foot Plexiglas barricade with a solid red wooden railing on top. He grabbed the rail, and swung over the barricade onto the ice.

Like many other things I suspect this man has been doing wrong most of his life, he didn't put as much thought into this as he could have. Consider the situation: you don't have skates on, you're attempting to flee by running across an icy surface, and to *get* to the ice you have to hurdle a fence.

Did he think he was going to magically land on both feet? Maybe he was trying to imitate the pose of the gold-leaf statue of Prometheus (another landmark of Rockefeller Plaza), that lovely Art Deco Greek figure sort of lying on his side with arms and legs so gracefully outstretched? Because right after Huckabee cracked his ass he went skidding off in roughly the same pose, just not as artistic. Now add to this the fact that at this time of year the rink contains the maximum amount of bodies allowable by law, and you get the idea that Huckabee wasn't the only one who ended up doing a brodie or two.

I, on the other hand, climbed very slowly and very

carefully over the same barricade, and was able to do so without injuring my back or my head or any other of my body parts, or getting run over by the rest of the skaters, who had already either scattered like pigeons or were now trying to become as vertical and as graceful as they had been before.

By then he was trying to crawl across the ice on his hands and knees but kept slipping and falling on his face. I was slowly and carefully maintaining my balance and made slow and steady progress in my objective, which was to catch up with him and wring his neck.

Jamie and Kelso were egging me on from the sidelines. And as you can imagine—with the number of tourists there—the flashbulbs were popping like it was half time at the Superbowl. People were screaming and the bad pop/rock versions of Christmas standards were still playing over the loudspeakers, giving some listeners a holiday feeling and others a migraine headache.

The five cops were also there. Four of them wisely stayed behind the barricade, though one of them was on the radio, calling it in. Two of them realized what Huckabee apparently didn't, that the only way off the ice was back the way he came—just down the right side set of stairs instead of the left. So they went over to that side to wait for him.

The tallest cop did what I'd done—he slowly and carefully climbed over the Plexiglas barricade and made his way onto the ice.

Then two security guards, from inside Rockefeller Center, decided to be helpful. They came onto the ice from an emergency exit at one of the restaurants, but had no skates on and no experience running on ice, so *they* fell down.

I finally got to where this sorry-ass Huckabee was

crawling along, and the best thing I could think to do to get the whole thing over with once and for all, was to just sit on top of him and not get up. So I did.

Once the roar of applause from the crowd died down I said to him, "You're a real pain in the ass. You know that?"

"Ow!" was all he said.

The cop reached us and helped me to my feet. Another round of applause. We pulled Huckabee up, then the cop cuffed him and asked me, "You want to come down to the precinct house with us now while we process him?"

"No," I said, moving slowly toward the exit. "Let the police back in Maine handle it. I have some dogs to walk and an important non-meeting to get to."

Jamie and I had to admit, though—as we laughed ourselves silly on the cab ride back to the hotel—this was one Christmas we'd never forget.

41

The office of Second World Studies on West 33rd Street was not only dark but completely empty, except for a steamer trunk with a telephone and a note left on top. I tried the light switch by the door—which had been left open—but there was still no light except the reflected ambience coming through the window from Herald Square, where we could hear a lonely saxophone player doing an aching, yet simple version of "White Christmas."

Frankie and Hooch wandered around the space, looking for interesting smells. I bet there *are* some inside that steamer trunk, I thought, as I went straight to it.

I picked up the note. It said, "Other people have dogs you care about, too. I want that key."

I showed it to Jamie. We had discussed my theory earlier at the hotel, but she still said, "What does it mean, Jack?"

"I don't know," I lied. Before the telephone could ring, as I knew it would—Peterman liked the dramatic flair, and probably had a listening device hidden somewhere in the room, or was hiding inside the steamer trunk himself, he was a magician, after all—I said, "Remember? He thinks I've got that key he says he lost."

"Do you?"

"No. And I don't know what dog he's referring to."

My cell phone rang. I clicked it open. It was Kristin.

"Jack! Daisy's been stolen."

"Oh, my god. What happened?"

"Marta was walking her to the park just now . . ."

"What's going on?" Jamie wanted to know.

I told her, then said to Kristin, "Go on."

"Well, Marta's hysterical, and her English isn't so good, especially when she's hysterical, so it's hard to get the whole picture, but two men came up beside her in a van, one jumped out, and took the dog and they sped off down Fifth Avenue and headed across the park."

"Really? At five o'clock? During Christmas rush? How the hell'd they do that?"

"Marta said there was a siren on the van."

"I don't suppose she got the plate number."

"No. Is there something you can do?"

"Me? I doubt it. You'll just have to get a new dog for Jen."

"What? Jack!"

"Well, nobody's attached to the dog yet, are they?"

"Just Marta a lot, and me a little. But Jack!"

It turned my stomach to do it, but I said, "Well, what can *I* do? If someone stole your dog, Kristin, file a police report, put up flyers. If the cops or someone who sees the flyers can find the dog, then you'll get her back. If not, there's nothing you can do."

"I can't believe you!" she said and hung up.

Jamie tsked at me. "You could have been a little more helpful or sympathetic, couldn't you?"

The phone on the steamer trunk rang. I clicked my cell phone shut and picked the other phone up. It was Peterman.

"I want to make you a little trade," he said.

"I don't have your key."

"I think you do."

"Think what you want." I hung up.

Jamie said, "Jack! What the hell are you doing?"

"What *can* I do? It's not my dog."

The phone rang again. I picked it up again.

"I know you better than that, Mr. Field. You love that dog. I saw you with her earlier today."

"Cool. You're a wizard and an amazing guy and you're everywhere at once and no place at all. But I don't have your key. I wish I did. I'd ram it down your flippin' throat."

There was a pause. "I'm getting tired of this."

"Fine. Me too." I hung up again.

It rang again. I let it.

I said to Jamie, "Let's go home."

"What? What about Jen's dog?"

"It's her dog, not mine. If *you* want to go look for her, fine. But it's not like she's lost. She's been stolen, apparently for the ransom, which we don't have."

The phone was still ringing. I picked it up. "You won the game, okay? You outsmarted me."

"Fine. I'll have my associates kill the dog."

"That'll look good on your résumé—'dog killer.' And best of luck getting your key back."

"I'm tired of this."

"Me too," I said.

Before I could hang up two very big men appeared in the doorway with automatic weapons drawn. One of them said, in heavily accented English, "Good-bye, Mr. Field."

The room filled with gunfire, Jamie and I fell to the floor, and in the ensuing silence I heard the clicking of Frankie and Hooch's toenails on the wooden floor as they came over to see what was wrong with us, and then the tinny sound of Peterman's voice, coming from the telephone.

Strangely enough he was asking me if I was okay.

42

We waited in the dark, not breathing, not talking, not wanting to make a sound—like a couple of kids waiting up for Santa Claus.

I heard a scraping sound. Jamie clutched my arm.

It was getting closer. We heard a little grunting, more scraping, and a little cursing. Then we heard the trapdoor open, the sound of someone heaving themselves onto the floor of the Brights' basement, then footsteps moving toward the wall. A moment passed then the lights came on.

Peterman couldn't see us because we were behind some moving boxes. He went to the washing machine and opened the door. He took a cloth bag from inside his coat and put it in the dryer. It clinked, as if it contained jewelry. Then he pulled the washer away from the wall, reached down behind the slats and pulled out the walking stick that had recently been purchased at the shop in Camden. He set it on top of the washing machine, then got down on his hands and knees and began searching the floor.

"Looking for this?" I said, holding a safe deposit key.

He turned, shocked, then his face became like mush and his whole body seemed to sag. "You're not dead."

"Nope. Doesn't seem like it."

Brad Bailey came through the basement door, accompanied by two uniformed Camden cops.

Peterman stood up slowly, saw Bailey and said, "You're not under arrest?"

"For what? Running a con game on you?" He looked at me. "I was a little worried about things until Jack's pals drove me to the airport and explained what was going on."

I shrugged and told Peterman, "I couldn't trust him with what we were doing. He's not a very good actor. You should have actually *seen* his Polish priest."

The uniforms put the cuffs on Peterman and I realized this was the first time I'd actually seen the man in person. I'd built this whole persona for him in my head, a semi-romantic figure with a lot of charisma and presence. All I could see now was a weak, rather nondescript old nightclub magician with balding gray hair and Gettysburg eyes.

They led him toward the door, he stopped for a moment in front of me and they let him. He said, "But you were in New York too. How did you get here ahead of me?"

"Good question. When you called the hotel this morning and asked us to meet you at five I figured you thought I had your safe deposit box key. I also assumed that you set up the dognapping scheme to either test me or get me to give you the key in exchange for the dog. I also figured that once you realized or believed I didn't have it, you'd hightail it back up here to search for it."

"Yes, but how did you know I was going to kidnap the dog?"

"I didn't. Not for sure. But Huckabee told me that you always go after what's most important to the mark, right?" He nodded. "You couldn't go after what's *really* most important to me—my fiancée—because that would involve kidnapping, which is a federal offense and would bring in all kinds of cops and FBI. So you had to go with what's *second* most important—dogs. Dognapping isn't even a felony, until you extort ransom."

"You really thought this through."

"Of course. Meanwhile, I couldn't be sure you weren't already on your way to Maine when we arrived at your office. The fake meeting might've just been a cover to keep me and Jamie in the city long enough for you to come back here, retrieve the murder weapon and look for your missing key. That's one reason I had Bailey 'arrested,' so he could fly back here, plant the fake walking stick, and wait for you."

He looked over at the washing machine. "That's not the murder weapon?"

"Nope. Bailey bought it in a little shop in Camden. The real one's in an evidence locker at the state morgue."

"Very smart," he said with a sad smile.

"Yes, it was. Then, knowing that you probably had set up microphones to eavesdrop on us when we arrived at your office, I had Kristin Downey call me as soon as we walked in the door. I'd called her earlier from the lobby and told her to wait thirty seconds, then call me back. When she did, we acted out our little telephone drama about the stolen dog. I thought it came off pretty good, too. We had an acting class together in college, you know."

Jamie tsked and shook her head. Peterman made no comment one way or the other. (Critics.)

"Then after Jamie and I were 'shot,' we had an ambulance waiting for us and the dogs, in case you or your cohorts were still watching. But the ambulance didn't take us to the nearest hospital. It took us to Teterboro. So that's how we beat you here."

"Well, Mr. Field. It seems as if you outsmarted me."

"No, you outsmarted yourself."

He nodded. "I broke my own rule."

" 'When the heat is on, drop the con.' "

He nodded, sighed, and looked around the room. "I should have dropped this a long time ago." He shrugged. "I just couldn't resist the setup. An underground tunnel? A wealthy mark who'll believe almost anything you tell her?"

I shook my head. "You got greedy and lazy. Not to mention the fact that you killed someone."

"Amy?" He nodded. "She was going to blow the whistle." His eyes changed. "Though that's not why I killed her. I lost my temper. I never *meant* to do it."

"No deals, Peterman. If you don't cop to second-degree homicide on Amy Frost we turn you over to the authorities in Kentucky, where they still have the death penalty. They'll go for first-degree and you'll get the needle."

"Kentucky?" He seemed dazed.

"Shirley Schwartzbaum?"

"Oh, well, I'd need to have a look at the case they have against me there before I make any decisions about my future."

"Sure. Throw the dice."

"Just keep in mind," Jamie said, "that your luck is on a bit of a downhill slide lately."

He nodded and gave her a sour smile. "All the same, I'll need to take some time to think it over."

"You'll have plenty of time where you're going," I said as they led him away.

After he was gone I took the Brights up to the third floor and showed them the game room and how all the tricks were done. I also showed them the little dorm room that Huckabee had described, with the two beds, the color TV, the dresser with a makeup mirror, a tiny bathroom, and a closet which held the elfin costumes. We also found some old pizza boxes, empty beer cans, and used condoms on the floor.

I put the costumes on Maxim and Fritz—who'd been waiting up on the main floor with Leon in case they were needed—and had them act as stand-ins for the little people, then stirred the water in the fountain with the walking stick, which made the dogs magically appear, as if from far away.

Ellis was furious that he'd been conned, though to this day I think Fiona believes her brother is still being held prisoner by elves, that they simply, and inexplicably, transformed themselves into Doberman pinschers for a day.

As to the con we'd pulled on Peterman, this is how it worked: by the time we'd gone to Ninth Avenue to locate Huckabee, I knew it was a setup. Huckabee hadn't bought donuts and beer with a credit card. He was an idiot, yes, but not about how to stay out of jail. Peterman was just seeing what he could get us to believe. And since I knew he had people watching and listening in on us, everything we said and discussed in that café was said to convince him that we believed his lies about Bailey. After all, one of the rules of a con game is to find something that's important to the mark. And since Peterman had spent $25,000 to convince us Bailey was on the take, it must have been important to him.

I concocted the fake contract Dmitri put out on me and Jamie to pave the way for the two Russians who showed up that evening at Peterman's office, firing blanks at us. It was also done to fool Peterman into thinking we were dead. I knew this would make him feel totally at ease about coming back to the mansion to retrieve the fake murder weapon and look for his missing key.

As for the underground railroad tunnel beneath the Brights' mansion, their attachment to the house was based on the idea that it contained a portal to a magical world, so a few weeks later, when the local historical society began the process of turning the property into a national historical landmark, Ellis and Fiona decided to donate the mansion as a place to house artifacts, a library, and a meeting hall for historical seminars. And since Leon was responsible for finding the tunnel, I suggested that it be named after him. They agreed. It's now called the Leon R. McMurfree Historical Museum.

He's been impossible since then, of course, but I don't mind. I kind of like the fact that he's so proud of himself. And don't tell him I said this: I think he *should* be.

But I'm getting ahead of myself again. This is a Christmas story, after all.

So here's what happened at Christmas . . .

Epilogue

The transplant surgery was a success, at least for Tim, although his father went into septic shock and almost died. (I shouldn't have felt good about this, but I did a little.)

The next day, I brought Hooch to see Tim. Because he was on anti-rejection medication and there was a high risk of infection, only one dog was allowed to visit. And Hooch had to wear a gown and surgical mask.

Tim said hello, happily, though tiredly, to the big dog, and played with his ears, causing Hooch to try to scratch his ass with his back leg. He nearly fell down doing it.

I laughed and said, more seriously, "I never did train Hooch to stand on his head, you know."

"Yeah," Tim said wistfully. "And you almost had me believing you could."

"Sorry about that."

"Ah, that's okay," he said. "Sometimes just believing in something is enough. That's what Christmas is all about, right?"

"I suppose so. But I thought you didn't believe in Christmas."

"I know," he said, smiling, "but things change."

The next day, I picked up my dad and my sister and her husband Barry and their four kids at the Portland airport, got them unpacked, then we drove down to Christmas Cove to have Christmas Eve supper with Jamie's dad and his second wife Laurie.

Annabelle wanted to go back early and get Dad and the kids to bed, but Jamie and I—who'd come in her car—put our parkas on and went down to the rocky, snow-covered beach to look at the ocean before driving back home. It was my idea.

"So, how's your Christmas cold, Jack?"

"It's gone. I think this is the last year I'll get it."

"Really?" She hugged me.

"Listen, could you show me your ring?"

She took her mittens off and held it out for me to see. "Why do you want to look at it?"

"Could you take it off for a minute?"

"Jack, what's going on?"

"I'm going to give you a Christmas present."

She shook her head and said, "Okay, but I don't want a new ring. I love this one."

"Oh, I'm not going to give you a new ring, don't worry."

"Okay . . ." She gave it to me.

I took it in my right hand and said, "I didn't really do this right the last time. So this is your Christmas present. Or one of them." I got down on one knee, took her right hand in my left, held out the ring, and said, "Dr. Cutter, will you make me the happiest man on earth and marry me?"

Her eyes got wet. "Yes, Jack Field, I will marry you."

I stood up and put the ring back on her finger. Then we kissed and I was reminded of a line from *The Princess Bride,* about which kisses in the history of the world were ranked the highest. There was now a new kiss at the top.

When our lips finally parted I said, "If your hands are cold, you can put your mittens back on."

"I don't care how cold my hands get. I want to look at my Christmas present." She didn't look at the ring, though. She looked at me.

Then somewhere far off in the icy, travertine waters a sudden, though subtle explosion of light caught my eye. I turned and saw a glow, coming from just above the horizon.

"Jamie," I said, pointing, "look!"

She did and said, "Wow! What is it?"

"I don't know." I looked at her. "Maybe Dr. Wacko was right. Maybe there really *is* an elfin island off the coast of Maine. One that can only be seen on Christmas Eve."

"It can't be. It has to be a ship or something."

"Honey, that's no ship. It's Christmas Eve and it looks like the aurora borealis, only it's sitting on top of the water."

"It's so beautiful. But still, it can't be."

We stood gazing in wonder for a while then the lights slowly disappeared in the fog. She shivered, put her mittens back on, took my hand and said, "Well, we know it couldn't possibly be an enchanted island, so there has to be a rational, scientific explanation for whatever it was."

"You're probably right."

We turned to go and she put her hands to my chest and said, "I know! It was bioluminescent dinoflagellates!"

"Of course," I said. "That has to be it."

"See?" she said. "And there was some disturbance in the atmosphere that made it seem like the lights came from above the water even though they didn't."

"You're right, honey," I said and we turned back toward the cottage and the long drive home.

"It *was* beautiful, though," she said.

"It sure was. Merry Christmas, darling."

"Merry Christmas, Jack."

We kissed again and I glanced up at the sky, hoping to see a fat man in a sleigh (or not so fat if you were to meet him in person). There was nothing except stars and clouds.

"Now what are you looking for, Jack?"

"Nothing," I lied.

She took my hand. "Don't worry. Santa Claus is real, if only in the feeling you get at Christmastime. Right?"

I nodded and we walked hand-in-hand up the rocky beach toward her car. But neither of us mentioned what we both knew: that it *couldn't* have been the magical, luminescent plankton we'd seen out there on the ocean.

They never show their lights in the wintertime.

Author's Note

Jack's approach to dog training, which is based on *Natural Dog Training* by Kevin Behan, works by stimulating positive, playful emotions rather than by using food rewards or dominance-based corrections. Food, markers, and even some types of corrections have their place, but food is not the "universal reinforcer" many trainers believe it is. And acting dominant, or alpha, is based on a complete fallacy.

Pavlov wrote, "Positive emotions arising in connection with the perfection of a skill, irrespective of its pragmatic significance at a given moment serve as the reinforcement." So it's not food, but positive emotion—usually stimulated by hunting games—that is the *real* universal reinforcer for dogs.

Max von Stephanitz, who developed the German shepherd dog as well as the sport of Schutzhund, and its underlying theory and philosophy, said, "Before we teach a dog to obey we must teach him how to play." And Nobel Prize–winning biologist Konrad Lorenz wrote, "All animals learn best through play."

So, if your trainer doesn't use a playful approach to training, find one who does. That's my opinion.

My website: www.leecharleskelley.com
Kevin Behan's website: www.naturaldogtraining.com
My e-mail address: kelleymethod@aol.com
Lou Kelso's e-mail address: louiskelso@aol.com
Adopt a rescue animal: www.strayfromtheHeart.org

Recommended Reading

Natural Dog Training, by Kevin Behan. Originally published by William Morrow and Co., 1993. Available again from Xlibris. The best book ever written about dogs and dog training.

Dogs: A New Understanding of Canine Origins, Behavior, and Evolution, by Raymond and Lorna Coppinger. University of Chicago Press, October 2002. The Coppingers have written that the logic behind the alpha theory is "just poor." They have also stated that pack social structure is related to prey size, and not about who's most dominant.

Play Training Your Dog, by Patricia Gail Burnham. St. Martin's Press, 1986. Shows the importance of playing tug-of-war and teaching a dog to jump up on command.

Dogs That Know When Their Owners Are Coming Home, by Rupert Sheldrake. Three Rivers Press, 2000. Hypothesizes that some dogs, like Hooch, may be innately telepathic.

"The Misbehavior of Organisms," by Keller and Marian Breland. *American Psychologist* 16 (1961): 681–84. http://psychclassics.yorku.ca/Breland/misbehavior.htm. An article by the inventor of clicker training, critiquing the philosophy of operant conditioning.

Emergence, by Steven Johnson. Scribner's, 2001. This book has nothing to do with dogs but may provide thoughtful readers a new way of looking at pack behavior.

The Emerald Modem, by Richard Leviton. Hampton Roads, 2004. For the curious, this book lists locations of sacred sites around the globe that are supposedly magic portals into unseen dimensions of reality. I can't personally vouch for this stuff. I'm a dog trainer, not a mystic traveler.